The Curse Of The Infinity Bracelets

(A Vienna LaFontaine Novel)

Juliana Andrew

Inquiries and Book Orders should be addressed to:

Great Writers Media
Email: info@greatwritersmedia.com
Phone: 877-600-5469

ISBN: 978-1-961416-28-4 (sc)
ISBN: 978-1-961416-29-1 (ebk)

Mademoiselle

Mademoiselle, will you come walk with me
Take my hand and I will lead you to our destiny
I told him no, no, no, a thousand times
For I was yours and you were forever mine

Mademoiselle, will you please come dance with me
Paradise is in my arms, you will surely see
I told him no, no, no, no, farewell, adieu
My dances were all reserved for you

Mademoiselle, let me take you from this life
Come with me to Vienne and be my wife
No, no, no, no, no, a thousand nos I cried
Let me go, leave me be, I am betrothed I lied

I left him there alone, so forlorn and wondering
I hadn't meant to be unkind but you were calling me
Tomorrow at dawn I must cross the seventh sea
Mademoiselle is coming home to you at Avonlea

For my amazing husband Roy...
Without him, there would be no love stories to tell.

Genre: Historical and Historical Fiction
Romance/Intrigue

Illustrated book cover by
Carrie Cudworth

Chapter 1

The Weddings

Rainey and I were married for the first time at 1 PM on June 11th, 1981 in Bridge Falls.

Our marriage was twenty one years in the making. I was thirty seven years old and Rainey was forty two. We had a daughter Ava who was nineteen. She had known her father for only five months. Rosalyn was twenty two. She was adopted, but I never considered her as anything but my own flesh and blood. Rainey had two sons, Morgan sixteen, and Mason fifteen.

We stood before our friends and family on a beautiful day in the garden of the home Rainey and I had purchased from my parents in January. His home had been in Vancouver and I had been living in Scotland for twenty years. No one, and certainly not Rainey or I ever thought this day would come. I had met Rainey Quinn when I was sixteen and fell hopelessly in love with him. We saw each other over a period of two summers. He never made any promises to me, and when he went to Italy to study architecture for four months in the autumn of 1961, I found myself pregnant. I believed there was no future for us as he had never once told me that he loved me. I would not jeopardize his career by saddling him with a child and so I fled my home in Bridge Falls. With my parents help I went to live with my Aunt Jannie in Scotland. I basically blackmailed my family to keep my condition and whereabouts a secret. I told them that I did not know who the father of my baby was. Rainey did try to find me but was not successful and eventually went on to marry a woman whom he wasn't in love with, but fathered two wonderful boys.

Rosalyn took me to be her new mother the Christmas of '61. Her mother Maveryn, had passed away before Rosy was two. I had met Maveryn when I was twelve on a previous visit to Scotland, and she became a dear friend to me. Rosy's father was Lord Jeremy McAllister, and he lived at Avanloch which just happens to be a castle. He was away most of the time and when he was home he spent very little time with his daughter. I presumed because she reminded him too much of his lost love. Unwillingly at first, I became a surrogate mother to Rosalyn, but by the time Ava was born four and a half months later, I considered Rosalyn as mine and could not imagine life without her. Jannie and I had brought her to live with us at Brackenshire Manor shortly after Christmas.

Lord Jeremy proposed that he and I should marry for the children's well-being and become parents to them. I weighed my options of how I could provide for my girls and agreed to marry him. On July the 6th 1962, I became his wife... in name only. Ours was a loveless marriage as Jeremy was still pining for his dead Maveryn and I was still in love with Rainey. He resided in the north wing of the castle and the girls and I had our rooms in the south wing. He was twenty five years my senior and never once considered me as anything more than a mother to his daughter. I was perfectly happy with the arrangement. I reflect back to those first years when I was still a teen and the mother of two and had a meaningless marriage. My life was pointless except for Rosy and Ava, and I took my duties as Mistress of Avanloch as an insignificant duty. I don't know when it was exactly that I began to realize that this was going to be my life and that I had better quit playing the role of a doomed damsel and accept the role that I had been given. I know I could not have carried on without the guidance of Aunt Jannie and the rest of the staff at Avanloch. Jannie and Uncle John lived at Brackenshire Manor which was at the bottom of the hill from Avanloch. They were both employed by Lord Jeremy. Jannie was in charge of Avanloch and the staff and John was his friend and solicitor.

My childhood remembrances of the castle and gardens were etched in my memory banks as one large playground. I did not relay my adventures to any of my friends back home in Canada as I was sure they would think I was making the whole thing up. Really, how many people ever get to have tea in a real castle and know the occupants personally? However, for some strange reason, I had once told Rainey that my aunt lived in a lesser castle in Wales. I always spoke of going to Wales…never Scotland. That little fabrication kept him from finding me. Even though I was the one who did the running away, I did so want him to come for me…but that did not happen. I had thought foolishly that if he truly loved me neither heaven nor earth could keep him from finding me.

I settled into life at Avanloch relatively easily. I turned the huge stone structure into a comfortable home for my girls. Jeremy was seldom around as he would rather be travelling around the world tending to his shipping business. I had carte blanche when it came to expenditures and over the years I changed the look inside and outside of the castle. I had the best staff in the world, and as far as the girls and I were concerned we were all one large happy family. Jannie gradually retired and I took over all her duties at Avanloch. Everyone had respected my privacy as to the reason why I had fled my home in Bridge Falls, Canada. I am sure they all suspected that I did not want the father of Ava to know of her birth, and they were right. I made a promise to myself that they would come to know each other one day, and now, thankfully it had come true.

I suffered through many bouts of melancholy; that is what I chose to call my illness. It was mine and mine alone to deal with until I started to lose time. Jeremy sent his therapist, Dr. Jai to me. She helped me to deal with my sadness, but I never told her of the real reason for my despondency. She encouraged me to have more contact with my family and friends and helped set up a relay postal box so that my best friend Lara could reach me, but still not know where I was. This way I could be informed of life and my friends back in Canada. Most of all I needed to know about Rainey. Lara pleaded with me to tell him of my whereabouts, but I was adamant that he not know yet. Then it was too late as he married and had children and my stubbornness cost me many years of sorrow.

After seven years of seclusion I made the trip back to Bridge Falls with Rosalyn and Ava. As soon as Lara saw Ava she knew that she was the daughter of her cousin Rainey. They both had the same azure blue eyes. One of my many lies was that of Ava's birth month so that the connection couldn't be made, but now Lara surely knew the truth. She knew that I wasn't ready to acknowledge it yet and kept my secret though what it cost her, I can only imagine. I was making her chose between her favorite cousin and best friend…who consciously does that?

Providence finally intervened and Rainey and I were reunited. I had wasted twenty years of our life together, not to mention that I kept Ava from her father. They have forgiven me. I think they are afraid that if they couldn't absolve me that I would slip back into the darkness again. That is so far from the truth, but I cannot convince them that those days of hopelessness are behind me. I have two beautiful daughters and am with the man that I have never stopped loving. I have never been happier. He has told me that I am the only one that he has ever been in love with and if he had of acknowledged it twenty years ago we would never have been separated. I keep reminding him that he wouldn't have his two sons then and I may never have become Rosalyn's mother. He understands my reasoning that this was the journey our lives had to take to arrive at where we are today but wants to take his share of the responsibility for our years of separation. I am afraid that department of culpability lies squarely at my feet and it will be my albatross to bear, but I try hard not to go to those dark places anymore.

Jeremy passed away on January the 26th 1976 after several years of battling tuberculosis. He had kept his illness from us until he could hide it no longer. He left me and the girl's heirs to Avanloch and McAllister Shipping Enterprises. I had no interest in the business and thankfully, his sister Ash and Uncle John and his sons, Grayson and Chandler took full command. Rosalyn was studying finance and corporate law and was already contributing to the company. Ava was only fourteen and had no idea where her future plans lay. I was content to continue with the preservation of the estate and keeping the mill and dairy in the Village operational.

Rainey owned a successful architectural firm in Vancouver which he entrusted to his colleagues to manage in his absence. He never intended to return to it. His divorce from the heartless Louise had been granted earlier than was expected. We would have been married immediately had I not chose to have the wedding in Bridge at this precise date. We would be returning to Scotland where we would be married again with our Avanloch family in the Village Chapel. We would stay here in Bridge for a few days until Morgan and Mason returned to Vancouver to finish up the school year. They would be spending the summer with us in Scotland. They had come over for a ten day visit on their spring break, and if it had of been up to them, they would never have returned to Vancouver and their mother. Their interest in the oddities of the castle surpassed any curiosities that the girls and I shared. We had not been triumphant at discovering any of the secret rooms, so they were determined that they were going to be the ones to solve the mysteries that lay hidden somewhere in the vastness of the castle walls.

When the boys had to leave for school in September, Rainey and I were going to embark on our quests to find the rightful heir to the Infinity Bracelets. Rainey had purchased the bracelets for me in Italy in 1961 as a Christmas present, but when he returned home, I was gone. He kept them all these years, and gave them to me when we were reunited. He did not know their history, but strangely, I did. One late sleepless, wintry evening as I was wandering the halls of Avanloch I ended up in the library and accidentally pulled out a book of unsolved love stories. I flipped through the pages and came upon a story that intrigued me. It was the 1850's and Anton, somewhat of a Spanish noble, fell in love and secretly married Katarina, a peasant girl from the Pyrenees. He had three silver bracelets made for her and sent them to her by courier while he was back on the war front in Spain. Sadly, when he returned to Katarina, he found that she had been murdered and their child had been abducted. The bracelets had been savagely ripped from her arm. He vowed that he would never rest until he found her assassins or his daughter. That was where the story ended. I had thought no more about it until Rainey presented me with the bracelets, and I realized from the inscriptions that they may very well be the Infinity ones from the account that I had read several years earlier. I had them authenticated as Austrian silver. They bore the date 1852, and had the names of Anton and Kat engraved on one. I felt that it was my responsibility to research them further and perhaps uncover what really happened to their daughter. Rainey warned me that it was going to be an insurmountable task but we would take the journey together.

Uncle John had recently discovered that LizBeth McAllister, the younger sister of Ash and Jeremy was still alive and living in the Netherlands. She was the supposed victim of a drowning mishap. She had been rushed from Avanloch some forty years ago by the doctor of the day. She was declared dead, and no one knew that she had survived except the doctor and her father, Bruce McAllister, who continued her care at a facility in Gloucester. Before he passed away he enlisted Jeremy to become her guardian and keep her existence secret. Although LizBeth would be fifty three, her world was one of a child of three or four. She had been transferred to Amsterdam where John had found her. It was Jeremy's sister Ash's wish that she be moved closer to home and she was now living out her days in a sanatorium near Edinburgh. She seemed perfectly happy as there were other children of her "age" living there. She was beginning to recognize us, and someday her doctors say that we can bring her home for a visit.

Poor Rainey, I am sure he never imagined what he was getting himself into when he agreed to come and live at Avanloch with me. He appeared to take it all in stride and never questioned the going ons of this storybook kingdom that I lived in. Although he did not believe in the concept of ghosts, I think he was somewhat disappointed that none had shown up yet. He still wanted to marry me and requested only two things of me; he wanted to be in charge of the wedding song and he wanted to create my bouquet. I shouldn't have been surprised as he was always coming up with new ways to impress me, but we never had a 'song' and wondered what he had in mind.

I had Ava help me design my dress and we had a seamstress in Waverly construct it plus the ones that my wedding party would be wearing. Mine was a simple summer frock with spaghetti straps and fitted at the waist with a full uneven skirt that fell just below my knees. It was made of a creamy white silk material with a delicate appliqué of cherry blossoms on a paper thin branch that ran from the hem to my shoulder. The girl's dresses were a cherry pink color. Rainey and I had decided that we didn't want our attire to be formal and I had a pretty good idea that he wouldn't divert much from his usual white shirt and tan pants, but I was in for a surprise.

Father met me in the conservatory and said that he was thankful that he was still alive to see me finally marry the man he had chosen for me many years ago. I laughed and said.

"Oh, you chose him for me did you? Well, you sure took your time making it happen!"

Mother met us at the door and took my other arm and handed me the bouquet that Rainey had arranged for me. I knew that he had enlisted the help of his Aunt Anne, Lara's mother, who ran a florist shop, for how else could he have preserved the cherry blossoms that highlighted the nosegay? Lily of the Valley and primroses and several stalks of heather made up the rest of the bouquet with one lavender perfect rose taking center stage. The tears started to fall because I knew the meaning of all the flowers.

Lily of the valley meant happiness, primroses stood for eternal love, the heather was for Scotland, and the cherry blossoms were Rainey's and my special signature because we had both smelled their fragrance the night we met and shared our first kiss. They stood for gentleness, and the lavender rose signified enchantment and love at first sight.

I stepped outside with my parents. Ava and Rosy, my bridesmaids, had gone before us and we were to follow after Lara, my matron of honor, but two grown women came from the corners of the porch and proceeded to lay a path of rose petals at our feet. Addy and Sissy, my younger sisters, were apparently the flower girls. I had not seen this coming…it must have been the conception of my two mischievous daughters. It was a delightful surprise as it was also to look down and see Rainey and his groomsmen attired in pale pink shirts and white pants and a frosted cherry blossom protruding from their lapels. I smiled my approval and slowly walked towards the love of my life to the amazing voice of Roberta Flack singing "The First Time Ever I Saw Your Face". I was so glad that I wasn't wearing mascara or eye liner as my tears would have been streaming down my face in black streaks. Rainey couldn't have chosen a more fitting song. As I reached the arbor that was alive with white clematis blooms, Rainey looked down at my feet and threw his head back in laughter. Pastor McMillan glanced at my bare feet and nodded his approval. He had a few words of welcome, said a short prayer for us and asked me if I was ready to declare my vows. I took Rainey's hands in mine.

Rainey Quinn, you are the light that crosses the shadow of the moon. For every day and every night that we've been apart I've kept your memory locked in my heart. I've missed your tender touch and the music in your voice. My love for you has never faltered and never strayed, and it never shall.

I have prayed that God would someday give you back to me and give me another chance. Today, all my dreams have come true and we truly will be one.

If you will have me, I promise to love you forever and I shall dance with you until the end of time.

I heard sniffling from the girls behind me. Rainey smiled and turned my hands over and placed his on top of mine. His eyes were shinning.

Vienna, my love, you have been my dream throughout these tumultuous years, never far from the recesses of my mind.

I have looked for you in the face of strangers and longed for you on sleepless nights. I heard you calling my name upon the wind and it kept me hanging on.

You once told me that happiness was to hold those you love in both hands and dance. I give you my hands to hold and ask if you will dance with me all the days of our lives for you are my happiness, my reason for being, and my destiny.

Vienna Lafontaine, you are my Lady, and I promise you that every day I will love you more than I did the day before.

Rainey kept hold of my hands as he turned me to face the minister. He was holding on so tightly that he would have brought tears to my eyes if I hadn't already been crying from the words he had spoken to me.

Reverend McMillan smiled at us. He spread out his hands and addressed our guests. "There are a few firsts for me here…never before have I been bathed in such a sea of pinks or seen so many happy, yet tearful faces." He looked down at my feet and said. "And, I certainly have never had the privilege to marry a barefoot bride who reigns over a Scottish castle. I have learned from Patsy and Lily, the mothers of Rainey and Vienna that these two took a very long detour to arrive here at their destination; twenty one years in fact. They wish to acknowledge everyone who helped them get here. Now, we best get this show on the road as I was informed by the groom that he and Vienna wish to be pronounced man and wife at precisely one o'clock and so without further ado…"

The old courthouse clock jubilantly rang out the hour as we were pronounced man and wife. Rainey took my face in his hands and said. "This is it Vienna. We are bound together forever in the eyes of God." I nodded as that was all I could do as we sealed the union with a long kiss. We were presented as Mr. and Mrs. Quinn to our family and friends, and amid cheers and whistles, we ran down the rose laden path through a storm of opaque bubbles. It beat being pelted by birdfeed.

Rainey pulled me up to the top stair of the veranda. "I need a few minutes alone with my wife…I'm sure you will all grant me this.

Yates, look after our guests please." With that he picked me up and carried me over the threshold of the conservatory door. When he put me down inside he said. "Lordy Lady, when did you put so much weight on?"

"Married two minutes and you are already complaining! Will you make up your mind; do you want me fat or do you want me skinny?" I retorted laughing.

"Mrs. Quinn, I will take you anyway that I can get you!"

"I think I have heard that before. Will you please call me Mrs. Quinn again? I think I am going to get everyone at Avanloch to address me as such."

"I love your dress Mrs. Quinn. So this is what you have been hiding from me?"

"Yes, but what about you? Pink and white…what a surprise. I am sure that everyone thinks we co-coordinated our outfits. I guess we just think alike. Thank you for the wedding song…I know all the words and it is just perfect. I love you so Rainey Quinn."

"As I love you my sweet, my bride…promise me that you will never leave me."

"Leave you…how could I? You have a hold on me stronger then the ropes that held Hercules. Now kiss me and let's go greet our guests."

"You are wearing the proverbial garter aren't you?"

"Yes, but I really don't want to throw the beautiful bouquet that you gave me."

"Well then don't."

"Oh no, I must follow protocol…we must not deviate from the rituals. Nothing can mar this perfect day."

"All righty then. Take my hand and we shall go and greet our subjects."

The tears were all gone and joyous laughter had taken over. Ava and Rosalyn were waiting for us when we opened the door. They hugged us and we beckoned Morgan and Mason to join us. Our families were now joined and the sun shone down brightly on us.

Somebody brought me a chair and I sat as Rainey put on a big show removing my garter. Yates Fielding, one of his childhood buddies, was the lucky recipient and it brought whoops and hollers from the male contenders. Rosy caught my bouquet and Rainey whispered to me. "Ah, there be hopes for a grandchild after all." I reminded him that one did not have to be married to have a baby. He said. "Touché."

The wedding supper and dance was to be held in Hawthorne, Rainey's hometown. It was a short eighteen miles from Bridge falls. The small town had graciously offered to host the event and we had wholeheartedly accepted. We had rented a school bus to transport the guests back and forth. The girls and I had wanted to bring a little Scottish hospitality with us so cuisine that we would have served at the castle at tea time was served for the luncheon. The little sandwiches were made of salmon, cucumber, cream cheeses, and our homemade jams. Lemon and raspberry tartlets, raisin scones, Highland shortbread, and a rich apricot mascarpone cheesecake decorated the three tiered wedding cake. For the hardier appetites we had made up what is known as a Ploughman's Platter, or as it was more commonly called 'pub fare'. It consisted of broken pieces of specialty breads, cheeses, salamis, ham and pickles and relishes and very tangy coleslaw. Hopefully, this would tide everyone over until the 6 o'clock dinner.

Jimmy Douglas, Rainey's best friend and best man rounded us up a little after three and said it was time to make our way to Hawthorne. Jimmy had been a very good friend to me also … before and after Rainey had gone away to Italy. I had kept in touch with him over the past ten years, but he too knew not where I was living. The fact that he had contact with me and never told Rainey did not win him any accolades with his best friend, but he had been forgiven. Rainey no longer harbored any resentment towards my family or his cousin Lara for their part in keeping my secret.

We climbed in the back seat of Rainey's old 1956 red and white Oldsmobile. He had been storing it at his parent's ranch for almost twenty years. His dad and Jimmy had made sure that it was in perfect shape for today. A multitude of memories, good and bad, saturated my mind. As soon as Rainey put his arm around me they all faded away. Today and tomorrow were all that was important.

Jimmy drove around the streets of Bridge Falls followed by several other cars all honking their horns in a random cacophony of tones. After the same thing in Hawthorne we went to the Quinn Ranch to relax before the evening's festivities started.

Morgan and Mason had some good news for us. They had been allowed to write their final exams the past week and so they were free to come to Scotland with us now. They, being the resourceful boys they were, had managed to be on the same flight home as the rest of us. We informed Jimmy, Yates and Lara that we still wanted to bring them over to Avanloch. The original plan was for them to come for our wedding, but now that we had already tied the knot here they all agreed that they would come over later in the year. I couldn't protest too much as I knew we were going to have a busy summer with the boys.

The Grange was elaborately decorated and had been recently painted and a new hardwood floor had been installed. It was twenty years since I had last set foot in it. Rainey had brought me to many a dance here. The first one was on New Year's Eve 1960; I was only sixteen. I only knew how to do the fast dances like the jive and the twist. I was scared to death the first time Rainey asked me to waltz with him.

"Relax Vienna, I'm going to hold you very close; just feel the music flowing through your body and let me lead you. See, I knew you would be a natural." He was right, I loved the closeness and wanted to tell him so but didn't because it wasn't that long ago that I had blurted out that I loved him and he wasn't prepared to deal with that and told me to forget him. I hadn't of course, although I tried. Then he had come home from university and asked me out just like nothing had ever happened. I was young and foolish and was willing to do whatever to keep him in my life.

The summer of '61 had been one to remember. I became more infatuated with Rainey and we became lovers. I thought that we would be together forever, but then he went off to Italy and I was convinced that he had found someone else. His letters didn't make it to me, and I assumed the worst. He had never told me that he loved me, but somehow I was supposed to know that he did. Twenty years is a long time to hold on to a dream, but I did, and am ever so thankful that I did.

The people of Hawthorne outdid themselves. The dinner was fit for a king and Rainey said he felt like one. I told him that he was going to have to settle for the title of lord instead because I was only a lady.

"Lord and Lady Quinn…I think I like it." He proclaimed. I knew he had no notion of ever taking on the title, but whether he liked it or not, it would be so.

Jimmy had me and most of the women in tears when he proposed his toast. He said that he had witnessed the growth of our relationship firsthand and had also suffered the agony of our demise. He spoke of how he had seen the loss of light in my eyes thinking that Rainey had found someone else and the turmoil that Rainey suffered through when he came home and found me gone.

"The minister today said that we had helped reunite Rainey and Vienna, but that is not entirely so. Some of us held the power to bring them together, but we were bound by promises and circumstance as to why we didn't. There is no one happier than Lara and myself that this finally came to pass. If they hadn't come to realize how much they meant to each other this past year, we were seriously thinking of kidnapping them and sending them off to some deserted island! I am pleased to say that love won out. For all of you non-believers that think love waits for no one, just look at these two…apart for twenty years and now together for eternity. I have taken my cue from them and decided to give love another chance because I want to be as happy as they are. Please raise your glasses to Vienna and Rainey. Their love story is an inspiration to us all."

There were more toasts from family and friends and then Rainey thanked everyone for coming and that they were all welcome to visit us at Avanloch in Scotland. Then he turned to me and said. "Vienna I cannot say this enough…I love you and I cannot wait to start our new life together. We are so much further ahead than most newlyweds because we have a readymade family; two extraordinary daughters and two remarkable sons. You are all my witnesses here tonight…never shall I let go of this woman again."

He bent down and kissed me and I told him that I loved him and that I was going to hold him to his promise. Jimmy had hired a band called "50/60". The first songs they played for us were I Can't Help Falling in Love With You and All I Have To Do Is Dream. We were finally dancing as we were meant to. A few hours later Rainey confessed to me that he hadn't made any arrangements as to where we were going to spend our wedding night!

I held him a little away from me. "Rainey Quinn, are you telling me that you forgot to do the second most important thing on our wedding day?"

He lowered his head and sheepishly said. "I'm an ass…please don't divorce me."

"Stop fooling round Rainey! But, please tell me that you are joking."

"I wish I was. Just out of curiosity, what was the first most important thing?"

"That you show up for the wedding."

"Was there ever any doubt that I wouldn't?"

"One never knows. Now, what are we going to do about tonight? We can't go to our house in Bridge as all my family will be there and all of yours are at the ranch. I guess we will just have to drive around until we find a motel or spend the night in the car."

"I would suggest the "line shack" but…"

"Rainey, that is perfect!"

"But Sweetheart, it probably hasn't been cleaned this year."

"So, we will stop at the ranch and grab some linens and coffee and we'll be set."

"You're sure?"

"Unless you come up with a better offer in the next hour or so, I think that's our only alternative, and it will be a nice change from the vastness of the castle, don't you think?"

"Thank you for forgiving my incomprehensible blunder Mrs. Quinn."

"Who said you were forgiven? I guess it will make a nice chapter for the grandchildren to read. Let's start saying our goodbyes to everyone …I am getting a little weary."

Rainey told Jimmy and Yates to keep the party going. Jimmy announced to the crowd that we were leaving but we must have one last dance. The band that he had hired for us had played all our old favorite songs from that time so long ago. Rainey took me in his arms as they played their rendition of our wedding song. I had never heard a male voice singing the words before and I must say I was overcome with emotion as was Rainey.

We finally made our way out the door among promises from our families that they would see us at brunch at the ranch tomorrow. It didn't even dawn at me as to wonder why they would be seeing us as they couldn't possibly know that we were spending the night so close.

Rainey and I would ride our horses up to the cabin in the meadow many years ago. We had spent several nights together there in 1961 when I thought I knew what I was doing, but didn't care one way or the other anyway. Tonight we had to take the rough gravel road and I hoped no harm would come to Gypsy Lady. Rainey had named his car for me as I had a fantasy about gypsies and he liked to call me his lady. After I had run off to Scotland, Rainey had put the car into storage, wanting to sell it but found that he couldn't. We arrived a few minutes before midnight. He told me to stay in the car until he got some lights turned on in the cabin. I said no and that I was coming with him.

"Vienna, will you please listen to me…just this once?"

I said all right but didn't know what the big deal was. I thought that he was gone an unusually long time. How long did it take to turn a coal oil lamp on anyway? I promised that I would wait and so I did. The whole cabin was gradually being lit up and I wondered how many lamps he was turning on. He finally came back for me and took my suitcase and the fresh linen from me telling me that I wouldn't be in need of it.

"Yes, we need them. I'm not sleeping in dirty sheets!"

"I'll come back for them. Come along then."

He took my hand and almost dragged me to the cabin door. "Rainey…"I protested.

He shushed me and told me to close my eyes. "Why?" I asked.

He picked me up and pushed the door open with his foot. "I'm going to put you down now, but don't open your eyes until I tell you to."

I was becoming a little annoyed with him but thought, what the heck; I'll let him play his little game, whatever it was. He told me to open my eyes and I did to a bright flash going off. He had just taken a picture of me and then he took another one as I became aware of my surroundings. The place was lit up like a Christmas tree; there must have been a hundred candles burning! The cabin had been transformed into a honeymoon cottage. The two beds had been made to look as one by an array of various bedding and pillows. A rose negligee and a kimono lay across it. A canopy was suspended over the bed and a web of sheer netting hung from it. Colorful braided rugs were strewn over the worn plank floors. The small table was draped with a beautiful embroidered cloth and a candelabra and wine glasses. A silver ice bucket with a bottle of champagne sat on it. I couldn't speak for a few minutes as I was in awe of the sight before me.

"Is it to your liking Mrs. Quinn?" My husband asked.

"Rainey Quinn, you are a mischievous boy! When on earth did you have time to do all of this? Do I like it? Nothing could be more perfect!"

"Oh, I had a lot of help. Don't think that I am this imaginative."

"And who pray tell were your accomplices?"

"That will be my little secret. Mom said she left something here for us under the pillows. Here …it looks like a photograph album." He opened it and on the first pages were pictures of me as a baby through childhood right up until I was sixteen. The next pages were of Rainey growing up. We smiled at each other as we mulled over how we once looked. The next entries were a complete but pleasant surprise to us. We didn't even know these images existed. They had been taken at the New Year's Eve dance in 1961. Along with the picture that Rainey's Aunt Mavis had given us both were a dozen other snapshots of that night. Three were of Rainey and I dancing, and the rest were of us with Jimmy and Yates and the rest of the gang. At the bottom of the page was a note from Rainey's mom saying that she had found them in Mavis's belongings. She and Uncle Saul had been in a deadly car accident a number of years ago. Patsy had kept them from her son because I had been long gone when she found them and they were sure to have upset him. The next entries had a note with them; they were from Ruth, Jimmy's girlfriend at the time. She had lost the film somewhere in the house that her and Jimmy lived in before their divorce. She had recently returned and discovered the undeveloped film while she was cleaning. There were pictures of Rainey and I the summer of '61 plus others of the barbecues and dances at the Grange. Neither of us could remember Ruth wielding a camera. We were both amazed and delighted beyond words that there existed a gallery of "us" from so long ago.

"Look at us Vienna…we were so young and we were happy, right?" Rainey was overcome as was I by the memories of yesteryear.

"I like to think that you were as happy as I was Rainey, but am not certain you were."

"How can you say that Vienna? Don't I look happy to you?"

"Yes, you do. You say we were so young; well, you were already in your twenties and I was just a naïve teenager in love with an older mature man. You knew then what you wanted to do with your life. You had all these realistic aspirations, and I had none. I didn't care if I ever finished school or had a career. I only wanted to be with you and please you, and have your babies. You would soon have tired of me and my dependency and so, I can now admit that we would have definitely come to a cruel parting of the ways. You would have broken my heart worse than I broke it myself."

"I think you are wrong my darling, but that is neither here nor there as we will never know. My life has been pieces of a puzzle fitting together. I had a loving home with wonderful supportive parents. I had a multitude of good friends, and am proud to say they still remain as that; especially Jimmy…who else would have put up with my callous behavior? I pursued my dream of becoming an architect and have a successful business and prestige and have enough money to retire with and I have Morgan and Mason. But, one piece of the puzzle was always missing, and that was the love of a woman whom I also loved. You are that missing part Vienna…you personify love, and I have so craved it for many years without really being aware that love was **you.** Although I thought of you throughout the years, it wasn't until I saw you in Hawthorne last January that I came to the full realization that I was, and had been in love with you all along. There was no way that I could have let you get away from me again. So you see my love, I am the needy one, and I can only hope you never tire of my passion for you."

"That is never going to happen as I have my own obsession for you." I said through tears. "Now enough of this talk on this our wedding night. Unzip my dress and I will put this gorgeous soft gown on. Did you have help picking it out?"

"I cannot tell a lie…Lara helped me."

Rainey undid my dress and kissed my neck and shoulders. I shuttered. "I have been off my medication for months now and so I can have a few sips of wine. I am not hungry but am sure I will enjoy that feast that is in the icebox for us later."

He smiled knowingly at me.

The party was still in full swing back at the Grange. Ava left the dance floor and sat down next to Jimmy. "I've had it! I couldn't possibly manage another polka. Whoever invented that dance had no mercy for the feeble."

Jimmy laughed. "Obviously, your sister doesn't share the same delicate constitution."

"She's had a lot more practice than me; you know she is three years older." Ava leaned her head against Jimmy's shoulder and said. "You know…if I was a few years older…"

Jimmy patted her hand and laughed again. "Yes, and if I was a few years younger and not trying to make a comeback with Ruth…"

"You know, I was not too impressed with you that night back in January when you wouldn't tell me about Rainey, but I have since come to realize what a stalwart guy you really are. I don't have any uncles…would you care to be mine?"

"I am flattered and would consider it an honor." Ruth joined them and Ava told her how happy she was for her and Jimmy.

"Hey, look who just walked in. Ava, have you met Yates's oldest son Cameron yet?"

Ava watched as a good looking strapping young man came over to their table.

"Uncle Jimmy, how did I know you'd be reigning over *the table*?" He hugged Jimmy and said how nice it was to see Ruth. He looked inquiringly at Ava while asking where everyone else was. "Please don't tell me I've missed Uncle Rainey?"

"Sorry Bud, he and Vienna are long gone to their cozy cabin in the woods. Will you settle for his daughter Ava?"

He introduced Ava to Cameron. He shook her hand and asked her to call him Cam. Jimmy explained that Cam had been up in the oil fields working and that this was his first holiday since late winter. Cam apologized to Ava saying he was sorry that he hadn't been able to make it back in time for the wedding. Ava assured him that Rainey would forgive him. He didn't look at all like his younger brother Frankie or Yates for that matter. As if on cue, Alexi, his sister and Yates appeared having spotted him from the dance floor. They joined the table and wanted to know all about his latest exploits. Half an hour later he complained of how hungry he was and where was all the food hiding.

Alexi laughed. "Same ole Cam; come on, let's eat."

Ava asked if she could go with them. "I'm sorry you missed the wedding too. I guess you never knew my mother?"

"No, but I know the story…sort of." Cam answered.

Mason joined them and whisked Alexi off for a dance.

"I guess you have known my brothers a lot longer than I have? We hit it off the first time we met and I feel like I have known them all my life." Ava said.

"I'm curious to know who was astounded the most…you, finding out that your father was alive, and that you had brothers, or Rainey finding out that he had a daughter."

"I think I was. Rainey was so happy to be finally getting my mother back that nothing would have fazed him that day." Before they opened the kitchen door Ava pointed her sister out to Cam as she came whirling by.

"She doesn't look anything like you."

"We are not blood related but are as close as two peas in a pod."

They fixed two plates of leftovers. Ava admitted that she was hungry also as she had been too excited at dinner to eat much. They sat down at the work table and ate and talked. Their long absence was not lost on the adults.

"What is that son of yours up to with my Ava?" Jimmy asked Yates.

"Really…**your** Ava? He's been at camp a long time you know. Wouldn't it just be the icing on the cake if something developed between the two of them?" Yates kidded.

Rosy returned and asked where her sister was. Jimmy explained and she said to Yates.

"So that hunk she went off with is another one of yours? Do you have an older one somewhere for me?"

"Fraid not Rosy my dear, two lads be all I got. Surely, there is a lad back in Scotland awaiting your return?"

"Umm, there might be but I don't think either of us is ready to take the plunge and admit our feelings yet."

"For the love of Mike Rosy, don't make the same mistake your mother and Rainey did! I am a true believer in the old quip; 'tis better to have loved and lost then never to have loved at all.' Jimmy quoted and looked at Ruth for confirmation and she nodded "yes".

We had overslept. I reached over Rainey to check the time on his watch; it read 10:15.

He opened his eyes and asked if I was feeling frisky.

"Really Rainey? It's after 10, and we need to get a move on. By the time we get out of here and get to the ranch and shower, breakfast, lunch, whatever, will be on the table. If it was raining I would just go outside and shower."

"Really?"

"Sure, I used to do it all the time when I was young. We lived in a few places where we didn't have running water and so that was the thing to do in the summer."

"You are not that old to have lived without modern conveniences."

"You have to remember that we moved a lot due to father's construction work and we ended up in some remote areas. When we were stationed in Quesnel Joe and Lily took quite a liking to the place and thought they would make it their permanent residence… well, we all know that didn't happen. Anyhow, father decided to build a house outside of town. We had to haul our own water while waiting for a well to be dug, and then we had to heat it up on the stove in order to have a bath. I can still picture myself with my knees curled up to my chest in that not so big galvanized tub. I loved the rain storms, minus the thunder and electricity, and it was reasonably warm. I did get caught once though by my boyfriend while I was running around in the nude."

"What…you had a boyfriend? How old were you anyhow?"

"I think I was nine or ten and yes, I had a boy slash friend. What is so odd about that?"

"I guess I thought I was your one and only."

"Sure you did. Anyhow, his name was Dennis and he was three years older than me. Apparently, I have always taken a liking to "older" men. He had a big crush on me but I liked him just as a friend as I had my eye on someone else."

Rainey raised his eyebrows. "So, you were a flirt way back then?"

"Do you think I'm a flirt? Well, I had no lady parts then so I wasn't too embarrassed, but poor Dennis was. He had come down the dirt road on his bike to give me one of his never ending presents that he was constantly making for me as I was running around naked. I almost ran into him. He turned beet red and I laughed and asked him if he wanted to join me. Of course he didn't."

"So you quit bathing in your birthday suit after that I take it?"

"If that is what you want to believe…let's hope we have a nice warm rain at Avanloch, and then you can draw your own conclusions."

"And you accuse me of teasing you…are you coming back to bed?"

"No! Get up, get up, and get a move on!"

We did manage to get cleaned up and dressed and make our way to Rainey's parent's house before everyone else arrived. Ruth and Jimmy were among the first. We had a group hug and thanked them for their contribution to the honeymoon surprise.

"I cannot tell you how much those photographs meant to us Ruth. There were times when I wasn't sure that I existed back then. You must have been the only one that had a camera. Lara and I don't even have many pictures of ourselves. I love you to pieces for supplying us with memories that we had all but forgotten." I said gratefully.

"The timing was perfect wasn't it? I come back to Hawthorne and start cleaning up our old house which had not been lived in for years, and lo, and behold, I find this roll of film. I had absolutely no idea what was on it, but was pleasantly surprised that it contained pictures of all of us from so long ago. That was a magical time for us all don't you think V?" Ruth couldn't have said it any better.

"Yes, and I thought of all of you throughout the years. I was very saddened when Lara told me that you and Jimmy were separating…I am so glad you have found your way back to each other. You can call me Vienna you know."

"Maybe I am a little nostalgic and still think of you as V. Just like you and Rainey, Jimmy and I never stopped loving each other; we just fell out of synch. We saw each other through the years because of our daughter Constance. The difference between us was that we always knew where each other was and you and Rainey didn't."

"I know I made a huge mistake keeping Ava and her father apart; a lesser man than Rainey would not have been able to forgive me. Constance is a lovely girl. I am so happy that she could attend the wedding and meet my girls. I understand she graduated this year and is going to live with your sister while she attends nursing school."

"We are very proud of her. She and your girls seemed to have become fast friends."

Rainey interrupted us and told me that my family had arrived. We visited with them and the other guests until we all sat down to brunch. I asked Rainey who the young man was that was seated next to Ava. He told me that it was Yates's eldest son and did his best to introduce us over the noisy throng. His name was Cameron. Just then, Cameron slid his chair back and came around to me and asked me if he could give his new "auntie" a hug. He said he had heard rumors about me for years but had really believed that I was a myth. We all had a big chuckle over that. He apologized profusely for missing the wedding ceremony. I liked him immediately, and I could tell by the smile on Ava's face that she did too.

During the scrumptious meal I thanked everyone again for the lovely surprises at the cabin; Lara for the lingerie, and Ruth and Patsy for the amazing photograph album. Rainey said he was delighted with the old pictures of us and scolded his mom ever so slightly for keeping them from him. She took it in good humor and said that perhaps she had made a mistake but it didn't matter anymore as her middle aged son had finally been united with the love of his life, and that he was at long last, happy again. She said she knew all along that I was the one for him. My father echoed the sentiment saying that he had picked Rainey out for me upon their first meeting.

Rainey looked at the two of them and replied. "Too bad you guys didn't let us in on your beliefs. Mom, did you just call me middle aged?"

"I think I did." Patsy laughed. "Now I know you specified no gifts but there are a few that have come for you and you are going to have to open them."

Rainey sighed and said. "They better be small. We'll tend to them and then Vienna and I are going to head out. We have decided to stay at least another night at the cabin. I know that it was inconvenient for some of you to be here on a Thursday for our wedding but Vienna wanted it to be on the anniversary of our first meeting which I think you all knew… we want to say thank you from the bottom of our hearts. We love you all and hope you will visit us in the near future. Thanks for the wonderful meal ladies. I hope you will forgive our hasty departure but I need to have some alone time with my bride."

Jimmy was not in favor of that. "Hold on there a second Buddy. You have already had five months with Vienna and you have a lifetime ahead to be alone with her, but what about the rest of us? Don't you think we have earned the right to spend a little more time with her before the two of you head back to Scotland? I'm sure Lily and Joe and her sisters would agree."

Rainey lowered his head as if he had been scolded by his father. I quickly came to his defense putting my arm through his. "Everyone has been so kind and I think Rainey is just overcome with all the emotion and attention that he forgot for a minute that we don't live in the next town. Certainly we can stay longer…right Honey?"

"You're right as usual Jimmy, I apologize. Of course I know how much you all love Vienna and I guess I am going to have to learn to share better."

"Hey, I misspoke…we love you too Rain, and are going to miss you just as much." Jimmy came over and hugged us both and Patsy suggested we go into the living room and make ourselves comfortable.

Rainey and I sat on the loveseat. He told everyone that I had shared a story with him earlier that morning that was very amusing and he thought that I should retell it.

"Really Rainey?" I knew he was trying to make amends and wanted to bring a little humor into the conversation.

"Really Vienna." He smiled and winked at me, and as usual he won, and I relayed my childhood nudity incident again embellishing it a little.

Mother and father remembered the episode and had a few choice words to add which led to more of my early encounters with the opposite sex. They had stolen the floor and had everyone laughing. Rainey kept waiting for me to deny the stories but I didn't. Instead I insisted that Jimmy and Yates and Rainey's parents relay some of Rainey's misadventures to my unknowing family. He protested, but it didn't do any good.

The day wore on and before we knew it the dinner hour had arrived. We ended up staying and enjoying leftovers from the wedding feast. We said our thanks for the wonderful day and said our goodbyes. It was 8 P.M. when we arrived back at the cabin.

As I prepared for bed I had a strange feeling come over me. I felt disorientated and had to clutch the wall to keep from falling. The dizziness continued for a few minutes and I sat on the bed hoping that Rainey hadn't noticed.

"Vienna, Vienna, wake up Honey, you're dreaming!"

It was Rainey's voice coaxing me to wake up. "Rainey, oh Rainey." I clung to him and he soothed me by rubbing my shoulders and kissing my forehead. "I had a horrible dream Rainey…I dreamt your dream."

"What do you mean…you dreamt my dream?"

"The one you used to have where I disappeared into nothingness." I was still shaking.

"Shish Honey, it's okay, I'm here. Can you tell me about it?"

"I was in a field full of flowers, and then there was nothing but rocks and I was stumbling trying to get over them and then I heard a roaring…it sounded like waves hitting against…I don't know what… then I was being propelled forward into nothingness. I was falling… falling, and then I heard you calling me. What does it mean?"

"It doesn't have to mean anything Sweetheart…it was just a dream, Shh, just a dream."

I lay in Rainey's arms for the rest of the night. I told him I wasn't going to go back to sleep, but I eventually did. I had my biggest enemy working against me; my mind. I had been plagued by many nightmares in the past and Rainey had not been there to comfort me. This one was most upsetting though as he was right beside me. Every time I closed my eyes a portentous feeling would envelope me, and I would shiver and Rainey would hold me tighter.

I awoke to the sweet aroma of freshly brewed coffee. It was the only vice I had outside of my voracious appetite for Rainey's love. He sat on the bed and handed me a steaming mug of the pungent brew. He stroked my arm and asked me how I was feeling.

"Well, I made it through the night thanks to you. I am such a baby. I don't know how I coped all those years without you to console me. But I guess most of my bad dreams back then were related to you. The girls have already told you that they continuously found me crying and calling out your name in the middle of the night."

"Yes, but you never have to do that again as I never plan on sleeping anywhere else but next to you."

I kissed him, but something was still not right with my chi.

We packed up and drove into Bridge Falls to see my parents and sister and niece off to Arizona. We had picked Morgan and Mason up from the Quinn ranch on the way. We were planning a quiet evening at the Palace with the boys and Ava and Rosy before heading to Potsdam the next day to start the first leg of our trip back to Scotland. As soon as everything had settled down I went into the conservatory to water all the plants so that they would not need attending to for several days. Lara had been the caretaker of the house for many years in my parent's absence and was going to continue to do so for Rainey and me. However, Sissy was leaving her husband and asked us if she could live here until she got her life back together. We welcomed the thought that someone was going to inhabit our second home and that we could aid her. I told her that we would continue to pay all the expenses as we would have had to anyhow. I opened a bank account for her just because I had the resources to do so. I had helped many people that I didn't even know throughout my years as Mistress of Avanloch, so I was only too happy to be able to help my own sister. Money was no object to me, but I did not take it for granted or spend it frivolously. Sissy was very grateful and promised she would take good care of the Palace for us.

Ava followed me into the conservatory and closed the door behind her. I turned and looked at her and knew she had something on her mind. "What is wrong Darling?"

"Nothing Mama. I want you to tell me again how it was for you the first time you saw Rainey?"

I smiled. "Come and sit down Ava and tell me what you really want to know."

"You say you knew that he was **the** one immediately…how did you know?"

"Something just came over me. I was weak in the knees when he took my hand and kissed it…that was not a common thing for guys to do. I felt like I was drowning in his eyes and when he spoke my name I heard music…I still do. Sounds corny doesn't it?"

"No. Mama, I think I may have found my Rainey and it scares me to death."

Ava had tears in her eyes. "Well, if it is so, don't make the same mistakes I did. Hold on to him with all you might and don't take anything for granted. Love is too precious."

"You know the only serious relationship I had before was with Randy, but I never once felt the tingling that I encountered when I first met Cam. I thought perhaps that it was just his rugged good looks that attracted me to him, but I soon found out he was a lot more than just handsome. I've only known him for two days Mama, but last night…"

I interrupted her. "You spent the night with him?"

"No, not that way Mama. We only talked and got to know each other. He is coming over soon; I hope that is all right. But, what should I do, what should I say?"

"Honey, your heart will decide for you."

"Suppose if I make a mistake and tell him how I feel and he doesn't reciprocate… what then? I'm older than him you know?"

I laughed. "Yes, by a few months…so what? You know your father did not tell me he loved me and he regretted it for years. Maybe it is not love you are experiencing but I think the feelings are strong enough to pursue."

There was a knock on the door. Ava nodded and I said. "Come in."

Of course it was Rainey. "I wondered where the two of you had gotten to."

"Darling, Ava needs to talk to you."

"Mother…I can't."

"Yes you can, and believe me, you really need to. He's the best listener and advice giver in the world."

I kissed her and then Rainey and closed the door behind me.

Rosalyn and I were playing some sort of invasion war video game with Morgan and Mason when the doorbell sounded. I answered the door and found Cam standing there.

"How nice to see you Cam; please come in."

"How are you today Mrs. Quinn?" His smiled broadly.

I took his arm and said "Let's go and find Ava shall we?"

As if on cue, she and Rainey emerged from the conservatory. They were both smiling and so I figured all went well. The phone rang and Rosy answered saying it was for me. I asked Rainey to take my place at the game and went into the kitchen to talk.

"Hello."

"Hello V."

I recognized the voice immediately. It belonged to Jack Jennings; the "almost" other man in my life. To this day I still wasn't sure if he was my rebound from Rainey both in 1960 and 1961, or if I had genuine feelings for him. He had told me that he was in love with me. We saw each other periodically when we were both back in Bridge. We would have coffee and talk. Jack had married and I believe had a son but the marriage was not working out as of the last time I had spoken to him. I hoped things had changed.

I did not miss a beat and said. "Hello Jack, how are you?"

"I understand via the Bridge grapevine that congratulations are in order. You finally got to marry the man that stole your heart. I am happy for you."

I turned to see Rainey with his arms crossed leaning up against the kitchen door. I knew he was not going to go away and so just smiled, and continued talking to Jack.

"Thank you Jack; how thoughtful of you to call. I hope you are well and that your life is more harmonious than it was the last time that we talked."

"Am I allowed to call you Vienna now?" He asked.

"Yes."

"I'm trying Vienna, I really and truly am. I think it is time that I put any thought of ever having a life with you to bed; twenty years is a long time to wait. If ever you should need anything, please know that I will come running…all you have to do is call. I wanted to hear your voice one last time." He sounded so lost, and I felt like crying.

"Thank you Jack, that means a lot to me. Thanks for calling. Please take care of yourself. Goodbye."

"Goodbye Vienna."

I laid the phone down gently. Rainey came over and put his arms around me and didn't say a word and I didn't volunteer anything. A girl has to have some secrets. We joined the kids in the living room and I asked who wanted to make dinner. Both boys looked at me as if I was bonkers. Rosy said that even if she wanted to there was nothing in the house to cook. We had already eaten the wedding luncheon leftovers. Rainey said he would go to the store and get some steaks.

"You know what? Tomorrow I have to quit eating and so tonight I think I want to have a big hamburger from the diner. What does everyone say?" I asked

"Why are you going to quit eating Vienna?" Mason wanted to know.

"Haven't you noticed that since you met me I have gained a lot of weight?"

"No." was the resounding answer.

"Well, I have and I have already had to buy a larger size. That is to worry about tomorrow; today, we feast again. Get everyone's order Rosy, no mustard or pickles on mine but everything else. Rainey, are you going to have onions?"

"Yes Dear, I'll have exactly what you are having. I'll go and pick the order up."

"No, I need you to help me change the bedding. Do you mind Rosy?"

"Of course not, I'll phone the order in. Do you think I should ask Ava and Cam?"

"No, you know what Ava likes and just get a double for Cam."

Rainey pulled out his wallet and asked her if she wanted to drive his car.

"The OLDS; really? I've been dying to."

The boys were on their feet before she could even ask them if they wanted to go with her. Rainey threw her his keys and told her to get milkshakes and lots of fries. As soon as they left he asked me if I was really serious about "making the bed." I took his hand and led him upstairs. I think he was a little surprised when I stopped at the linen closet.

"You weren't kidding?"

"No, I wasn't." I passed him a fitted sheet and asked him how he made out with Ava.

"Honey, I have never had to give relationship advice before, especially to a teenage girl who just happens to be my daughter, and who thinks she may be in love. I told her the only thing I could and that was that she must not deny her feelings the way I did because look what it had cost me. You know what she said to that don't you… the same thing you always say…that there would be no Rosy, no Mason or Morgan. God, you two are so much alike. Anyhow, I told her that we couldn't change the past but this was the here and now and she should follow her heart. I'm sure you told her the same thing. She is worried about a long distance romance working out but she is really smitten with Cam. I told her that he is exactly the kind of boy I would choose for her. She liked that."

"That was nice Rainey." We finished making the bed and I walked over to him and took a pillow out of his hands. "Give me that…it is torture watching you try to slip a pillow."

He asked me if I was angry with him. I asked him if I should be.

"I was very rude when I eavesdropped on your phone call from Jack. It was personal and I apologize."

"No need to. You know that I had a relationship with him don't you, but that it didn't go anywhere because after that New Year's Eve dance there was hope for you and me again? Of course we know that didn't go according to my plan did it?"

"You still haven't forgotten my interlude with Priscilla have you?"

"Interlude…is that what we are calling it now?" I'm sure I sounded bitter.

"You are throwing that up in my face because of Jack aren't you? I think that maybe he meant a lot more to you than you are letting on."

I had to nip this in the bud. Rainey was disturbed over the phone call, and I needed to assure him that Jack had only phoned to wish me happiness and nothing more. I would never tell him that there was a time not very long ago when I had considered becoming the "other woman" in Jack's life because I was so lonesome. I knew that he would have left his wife for me in the blink of an eye. Now, I know that Rainey would have also, but I never saw myself as a home wrecker so I never did anything about my fancies.

"Jack was there for me after you told me to forget you and in the darkest hours before I went to Scotland. I did not confide in him that I was pregnant…if I had, he would have offered to marry me; there is no doubt in my mind about that. I have told you that there has never been anyone other than you in my bed, but I don't think you believe me."

"I believe you about that and it shouldn't matter to me anyhow if you had a lover, but it does and especially because Jack is still in your life. Do you not believe that I wouldn't have wanted to marry you?"

"Oh, I knew you would but I didn't want you to feel obligated… you know that."

"I would not have felt obligated, but I know there is no way I can convince you of that."

"Well we are married now. I love you, and I am still hopelessly in love with you. My God, do you doubt my feelings? Jack is just a friend, but if it is your wish, I shall never have another word with him. I will make sure he never contacts me ever again." I wanted this conversation to be over with and I am sure that I sounded annoyed.

"I would never ask you to stop having a friendship with anyone, not even Jack. How asinine do you think I am?"

"I would do anything for you Rainey. I do not want this to be a problem for you."

"It won't Vienna, I promise. Will you forgive my stupidity?" He had put his arms around me, but I am afraid I was a little stiff and he could feel it and let go of me.

I was a little surprised that I was harboring some resentment of him intruding on my conversation with Jack. I would have liked to have another talk with Jack, but I didn't want to upset the apple cart and so I had better let the whole thing go.

"Have we just had our first disagreement Rainey?"

"I am not so sure that I would call it that, but more of a question and answer session."

The kids were home and they announced it very loudly. I did an about face and put my arms around Rainey and told him that he was never to feel insecure about my love again.

He said he would try not to be jealous of my male friends, but it wouldn't be easy.

I told him that I would probably have felt the same way if one of his former lady friends had called him. He told me that was never going to happen as he had no lady friends. I asked him if I had answered all his questions sufficiently and he said "Yes."

"I have one little bone to pick with you however. For your information, eavesdropping is listening behind closed doors, or hiding behind one…you were out and out hanging on my every word, and in plain sight."

"I stand corrected and I shall not invade your privacy again."

Now I felt rebuffed and I should have because I had hurt Rainey's feelings and wondered why I had said what I did. Was he always going to be the one to back down and apologize? What was wrong with me?

As if nothing had transpired between us, he asked me not to lose too much weight as he didn't want me to be skinny. I assured him I didn't want to go there again neither and that I just wanted to be able to fit into Jeremy's grandmother's clothes again. Miss Mary had a wardrobe that dated from the 1800's and I was the only one who was close to her size. Jeremy had insisted that I make use of the attire that had hung in the closets since 1939 at her tragic passing. Every outfit was as if it had just been purchased and never seemed to go out of fashion. It was never clear to me why her closets were kept intact. I could have donated them myself, but so far had not been able to do so. It was as if they were the castle's legacy and I best not mess with karma.

Lara and her husband Coop came over to bid us farewell that evening. While she was helping me with the coffee and leftover cakes I told her about the phone call from Jack and the subsequent confrontation from Rainey afterward. She understood but told me not to be too hard on him. Somehow, she was sure that he blamed my sudden departure of so long ago on Jack. That made no sense to me what so ever.

I could not say goodbye and so I said. "Vaya con dios." I had adopted the phrase from my Aunt Jannie. I had mixed feelings about leaving Bridge Falls as I felt totally safe here. I hated to leave Lara and Jimmy and Rainey's parents, but Avanloch was calling me home again and though I felt apprehensive. I must go and pray these feelings that something ominous was waiting me would go away. I slept close to Rainey all night long and he welcomed the intimacy.

Chapter 2

Forebodings

The whole trip back to Avanloch was tedious and though I tried to contribute to the conversations, I did not do a very good job. Even Ava who had just left her new relationship with Cam behind was more animated then I was.

When Winston picked us up in the limo at the train depot in Waverly I questioned him right away about the going ons at the castle. Nothing unusual had happened while we were away. I was not pacified as the feeling of impending doom was following me.

Rainey insisted upon carrying me over the threshold once again. This was the third time! Once inside the grand entrance the kids encouraged him to carry me up to the second floor. I begged him to put me down as I was too heavy and I didn't want to go upstairs anyhow. He lowered me to the floor and as he did so I felt as if the walls were closing in on me. I heard voices that seemed to be emanating from the century old portraits. Rainey said something to me, but I couldn't understand what it was. I was slipping through his arms and I promptly fainted.

Rainey knew she was light headed; he could see it in her eyes as he felt her body go limp. He gathered her back in his arms and carried her into the small drawing room and laid her down on the divan. Ava and Rosy were fretting and the boys kept asking him what had happened; what was wrong with Vienna?

"I'm sure she is just fatigued and I know she didn't eat much today. Rosy, why don't you go and see what you can find for a snack and bring her some water okay? Ava, just as a precaution, perhaps we should call her doctor…this is the second time she has passed out in the last few months." He was trying not to show how concerned he was.

Mason had followed Rosy and he ran back with a pitcher of ice water. Morgan had gone into the powder room and returned with a damp, cold cloth. Rainey told him that was smart thinking and applied it to Vienna's forehead just as she was starting to open her eyes. Ava had returned and said they were in luck as Dr. Mac was in the village and his receptionist said she would track him down and send him over.

I was confused. Why was everyone hovering around me, and why was I lying on the sofa in the drawing room? I tried to right myself, but Rainey cautioned me to take it easy and held me from fully sitting up. I did not fight him, but I had a lot of questions.

"It's all right Darling; you had a little fainting spell again." Rainey explained.

"Mama, are you okay? We were just joking, I'm sorry." Ava was in tears.

"Whatever are you talking about Ava? Please don't cry…I just fainted, right? I didn't fall down the stairs or anything did I?"

Rosy and Mrs.D arrived with some soup and crackers.

"Miss Vela, are we a little woozy then? This will fix you right up. Rosy near to scared me out of me britches. Sit up a tad luv." Mrs. D had taken over. "Now everyone out and give the lass some room to breathe!"

I laughed and watched as they all fussed but left anyhow. I saw the look on Rainey's face as he glanced back at me and I saw fear. I smiled and said. "I want you to stay… please Rainey." I reached out for him and he came and sat next to me.

Mrs. D left to make a pot of tea.

I ate a little of the broth and made a face saying it was "bloody awful."

Rainey smiled. "That's my girl." He took the bowl from me and asked if I could eat a few crackers.

"I am not nauseated…I used to live on these when I was pregnant."

"There is that "pregnant" word again, but I know you're not… right?"

"I'm not. Please, I want to go upstairs." I said clinging to him.

"What is it Darling…you're trembling. You have nothing to be sorry for."

"Yes I do. I was so mean to you the other day and you didn't even get mad at me."

"You, mean? Now that is funny! You let me know how things are, and if you gave me a little tongue lashing then it was nothing less than I deserved. There is nothing you can say or do that will make me angry; don't you know that? All of these years all I wanted was to have you back in my life, and I am not going to waste a single moment being cross with you…exasperated maybe. This fainting is starting to worry me though."

The doorbell chimed. Rainey said. "That will be the doctor."

"What? And just who was the one that called him?"

Amma arrived and admitted Dr. Macintosh into the drawing room. She introduced him to Rainey and went over and kissed me on the cheek.

"Welcome home Mrs. Quinn; you make quite an entrance."

I kissed her back and asked her to return later so I could tell me all about the wedding, but first she had to assure everyone that there was nothing to worry about.

"How about if I be the judge of that Miss Vela? Now what is this that I hear you have run off and got yourself married? I thought you and I had an arrangement; does your young man know about us?" Dr. Mac teased.

"Shh, he is right here you know?"

Rainey grinned and excused himself, but I called him back.

"I want him to stay Mac." He knew better than to argue with me.

"Certainly he can stay and hold your hand, but not until I have taken your blood pressure." He smiled as he pumped up the blood pressure cuff. Satisfied he felt my pulse and did a facial and neck exam. He found nothing out of the ordinary and told everyone so saying he was glad that I didn't appear to have any head or neck injuries and that I must have fell on something soft.

"Just me Doc.; I've caught her both times she has collapsed." Rainey informed him.

"Whoa there…this isn't an isolated event then? How often has this happened Vela?"

"Only twice, but I should tell you that I have had several dizzy spells though…sorry Rainey, I didn't want to worry you." I confessed.

Rainey scowled. "You can forget that because I am openly worried. Should I be Doc?"

"Not necessarily. Vela, is there a possibility that you could be pregnant?"

"I am not. It is not that kind of dizzy. I feel like something is tossing the inside of my head around, and I have the feeling of impending doom."

"Are you telling me that you are having premonitions?" Mac asked skeptically.

"No; I don't see anything happening. I don't know how else to explain it except it is very unnerving. I started to experience these strange sensations a while ago, but they have become more frequent since the wedding." I looked pleadingly at Rainey hoping he would understand why I hadn't confided in him.

"Perhaps this is something that you should discuss with Dr. Jai? I do want you to come in for a full physical however. Can you see that she does that Rainey? For now, I want you to get plenty of rest and nourishment. I do not want to see you as slim as you were last year. Yes, yes, I know you are very active. I like your new look. One more question…are you taking any new medications that I am not aware of?"

"No."

Rainey was quick to point out that I had been off the pills that I had been taking for despondency for several months.

Mac frowned and asked her if Dr. Jai was aware of my decision.

"Rainey not being in my life was the reason for my melancholy. We have been back together for five months now, and I do not need a placebo anymore." I squeezed Rainey's hand, and he brushed the hair back from my face and kissed my forehead.

"Well let's leave those kinds of decisions up to the professionals shall we? You may be having some sort of withdrawal symptoms. I think you should discuss it with Dr. Jai."

Rainey promised that he would have me in for a check-up later in the week as he accompanied Mac into the hallway. I got up, and ran to him as soon as he closed the drawing room door behind him. I stood on my tip toes and entwined my hands around his neck. I started kissing his neck and face and whispering in his ear.

"I want to go upstairs with you Rainey. I want to be alone with you."

"I want to be with you too Honey, but first we have to deal with the kids. They are worried about you just as I am. Do you remember what you said to me when we left my parent's place last winter?"

"I'm sure I said a lot of things as you had a hundred questions for me."

"This was not an answer or a question; you said that we had to start acting like adults, and I think that applies to right now. We have the rest of our lives to be alone together but right now we have to inform everyone that you are all right. What do you say?"

I released my hold on him and sighed. "All right, where are they?"

He took my hand and led me into the grand hallway and pointed to the four anxious figures leaning over the second floor balcony. I motioned for them to come down. The boys were gentlemen and let the girls descend before them.

Rosy and Ava hooked their arms through mine and in unison asked how I was feeling and what did the doctor have to say.

"Are you sure these two aren't twins?" Rainey asked.

I laughed while telling them I was fine; just fatigued. Amma and Mrs. D escorted us into the kitchen where tea, juices, sandwiches and cookies and a steaming pot of coffee awaited us. Ava called Duffy in to join us. Amma said that Johnny was out riding checking on the cattle and sheep in the pasture on the lower forties. Rainey stated that he should be with him.

"Tomorrow is early enough Dear and I think I might join you as I haven't been down there yet this year. The fields should be alive with the spring calves and newly born lambs. Do you *kids* want to come along?" I inquired.

Rosy looked at her sister and said. "How long do you think she will keep referring to us as *kids*?"

"It's easier than saying boys and young ladies."

"We don't mind Mother." Ava admitted.

"Tell us all about the wedding as we are dying to hear." Amma coaxed.

Each of them contributed to the momentous occasion. After almost an hour I said that I simply had to go and lie down for a while. Rainey said that he would join me so that he could keep an eye on me..

Mrs. D told us that supper would be ready in two hours, but that they would all understand if we were still too tired to join them.

Ava pulled out the wedding album that she and Rosy had already put together. I kissed everyone on their brows and said I would look at it later. Rainey took my hand and we took the lift to the second floor. As soon as we alighted I ran down the hall laughing. Rainey caught me at the bedroom door and said that I was going to wake the dead.

"I've got news for you Darling," I said breathlessly, "the dead are already awake."

I held him against the bedroom door. "I love you Rainey Quinn."

"I love you too Vienna LaFontaine Quinn." He picked me up and carried me to the bed.

It was nine o'clock in the evening before we made it downstairs for supper. After a fare of cold chicken and salad we went in search of the children and found them in the games room playing billiards. We visited for a while and then returned to the bedroom to get some much needed sleep.

I was awakened at three a.m. Before I even opened my eyes I knew that Maveryn was in the room. Gently I aroused Rainey and immediately he was awake thinking something was wrong with me.

I pointed to the end of the bed where he encountered something he was sure didn't exist. There, in a long white gown which seemed to be made of gossamer stood…no, floated a vision of sheer beauty. Her flowing hair was as red as Rosy's and her countenance was one of beauty. Her arms were outstretched as if welcoming us into her fold. Then she came closer, and with her hands motioned for us to follow her. I was out of bed in a flash and grabbed Rainey as he came around the corner of the bed, and hastily put his robe on. I was not as modest and yanked a sheet from the bed and draped it around myself. Somehow the sitting room door opened. We followed her and noticed that a page was open to some sort of journal on the desk. We didn't have time to peruse it as Maveryn was already on the move and floating down the hall. She stopped at Rosy's room where we found Rosy in one bed and Ava in another. Maveryn's persona lit up and she folded her arms as if they were wings and slowly backed towards the window and then… she was gone.

Ava woke up first and then Rosy. I spoke in a whisper that Maveryn had made a visit and Rosy yawned and said. "Oh, is that all?" She rolled over and went back to sleep as did Ava.

We walked back to their bedroom and sat on the bed.

"Am I dreaming Vienna? Please tell me that I am for what I think I may have witnessed simply cannot be." Rainey begged.

"If it is possible that two people have had the same dream, and if it eases your mind, I will tell you that yes, you are dreaming. Did you place Maveryn's diary on the desk? I didn't and so if it is there and opened I would say that she was indeed here. There is only one way to find out…come, and we will go and see."

Reluctantly, Rainey tagged along behind me, and sure enough the diary was open on the desk. I was astounded to see what was written on the exposed page, and read it out loud.

There will come three strangers to the doors of Avanloch. One will be invited and one will have a mission to fulfill. The third, though welcomed, will deliver a message of extreme peril …do not ignore it or the consequences will be grave and much grief will fall upon the house of Avanloch.

"What the hell! Is this somebody's idea of a joke?" Rainey was astounded by the look on my face. "Vienna, what is it?"

"I've never seen this page before. It looks like Maveryn's writing, but I don't think it is. What could it mean and how did it get here?"

"You're the one who consorts with ghosts so you tell me."

"Do you think this has something to do with the feelings of impending doom that I have been experiencing?"

"If I thought that then I would have to admit that your subconscious knows things that no one else does, or that you have hidden powers, and I am not ready to go there yet. Let's go back to bed and look at this in the light of day, okay Hon? Maybe we just imagined the whole thing."

"Tell me honestly Rainey; were you frightened by Maveryn's appearance?"

"Yes and no. She herself did not scare me but yes, if she was really here then I think that I have entered another realm, one of which I don't believe in. I went along with all your stories of her visitations, but I have to admit that I did not believe you. You are such a great story teller that I don't think I stopped to consider that there was a possibility that you were telling the truth. Now, I honestly don't know what I believe anymore. I am hoping I am still dreaming."

"You have heard the girls speak of seeing her also, so now I think you need to hear from others as well. You will find that no one finds her visits upsetting…now the Black Russian… well, that is a different story. Did you not experience a feeling of peace and tranquility with her visit?"

"Vienna, you are asking me something I cannot answer. If I can't admit that *she* was here, how can I tell you how I felt? I can just imagine the boy's reaction."

"I think you need to read some stories of other people's encounters with the spirit world, and I think you will be surprised to learn that there are many scholars who have had experiences that could not be explained."

"I know that Sweetheart, but how many treat the apparitions as an everyday occurrence and don't question how it is possible. It is like you have your own guardian angel."

"Now you are getting it Rain."

I awoke to hear swearing coming from my sitting room. "Oh, oh, what has he discovered now?" I threw my robe on and found him sitting at the desk scowling.

"What is it Sweetheart?" I asked him.

"I'm sorry Love, I didn't mean to wake you; come, look."

"What? Oh, it is the strange notation. What else is in the journal?"

"That's just it Vienna…there is nothing else in the book…not a single, solitary thing!"

"Strange; does this mean you are ready to omit that you weren't dreaming last night?"

"I am not ready to admit a damn thing! I'll tell you one thing though; I am going to get to the bottom of this. Someone in this house is going to answer for this." His tone was one of determination.

I smirked. "Good luck with that."

"Does this not upset you? It is obviously a warning of some sort."

"I say, let's wait and see if three strangers come to our door." I said rationally.

We took the back stairs to the kitchen where we found Mrs. D flitting around like a busy bee. Her work station was a mess with flour, spices, fruit, and a rolling pin. We said good morning and discovered the coffee pot was empty.

"Can we make our own breakfast Mary; we promise not to get in your way." I vowed.

"Naw, naw, tis be naw cookin on yous honeymoon! Tis all been takin care of. The girlies have all under control. Shoo with you now, your breakfast will be getting cold as peas porridge."

Rainey smiled at her and said. "Right you are then."

She picked up her rolling pin and shook it at him. "Boutin time there was some blokes in this house to appreciate good vittles. These wummin they have to keep their figures ya know. You like roast pig-let Mr. Rainey with cabbage and turnips?"

"Sounds delicious. Can we come back and help you? Can't you just call me Rainey?"

"Off with you then. My scullery no place for a man."

We pushed open the swinging door and found the young people already at the table.

"I hardly expected to see you all up so early." I said pouring coffee for Rainey and myself. I sat down next to him and inhaled the delightful aroma of hazelnut. "I know Mrs. D did not make this coffee…"

"I did Mama." Ava said.

"And who made this appetizing breakfast?" I inquired with tongue in cheek.

"Let's see; Mason made the orange juice and Morgan made the toast and Rosy set the table and I opened up the cereal boxes. Now eat before it gets cold!" Ava laughed.

Rainey poured corn flakes for us and topped the bowls with strawberries and creamy milk. "Did every one sleep all right?" He asked.

Rosy looked at us. "Yes, but we had some visitors in the early hours."

"What kind of **visitors**?" Mason asked.

"Not the kind you are hoping for. It was *only* Rainey and our mother."

"We had a visitor too Rosy. Your mother Maveryn came to see us last night and she took us on a little tour. First, she beckoned us to follow her into Vienna's parlor where we found a strange message in an open journal and then she had us follow her to the bedroom where you and Ava were sleeping." Rainey looked at his boys as he retold the ghostly visit. They both just stared at him and he wasn't sure if they believed him.

Finally Morgan said. "You're joshing, right Dad?"

I interjected. "No, he's not; Maveryn was here. Your dad is still trying to come to terms with the fact that someone from another dimension paid him a visit. She was here for him, not me. The message in the journal is very cryptic and I want you girls to see if you recognize the handwriting. Rainey thinks someone in the house is playing a cruel trick."

"No one on this entire property would do or say anything to harm you Mama, you know that. What did it say?" Ava asked.

"Later Dear. What are everybody's plans for the day?"

"Aren't we all going riding?" Mason asked.

"Yes, let's; it looks like a beautiful day." I agreed.

"I want to see the journal first so I don't wonder about it all day." Rosy declared.

We cleaned up the table and went upstairs to my parlor. We stood back as one by one they all read the notation. Rosy was the last, and when she had finished she flipped through the booklet and turned it upside down to see if there was anything else in it. She discovered as we had, that there wasn't.

"Where did this come from and how did it get here? Surely Maveryn is not to blame."

"Of course she isn't!" I declared.

"What are you going to do about it Mama?" Ava asked.

"There is nothing to do. Rainey wants to question all the staff which he certainly has the right to. Me, I am going to wait and see if three strangers come to the door."

"Your mother is not taking this serious, but I guarantee you that I am." Rainey vowed.

"Well, I think if someone wrote it as a joke and we find out who they are they should be put in with the Black Russian!" Mason declared.

"Yeah," Morgan conferred. "it's a bunch of crap!"

We left for our horseback ride humored by Mason's suggestion. We met Johnny at the stables and after he congratulated us, he and Rainey and the boys went to saddle our mounts. I usually was in charge of my own horse but decided to let the guys do it for me today. Amma met us and said that she was on the way up to help Mrs. D with the dinner preparations as all the other girls were off today for one reason or the other. I offered to stay and assist but she wouldn't hear of it.

I knew that Rainey wanted to get Johnny's take on the events of last night and so we let them take the lead. Mason and Morgan had been riding since they were knee high to a grasshopper, but I still kept an eye on them to make sure they were comfortable with the horses that they had chosen.

In the months prior to our wedding in Bridge Falls, Rainey and I had come riding every day that the weather permitted. Because I had been a solitary rider before I had not ventured too far off the beaten track, but together we had discovered new and inviting trails to pursue. Once we got caught in a sudden down pour and had to take shelter in an old run down shack that I never even knew existed. It was full of last years' hay so someone was making use of it for storage. We stayed until the rains had tapered off and made good use of the bed that Rainey fastened out of the bales. I smiled in remembrance and rode up alongside of him and Johnny and inquired if Johnny knew about the little hovel. Rainey grinned as he knew what I was thinking. Apparently, several of these little lean-tos were scattered around the range.

"Something like line shacks," I said. "just not as comfortable." Johnny asked me what I meant, but for an answer I took off galloping.

We arrived home in time to have a quick shower and change before supper. Rainey wanted me to wait for him while he cleaned up but I daren't as I knew what would happen and I wanted to get down stairs to help with the table. Amma and Johnny joined us for the meal as their girls were all with Granny Kay in the village. Amma told us of the plight of one of the young women from the village. Her and her four year old daughter were living with her parents as her husband had left her, and now she had been diagnosed with a cancer that required four to six weeks of treatments. She could only receive them in London and was going to have to live there which she could not afford to do. I was well aware of Elsa McCracken's illness, but did not know that it had come to this.

"She won't have to worry anymore as her and her family can have our flat in London." I announced.

"But Mama, where will Rosy stay?" Ava questioned me.

"I wasn't aware that she was still using the apartment. Pass me the gravy boat please Mason and I will refill it."

Mrs. D said she would do that and I placed my hands on her shoulders and told her that she had done enough for one day. Rosy pushed her chair back and followed me into the kitchen. I heard Mason ask how many people it took to get a pitcher of gravy. His father told him to mind his manners.

"Mama, I didn't mean to keep anything from you. You and Rainey had just found each other, and there was so much to get used to and plans to make for your wedding, I didn't think the time was right for me to tell you."

I opened the back door and suggested that we take a little walk.

"What about the gravy?"

"Let them get their own." I smiled and took her hand and we strolled towards the pavilion. She asked me how long I had known. I told her ever since she brought Evan home last summer. She was quick to say that they were only friends then and things didn't change until just before Christmas, and again, she asked me how I knew.

"Well my dear, I have known ever since you were a teenager that Evan had a thing for you, but he held his feelings back because you were so young and he was much older. Perhaps he was intimidated by Jeremy and me because he worked for the company. You were spending so much time on the telephone when you were home, so I assumed something was up with the two of you."

"Do you think Evan is too old for me?"

"There is no age difference when two people love each other. Women have been marrying much older men for centuries. Rainey is five years older than me, and I used to think that perhaps I was too young for him, but that was just silly. You are twenty two and Evan is what, twenty nine or thirty? Jeremy was much older than that."

"Yes, but Mother, you did not have a physical relationship with him."

"No I didn't. Sex with the person you love is very important to the relationship, but trust and patience and understanding play an important role also, and you always have to be a good listener and be able to forgive. There is no room for suspicion or resentment of past events. Are you and Evan in love?"

"Yes Mama. I may have found my Rainey."

I threw my head back and laughed. "Your sister said the exact same thing about Cam."

"The way you and Rainey look at each other and talk as if there is no one else in the room has inspired us to want the same kind of love for ourselves. I will never be able to fathom how you had the willpower to stay away from him for twenty years."

"It all worked out didn't it, and it will for you too if it is meant to be. You shouldn't be ashamed that you are co-habiting when you are in London. I think that once your relationship is revealed you will be able to relax a little more. Do you want to tell me anything more or shall we return to the family? You do know that you can ask or tell me anything don't you?"

"Yes Mama, I do. I love you and I am sorry I didn't tell you sooner about Evan."

"I love you my darling Rosalyn and you only thought I didn't know. You have been unusually sweet and considerate and only love can make a woman smile as you do."

We took our seats back at the table and no one acted as if we had been gone at all. I placed the boat with the cold gravy back on its platter. Rainey looked as if he was going to break out in laughter as they were all starting on dessert and coffee or tea. Ava poured me a cup saying that it was decaffeinated. I told Mrs. D that her pies looked delicious but I would pass for now.

"Amma, would you like to accompany me to the McCracken's after coffee? Will you girls do the cleanup please?"

"Yes Mama." Ava and Rosy said in unison, as usual.

Rainey offered his and the boys services. He winked at me.

Mrs. D said. "Men and boys in the kitchen…what'll they think of next?"

Amma and I had a very nice visit with Elsa and her parents. It was early evening, and her little daughter was not yet in bed. Her name was Tanny. I knew her from Sunday school. I asked her to come over and sit on my knee after all the arrangements had been made with the McCracken's. I asked her if she would like to come and stay with me and the girls at the castle while her Mama and Granny and Grandad were in the big city because it was no place for a bonny little lass. Her eyes lit up and she asked her mama if she could. Elsa said she couldn't ask such a thing from us. I told her it would be a delight to have a "youngin" in the house again. I told them that I had a special room downstairs set up for day care which both Amma's and my girls had used, and that she could sleep in the same room as Ava. I guaranteed them that Tanny would never be left alone. There were a lot of tears shed and they wanted to know how they could ever repay us.

"Just get healthy Elsa; that's all we ask. I could use some help in finding suitable girls to come and work for us however. Shalla has moved away and I fear that Cyn will be leaving us soon also. There were some very lovely girls who came to help out at Henry's retirement supper…one of them I knew as Kelly, but the others were unknown to me. If you can recommend anyone I would be most appreciative."

They promised they would give the matter serious thought. Mr. McCracken said he was worried about taking so much time off from his job at the flour mill but I assured him he had nothing to worry about. I made a note to myself to approach the foreman tomorrow. We left feeling we had did all that we could without offending their dignity. I walked Amma to Brackenshire as I wanted to take the long way home and meander through the rose gardens. When I arrived back at Avanloch it was half past eight. I found Rainey and the boys in the grand hallway taking measurements.

"How goes the hunt for the mysterious secret rooms?" I asked.

"Not very well Vienna." Morgan sounded down hearted. "Dad has got us measuring and taping everything that doesn't move. Tomorrow we descend into the cellars."

"Good luck. I would assist you but I am just too tired. See you tomorrow boys. Will you be coming up soon Rainey?"

He said he would be up in a jiff. I was already in my night clothes and brushing my hair at my dressing table when he opened the bedroom door.

"Is Vienna back?" He asked me.

"What a strange question; you can see I am here, and why did you phrase it like that?"

He relieved me of my task and gently did the brushing while watching me in the mirror.

"Why? I think your other personality showed itself at the dinner table tonight."

"Whatever are you talking about?" I frowned at him in the mirror.

"Perhaps I am overreacting…were you not a little testy with Rosy? I am not accustomed to hearing annoyance in your voice when you speak to the girls."

I reached up and took hold of his hand. "I did not mean to sound cross; I hope no one else interpreted my words as such. Shall I tell you of our conversation?"

"Only if you want to and it is not infringing on mother/daughter confidences."

"It is not Darling, and you would find out sooner than later anyhow. It appears as if we have another daughter who is in love." My reflection smiled at him.

"I like it that you refer to her as ours and I hope that someday she will come to think of me as a father. Who is the lucky fellow?"

"His name is Evan Govern; he is our pilot. He was a bush pilot in Australia before coming to work for the company some years back, not long before Jeremy became ill. He is a very nice young man and has no family; at least none that he speaks of. Jeremy and I welcomed him into our lives and our home. I am very fond of him and have known that he has thought of Rosy as more than a sister for some time."

"Your pilot…does that mean that you own a plane?"

"It's a small jet and it is owned by the company, not me."

"A small jet; just how small? Do you, oh pardon me, the *company*, also own ships, and maybe a yacht or two? The girls weren't exaggerating about your wealth were they?" I was surprised to hear the testiness in Rainey's voice.

"There are no yachts that I know of. McAllister Holdings does own freighters. The jet is only used for business. I am not keeping anything from you Rainey. Are you angry with me for not telling you before? Tomorrow I will introduce you to all the ledgers that have an accounting of what Avanloch and McAllister Holdings are worth."

"I do not need to know any of that Vienna. In truth, it is none of my business."

"Wrong; whether you like it or not, you are the Lord of the lair and I know you have a knack with numbers so I need you to watch over the finances. Should anything happen to me, the girls will need guidance."

"Will you quit talking like that? I will do whatever you need me to, but I do not want to step on anybody's toes. Now, tell me more about this Evan and when am I going to meet him? Do you think there is a wedding pending, and speaking of that, when is ours?"

"I have been thinking that it should be soon…what do you say to two weeks from now? I need to hire more staff, especially a helper for Mrs.D. I was sure that she was going to retire but she assures me that is not going to happen anytime in the foreseeable future. She said that just because she is sixty something doesn't mean she's ready to be put out to pasture. Reita's final farewell was Henry's dinner. Mrs. Sharpe is also retiring and so we need to find a new cook for Brackenshire also. Millie and Emma are ready to pack it in, Shalla is gone and I fear Cyn is about to make a home for her and her young man in Waverly. Oh, why does everyone have to leave at once? Most of them have been here for as long as I can remember. I don't know if I am up to interviews with strangers."

Rainey laid the brush down and turned me to face him. He wiped the tears from my eyes with his hands. "Oh my poor, little rich girl; all she has to worry about is replacing the staff. I will help you my love but you are not to consider doing anything until you have had a complete check-up, do you hear?" I liked it when Rainey was assertive with me.

I told him to quit teasing me about being rich. It was going to be very difficult to replace the staff who had been part of my life for so long. I asked him if he understood. His answer was to take me in his arms and ask me to dance with him. I was dead on my feet, but could not refuse him. He had chosen to play a piece from the fantasy overture Romeo and Juliette by Tchaikovsky. I did not understand his choice of music unless he was insinuating that we were doomed lovers, but I did not question him. As we slowly waltzed around the room I informed him that a little girl was going to come and live with us for a while. His response was not what I expected.

"Is this to be a trial run for the child that you want us to have and does she count as one of the strangers? If she does, then I am all right with it."

"She is not a stranger Rainey because I know her, but if you want to consider her as the one who was invited, then that's okay. I do think that we need to talk more about Maveryn's visit though."

"There is nothing to discuss; she was either here or she wasn't, and I still cannot comprehend that she was. I do not know how to explain the events of that night. I don't know how you embrace the spirit world so readily. Can you explain that to me?"

"Yes I can. It was a long time ago, and I was very lonely and perhaps susceptible. I think I told you that the first time I felt an unexplained presence was when Ava was born. I cannot explain the feeling of peace and love that I was left with. When Maveryn first came to me I thought that there was nothing else more wondrous in the whole world. I was reunited with a dear friend. She had trusted me enough to let me see her. I felt loved again. I accepted her into my life, and whenever I have been troubled she has come to me. She doesn't speak, but I swear we communicate telepathically. I am always reassured after one of her visits. I do feel that her visit the other night was a warning of sorts and will have to try and figure out what it all means. It doesn't matter to me whether you believe or not because the mystical world is not something everyone can embrace. Does that answer your question because I could go on and on?"

"It will suffice for now. Shall we go to bed?"

"Yes, just one other thing I forgot to tell you. Rosy said that she thought she had found her Rainey in Evan."

"You have to be kidding…Rosy said that?"

"No, I am not and she also said she doesn't understand how I could have stayed away from you so long for you were quite a catch."

"Well that is certainly true; I am a catch and I too wonder how and why it took you so long to realize it."

"Rainey Quinn…you conceited so and so!"

"And you love it when I'm right, don't you Baby?"

The next morning at breakfast I asked the boys if they had ever wanted a little sister. They looked at me as they usually did when they thought I was kidding.

Morgan answered for the two of them. "Well, it is too late for that. You and Dad are way too old to have a baby…right Dad? Vienna, you have a very bizarre sense of humor."

"Too old; Morgan thinks we are toooo old. Do you think we should tell them or not?"

Mason hit his forehead with the palm of his hand. "Jeeze, are we ever dunce Morg. It was Vienna's subtle way of telling us that she was going to have a baby when she asked us if we noticed that she had gained weight."

Morgan clued in to what his brother was insinuating. He looked at his Dad who was hiding behind a newspaper. "Is that so Dad, and you already know that it's going to be a girl?"

Rainey put the paper down and with eyebrows raised, looked at me and said that it was my story to tell.

"It's not really a story; a little girl is coming to live with us. She could arrive at any minute and we have to make plans for her arrival."

"She can't be here that soon!" Morgan exclaimed.

I decided to keep the ruse going. "You boys still haven't told us how you feel about a small child in the house. I promise you that it won't interfere with your sleuthing."

I think the boys were confused as to how their dad and I could be expecting so soon. Mason was still putting things together.

"No wonder you were so worried about Vienna when she fainted Dad. Is that what happens to women who are going to have a baby? Are you all right now Vienna?"

Rainey said that I was just fine and that they need not worry and perhaps it was time that I come clean with them. He grinned and said. "Vienna, do you want to explain?"

"Sorry boys, I was only having a little fun with you. We are not having a baby…but there is a little girl coming to stay with us for a while. She is four years old and her mother is very sick and requires a lot of treatment in London, so I have invited her to live with us here until her mother is well again. I promise you that she will not get in your way. I could use some help setting up the playroom and finding a suitable bed for her though. She will be sharing Ava's room right next to your Dad's and mine."

"Of course we will assist you, won't we boys? We can put our explorations off for a few hours; those stairs and cellar aren't going anywhere. Your wish is our command my Lady." Rainey winked at me and I gratefully acknowledged their help.

"We never did answer your question about wanting a baby sister did we?" Mason asked.

I put my arm around his shoulder as we walked towards the storage closet. "I am sure that is the last thing that teenage boys would ever think about. I don't really expect an answer. As we say over here, I was only pulling your chain."

"You're right though Vienna, we never thought about having a sister as we knew Mom and Dad would never have any more children. I think if you and Dad want to have a baby that is your business and not ours. We have Ava and Rosy and they are the best sisters in the world, so another one would be great, right Morg?"

"We could have done a lot worse." Morgan said.

Rainey cuffed him lovingly on the head.

"You shouldn't be worried about what we think Vienna. We are only here for a few months and you and Dad have a lifetime ahead of you. We will do our best to help you with the little girl." Mason promised.

"Of course I worry about what you two think. You are a very important part of our family. I do want to warn you though that I do want to have a baby with your father and if God chooses to bless us, we will be overjoyed …it better be soon though as I am getting long in the tooth…right Morgan?" He blushed and Rainey smiled and kissed me.

Two hours later we ready for Tanny's visit. The playroom was once again furnished with everything that any young girl could possibly want. It hadn't been used as such since Amma's and Johnny's girls were young. We had most recently used it to store items that were to be donated to charity. It would be nice to see a young child on the premises again. I could not expect Ava and Rosalyn to babysit her all day however, and thus my problem of hiring suitable staff arouse again.

Ava had selfishly offered to share her bedroom with Tanny and that meant that she would be her night nanny relieving me of the worry. Her exact words to me were, "You cannot expect Rainey to share you with a child; after all you are still on your honeymoon." Rosy said that she would take up the slack and they would both help out in the daytime as long as they were around. That was it exactly…I couldn't ask them to give up their summer for something that was my idea. Tomorrow would be time enough for me to actually do something about finding help for Avanloch.

I decided to ignore it for the time being and joined the boys in the cellar leaving the girls to rearrange furnishings in Ava's room. I found the trio standing by the doors that opened into the wine storeroom. Rainey had the huge key ring in his hand and told the boys to prepare themselves for the smell that was going to greet them. Mason asked why.

I explained that these cellars that housed the wines were very old and that many bottles had been dropped and broken throughout the years, and that because the floor was dirt there was always a sweet earthy odor escaping as the doors were opened. I assured them that it would dissipate soon.

"Holy crap!" Morgan exclaimed. He and Mason followed their father as he led them through the vaults that seemed to go on forever.

"How many bottles do you think there are Dad, and why in the world would anyone need so many?" Mason asked

"I think Vienna can answer that question better than me."

I showed them a chart on each row that was supposed to show the name and vintage of each wine. Whenever a bottle was removed or a new one added the date and any other info. was to be recorded. I told them that I had no idea as to how many bottles there were. There really isn't any sense to keep track anymore because I don't drink and the girls seldom do, but that Rainey could take up the task if he so desired.

"Before my time many a gala event was held here and I am sure numerous flagons were consumed on a regular basis. Mr. McAllister and I only entertained a couple of times a year and he was responsible for the maintenance and restocking. The temperature never seems to fluctuate at all down here as apparently wine is supposed to be kept at a constant temperature. Ash and her friends like to raid the vats and so she has been in charge, but now that your dad is here I think he can assume the responsibility of keeping the stock up to standards. Don't ask me what that means because I do not know. Speaking of such, Rainey perhaps you would like to bring a bottle up to dinner? Anyhow, I am going to leave you to do your spelunking or whatever. The girls and I have gone over this room with a fine tooth comb and found nothing…I hope you will be more successful."

"What are you going to do Vienna and do you require my help?" Rainey asked.

"I'm going to have tea with Amma and go over some menus with Mrs.D, that's all."

Amma and her eldest daughter, Alexa were waiting for me in the kitchen.

Amma poured me a cup of tea even though she knew I did not care for it. I sat down and added cream and a cube of sugar knowing full well it was not going to improve on the flavor. My mother had enjoyed her afternoon tea fix and I pretended to when we served guests from the village that would arrive once a week for the tradi-tional "high tea" affair.

Occasionally, a pot of coffee would arrive for my benefit if Mrs.D felt so inclined. I had so enjoyed the teas at the castle when I was young, but I guess I was only playing out a child's fantasy pre-tending that she was the princess in a fairy tale world.

"Tia," Alexa said. "Can I come to Avanloch and work for you in whatever capacity that you need?"

Alexandria was Amma and Johnny's eldest daughter. She could not say Vela when she first started talking; it came out Veeah and eventually Teeah and so I took on the persona of Tia which of course meant auntie. All the girls referred to me as such and seeing I was their Godmother, the name was fitting and they still referred to me as such.

"Alexa, I cannot think of anything that would make me happier. I thought that you were pursuing a part-time job at the hospital in Waverly?"

"That's just it, it would be part-time and I would have to be 'on call', so I would have to live there, and it would cost too much. This way I can live at home and keep all my earnings to help with schooling in the fall."

"You are the answer to one of my prayers my dear. I am delighted to have you on board and you have come at a most critical time. Did your mother tell you that Elsa McCracken's little girl is coming to stay with us for a spell?"

"Yes she did, and you know I have helped raise my two sisters, and so if you wish, I could be her companion."

"That would be wonderful because I am going to have my hands full with the wedding plans and the boys here, not to mention we need to organize the cleaning crew to come in and do a complete overhaul. I wanted to suspend the "teas" until autumn, but the girls said they will host those and so I guess that is going to carry on much to Mr. Rainey's dismay. As long as they, "the tea grannies", he calls them, don't interfere with his and the boys quest of finding the secret rooms, he will tolerate it." Amma laughed. "He didn't really say that did he Vienna?"

"Along those lines; now let's drink this dreadful dishwater and be on with the day. Alexa, can you start right away?"

She said she could and Amma told me not to worry about the cleaning crew as she already had that under control. I asked Alexa if she knew Kelly from the village and did she think that maybe she would like to come and work here also. No sooner had the words left my lips when Cyn appeared at the kitchen door with two girls in tow. One was Kelly and the other was a school friend of hers from outside of Waverly. They were looking for employment. I hired them on the spot after a brief interview. They understood that their duties were to be that of chambermaids but may be called upon to assist in serving and cooking. They agreed readily and were most eager to begin immediately.

They thanked me and I told them that we would talk after they had the tour of Avanloch.

That was almost too easy. Half of the staffing problem had been taken care of … surely everything else would fall into place. I could hardly wait to tell Rainey.

Amma took Kelly Flynn and her friend Yvonne Macready into the office to get their pertinent information from them. Something occurred to me and I thought that I had best discuss it with Rainey and went in search of him. He and the boys were nowhere to be found. They were not in the cellars that I could see and they definitely had not passed by me. I went to the Butler's call box in the kitchen and one by one rang each room that was equipped with an answering device. Ava, Rosy, Amma and Duffy answered; none of them had seen Rainey since earlier in the morning. Mrs. D hadn't either. I felt a tinge of excitement wondering if they had come across one of the secret rooms. I recalled that Rainey had said they were going to check out the hidden stairwell by the McDuff suite to see if it truly did hook up with the one from my parlor. I asked the girls to join me as I was not at all comfortable descending into the tunnels by myself.

By the time I arrived in my parlor they had already unlocked the drawer that held the key to the concealed door. Ava located the obscure button that was camouflaged among the roses in the wallpaper that opened up the entrance to the stairs. She reached in and turned on a light switch, and just in case the electricity unexpectedly went out, we had our trusty flashlights as backup power. Rosy asked if I was worried about Rainey and the boys and I said I wasn't, but if they had discovered something then I wanted to be there at the get go and they agreed.

A musty damp odor greeted us as we descended deeper into the subterranean. Motion lights had been installed and greeted us warmly at every level. As usual we held hands and kept up a loud conversation…just in case. We had made this journey many times before and were always creeped out by the eerie feeling of being in a vast cavity. We entered the tunnels and wound our way through the passages meeting up with the stairs from Jeremy's quarters and then the ones from the main hallway that were disguised behind a closet. Nothing, no sound, no movement, not even a mouse. Down we went into the cellars where I had started my search earlier.

"Listen." Rosy cautioned. "Do you hear that? It's coming from underneath us."

We came to a stop and silently listened. Sure enough there were voices coming from below. "How can that be?" I asked. "**This** is the cellar!"

"Apparently not." Ava said.

We went to separate walls and listened but there was no sound coming from any of them. "Enough of this!" I said and called out Rainey's name.

Rosy covered her ears. "Mother, you practically deafened us!"

"I only hope she hasn't awakened any of the sleeping ghouls." Ava said.

"I'll get you for that my pretty and your little dog too." I croaked in my best wicked witch voice.

We heard a noise that appeared to be coming from the wine vaults, and we started for them. Sure enough, Rainey and the boys emerged. They were covered in dirt but it couldn't hide the smug look on their mugs.

"We were just thinking of coming to get you in a few minutes when we heard this piercing scream… we thought it was a banshee and decided to hightail it out of there immediately. Did you gals hear it too?" The devil was in Rainey's eyes as he smiled.

I hit him. "That is one thing the good Lord blessed me with…a good strong voice and I see it has come in handy. Now, suppose you enlighten us as to where you've been."

"It happened by accident. I was checking out the wine inventory and came across some intriguing labels and thought I would try one from Tuscany. There was one named Red Sails and another was

Burgundy Brandywine, but the one that I chose was Ruby Passion. However, when I went to draw it out I discovered that the bottle held nothing but pale colored water. It had a sticker on it that read: "DO NOT REORDER. DO NOT REMOVE ; needed for balance." I found that a little strange and removed the bottle anyway and heard a clicking noise. I thought the boys had done something but they said 'no.' Next thing I knew the wine rack slid back like a folding door to reveal a black hole. You can imagine our enthusiasm as we thought we had discovered one of the hidden rooms. We shone a light into the hole and could see a set of steps. One by one we squeezed through the narrow opening unto a rickety set of wooden stairs that led to another subterranean floor. I'm afraid we didn't get very far as our flashlight conked out. We had to feel our way back to the stairs and had just reached the top when we heard you yelling. Unbeknownst to us, the cellar door had shut behind us. Luckily, Mason had his Boy Scout pack as it included an emergency light and I was able to find a panel that reopened the door, and that is about it. We really didn't find anything earth shattering but plan on exploring the chambers another day and need I say, armed to the teeth with many more lanterns."

I was a little alarmed at Rainey's account and told them that they had better leave instructions as to where they were going the next time. We followed them back into the wine vault and he repeated his procedure for our benefit. I wondered what other secrets this castle was hiding and what was beyond the newly discovered tunnels. It would have to wait for another day as the guys were hungry and thirsty, but first they needed to clean up. Rosy and Ava went to the kitchen to make sandwiches. I followed Rainey upstairs and mentioned that we needed to have a family powwow.

I decided to open all the windows in the bedroom and the parlor while Rainey was showering. An idea came to me and I filed it away hoping I would remember to mention it to Johnny later. I sat on the bed and waited for Rainey.

He came out half-dressed and toweling his hair. "You weren't worried about me were you Babe?"

"Maybe a little; I wouldn't want you getting lost in my castle." I took the towel from him and finished drying his hair.

"I wasn't worried when we found ourselves shut off from reentry because I knew that you would come looking for us sooner than later, and I was right wasn't I?"

"I spent an awfully long time in the past wishing that I could see you for just a moment, but now I don't have to wish anymore. All I have to do is call your name and you are here. But you didn't answer me this time and oh, I forgot to secure the doors in the parlor." I got up and Rainey followed me.

"Did you go down these old stairs looking for me?"

"Yes, but don't worry, the girls were with me and we had flashlights. Unlike your newly found passageway this one has lighting and I have been through it dozens of times."

We locked up and Rainey decided that he really wasn't hungry at all except for me. I had to put a damper on that reminding him that we had a meeting planned with the children. He relinquished but pretended to pout all the way downstairs.

The girls had made us salmon and watercress sandwiches with freshly cut raw vegetables on the side and potato chips for the boys. We had iced tea with lots of lemon and sugar. It was so much better than hot tea. While they were finishing up with blackberry pie and ice cream, I went to the office to retrieve the small bulletin board on which I had written a rough plan of the summer's events. I propped it up against the bread box in the kitchen.

The list consisted of: The wedding July 4th

> Rainey's Birthday July 14th
>
> Highland games July/August
>
> Trip to London to visit the sites

Rainey immediately topped the list with: Vienna's Doctor appointment.

We discussed the agenda and I asked if anyone had anything to add and could do so at any time. I informed Rainey that Amma had already booked an appointment with Mac for the next day and he asked me when I was planning on seeing Dr. Jai and I told him there was no need to. He disagreed with me, but said we would discuss it at another time.

Amma peeked in the door and said that Alexa had finished her orientation with Kelly and Yvonne and would I have any further instructions for any of them. She told Rainey that his friend from London had called and that Elsa had also. She was to start treatment in two days and so was it convenient for Tanny to come tomorrow? We told her we would return the calls and walked with her back to the office where the new girls were waiting. Kelly smiled as she noticed that Rainey and I were holding hands.

"I hope we didn't disturb you Ma'am." She did a little curtsy.

"No, you did not. We have to lay some ground rules here. First, I am not **the** Queen and so there is no more of that, and please do not call me ma'am."

Rainey told her jokingly that he had called me ma'am once and was still regretting it. I think that made the two of them feel more at ease.

"What should we call you then?" Kelly asked.

"Some people, such as Mrs. D still call me Vela as that was what I use to be known as, but now I am Vienna and you may address me as such."

"My mother told us that we must be respectful and we should call you Lady Mc…sorry, I guess it is Lady Quinn now."

"I am just an ordinary person who happened to marry the Lord of Avanloch; I did not come by the title of Lady by birth. Lady Vienna sounds so stuffy …I thought that I might call you girls K and Y, what do you think?"

They both smiled and said that is what they called each other already and they would be pleased if I did and could they call me Lady V then? I asked Rainey if it was all right with him and he said it was and they were to call him Rainey and only Rainey. I suppose they wondered why I had asked his approval for they could not know that is what he used to call me when we first met and I wasn't sure whether he would mind or not.

They started to leave stating that they had to go and track down a tent as they were going to be living in it on Kelly's parent's property for the summer. I asked them why. Kelly said that the house was too small and that she was already sharing her bedroom with one of her sisters and that they would like a little more privacy. Yvonne did not drive and the distance was too far for her to walk every day.

I asked them what they would think of an alternative that we could offer them.

"What do you mean Miss Vienna?" K asked me.

"I like that…yes; you could call me Miss Vienna. It is not as stuffy as Lady. We have a vacant manor house which is known as Willowisp. Amma and her family have been living in it for twenty years but have moved to Brackenshire Manor since my aunt and uncle moved into London. I hate to see it empty and I think it would be perfect for the two of you and perhaps even a third girl. You would be responsible for keeping it clean and neat but you may take all of your meals here if you would so desire. We are hoping to hire another cook and helper soon. Is this something that the two of you may be interested in?"

The girls were speechless. Kelly finally stammered. "Are you serious, a house on the property? Surely, you jest?"

"I am serious. Would you be interested? You may think about the proposal for as long as you like."

They squeezed each other's hands and said they did not need to think and could they move in immediately. Amma offered to show them the house and left to get the key.

Yvonne had a question for me and she timidly asked it. "Miss Vienna, I don't know quite how to ask this, but…are there any ghosts at Willowisp?"

"That's a perfectly reasonable question Y. I have never heard of any but let's ask Amma when she returns. I suppose that you have heard that Rosalyn's mother Maveryn visits us here periodically?"

Kelly said that she had but didn't know if there was any truth to the tale. I told them that it was true but they had nothing to worry about as she was a friendly entity.

"You will probably never encounter her as she only comes at night and that is to check in on the girls and see that all is well in the castle. Mr. Rainey has already made her acquaintance." I tried to stifle a little giggle.

Rainey was quick to reply. "Don't let her scare you girls…I am not sure I experienced any such visit; I remain a skeptic."

"Oh, we are not frightened. This is an old castle and there are probably many lost souls wandering the halls. We wouldn't be here if we were skitterish. Just wonder if we have to watch out for any at Willowisp that's all." Yvonne said.

Amma returned and told the girls that her and her family had never encountered any ghosts in all the years that they had lived there. The girls asked if they could hug me but maybe that was against the rules. I told them there were no such rules. They gave Rainey and me polite hugs and ran off giggling and whispering.

We met Ava and Rosy coming out of the kitchen with drinks in their hands. Rainey asked them where they were going and they said that Morgan and Mason were playing chess on the giant board in the tower courtyard and they were taking them refreshments.

"Will it be all right if we take the boys and Amma's girls into Waverly for a burger and a movie tonight?" Ava asked.

"Of course, sounds like fun. What do you say Rain?"

"You girls are really spoiling them you know?"

"As if you haven't already!" Rosy exclaimed.

We rode up in the lift together and I said I was going to have a long soak in the tub.

Rosy asked Rainey what he was going to do.

"I am going to join your mother."

"Really?" Rosy teased.

"He has a standing order to wash my hair, and then he has a hundred other things that need to be taken care of and so he'll be busy. He can't freeload all his life." I left them and ran down the corridor before he could offer a contradiction. I tried to lock the bathroom door but he was too quick for me and pulled me into his arms.

Laughing he said. "Was that for the girl's benefit? I sure hope so because I may have other plans for you my Lady."

I started the tub and told him that I was serious. "Now that the kids will all be gone I thought that we could invite Amma and Johnny over for dinner and seeing Mrs.D is gone, why don't you make your specialty fondue? And, since you inherited the pool upkeep from Johnny, I think the ph. needs checking. We do want to swim later don't we?"

"You're becoming a slave driver, but I am yours to command at will and so my Lady, it will be done."

"I hope I haven't made a mistake by hiring the girls."

"You mean Kelly and Yvonne…why would you say that?"

"Well they are no more than seventeen or eighteen and they along with Alexa will be here almost every day and then we have Morgan and Mason…do you see where I am going with this?"

Rainey was applying the shampoo to my head and I already knew that this was a bad idea. I tried to ignore the sensation of utter elation that was radiating through my body as his sensuous hands continued to massage my entire scalp. I escaped the stimulation by immersing my entire head underwater. I stayed submerged until my last breath was gone.

"Are you testing my patience by staying under for so long? I don't even like to think of you in the pool alone…you are not Houdini you know?"

"Oh Rainey, don't be such a worry wart! I have heard though that drowning is a very peaceful way to die."

"Vienna, I will not have you talking like that! Now sit up and let me finish your hair!"

"Yes Sir! So what do you think about the boys and their hormones with all these pretty young fillies under foot?"

"To be honest I have not given it any thought. At home they are only interested in sports and video games and so I don't think it will be any different here. Their only mission right now is to locate the mysterious secret rooms."

"Says you…don't tell me that you weren't ogling the girls when you were their age?"

"Honestly Honey, I wasn't. All us guys were too busy with hockey, or basketball, or soccer depending on the time of year, and on the weekends and holidays we were camping and hiking and fishing…you know, outdoor stuff."

"I find that hard to believe. I was already hopelessly in love by the time I was sixteen."

"Oh really, anyone I know?"

"Let's see, how do I describe him? He had sandy brown hair with a little curl that fell over his forehead. He had this lean yet muscular build and blue eyes that one could drown in. He was older than me and very worldly, but he was ever the gentleman. He won me over with his charms. Oh wait…I think he still holds me in captivity."

"You're wrong; it is I who is being held hostage by an enchantress in a mystical castle."

"Ummm, I think I like the idea that you are my prisoner."

"Yes I am Darling…a prisoner of love. Now, do you want me to stay or not?"

"I want you to stay but the hour grows late and we have much to do. I'll be down to help you in two shakes of a lamb's tail. I want to have dinner in the tower courtyard so I'll have to go up and see that the chess people are all in their beds and set the table."

"I think they are called chessmen. Do you really want to haul everything up there?"

"I believe the Queens would take offense to you calling them men. And apparently you have forgotten again that the dumb waiter goes to the towers and that the linens and tableware are all there also."

Rainey held my robe out for me as I climbed out of the tub. "I stand corrected again; chess people they are. How long did it take you to familiarize yourself to all the idiosyncrasies of Avanloch? I have been here almost half a year and I can't seem to remember what goes where or what room I'm in half the time."

"Don't be silly, you have discovered things that most of us didn't even know existed… like the cellar below the cellar and you have opened up LizBeth's room. Speaking of her, I think I would like to stop and see her tomorrow on the way back from that unnecessary doctor's appointment. Are you ready to meet her?"

"If you think she can handle meeting another new person then yes, I would. Are you still planning on bringing her here for a visit?"

"Yes, maybe in autumn, when all the craziness is done with."

We watched the children from the front door as they were leaving for their night in Waverly. Rainey shook his head in wonder as he watched Rosy hug and say something to Zeus and Zoar, the two stone lions that guarded the entrance. He asked me if she always stopped to chat with them and I replied that as far as I knew she did.

"What do you think she tells them?" He asked.

"That's between her and them but I think she tells them to watch over Avanloch."

We had a pleasant evening with Amma and Johnny. Towards the end of the meal I sprung my plan on them. "Today when I was in my parlor I thought how nice it would be if I …we, had a balcony. Why do you think the family never included any off the bedrooms in the construction plans?"

"I can't answer that for you Vienna. I am sure that it wasn't a priority." Johnny stated.

"How difficult would it be to add one now?" I looked back and forth at Johnny and Rainey. Amma had an amused smile on her face.

Johnny also seemed entertained by my question. "You're the architect Rainey, what do you say? Is it an impossible task?"

"I can tell you how to build it, but it will be a lot of work. You are going to have to start from the ground up and it is going to take some time and a lot of manpower and it will be quite pricey."

"That's all I wanted to know…if it could be done. Money isn't an issue and I'm sure there are a lot of men who need work. However, there are way more pressing things that need attending to than one of my impractical whims."

"Is that it, you just wanted to know if it could be done?" Rainey asked me.

Johnny answered for me. "If I have learned anything in twenty years, it's that if Vienna wants or asks for something Vienna gets it." He smiled at me and I smiled back.

We invited everyone to come for a late night swim but the kids were all too tired from their outing in Waverly and Amma and Johnny took a pass also. Rainey and I had the pool to ourselves. The semi warm water was the perfect temperature for a few laps without exhausting me. Rainey did not swim but waited for me on the third step. I sat down beside him and asked why he wasn't swimming. He didn't give me a reason, but instead asked me a very disconcerting question.

"Vienna, should I be worried about the relationship between you and Johnny?"

"Please tell me that I didn't hear what I think I did?"

"It's just that I have noticed the way you two look at each other and I can't help but feel that there is more to your feelings for each other than meets the eye."

"Rainey Quinn, how can you even insinuate such a thing! Amma and Johnny are my very best friends over here and the three of us are very close. Johnny is the brother I never had and I am the sister he never had. I thought you were clear on that, but apparently I was wrong. We have shared many things in the past two decades but never anything such as you are suggesting! You are still not convinced that I didn't have lovers in the years that we were apart are you?"

"Please don't be angry with me Vienna; I had to ask."

"If I remember correctly we have already had this conversation. I thought you were going to ask Johnny to be your best man…well, I guess that is not going to happen now." I climbed out of the pool and left without even toweling off or changing. I heard Rainey calling after me but I was in no mood to talk to him anymore. I stomped into the hall and took refuge in the Harem Room. It was the last place anyone would look for me. I cloistered myself behind one of the curtained niches and curled up on the divan and cried.

The door opened. "I know you're in here Vienna because you left a trail of droplets. You must be some pissed with me to have come to your least favorite room."

I tried to escape through the other door but he found me before I could reach it. I fought him as he tried to corral me in his arms and even though I was fuming, he was too strong for me. He held me until I went limp and then sat me down and apologized fervently.

"I have spent half our life together asking, no, begging you to forgive me and here I am again. I am envious of every man that is in your life and I do not know how I am going to come to terms with my jealousy, but I promise you I will. I love you so much that sometimes I become blinded to the fact that you had another life without me. Look at me Darling; I need your help to conquer my uncertainties that you won't leave me."

"I am deeply hurt that you do not trust me. I have told you a thousand times that I love you and will never leave you, but you still don't believe me. I will no longer be able to be alone with Johnny or hug him without having you question my intentions."

"No, I do not want that to happen and I do want to have him as my best man. I do trust you. I'm sorry; I am such a fool."

He laid his head in my lap and I surrendered and comforted him. Lordy, how was he going to react when he and Roberge crossed paths? I didn't want to think about it.

The next day dawned and it was if last night hadn't happened. Dr. Mac found nothing wrong with me but took some blood tests anyway. We had a pleasant visit with LizBeth and Rainey informed me that his friend Stu and wife Daisy would be coming to our wedding. We arrived home to find Ava and Rosalyn entertaining Tanny.

Chapter 3

The White Witch, The Duke, and The Clairvoyant

It was June the 18th. I awoke with one of my peculiar sensations that something was about to happen. I had not slept well as the moon was full and it seemed to influence my moods and sleep pattern. I dressed quickly without waking Rainey and crossed through the adjoining door that led to Ava's room. She and Tanny were already awake and talking. I told Ava that I would take Tanny off her hands for the day. I had purchased several outfits for her yesterday and let her choose which one she wanted to wear. We went down the lift to the kitchen where Mrs.D was preparing breakfast. Tanny said she wanted cereal and I let her have her pick. Rainey came in and kissed me and asked me why I hadn't woken him. He said good morning to Mrs.D and ruffled Tanny's hair. She pretended to ignore him. He asked me what my plans were for the day and I told him I was going to have a much needed play day now that I had someone to play with. He smirked and asked if he could play too. I reminded him that he and the boys were going to continue their tour of the cellars.

"I haven't forgotten. Actually, I have invited Johnny to join us."

"Really; you're not planning on losing him down there are you?"

Mrs.D looked at me inquiringly and I told her it was a joke between Rainey and me. She shrugged her shoulders and said. "You two, such mischievousness I never have seen."

At eleven I took Tanny outside and introduced her to the lions and suggested that we hang out at the faerie fountain and clean up some of the leaves that had blown into it. We took off our footwear and waded into the shallow water. I shut the jets off so we wouldn't be soaked by the spray. Tanny inquired as to the names of all the faeries just as Rosalyn had done so many years ago. I told her I only knew that Loralei was the queen but that I had forgotten the names of the rest of them. She was making up names when a large black limousine came through the gates and stopped half way up the drive. It was a very hot day and so I was a little surprised to see a young woman clad in what appeared to be a nun's habit complete with head dress, emerge from the car. The dress and cloak were white and appeared to be made of a heavy fabric. I presumed that she was a nun; perhaps a nurse. I couldn't have been more wrong.

She walked over to us and asked me if I knew if the Lady of Avanloch was home. I asked her if she had an appointment thinking that Amma must have forgotten to tell me.

"I am a feared that I came unannounced. How rude of me; my name is Tathia and I have come to take my mother home. If you are employed here would you be so kind as to ask the mistress if she would be so gracious as to grant me an audience."

I did not recognize her accent, but she certainly was not from Scotland. No one that I knew would ask to be granted an audience with me, and what was this about her mother?

"I am Vienna Quinn, the current Lady of Avanloch. I am pretty sure that your mother is not here."

She asked if she could join us in the pond and promptly shed her robe and sandals and pulled her dress up to her knees and sat down on the rim between Tanny and me.

"I like the faeries." She said. "I like to think of myself as a sort of faerie, but in actuality I am a witch; a white witch, of course."

She said it so casually that I wasn't one bit phased. "I was not aware that witches came in different colors."

"We must assign a color to ourselves to differentiate between good and evil. As a white witch I only practice positive magic, and I can do no harm to anything or anyone. You may have heard others refer to us as Wiccans. Then there are witches such as Isobel Gowdie the famous Scottish witch who could command brooms and other paraphernalia to fly. She was a black witch so to speak. I must say that you do not seem to be upset that I have just informed you that I am a witch of a different sort."

"I live in a castle that is inhabited by restless spirits, and so meeting a witch fits into the picture quite comfortably. To be perfectly honest after making my home here for twenty years, nothing surprises me anymore. I do not know the name Isobel Gowdie though."

"I did not expect to meet someone with such an open mind and so am sure that we will be able to work together satisfactorily."

"That all depends on what you have in mind."

"My mother is Tatylyanna Speshiloff and I have come to free her soul and return it to her home in Russia."

Now I was astounded. "Excuse me…you what?" Had I heard her right? "Are you trying to tell me that Lord Jeremy McAllister is your father?"

"I suppose I should start at the beginning."

"That would be a good idea. Would you like to come inside?"

"I am quite comfortable here if it is to your liking."

I asked Tanny if she wanted to go inside and she said no. "Very well, please continue."

"Lord McAllister is not my father. Before my mother's involvement with him she was in love with my father, Ivan Devansky. He was a soldier and was deployed to the other side of the country to defend the borders. While he was gone I was born and my mother's family came upon hard times. They once had considerable wealth and could not face living in poverty. My grandfather came up with this plan to marry his three daughters off to men of means. He did not care that they were in love with others; it was their duty to save the family from financial ruin. It proved to be quite a dilemma for my mother and aunts, but they being the obedient daughters went along with the plan. Once they had procured sufficient funds from their marriages they planned on returning to their loved ones. Unfortunately, my mother never got the chance and met with her demise here. I know that Lord McAllister discovered that she was only interested in him for his fortune and dissolved the engagement. My grandfather made her return here to try and make amends but she never got the chance. According to one of my aunts, my mother became a spiteful and intolerable woman. Probably no one here was sad that she fell to her death. When I was seventeen I started having vivid dreams about her. They were not upsetting, but always ended with her calling for me to bring her home. Her body was already resting in the family plot and so I did not know what she meant when she was asking me to bring her home. Two years later I journeyed to Egypt on a student visa and accidentally met some people who practiced Wicca. They worship nature and believe that all creatures are sacred. One of their objectives was to end the negativity assigned to witchcraft. I liked their philosophy and jumped in with both feet planted firmly on the ground. I soon realized through meditation that my mother's soul had not returned home with her body."

She stopped talking long enough to catch her breath and then continued. "My dreams of my mother continued and with the help of the masters who practiced Wicca, I came to an understanding of what they meant. My mother's soul was suffering from the actions that she had taken and was in limbo. It has taken me almost five years to gain enough knowledge and confidence that I feel I can free her. I should have been here yesterday as it was the full moon. My flight was delayed and so I am one day late, but I feel that there is still enough energy in the cycle to lift the veil that separates our world from the next. October the 31st is when the veil is the thinnest, but I do not want to wait that long. With your permission, I am hoping to be able to visit the astral plane that possesses her soul and convince her that it is time for her to be at peace."

"What do you require of me and how will you know if you are successful?"

"Has she done any mischief here and has anyone ever made contact with her spirit?"

"Yes; Lord Jeremy's first wife was plagued by her tauntings and wrote about them in her diaries. She is supposed to be responsible for an accident involving a worker. I am told that the ghost of a previous inhabitant is responsible for Taty's death. Maveryn, that was Jeremy's wife, believed that Taty's spirit made her home in room six. Maveryn had the room sealed and it has not been opened except for renovations which resulted in the accident, which incidentally happened on the very stairs that had claimed her life. After that incident we brought in an expert who said he could extradite her from the castle. Four of us went in to accost her and she chose me to be her intermediary and told us all to leave her room and that she meant us no harm. I have no recollections of her taking over my body and we have never opened the room since nor have we ever heard from her again. I still fail to see how we can keep a dead person's spirit behind locked doors."

"I take it that was her bedroom whenever she visited here and so I believe she thought of it as her own and so her soul made it her sanctuary. Tell me how did you find the room when you were in it?"

"We did not turn any lights on so I did not see a thing. The room was bitterly cold and I felt completely helpless. Jeremy and my friend Johnny were with me. Johnny held on to me the whole time and later told me that my body went limp. When they told me that Taty had used me and my voice to communicate I was dumbfounded. I would be most indebted to you if you can remove your mother's presence from Avanloch, but I cannot apprehend how this can be done. Is soul capturing a common practice among Wiccans?"

"I can't really answer that as I do not know. No one I have met has ever admitted to it, and so I do not know if it can even be done, but I must try as I want these incessant dreams to stop. I do not want you in the room with me. I will only need you to keep watch for once I begin as I mustn't be disturbed. The exorcism, so to speak, will take place at the midnight hour. Will that pose a problem for you?"

"No. By the way, your mother is known as the Black Russian by everyone here. Will you be spending the night, and why are you driving a limousine?"

She was not fazed by my telling her that her mother had been nicknamed the Black Russian. "I will be gone the minute my task is completed. This was the only rental available. How will you explain who I am to your family?"

That was a very good question. Rainey always told me that I was a good story teller…well, my prowess was about to be tested. "Let's go to lunch."

I had five minutes to come up with a plausible story from the moment I opened the doors until we reached the kitchen. I stopped at the lavatory and passed a towel to Tathia and dried off Tanny's and my feet. I looked back and realized that we had left a somewhat watery trail. Oh well, I suppose that is why we have help.

We heard voices coming from the family room where we took most of our meals. Sure enough everyone was seated around the large wooden table. I was happy that Rainey was not among the luncheon congregation.

I told Tathia to follow my lead and hoped that she could improvise.

"Everyone, I would like you to meet Sister T. She is on her way from Egypt to her family home on the Baltic Sea and thought she would stop in Scotland and visit with an old family friend. Unfortunately, word never reached her or her family of Jeremy's passing. I have invited her to spend the night. Please make her feel welcome as she has had a long and arduous journey only to learn that Jeremy is no longer with us."

They all echoed hello and no one seemed surprised to see a nun at the table.

Mrs.D was first to ask questions. "The Baltic Sea…that is in Russia is it not?"

My heart stopped for a second as I was sure she was going to ask her if she knew Tatylyanna Speshiloff. Tathia told her that it was and that she had not been home for many years as it was far too expensive.

"Sister T, that is an odd name even for a woman of the cloth… sorry Sister, I dinna mean to be disrespectful." Mrs.D stammered.

Tathia laughed. "It is the name assigned to me; it is spelled T E A just like the beverage. The meaning in Egyptian is 'white flower'."

I almost choked on my soup when she said 'white' as I was sure she was going to add 'witch'. She played along all through lunch. No one was interested in her 'calling' but wanted to know all about life in Egypt. Thank the Lord I hadn't made that up. As it was I was going to have to do a lot of explaining tomorrow.

I managed to get a word in and asked if the guys were still in the cellars. Amma said they hadn't heard a peep out of them yet. Tanny piped up and said that we had all been in the faerie pond and that our shoes were all wet.

"Which reminds me, I am sorry but we left a bit of a mess in the lobby."

"Not to bother Miss V, Y and I will see to it." K volunteered.

I suggested that perhaps Sister Tea would like to see her room and rest for a while. She heartily agreed as I hoped she would for we still had the details of her quest to discuss. I left Tanny with Amma and asked Ava if she would retrieve the Sister's valise from her car and perhaps turn the car around and leave near the gates as Sister Tea was going to be leaving very early and did not want to awaken any of us.

"You can drive a limo right?"

"A limo?" Ava inquired looking at Tathia.

"I will explain later. Shall we take a pot of tea with us Sister?" I asked.

"That would be lovely. Thank you so much for the delicious luncheon and your hospitality. I will remember you all in my prayers." Tathia gracefully acknowledged them as she followed me out into the hall.

When we were in the lift she asked me how she did and I replied "Excellent, now we just have to get by my husband. I will have some explaining to do but I can handle it."

I didn't have much choice as to what room I could assign to Tathia. I didn't want her near the boys or Rosy, Ava and Tanny, and so the only room that was suitable was Jeremy's. According to her she wouldn't even be spending the whole night and just needed a place to prepare for her mission and to rest. We were pretty well done with our plans when I heard Rainey calling for me. I asked Tathia to excuse me and went to greet him. I found him knocking on the doors of unoccupied rooms.

I shut the door behind me. "I'm here Darling." He had reached Miss Mary's room.

"Oh, you put our guest in Jeremy's old suite?" He seemed surprised that I would do so.

"It seemed to be the best bet. She plans on being gone before any of us are up and from there she can make her escape without disturbing anyone."

"Escape…that's an odd way to describe her departure. When do I get to meet her?"

"At dinner; she is resting now. She has had a very long day. Come, I am dying to hear about your adventures today."

We walked back to our bedroom and Rainey lay down on the bed and asked me to join him. He had already changed his dusty clothes while I was ensconced behind closed doors with Tathia as she prepared me for the bewitching hour.

He enclosed me in his arms and asked me why I was so tense. I told him I hadn't realized that I was. He then reiterated the events of the day to me. The tunnel did not reveal anything and it ended at the mausoleum.

"What?" I asked. "That has to be a mile away!"

"Not quite Darling. Anyhow, it ended there and there was no exit that we could find and so we had to come back the way we had gone. So that is another dead end, but not the end of our quest. That is not what I wanted to talk to you about though. After we returned and had a bite to eat Johnny asked me if I would accompany him on a short walk. I must say I was a little taken aback at what he confronted me with."

I knew what was coming next and I told him I was sorry.

"No my darling you have nothing to be sorry for; I'm the culprit as usual."

"Rainey …" I pleaded.

"Shh, I am not angry with you. Johnny told me that you seemed to be aloof this morning and when he confronted you, you told him about my suspicions regarding your friendship. Needless to say, he let me have it with both barrels and called me a pompous ass. I'm afraid I burst out laughing at that insinuation telling him that I had been called that many times over, and that it was true. He told me that next to Amma you are his best friend and have been for almost as long as you and I have been apart. He told me to take the blinders off and stop being such a fool. If I couldn't see what was right in front of me…that being that you were hopelessly enamored with me, then I should catch the next freighter back to Canada. Then do you know what he said?"

"No." I whispered.

"And I quote. "I will not give up my friendship with Vienna just because you can't bear to see another man smiling at her. We have worked together for a very long time and so there will be moments, and you can't be jumping to ridiculous conclusions every time we share a memory. So put that in your pipe and smoke it!"

I was afraid to ask what happened next, but I did and he said. "I asked him if he would be my best man and he asked me what took me so long to ask him."

I hoped Johnny's words had put an end to Rainey's suspicions. Tathia excused herself shortly after dinner but not before she had been bombarded with more questions about Egypt. I walked her to her room and told her I would meet her outside room six just before midnight. Rainey was used to waking up and finding me gone so I could only hope that this would be one of the times he didn't come looking for me.

I willed myself to stay awake keeping an eye on the clock. I never concerned myself with the time and kept the clock turned away from me so that the light wouldn't bother me. I could not afford to do so tonight. I started creeping out of bed at 11:30. I had left the parlor door ajar so I could make my getaway from there. I didn't want to open or close any doors. I peered back at Rainey and whispered. "Sleep my darling… sleep."

An hour later I snuck back into bed. Tathia was gone, and hopefully, so was Taty.

I clung to my side of the bed as I was shivering uncontrollably. My shaking aroused Rainey and he pulled me close to him.

"You've been on one of your midnight strolls haven't you? Why do you smell like smoke?" He asked me in a dream like trance. I told him to go back to sleep.

We awoke to the blood curdling screams of the boys in the morning. "Dad, Vienna!!!"

"What the hell?" Rainey jumped out of bed and yanked on his pants and ran to the door.

I was in no such hurry but nervously followed him into the hallway where Morgan and Mason stood across the landing from us pointing to room six. I went back inside my room and prepared myself for the onslaught that was surely coming. I took a deep breath and waited for Rainey. He found me in the closet choosing an outfit for the day.

"Vienna LaFontaine, what have you done?" He was fuming. Ava and Rosy had followed him in and the boys stood outside in the corridor.

"For your information, my name is Vienna Quinn and I would appreciate it if you would lower your voice as there may be several people who are still asleep." I went into the dressing room and shed my night clothes. I stepped into the powder blue gingham dress I had picked out. The girls backed out saying they would tend to Tanny.

Rainey grabbed hold of my arm as I attempted to leave. "You are not going anywhere young lady until you explain what is going on here! What is it with you…we just get over sorting one thing out and then you go and do something that is beyond comprehension… you unlocked **the** door and let that so called nun in didn't you, and to what purpose? You are in cahoots with her aren't you? How long have you been planning this…did you forget how dangerous **she** is?"

I was more afraid of Rainey at that moment then I had been at opening Taty's room.

"For someone who doesn't believe in another realm you are acting rather outlandish. I would think you would be happy that Taty is gone. You refuse to see the ways things are here. Do you think that you could loosen your grasp on me?"

"I'm sorry; I didn't mean to hurt you. What do you mean, gone? How can she be gone; she wasn't even here."

"No, but apparently her soul was. You didn't hurt me. If you will give me a chance I will explain everything to you and the household. Now I need to go and call Johnny as I need his help."

"Of course you do because you can't confide in me and I can't help you." He said sarcastically.

"Don't you start on that again Rainey? I am in no mood to appease your childish inadequacies." I knew I had said the wrong thing the second it was out of my mouth.

"I am so sorry Lady Vienna, I forgot my place. This is **your** castle and I am but a peon."

"Now you are just being ridiculous." I refused to be baited any further by the man who was my world and asked him if he would accompany me to room six. I told him that it was perfectly safe and that I wanted to open the window to let the fresh air in, but that it was stuck and that is why I needed Johnny. I walked by him as he muttered something. I stopped at the girls' rooms and asked them to collect the boys and meet us in the family room. Rainey did follow, albeit hesitantly. He attempted to open the window but could not pry it loose.

"You are right, you need Johnny."

I was trembling as he walked coldly by me. "I don't need anyone but you Rainey."

To my amazement he attempted to smile. "I know that Vienna and someday I hope that you will come to realize that you can tell me anything and I will do my best to understand and support you. It's not going to be easy as you are very willful and destined to act on impulse. I'm trying to adjust to your whimsical castle in the sky and all of the idiosyncrasies that go with it…I thought I was doing relatively well, but maybe I'm only fooling myself."

"I've had a lot more time to adjust to this way of life; actually, I never had to adjust at all. I just accepted it the same way I accepted marrying a man I didn't love because I didn't have anything else after I lost you, or thought that I had. I'm sorry I didn't confide in you but when you hear the whole story you will understand why I couldn't."

He reached for me and I went eagerly into his arms. "Is this the way it is always going to be with us Vienna, you doing something impulsive and me jumping to conclusions without giving you the benefit of a doubt? And one of us is always saying their sorry?"

"I don't know Rainey; I can't imagine life without you."

"Nor I without you. I am going to worry about you no matter what you do or where you go. Can you understand how hard it is for me to wrap my head around the supernatural?"

"Believe it or not Rainey, what transpired here tonight is way beyond my acceptance of the paranormal. Ghosts are one thing, but capturing one's lost soul is incomprehensible."

"What are you saying Vienna?"

"Come and I will tell you the tale of Tatylyanna Speshiloff and her plight to return home. You still like my story telling don't you Rainey?"

"I do and I think this one is going to be a corker."

We found everyone waiting for us. Mrs. D had already called Amma and Johnny and told them that something very strange had taken place overnight and they best get up here right away. Rainey went to the sideboard and poured us each a cup of coffee. Ava squeezed my hand and I knew that she was glad that her father and I were still talking to each other. I took my coffee from Rainey and wished that I drank because I could sure use a little fortitude. I went to the window and looked out towards the gardens. No one said a word. I turned and started at the beginning… that being when the limo pulled into the drive and a young woman clad in white stepped out.

"Her real name is Tathia Devansky and she is Tatylyanna's daughter."

Mrs.D gasped and stood up. "I knew it! I knew there was something sinister about that woman; I could feel it in me bones!"

"Let the girl continue Mary." Duffy suggested patting his wife's hand.

I smiled half heartily. I made sure that they knew that Jeremy was not Tathia's father. I told them that she had revealed to me her vivid dreams of her mother when she was about seventeen and that they always ended with her mother begging her daughter to bring her home. She was a very young child when her mother died and her memories were mostly those that her father and family instilled upon her. I hesitated before I continued.

"Do any of you know about the practice of Wicca as a religion?"

Johnny and Amma said they knew the name but that was about all. Mrs.D. crossed herself, Rainey nodded, and by the look on the girl's faces I think they knew very well what a Wiccan was.

"Tathia accidentally met some people in Egypt where she learned its philosophy. It seemed to have the answers to the questions she had been asking. It took her almost five years but she is now a self-proclaimed White Witch."

"What the hell does that mean Vienna?" Rainey's ire was rearing its ugly head again. "I thought she was a nun…what's with the "Sister" title?"

"I never told any of you that she was a nun; you just assumed that from her dress. I didn't mean to confuse you by calling her sister; that was a mistake on my part. She really is just an ordinary person who was seeking an answer for her mother's pleas."

I looked directly at Rainey whose eyes told me that I was out of my mind if I really thought that Tathia was like anyone of us. I am sure he wanted to leave the room but was too polite to do so. Johnny encouraged me to go on.

I explained the ideals behind Wicca and that their motto was to do no harm and that all creatures were sacred. White magic is used to bring good and to protect people from curses and spells. Their protection spells remove negative energies, and that they worship Mother Nature.

Mason had a question. "Is she like Belinda, the good witch in The Wizard of Oz?"

"I think you mean Glinda. Well, she didn't come in on a bubble and I didn't see any magic wand. I do not know what went on in room six because I was not allowed to be present and am thankful that I wasn't."

"Amen!" Johnny uttered and I knew he was remembering our previous encounter with the black Russian.

"My whole part in the affair was to stand guard which I did and very nervously, I might add. It seemed like hours passed, but in actuality it was only fifteen minutes until Tathia opened the door and asked me to come in. I really did not want to do that." Johnny's and my eyes met and he was telling me it was all right. We shared something that night so long ago and now the events of last night had brought it back into focus.

"Somehow I managed to get my feet to work and followed her into the condemned room. It was ablaze with the light from dozens of white candles that formed a circle. Inside the ring were four bowls; one contained water and one held salt, another one contained crystals and the last one seemed to be of earth and an herb…sage, I think. The heavy drapes had been opened and though it was past midnight the moon's light was illuminating the room. It was no longer the bitter cold that I had experienced before. The only thing I can tell you all is that when Tathia entered the room earlier she said:

"Mother, it is me Tathia and I am here to take you home."

"What happened when you were in the room Mama?" Rosy asked.

"I knew immediately that Taty was gone though I knew not how or where. The look on Tathia's face was one of pure radiance. So much for her being a witch for she looked like an angel. I helped her pack everything up into her valise. When she bent down I noticed an amber talisman dangling from around her neck and a crucifix was protruding from a pocket in her robe. When I spotted the cross I thought perhaps if all else failed she would call on God to help her. That's it, I know no more. She hugged me and thanked me and told me that I would never be far from her thoughts and if I should ever need her all I had to do was call. She slipped quietly down the stairs and into the night."

The room was silent until Mrs. D rose and came over and embraced me. "Lady Vela, you are the bravest woman I know and I thank thee for delivering the house from evil. Breakfast will be in an hour." She marched into the kitchen with Duffy echoing her sentiments.

Rosy and Ava and Amma were all trying to hold back tears and one by one they kissed me and told me they loved me. The boys didn't know what to say and so they just smiled.

Ava corralled them to help out in the kitchen. Amma picked Tanny up who had been playing with her dolls on the floor the whole time.

Johnny came over to me and kissed me on the forehead. "Well done My Lady. Now, what say we go up and air that stuffy old room out?" He took my hand and said. "Are you coming Rainey?" I knew then that he didn't care what Rainey thought about our relationship and at that moment, neither did I.

Johnny let go of my hand in the lift. Rainey hadn't said a word. The two of them managed to pry the windows open and sweet smelling air filled the once sinister room.

"I can see I am going to have a few weeks work in here and so I had better get started on hiring a new hand. I don't think I have to tell you Rainey that you have captured yourself one remarkable woman. See you both later."

Johnny left and Rainey and I were alone. "What now?" I asked.

It was Rainey's turn to take my hand and we walked together down the hall to our bedroom. He shut the door behind us. I asked him if I should be afraid.

He held me and said. "I don't think you are afraid of anything my love. I'm not very understanding am I? Not once did I stop to consider what this ordeal was like for you. You wanted to free the house of the Black Russian and so you jumped at the chance no matter how farfetched the idea was. You knew if you discussed the plan with me I would have forbidden it and then you would have had to go behind my back and follow through with it anyhow. I realize that you felt you couldn't confide in me because of the dire nature of the plot. I do not want you to ever feel that way again. I promise I will listen to whatever cockamainy plan you may come up with. I might not agree, but I will give it the old college try. I love you Vienna and if anything should ever befall you when you are on one of your hair brain escapades I could never forgive myself for not being with you. Promise me you won't do anything so foolish again without me?"

"I'm sorry Rainey; I can't in good faith promise that I will never do anything impulsive again. That's just the way I am, but I will try and talk things through with you first."

"That's not good enough Sweetheart; I really need your word."

"All right, I promise."

"Are your fingers crossed Vienna?"

He knew me too well. I didn't answer him but instead said. "You are wrong when you say nothing fazes me… I don't think I breathed the whole time that Tathia was in the room alone with that woman. I had never been so uneasy in all my life before. I wanted to run to you and have you hold me but I knew I couldn't, and not only that, but I felt as if my feet were glued to the floor."

"I wish you had of come to me. Now I know why you were so cold in bed last night; you're still shivering. I'm going to draw you a warm bath and hopefully that will warm you up. Do you want me to wash your hair?"

I told him it didn't need washing and that I was just going to soak. I climbed into the warm soothing water and Rainey placed the bath pillow behind my head and said he'd be in the parlor. I supposed that he was going to read more of the letters I had written to him or my journals. I let the water rise up to my neck before I shut the taps off. Something was playing tag with my mind but I couldn't catch up to what it was. I closed my eyes and found myself back in room six; only the memory was not from last night but another time that I thought I had filed away forever. How long ago was it that Jeremy and the so called expert on paranormal activity Allister, and Johnny and I had entered that room? Jeremy had instructed Johnny to watch out for me once we were inside the room. Johnny had said that he didn't need to be asked twice. I remember holding on to Johnny and complaining about the glacial cold that accosted us. He had opened his coat and folded it and his arms around me. "I will never let anything harm you Vienna …never." I think I touched his hand just before the lights went out inside my head. The next thing I recalled was being out in the corridor and Johnny placing my feet on the floor. Had he been carrying me? Someone had yelled from the bottom floor. "What's wrong with Vela, Johnny?"

I told them that I was all right and then Jeremy ordered us all to follow him into his suite where they told me that Tatylyanna had spoken through me. If I recall correctly, I was not terribly upset with hearing that I had been her instrument to convey the message that she was no threat to anyone in the house. It was later that night when I was nestled in bed with two hot water bottles to warm me that a most perplexing revelation came to me. I had pulled one of the extra pillows close to my body as I always did pretending it was Rainey but instead of whispering his name I had murmured Johnny's. I sat straight up in bed startled at what I had just said. I reiterated what had happened earlier and convinced myself that I had imagined it all and pushed it to the back of my confused mind. Amma was my best friend and Johnny was my most trusted employee. We never spoke of what had transpired in room six and eventually I was able to continue my special friendship with Johnny again. I had wiped that night out of my memory, or so I thought. On the other hand, maybe it never happened and it was just my overactive mind playing tricks on me. So what brought the episode to light again…it had to be Rainey's curiosity about what Johnny and I shared and the kiss he had given me earlier. Something odd just occurred to me…had Johnny called me Vienna that night a hundred years ago? No, I must have imagined that too; no one over here had ever called me that.

"Vienna, Vienna!" Rainey snapped me out of my dream state. "Where were you Darling; did you fall asleep?"

"Rainey?" I looked at him out of the corner of my eye.

"Of course it's me. Were you expecting someone else?" He sounded concerned.

"Don't be silly…who else would be in my bathroom?"

"No one I hope." He held my robe out for me and I climbed out of the tub. He patted me dry and sat me down on the chaise longue and dried my legs and feet. I was still cold.

"Whatever am I going to do with you? I am going to suggest something and I know you are going to hate the idea, but will you please take it into consideration?"

"I think that depends what the suggestion is."

"Until we get the test results back from the doctor I would be most pleased if you would not bathe or go swimming alone. Suppose you were to have one of your "spells" while you were under water…I can't even comprehend that."

"I think you are right Rainey. I don't want to worry you and I must admit I have been preoccupied lately though I know not why." I wrapped my arms around him and for no reason started to cry.

"Hey Babe, what's this all about?" He kissed my tear stained face.

"I know you and others think that I am this hardheaded woman who is not challenged by anything, but that is so not true. I can deal with most everything, but I am still afraid that one day I will blink and you will be gone. I have this imminent feeling that something or someone is going to come between us." I was blubbering like a foolish child.

"I was hoping those sensations would have left you by now but I see they haven't. What can I do or say that will convince you that I am not going anywhere no matter what. There will never be anyone for me but you and I have told you that a thousand times. And if you were to tell me that you loved someone else I would fight for you until my last breath for I have waited much too long to ever give you up."

"I love many people Rainey but I am *in* love with you and only you so you will never have to fight for me. My hormones are working overtime so please forgive me…again."

"This may sound sexist but I like it when you are a little bit dependent on me. Now let's get you dressed; they are waiting for us downstairs."

On our way to the elevator Rainey stopped. "Vienna, will you come away with me?"

"Why Rainey Quinn, are you remembering the first time you asked me that?"

"Yes, I have been thinking about our trip to Avastavalley and I believe it was about the same time of year as our upcoming wedding. Am I right?"

"It was a little later but that does not matter. I would love to go away with you now just as I did back then. What do you have in mind?"

"I'm not sure…I may need a little help finding the perfect private get away. I know you won't want to be gone too long because you have an obligation to Tanny, but I feel we need some complete alone time. Do you realize that we have not been totally alone since our reunion?"

"We had our nights, but you are right, it has never been just you and me and I don't want to wait until September and Andorra.

I want to do something for you too. You told me you came to enjoy the opera when you were in Italy and so my wedding present to you would be to take you to the Royal Opera House in London. You are going to love the architectural style…have you been there already on your trips to visit Stu?"

"No, I haven't and I would like that very much especially because I'll be with you."

"Wonderful, I will check the calendar and see what is performing; I hope it won't be one that you have seen before."

"That doesn't matter for I am not an opera aficionado. I started going because it was the thing to do in Milan and frankly, I was bored. To my great surprise I discovered that I really enjoyed the performances. Someday I would like to take you to the great opera house in Vienna."

"You are still the romantic aren't you?"

"Only where you are concerned my love."

We entered the breakfast room hand in hand. Amma said. "Now don't you two look like the picture of happiness?"

"We are Amma; Rainey has asked me to go away with him."

"Really Rainey, and just where do you think you are taking our mother?" Rosy asked.

Rainey laughed. "Wouldn't you like to know little miss nosey Rosy?"

That brought an amused smile to my eldest daughter. "Good one Rainey."

"It is an anniversary of sorts for us and if I may impose on you ladies to mind Tanny while we are away, I will be in your debt as usual."

"You never mind Miss Vienna, she be in good hands with us." Mrs.D assured me.

The girls and Amma echoed her sentiment. Mason wanted to know when we were going and Rainey said. "After our wedding supper if that meets with everyone's approval and too bad if it doesn't."

Ava answered for everyone. "Of course it does. You two deserve a honeymoon and we can certainly hold the fort down while you're gone."

"Now I know I sometimes come off as a stuffed shirt and you probably all think that I have never encountered ghosts and witches before…well ghosts, I have not, but I do know a witch." Rainey's statement astounded us all.

"What are you saying Rain?" I was slightly amused.

"I suppose you think we don't have witches in Canada…well, I am here to tell you that we do, and I have met a modern day one. Her name is Gretchen and she is my secretary's niece."

"Do you mean Sylvie?" I asked.

"Yes, the whole family is very superstitious and I don't just mean the usual black cat and ladder thing. They follow the predictions of their horoscopes and consult an Ouija regularly." Rainey noticed the stunned look on some of our faces and grinned.

"Sylvie…really Rainey? I have met her and I found her to be a very down to earth person. Surely, you are jesting with us?"

"No Vienna, I kid you not."

It was Morgan's turn to question his dad. "I have met Gretchen Dad and there is nothing unusual about her."

"Well of course not. She doesn't dress in black robes or have a pointed hat or anything quite so obvious, but she follows strict ordinances. She and others like her observe certain days as sacred to their religion; those being the spring and fall equinoxes and the summer and winter solstices, and of course Halloween which is their New Year. I only know this as Sylvie has told me that her niece will not work on those days and takes them off. I never questioned her anymore as I thought the whole premise was absurd."

"I take it that she is a good witch then. I wonder if she wears red petticoats." Ava said to no one in particular.

"I beg your pardon Ava, what did you say about red petticoats?" I asked her.

"I heard or read somewhere that red is a magical color to witches and so they like to wear red petticoats… that's all I'm saying."

There were a few giggles at the table until Mary McDuff wagged her finger at the non-believers. "Now don't ya be a jousin the lass for she be right. I donc did hcar that mysclf along with a lot of other crazy things."

"Mary, do you know anything of the legend of Isobel Gowdie?" I asked.

"Well ever since "Sister Tathia" and I say that with tongue in cheek, mentioned the name the other day, I decided to familiarize myself with her saga. I cannot attest to the accuracy of the account that I found in one of Mr. Jeremy's history books, but here is what I learned. She was not what one would call a white witch, just the opposite. Oh, she had a religious upbringing all right but later in life claimed that she made a pact with the devil. She was born in the early part of the 17th century and was apparently well educated and was reputed to be very beautiful with flaming red hair." She smiled at Rosy. "Anyhow, she was forced into marriage by her father to a very religious man. She met a woman Margaret something or other and they became friends. Margaret's mother was a gypsy and Isobel learned much from her. According to Scottish history, Isobel became the devil's mistress and would cavort with him at the ruins of Inshoch Castle. Much of what we know of witches in Scotland came from Isobel's confessions. She tells of travelling to Elf land and being a guest at a ball held by the King and Queen of Fairyland. She told stories of turning cornstalks into horses and how to transform cats, and crows and hares. She was arrested in April around 1664 and signed her own death warrant by confessing to crimes of being a witch who had by her own admission been baptized by the devil. She also admitted to killing a ploughman with elf arrows and using bags of toad entails to cause infections and of course stating that she could fly. For these offences it was reputed that she was condemned to death and strangled and then burnt at the stake on Gallows Hill outside of Auldearn. Margaret and her mother were also tried as witches. Makes a fascinating story doesn't it? How much is true…who knows, but I am sure that the tale is being told and added to today. And that is the presumed account of Isobel Gowdie. If you want to read more I can point you in the right direction."

"Thank you Mary for enlightening us. I have never known you to go into so much detail about an event before." I told her.

Duffy laughed and said that this was not uncommon for her as he got to listen to her every night retell the events of the day blow by blow.

Rainey said. "I think we have had enough of sorcery for one day."

"Well Darling, you started it." I kidded him.

"You're right I did. Mrs. D, you have outdone yourself with this brunch and you are banished from the kitchen for the remainder of the day. I do a mean barbecue as the boys will contest to and if it suits you all supper will be served in the pavilion at six."

I asked Tanny if she wanted to come and help Rainey and I gather flowers and vegetables. She was on his lap in no time asking him to help tie her shoes. I smiled at the thought that someday he and I would be parents again. The hope made my heart sing.

We had a delightful time in the gardens with Tanny. She wanted to smell all the roses and pick one of every color. Our baskets were overflowing with blossoms and buds before we reached the end of the paths. Tanny said that she was too tired to walk any further so Rainey picked her up and carried her back to the house. I walked with them until I reached the cobbled walkway that would take me to the vegetable plots. I chose everything we would need for the evening meal and washed them in the outdoor sink and deposited them in the kitchen basin to dry. I checked on Tanny and found her fast asleep in the playroom so decided to spend some time going over ledgers in the office. I was interrupted soon afterwards by Johnny.

"Are you busy Vienna? I can come back later if you are."

"To tell you the truth Johnny I have no idea why I even came in here. Please come in and tell me what is on your mind. We never heard two peeps out of you at breakfast…is something wrong?"

He sat in the leather chair that was once Jeremy's. "Are we all right Vienna, or did I put my foot in it?"

"I am sure that I do not know what you are referring to." I did, but did not want to acknowledge anything. "There is nothing wrong with us…why would there be?"

"You know how I feel about you and I would never want to do anything that would damage our friendship or our working relationship. I may have overstepped my boundaries when I told Rainey that

I was not going to give you up no matter what. I hope that I set him straight and that he has nothing to feel insecure about. I want to be his friend but I can't stop treating you the way I always have. We will always have moments where only you and I know what is going on and so if we look at each other knowingly it doesn't mean that we have a secret. On the other hand, I suppose I wouldn't be comfortable with another man sharing special memories with Amma. Tell me if I need to make further amends with Rainey."

"Oh I think he is perfectly fine with what you told him. He has never had a friendship with another woman except his cousin so you will have to excuse his inability to accept that two people of the opposite sex can just be friends. He has promised not to jump to conclusions anymore. He never had any doubts before we were married but a little incident that took place in Bridge Falls caused him to be suspect of my male friends. I believe that he has come to a new understanding so don't you dare start avoiding me!"

"I never had any intentions of doing so. Now down to the matter of business. I have put feelers out and about to aid me in finding a new charge hand that is a Jack of all trades. Also, it appears that we need to hire an assistant for Mrs.D. and a housekeeper and a part time cook at Brackenshire. Have you any prospects?"

There was a rap on the door. "Come in, it's open." I called.

It was Rainey. "Am I interrupting?"

"No dear, Johnny and I were just discussing the sad state of our lack of help. I am afraid I have been neglectful of not addressing the matter sooner."

"I don't think you can be faulted for that Vienna. You have had other things on your mind; like the weddings. For some unknown reason people are not banging on our doors looking for work anymore." Johnny said.

"I'm pretty handy Johnny, so don't hesitate to call on me for anything." Rainey said.

"I appreciate that Rainey and you have already been a big help on the range. The usual extra hands will be here for the haying but as I was just telling Vienna, I need to hire someone who is willing to stay on full time and is adept at all things including carpentry if we are to get started on her balcony."

"That was just a whimsy of mine Johnny and certainly it is not a priority."

"It will get done Hon I promise. Right now I could use Johnny's help at the pavilion if I might steal him away?" I was glad to see that Rainey was in a very good mood.

"We're done here aren't we Vienna? We won't be solving any staff problems today. My next stop was to see what I could do for you Rainey."

"And me, what can I do?" I asked.

"The girls are making the salad and getting the condiments assembled so you and Amma and Mrs.D are just to take it easy the rest of the day. By the way, Rosy has just informed me that Evan will be arriving for the weekend…did you know that?"

I walked them to the door and heard Tanny rumbling around. "I was hoping that she would invite him. You'll like him Rainey, he is a very pleasant young man isn't he Johnny? See you all later."

After Tanny and I had a snack we decided to go and seek out K and Y. She ran ahead of me down the long hallway. I caught up to her just as the doorbell sounded. I scooped her up in my arms and opened the door to find Roberge Farradan, the Duke of Shaunessey, standing there.

He did his funny little bow to me as he usually did. "Lady McAllister, how absolutely delighted I am to see you!" He nodded to the tot in my arms and commented that I was a fast worker. "I hear congratulations are the order of the day. What is the name that you are going by these days?"

"Please do come in Roberge. I thought perhaps that you would have called first but you are most welcome. You may call me Vienna as I am trying to get everyone into the habit of calling me that. I do say that was a very long cruise that you and your lovely wife were on." I motioned for him to take a seat on the little red velveteen sofa and I rang the butler's box hoping someone would answer so that I could offer refreshments.

He was still laughing at my absurd remark about his wife being lovely when Kelly appeared and asked how she could help me. I asked her to bring ice tea and whatever else she could round up. Roberge assured us that tea would be sufficient. I knew that he would prefer something a bit stronger, but first I must conduct my business with him. We made polite chit chat while waiting on K. When she arrived with the tea I asked her to take Tanny and was about to usher Roberge into the parlor when I was aware of someone else coming down the hall.

"I thought I heard you talking to a man…who is our guest Darling?" How he could have heard voices was beyond me as he was supposed to be in the back courtyard.

"Rainey, this is the man I have been telling you about that I am hoping can help us with our quest. Roberge Farradan, this is my husband Rainey Quinn."

"I am most pleased to make your acquaintance sir." Roberge offered his hand. "Any man that could win the heart of this fair lady must be bravura!"

Rainey extended his hand and said welcome but his eyes were not at all friendly. I hoped I wouldn't need to assure him about my relationship with yet another man.

"So the elusive Duke has returned home to Britain. Vienna was beginning to be concerned for your welfare. I am happy to see that you appear to be unscathed."

"There was no cause for worry, but I am happy that my long absence was noted by your beautiful wife." Roberge smiled at me and continued. "I do not know if Vela, excuse me, Vienna, has mentioned to you or not but our last meeting was not one that ended well and so when I returned home and found several messages from her I was most curious."

"No," Rainey answered. "She did not mention anything out of the ordinary. Is there something I should know Vienna?"

"Roberge and I have been known to have some heated disagreements and I suppose that our last encounter was such, am I right Roberge?"

Rainey didn't give him the opportunity to respond but made his apology saying that he was busy in the backyard preparing supper and must excuse himself. "It was a pleasure Sir, and I trust we will have the opportunity to converse later. You will stay for supper will you not? Actually, why not spend the night? You have come a long way, have you not? I really must get back…you will see to our guest won't you Vienna?"

He hadn't given me much choice and had not waited for Roberge to reply. I asked Roberge if he would wait for me in the parlor while I discussed something with my husband. Rainey was already half way down the hall when I caught up to him.

"Rainey, are you going to leave me alone with him?"

"Is there some reason I shouldn't? You would have been alone with him anyhow if I hadn't come in." His voice indicated that he was a tad annoyed with me.

"I did not know that he was going to show up. I don't want you to become upset again."

"Then don't give me any reason to be. Have your tea and perhaps you can have one of the girls set him up in a room so that you won't be alone with him upstairs."

"That was uncalled for Rainey!"

"Yes it was and I should have my tongue removed for it seems it has a mind of its own."

He kissed me hard and said. "I love you and don't forget who you belong to."

He turned and I was left utterly befuddled again. I rejoined Roberge and apologized for leaving him alone. I think my face was probably red as I was still mortified by what Rainey had so blatantly implied.

We sipped our tea and I explained the reason why I had contacted him.

"Are you telling me that you are still on the hunt for an heir to those bracelets? My dear Vienna, we do not even know if they exist."

"But we do Roberge…you see, I have them."

His interest was suddenly aroused. He leaned forward. "Are you telling me that you are in possession of the Infinity Bracelets? That is not possible."

"Why do you say that?"

He sat back in the chair. "Because there is no proof that they ever existed and if they did why would they suddenly materialize one hundred and thirty years later? I am afraid you have been duped my lady."

"Roberge, you pride yourself on being somewhat of a history buff right? Surely you have heard of countless treasures resurfacing centuries later. Archeologists are continuously finding new treasures…most recently, the tomb of Tutankhamen. What if I was to tell you that Kat's bracelets were found in a musty shop in Italy many years ago?"

"Then I would tell you that although there is a scant chance that this might be true, the odds are not in your favor. You came across this romantic fairy tale a few years back and chose to believe that the legend of Kat and Anton really existed when in truth there is no evidence to support it. I hate to burst your bubble my pretty, but you need to come down off your cloud and face reality. You have your prince and your castle so I fail to see why you are still enchanted by a long forgotten love story that may never have even existed."

"Because my instincts tell me the story is true and with your help I intend to find what became of Katarina's daughter. We have just begun to investigate."

Roberge laughed. "I have not agreed to help you and why would I? What is in it for me…if you were the prize I might consider it, but alas I fear that is no longer a possibility, so why would I want to indulge in such a whimsical quest?"

"You will not be so quick to dismiss me and my beliefs after you have seen the bracelets; mark my words Roberge Farradan."

I could see K waiting in the foyer and I assumed she had made sure a room was properly neat and clean for our guest. I asked her to come in.

"I have put Monsieur Roberge in room three; is that acceptable Miss V?"

"Perfect, thank you K. Will you please ask Winston to have his car moved to the garage? Roberge, do you have anything to retrieve before it is moved?"

"Yes, just a petite paquet and an overnight bag. I am always prepared."

"Very well then, K will show you to your room and I will wait for you in the kitchen."

There was nothing left for me to do. The salads had all been made and I assumed were already in the outside cooler. I felt a headache coming on and went to the medicine cabinet in the hall lavatory to find an aspirin. I caught a glimpse of my reflection in the mirror and wondered when I had last combed my hair or applied any make-up. I fumbled in a drawer and found a small bag that contained a few cosmetics. I hastily applied eye liner and a green shadow and a red lip gloss. I pulled my messy shoulder length hair into an up-sweep and loosely pinned it in place. There, I looked reasonably presentable for the lady of the house; that is if it was a house of ill-repute. I laughed at the suggestion and decided to head upstairs and change my clothes.

I met Roberge at the lift and asked him to wait for me while I dressed. He handed me a box wrapped in golden paper. "For you Mademoiselle."

I thanked him and ran down the hall to my room where I quickly slipped out of my homely dress. I pulled on a pair of tight jeans and a white peasant blouse which did not leave much to the imagination. I was sure that Rainey was going to send me back to my room to change. Roberge whistled when he seen me.

"I wouldn't advise you to do that in front of my husband."

"Certainly not my dear…I'm a lover not a fighter. But if you are trying to get his attention I think you have succeeded."

"Maybe I am just tired of being me."

"The world is teeming with women who wish they were you. Have you forgotten how beautiful you are? Has married life taken the life out of you already?"

I did not answer him but changed the subject asking him if the room was to his liking.

He said it was and he noticed that the door was open to Tatylyanna's old room and was there some significance to that.

I told him that her daughter took her home, and that it was a long story. Her evil spirit, if indeed it was evil, has vacated the premises and that was all that mattered.

"I wasn't aware that you knew about room six, or that you even knew her?" I queried.

"Many times I am sad to say. I think I saw through her act the very first time our paths crossed. Jeremy had brought her to one of Lauren's fancy parties and you're going to love this…the two of them became friends. I say that very loosely as I do not believe a woman such as Tatylyanna could ever have a friend unless it was advantageous to her. Jeremy must have told me about room 6. I must hear more."

We entered the courtyard to find everyone milling around with drinks in their hands.

Continuing with our conversation I told Roberge that Taty's father had torn her away from the man that she truly loved to find a rich husband as the family was in financial ruins. According to the daughter that had turned her into a bitter and scornful woman and she died trying to save the family's reputation.

"Only you would vindicate her actions. I for one am glad she is gone. I am thankful that the two of you never met."

"Oh, but we did!"

He didn't have a chance to respond as Ava and Evan came over to say hello.

Evan took my hand. "It's a pleasure to see you again Mrs.…. Rosalyn says that I am to call you Vienna."

"Yes you should Evan, and I am delighted that you could join us for the weekend. Rosy, you remember Roberge Farradan don't you?"

She said she did and introduced the two men. We walked over to where Johnny was pouring drinks. I asked Roberge if his pleasure was still Chardonnay and regretted it the second it was out of my mouth. I should not remember another man's taste in wines.

"You know me too well my Lady." His meaning was only obvious to me I hoped.

I asked Johnny for a coke with a splash of Scottish Whisky. He asked me if I was sure.

I knew my made up face and tight clothes had not gone unnoticed by the way he smiled at me. I had the feeling he was thinking there was trouble in paradise again. I told him I was sure about the drink and took it and headed in Rainey's direction.

Rosy waylaid me. "Are you all right Mama?"

"Why do you ask?"

"For one thing, you don't drink, and you are dressed rather provocatively …are you trying to ire Rainey?"

"Why ever would you say that? I'm just having a little fun. Please keep Roberge company while I talk to my husband."

I walked over to Rainey who had his back to me. "Hello Darling." I purred.

He turned with a spatula in his hand. "Hello yourself." He was very quick to respond to me. "Who are you again? Ah, Jane Russell it is!"

I smiled at the reference to such a sex symbol. "Will you be joining me at my table Sir? I will be over there with our guest."

"I would rather meet you in the hay loft."

I was delighted at his reference to the movie "Outlaw" that had launched Jane Russell's career. "Take a number." I teased.

He grabbed me and said. "You only have one number Lady and don't you forget it!"

I reached up and kissed him just as hard as he had kissed me earlier. I think I bit his bottom lip. I turned to leave and he hit me soundly on my backside with the spatula. I was so startled that my glass flew out of my hands throwing its contents to the wind as it fell to the ground. I was just about to respond to Rainey when Ava caught my arm.

"What are you two doing? I can't tell whether you are fighting or playing! Behave yourselves; we do have company you know."

"Yes daughter." Rainey sheepishly promised. "Sorry I spilled your drink Jane…see you later okay?" He winked at me.

"Sure Kid." I said.

"Is that another private joke Mama?"

"Not really…we were just role playing. Earlier this spring Rainey and I watched a marathon of old movies and one was The Outlaw starring Jane Russell and her love interest was supposedly Billy the Kid. It was way before your time honey, heck it was before my time. I guess the way I am dressed reminded Rainey of it."

"Well Mother, you are looking rather provocative…"

"Your sister said exactly the same thing."

"I guess we have to get use to seeing a different side of you now. You're no longer the reserved person you use to be."

"Ava, is that your way of telling me that I was a prude?"

"No mother, you were never snobbish, just more modest. I can't remember seeing you with made up eyes and tight clothes before. Was it for Rainey or someone else?"

"Ava Lane, how dare you suggest such a thing?" I wasn't scolding her but pretended to be offended. "Lighten up Sweetie…I'm only letting my hair down a little."

"Have you been drinking Mother?"

"I think your father seen to that. Quit calling me mother and come and say hello to Roberge while I clean up the broken glass."

By the time I returned from the kitchen with a dustpan and gloves the broken shards had already been discarded. Rainey apologized.

"Sorry Babe, I didn't mean to hit you so hard."

I kissed him, lightly this time. "And I didn't mean to bite you."

"Are you sure about that?"

"Get back to your cooking, I'm famished."

I joined Roberge at one of the tables across from Amma and Johnny. There was another drink awaiting me and my first sip told me it was sans alcohol. "Really Johnny?" I asked.

He only smiled. We kept the conversation light, talking about mundane things while we waited for the steaks to be done which wasn't very long. Rainey served all the young people first which included his boys and Amma's girls and Ava and Rosy, Evan and Tanny. We had also invited K and Y to join us who were delighted to be included. Duffy and Mary joined us at our table. Rainey pulled a chair up close to me and handed me my well done steak. Apparently, I was the only one who liked their meat cooked.

After the potatoes were all dressed and the salads passed around Roberge commented on the fine tradition of the North American barbeque.

"I don't think it was invented by us Mr. Farradan. I am sure the Europeans have been cooking outside for centuries." Rainey said. "What do you think of Vienna's bracelets?"

"I have yet to see them, and if we are indeed to believe that they really existed, I am dubious to that as Vienna wells knows. How would one ever prove they were Kat's?"

Amma told Roberge that once he saw the bracelets his doubts would be gone as to their authenticity.

"And you have the expertise to corroborate that they are the genuine article my dear?"

"No, but Vienna does."

"You did not tell me that Vienna, when and by whom?" Roberge asked.

"I had to leave room for some intrigue. They could only be authenticated as to the silver content, the year, and that they were genuine Viennese silver. None of the jewelers that I took them to in Vancouver had ever heard of them but they were all extremely interested in learning of their presumed heritage."

"How exactly did they come to be in your possession?"

"That is where I come in." Rainey told him. "I bought them for Vienna in 1961 in a run down curio shop in Rome."

"So you have had them all this time Vienna but never mentioned it until now?"

Rainey answered for me. "That is not true Mr. Farradan as I have had them locked up in a safety deposit box until this past year. Vienna did not know of them until last January. I am just grateful that I chose to keep them as they were a painful reminder of her, but I guess I hung on to the premise that I would find her someday."

I felt guilty again and put my hand over his and he squeezed it.

Roberge realized his error and acknowledged it by saying. "Right; my apologies to you both. I am but Roberge, Mr. Quinn."

"And, I am just Rainey. There is no need to apologize. As soon as I have finished eating I shall fetch the bracelets and you can decide for yourself if you can, or want to help us."

Ava overheard our conversation and said she would get them.

"I realize that you feel like you must return them to the rightful heir, but you will forgive me for not fully understanding as I am afraid I am not that noble. You do realize that I have only seen a faded somewhat questionable sketch of them and that was many years ago? I cannot be sure that the drawing still exists or could prove anything."

Amma asked him how he had come across the story and the drawing.

"My mother's family is Spanish and many stories have been passed down through the years. This one comes from my grandmother whom I am happy to say has just celebrated her 92nd birthday and is still as sharp as the day she was born. I was there for her celebration, and had I known about these bracelets then, I would have questioned her for more information."

"Do you think she would be willing to tell us what she remembers?" I asked.

"I don't think; I know she would be absolutely delighted to meet you, and if the bracelets appear to be genuine, she would do everything in her power to help you locate the heir. There have been many who have gone before you to try and find out what happened to Catalina Christoval, but to my knowledge no one has succeeded."

"Just a question of curiosity Roberge, do you have any idea as to why your family would have a picture of the bracelets?" Rainey leaned across me to ask.

Just then Ava returned and handed the precious bangles to him. He took his time examining them with the magnifying glass that Ava had thoughtfully brought with her. When he finally put them down he turned to Rainey and said. "To answer your question Sir, my grandmother's maiden name is Christoval."

All eyes were on Roberge. He did not offer anything more and left us all speechless.

Rainey squeezed my leg and pushed his chair back and stood up. "Did you know this Vienna?"

I assured him that I did not.

"All righty then, I think this calls for a drink as the plot seems to be thickening." He held up his glass to see who would join him. They all declined. "Vienna?"

I said I was waiting for Ava to return with the coffee. I didn't like it that Rainey was still drinking.

Ava rejoined us at the table while the rest of the young people had gone off to play croquet or some other lawn game. Rosalyn and Evan had escaped to be alone.

Rainey returned with a full glass of whisky and plopped down. "What did I miss?"

"Nothing," Johnny told him. "we were waiting for you and Ava." He looked at Roberge.

"Well, out with it; are you telling us that you are related to Anton Christoval? Why did you omit telling Vienna that fact when she first asked you if you had any knowledge regarding Anton's and Kat's story?"

"I didn't want her to… how is it you say, be off on a wild goose trail. Shall I tell you what I know?"

We all said "yes" in unison.

"Stories are past down from one generation to another as you are all aware of, and my family are no different. One of them is of the disappearance of the Infinity Bracelets. According to my Grandmother Abella, Anton and Katarina were married at the time of a very ruthless war between France and Spain. It appears to be true that Anton was sent to wait out the conflict at a monastery some-where in the Pyrenees, and that is where he met Kat. Abella's mother told her the story of the bracelets he had made for his wife and yes, there does exist a faded sketch of them though I know not where it is. My great grandmother was a cousin to Anton's father and seeing that Abella was born around 1890 that would put my great grandmother alive during the time in question being 1850 or so. I do not recall any details as I have not heard the account for a number of years and quite honestly, I did not take much of an interest in the fable at the time. However, I must say that seeing these exquisite bangles has aroused my curiosity. I feel I have an obligation to pursue their heritage and so the answer is yes…yes, I will do what I can to help you find the rightful heir Vienna providing that my grandmother can provide a few more details."

"I can ask for no more Roberge. I look forward to meeting with your grandmother and hear her telling of the tale. We will not be able to pursue the matter until September as our summer calendar is already overflowing with activities. I trust you will speak to your grandmother on our behalf…I hate to put the visit off but it cannot be helped. Now let's put the story to bed for the evening and speak of other things."

The hour was nearing midnight when Rainey and I made it to our bedroom. He found the wrapped parcel on the bed where I had flung it earlier.

"What is this Vienna?"

I told him that Roberge had brought us a wedding present.

"How touching. I assume that he is the man in your song Mademoiselle, am I right?"

"Really Rainey, are you going to go there again? Will you ever be satisfied with what I have told you of my twenty years without you? You're going to drive me to drink. Now go to bed and sleep your liquor induced stupor off! I'm going to my balcony."

"You don't have a balcony Vienna."

"Exactly, and if I did perhaps I would throw myself off it." I turned and walked away from him intending to slam the door but he was too quick for me and held on to it before I could do so.

"Don't make idle threats; you know you would do no such thing. I am not drunk and I want you to come to bed."

"Well, I don't want to. There are at least a dozen other beds in this gin joint that I can sleep in, or maybe I will go for a nice long swim." Again I tried to leave.

"You promised me that you wouldn't go in the pool without me."

"Oh yeah right, well, you promised me you would quit asking inane questions about my past so I guess you see how that works."

"I'm an idiot and I think that fact is well documented. You haven't been out of my bed for five months and I don't want tonight to be the first. I'll go have a cold shower if you will stay with me. I can't say I am sorry again because it's getting old hat and surely you are growing weary of my apologies."

"I wouldn't be if they were sincere, but I believe we both know that they aren't always. I am getting tired of arguing with you and making up only to start anew the next day. So how about if I tell you this; not only were Jack and Johnny and Roberge my lovers, but so was Jimmy and Reverend Peters!"

I left an astonished man to ponder that for awhile and walked past him and into the bathroom and unlocked the adjoining door to where Tanny was sleeping and tip-toed down the hall and kitchen stairs. I picked up a flashlight from the pantry and quietly let myself out the back door. The air had a biting chill to it and I wished I had brought a sweater. I remembered that I usually kept a shawl in the conservatory so I wound my way around to the back entrance. A spare key was kept under a flower pot and I removed it and unlocked the door and found my wrap. I relocked the door and followed the path to the mausoleum. The moon was still almost full and so its light illuminated the walkway. The structure loomed before me in an incandescent glow. I was trembling as I fumbled with the latch on the heavy door. Please God, not now…don't let me faint. I clutched the wall and fought the dizziness, but the sensation of something menacing was with me again. I was in a tomb filled with souls from another lifetime in the dead of night…what was I thinking by coming here? I switched on the light on the stone wall and took a deep breath and found my way to Maveryn's niche. I lovingly placed my hands on her plaque and spoke to her as if she was right beside me.

"Maveryn, you once told me that I was going to find my prince and that I would know what true love was. I found him a long, long time ago, but I had to let him go. Now we are together again and I can't bear the thought of losing him and yet I fear I am going to. I know that just as well as I know that the sun is going to rise tomorrow and I also know that I am powerless to stop it from happening. Is my fear going to be the catalyst that stands between us and everlasting happiness? Rainey loves me, but he doesn't trust me and that lack of faith is wearing on me and I feel we are on the path to destruction." For a brief second I thought I heard a rustling and another shudder enveloped me. I wrapped my arms around myself. I had placed a large block of rock against the door just as I always did because I was afraid that it couldn't be opened from the inside although I was sure it could be. It was probably just the wind playing with the leaves in the trees.

"I never thought I would ever be as happy as I was when Rainey told me that he loved me Maveryn, and had all the years that we were apart. But the day we were married passed all expectations and we are going to have a second wedding here and I hope you will be with me. I will know if you are there because I can always feel your presence. You did not leave that ominous message for me did you Maveryn? I thought I was being cautious and yet I let a witch…a good one mind you, into the house. Are you aware that your nemesis has left the castle? Now, if I could only figure out who and what the third stranger's forecast will be…I best be going Maveryn as I fear I have more fences to mend. I only pray my willful nature won't be my comeuppance. I miss you so."

Perhaps I do have the sixth sense for I knew someone was outside the crypt and so I was not startled to find Rainey leaning up against the building waiting for me.

"Hi Gorgeous." He said nonchalantly.

"How did you find me?"

"I hope I will always be able to find you Vienna. This time you left your imprint in the wet grass that bordered on the path. You came to talk to Maveryn didn't you? I did not eavesdrop on your conversation in case you are wondering."

"You wouldn't have heard anything that you do not already know, and that is that I love you and am so afraid of losing you. I will be the cause of our demise won't I?"

He pulled me close to him and and rubbed my cold body. He kissed my forehead and my eyes as he always did. "You sobered me up in a hell of a hurry Sweetheart when you said what you did and ran out on me. I am so full of meaningless excuses for my never ending jealousy that I am ashamed of myself and quite rightfully you should be thoroughly disgusted with the way I attack you. Is this what love does to one? I thought it was going to be one never ending honeymoon and that we wouldn't be apologizing to each other at every turn."

"I need you to trust in me Rainey and believe that what I have told you is true…can you do that?"

"I'm working on realizing that you had a life without me. I couldn't live without you Vienna or would even want to, so if we have to keep having these futile spats then it is still better than the alternative because I love you dearly."

I smiled up and him and told him what he needed to hear and that was how much I loved him and that there had never been anyone else. He said he knew. Then I asked him to take me home.

I woke up to find myself alone in bed. It took me a few minutes to recall the events of last night and when I did I was out of bed like a Jack rabbit! I slipped a long housecoat on over my flimsy nightie and bolted for the stairs. I could hear loud boisterous voices coming from the breakfast room and opened the door expecting to find Rainey and Roberge in a heated argument. Instead they had their heads down and were chuckling like school children. Rainey spotted me first and motioned for me to come and join them.

I asked to be excused for a minute and went to the lavatory where I washed my face and combed my ratty hair. I let out a long sigh of relief as I wasn't up to any peace keeping missions this morning. Roberge and Rainey both stood up as I entered the dining roomagain. Rainey held my chair for me and Roberge brought me a cup of steaming coffee.

"Thank you. What was all that laughter about?" I asked.

"Roberge was relating some hilarious tales regarding his aristocratic relatives. Apparently their blunders are just as comical as are ours of the lower classes."

"I assure you that royal blood does not run through my bones just because I am married to a woman of nobility. I would love to stay and chat a while longer especially now that you have joined us Lady Vienna, but I must take my leave if I am to make London at a decent hour. Thank Mrs. D for the hearty breakfast for me will you Rainey?"

Roberge collected his valise from the floor and we walked him to the door where his car awaited him. "Thank you for the interesting evening and I will be in touch as soon as I have word from Grammama. It was a pleasure to meet you Rainey." He took my hand and bestowed a kiss upon it. "With you my dear, it's always a delight. We will have the opportunity to be working on our little endeavor soon I am sure. Au revoir mes amis."

We said our goodbyes and turned to see a pajama clad Tanny running down the hall towards us. Ava was hot on her trail.

"Tia, Rainey, save me from the bad witch." She tried to climb up on me but Rainey grabbed hold of her and told her that he would save her. She was giggling and pretending to be afraid of Ava.

Playing their little game I said. "Get ye far from this child oh wicked one. Your powers are no good in this kingdom."

"The soup will be no good without her my Queen. I need those tender little tootsies and fingers…they are so tasty. Will you not give her back to me?" Ava croaked.

"Be off with you before I turn you into a frog."

"I don't like frogs. Tia, don't make Ava a frog." Tanny cried.

"We are only foolin Honey. How would you like to come upstairs with me and we can both get dressed in our outdoor clothes?"

We were standing before the grand staircase and Tanny made it known that she did not want to climb those big old fat steps as her legs did not like them.

"Rosy and Ava never liked these stairs when they were young either. I do not know why the old people made these steps so far apart and hard for little people. Let's take the lift."

"Or, how about if I carry you up these big ole steps and Tia takes the lift and we will see who wins?" Rainey coaxed.

Tanny laughed. "Hurry Rainey cause Tia is fast."

I wasn't that fast and it made her happy that they beat me. I thought we would take Tanny down to the ponds to feed the wildlife and then for a boat ride. I told her we would stop by the kennels and pick up Barrett and Browning, the two golden retrievers. They had been neglected lately as Johnny was training two young pups and hadn't had much time to spend with the older dogs. I decided right then that I would keep them with us at the castle and they could be our watch dogs again. I felt badly that I had been away so much and that they had been banished to the kennels.

Rainey asked Tanny if she could help me with the bed while he showered. She spotted the open dresser drawer where the golden wrapped gift from Roberge protruded. She picked it up and brought it to me asking what it was and I explained that it was a wedding present. She wanted me to open it and I thought that it was as good a time as any with Rainey out of the room.

"What is it Tia?"

"I'm not sure Honey." I removed the last of the protective wrap and was astonished to find a small portrait of myself staring back at me. "Oh." I stammered.

"Is that you Tia?" Tanny asked. "You look funny."

"No, it is not me. See this lady has very long black hair and she is wearing clothes from a long time ago. Let's see what the note says." I read it out loud:

Lady V, I came across this in a petite Shoppe in a remote village in France and noticed the likeness to you and had to have it. I have had a copy made and have taken the liberty of researching the name of the enchantress. Does the name Angeliqua Novia have any meaning to you?

Your humble servant Roberge

"Who is the lady Tia?"

"I don't know Tanny, but it is not me. Monsieur Roberge only gave it to me because he thought the young lady looked like me. Come on now we must get to work."

As soon as Rainey returned Tanny ran to him with the picture. "Look Rainey, a picture of Tia a long time ago."

"Where did this come from Vienna?"

"From Roberge…he seems to think I bear a resemblance to the woman in this ancient lithograph and thought I might like to have it…why, I do not know."

"The resemblance is uncanny to when you were sixteen." Rainey read the note. "Could she be a relative of yours? Is the name French or Spanish…do you know? How much do you know of your father's heritage?"

"He did not speak much of his ancestry and I do not know why. I am sure that everyone shares a likeness to someone else from times gone by but it doesn't mean that they were related. What would it matter anyhow?"

"I think I would like to know who this French/Spanish beauty is who resembles my wife so much. Kudos to Roberge!"

"Oh Rainey, let's not get started on another tangent; we have enough on our plate right now. But seeing we are on the subject… what do you make of the fact that you and Johnny could be related?" Let's see what he had to say about that.

"We have discussed it, and I do believe when there is time we will delve into the matter further. Right now we are discussing you… this portrait is captivating for it is you from another period in time. Surely you are a little bit curious?" Rainey laughed. "She looks regal to me; perhaps you are a descendant of kings and queens!"

"Perhaps we all are Rainey. Do what you want with the picture. If you want to be a co-conspirator with Roberge… go for it. Now I am going to get myself and Tanny ready for our outing."

Rainey said he was going to show the aged photo to the girls and would meet us downstairs. I had the last word. "By the way, Novia was my great grandmother's name."

He turned around and was about to say something but was interrupted by Morgan and Mason running down the hall. They stopped short in front of him and in a barely audible voice whispered. "They're here…we saw them."

"Whoa boys; who is here, and why are you so out of breath?"

Mason looked past his dad and said to me. "You know don't you Vienna?"

"Perhaps I do but you had better give me a clue as to what you are referring to?"

Morgan had regained his composure and explained. "We were in the tower courtyard playing chess as usual and then all of a sudden **they were there**. We both saw them; there must have been half a dozen men dressed in full regalia armor. They came from out of nowhere and disappeared just as fast as they had come."

Mason chimed in. "They were carrying swords and shields and appeared to be going into battle. I dare say I was scared to death. I thought I was hallucinating until I saw the look on Morg's face. They were just as real as you and I."

Rainey looked at me with an amused smile. "I think it is just your overactive minds playing tricks on you. The both of you have been hoping to encounter ghosts and …"

Morgan didn't let his father finish. "How do you explain that we both saw them Dad?" Then he turned to me. "You know about them don't you Vienna?"

"I have never seen the warriors myself, but Jeremy told me that he and Ash had many encounters with them when they were young. At first they were terrified but soon came to accept them as the ghosts of fallen soldiers. I cannot explain why they materialized today. Possibly the arrival of the summer solstice has something to do with it. Apparently, it is the time for magic."

Rainey was not pleased with my explanation. "Vienna, you are not helping any. Boys, let's just chalk what you thought you saw down to wishful thinking. You know that what you described is impossible don't you?"

"Sure Dad, in the real world, but Avanloch is a castle and has an unusual history. Battles took place here and many a life was lost. Is it so alien to you that their spirits pass through the walls now and then?" Morgan was trying to convince his father that they had witnessed something incredible and that he should acknowledge that it was true.

Rainey's eyes said it all without him having to utter a word. He had heard all of the stories but could not put credence to any of them, and now his look was accusing me of putting ideas into Morgan's and Mason's impressionable minds.

"Your father is trying to be the voice of reason as usual boys." I took Rainey's hand and smiled. "He still has not come to terms with the night Maveryn visited us. He does not believe in the unexplained, and I don't know what it will take to convince him that there are spirits among us. Are you boys afraid to go back to the courtyard?"

They said they weren't and were going to ask the girls why they hadn't told them about the phantoms. I told them that as far as I know Rosy and Ava had never encountered them probably because they had hardly ever played upstairs.

Rainey said he would go back with the boys if they wanted him to. They both agreed that he needn't and that he, being a non believer would probably only anger the spirits. I laughed and agreed.

"Don't you have to get dressed Vienna? Quit adding fuel to the fire." Rainey retorted.

"Yes Dear. I will meet you down stairs unless I am waylaid by the Lady in Grey."

Rainey arched his eyebrows. "Should I even bother to ask who the grey lady is?"

I blew him a kiss and said "Later."

As soon as Tanny and I were dressed we went to the kitchen to pack a small picnic lunch. Mrs.D was nowhere to be found and it occurred to me that she was hardly ever around anymore. Perhaps it was her way of preparing us for her retirement.

The day was perfect. Rainey picked up the dogs and joined Tanny and I on the garden path. She ran ahead of us calling for Barrett and Browning to follow her. Rainey picked a red rose bud and tucked it into my hair.

"For my love only because there aren't any cherry blossoms." He said in a soft voice.

I smiled and took his hand and we ran to catch up to the trio in front of us. The meadows were alive with purple lupines, white daisies, blue corral bells and orange tiger lilies. Yellow iris, pink Mayflower, lavender violets and lily of the valley were in full blossom along the water's edge and the water lilies were flowering profusely. Tanny wanted to pick flowers but we told her they would not be happy without water and we could gather a bouquet on the way home. We roamed around for an hour or so and then placed the dogs in the kennel by the man- made lake while we toured around in the canoe. The swans had returned and put on quite a show for us. Two does came to the edge of the water to drink leaving their newly born fawns hidden in the underbrush.

Rainey released the dogs while Tanny and I set up the lunch on one of the picnic tables. Later we fed the scraps to the waterfowl and started the climb for home. Tanny was one knoll ahead of us and yelled down to us. "Look at me!" She proceeded to lie down and curled up in a ball and rolled down the hill. Rainey caught her and carried her to the top.

"Watch me Rainey." She squealed as she broke free of him and tumbled down the hill again with the dogs in hot pursuit.

Rainey and I sunk down into the cool deep grass to watch the antics of a four year old child. "How long do you think she can keep this up?" He asked.

"I have no idea." A tear formed in my eye as I lay my head on his shoulder. "This could have been you and I with Ava if I hadn't been so pig headed for all those years."

"No you don't Vienna; you don't get to spoil this wonderful day by regretting the past. Look at me…do you hear?"

"Yes, but I still want to give you the chance to raise a child with me."

"If it happens it happens, but if it doesn't I am perfectly happy with the family that you have already given me. Tanny will be a part of us from now on I am sure. Tell me you are happy with our life Vienna?"

"Oh yes, I am happy Rainey. I am as happy as a witch is in a broom factory."

He broke out into laughter. "Where do you come up with these things?"

Tanny had made it back up the hill and jumped on Rainey tickling him. The dogs, barking loudly joined in running around him."

"Help me Vienna…help me." He pretended to plead.

"I'll help you all right!" I assisted in the assault until Rainey said he gave up and managed to roll away from us.

"You girls are too much for me. Shall we pick those flowers now Tanny?"

She agreed and we gathered an armful of colorful posies and then Rainey picked her up and put her on his shoulders. She said. "Getty up, getty up, faster, faster."

They trotted on ahead of me as I struggled with the large armful of flowers. At the entrance to the pavilion Rainey stopped and put Tanny down. I caught up to them and could see that he was lost in thought. I asked him what had him so engrossed.

"Tell me if I am imagining it, but does the left turret protrude further out from the castle then the right one?"

I told him that I couldn't be sure but asked what difference would it make if it did?

"There are no entrances into the bartizans from inside that you are aware of are there?"

"First of all, I have no idea what a bartizan is, but if you are asking if we can get into the turrets from inside, the answer is no… not that I have any knowledge of anyway."

"Sorry Darling, a bartizan is an overhanging structure mostly found in French and Spanish fortifications; just another word for turret, but they can contain rooms and staircases. I think I need to start concentrating more on the makeup of the outside of Avanloch and what possibilities might lay within these abutments or even some of these projecting windows."

"As far as I know Rain, the turrets and elaborate windows are strictly for decorative purposes, but if it will satisfy your curiosity then you had better get your measuring paraphernalia out again. The boys have gone with Rosy and Ava to Waverly to see Evan off on the train and so you are stuck with me as your sidekick."

"I wouldn't exactly call it being "stuck" as I would rather have you by my side than anyone else. Your expertise on Jeremy's rooms would be most appreciated. I know the suite has been searched many times before but who knows, we may just find the hidden clue this time. How about I take the dogs back to their kennel and you see if anyone is around to take care of Tanny and then we'll meet up?"

"The dogs are not going back to the kennels Rainey; I want them back in the house. I am going to restore their sleeping quarters by the back stairs."

"Is something worrying you? Has all this talk about ghosts unnerved you, and what is this grey lady thing?"

"No, I am not anxious, I just want them near and Tanny loves them so. I will fill you in on the Grey Lady later."

"I am going to hold you to that. Will Mrs.D be okay with the dogs in the house?"

"They have taken up residence here before. Johnny took them to be parents to the new pups but they are fine on their own now. I think you are forgetting something…contrary to what some people believe, I have the final say in matters regarding what transpires in this house, and if I say the dogs stay, the dogs stay."

"Yes Ma'am. I'm sorry…please forgive me." Rainey jested.

"Did you just call me ma'am? Don't answer that. Tanny has fallen asleep on the chaise. Can you take her upstairs while I find Alexa? The dogs can run loose."

By the time we found our way to Jeremy's rooms, it was almost 4 o'clock and the boys would be returning any moment and so I wouldn't be crashing in on their thunder for very long. I needed to have a conversation with the girls about renaming this suite; we couldn't keep referring to it as Jeremy's rooms.

"Where do you want to start Rainey? The turret is in the far northwest corner and so it should be on the outside of the bedroom wall."

"Exactly, and that is where we shall concentrate our search. Keep your mind open."

"What exactly does that mean?"

"I just meant for you to watch for any inconsistency in the wallpaper, the wainscoting or around the window casings. You know how the wallpaper in your parlor conceals the button that opens up the stairs…well, there is probably one here that does the same."

"The girls and I have gone over this room with a fine tooth comb on numerous occasions and found nothing, nada, zilch, zip. What makes you think that this time will be any different?"

"Patience my love; just be diligent. Can you search and talk at the same time or should we sit down for a few minutes while you fill me in on the grey lady?"

I tried to conceal my amusement and told him that I could only really do one thing at a time and pulled him down on the bed.

"Well this will certainly accomplish a lot won't it?" He started kissing me and I had a hard time resisting.

"You silly goose, do you want the kids to walk in on us?"

"Frankly my dear, I don't care if they do."

"Do you want to hear about The Grey Lady or not?"

"That isn't my first choice but go ahead."

I sat up and composed myself. "You can thank **her** for my final decision to go to Bridge last winter. The girls thought they had convinced me to go and I let them believe that, but the truth of the matter is that I was worried about my state of mind. A week or so prior to their suggestion that I needed to get away I was experiencing strange dreams…at least I thought they were dreams until I started seeing things in the middle of the day while I was wide awake."

Rainey held me tightly and kept both of my hands in his. "What did you see?"

"The first time… I was in the grand entrance arranging wintery greens and alone of course, and out of nowhere these Scottish pipers came parading. They were playing some mournful song. They marched through the doors into the harem room. I ran after them, but they were nowhere to be seen. Another time I saw them traipsing down the staircase and again they simply vanished into thin air. I asked Mrs. D and Amma if they had ever seen such a thing and they said they hadn't but that they had heard stories of mysterious pipers appearing in the village during certain times of the year. Wonderful I thought, and then I started to have visitations from the Lady in Grey. I wrote about them in my diary and so you may come across her as you continue to read the journals. She wasn't menacing and I was not afraid of her. She was a very restless spirit and her misty shape would wander in and out of wherever I was. I believe she was grief stricken as her mood was always sorrowful. I believe she was on a never ending search for someone…her lover or a child. I don't know why she chose that particular time to appear to me unless she was mimicking what I was going through in my desire to be with you. Her visits always left me with a sense of hopelessness. She has not returned since I've been back."

"I think you were right when you said she was feeling your sorrow. You know how I feel about these sightings Sweetheart, but I am beginning to believe that there are forces at work here that we will never fully comprehend. Perhaps the boys' experience was not a hallucination and neither are yours. If this lady brought you to me then I am grateful and will forever be in her debt. I think I would like to meet these pipers myself."

"Oh you would, would you? Be careful what you wish for it might come true and then you could deny seeing them just as you do Maveryn… so what good would that be?"

"If it wasn't for that message in the otherwise blank notebook, I'd believe it was all a disturbing dream; you know like the ones Scrooge experienced."

"Those ghosts that visited Scrooge were there to show him what a pitiful life he had lived and that things would only get worse if he didn't make amends. You, on the other hand have lived a respectable and admirable life. You did not achieve your accomplishments by taking advantage of your fellow man."

Rainey snickered. "Are you sure about that? Anyhow, to change the subject…I have a question that I want to ask you; it is about your song Mademoiselle."

"RAINEY QUINN; are you REALLY going to go there AGAIN?" I wish I had never wrote that song or sent it off to Gizelle Marchant. Never in my wildest dreams did I ever think that she would put it on an album or that you would ever hear it even though I wrote it with you in mind. She is one of your favorite singers and you even attended one of her concerts, but how was I to know that? I thought that I had finally set your mind at ease about the gentleman whom you think is pursuing me in the song, but apparently I haven't." I pushed myself away from Rainey but he pulled me back down.

"Don't get so hostile…I'm done with all that, but this is about your mention of the city of Vienne. Why did you pick that particular city?"

I let out a sigh relieved that we were not going to visit that forbidden subject again. "I haven't the faintest idea…I didn't even know if it was a real place or not."

"It's a real place all right for I have been there. It is the French spelling of Vienna."

"Are you suggesting that I subconsciously wrote Vienne somehow knowing that it was the French version of my name?"

"I don't know, but I have a hunch that you were named for that French town and not for the Austrian one. When you talk to your father about the name Novia ask him about Vienne. I think the two may be connected."

"Why do you think that Rainey? My name is Vienna; my mother named me."

"Correct me if I am wrong, but your mother was against your father speaking French or teaching you or your sisters his native tongue wasn't she?"

"Yes, that is true. So, you are saying that she may have liked the name Vienne but didn't like that it was French and so she added the 'a' to make it sound more English? Have you been doing a lot of thinking about this?"

"Not really, but ever since seeing the likeness of the woman in the photo to you I have been somewhat preoccupied with the idea that she could be related to you."

"Why me Rainey? Shouldn't you be researching your own roots? I think that your Irish origins are going to be a lot more interesting than mine."

"Perhaps, but right now I want to concentrate on you and see if Roberge comes up with any more information on this captivating woman Angeliqua Novia. I will be most intrigued if there is a connection to you."

"Rainey, haven't we enough on our plate right now? Do you really want to go digging up skeletons in the attics?"

"Aha, so you admit the LaFontaine name might have a dubious past?" I hit him.

"Didn't we come here to try and find an entrance to the bell tower?"

He had started for the door and was going to say something but left the words hanging in the air. He came back and sat down again with a puzzled look on his face.

"Why did you call the turret a bell tower?"

"I don't know, perhaps I heard it called that before."

"You do know what a bell tower is don't you?"

"Of course silly, it's a tower where bells are rung."

"Okay Miss Smarty Pants…what would bells be doing in a turret?"

"How would I know Rainey? I seem to remember Jeremy telling some old geezer from the village that the bells had been removed after the war because they were driving his parents crazy. Apparently, they would sound at every little breeze and were constantly waking them up. Knowing me, I probably heard wrong and they were removed from the tower room and not the structure outside of their bedroom. That's all I know…"

"Vienna, you have an amazing memory and if you are right you know what it means?"

"Oh heavens no; do tell me kind Sir."

"You're still the little imp aren't you Lassie? I'll tell you what it means…there is definitely an entrance into this so called turret."

He got up and pulled me along with him to the far corner of the bedroom. "What would you say if I took a power saw to this wall?"

"I would say you're out of your pea pickin mind! What kind of an architect are you anyway? Did you ever stop to consider that maybe the key that will open the wall is controlled by something else?" I walked over to the butler's box on the wall. "Like inside here or certain combinations of numbers?"

He seemed intrigued by my suggestion and looked the outdated system over carefully. I couldn't be sure but I think he may have fiddled with some of the buttons. "When did you get so methodical… don't answer that because you always have been. I think we may be going at this all wrong. The way in may be under the floor. Wait here, I'll be right back."

I asked him where he was going but he ran out of the room leaving me with my hands in the air wondering what the heck he was up to now. By the time I entered the hall he was nowhere in sight. I heard the dogs barking and headed for the back stairs to find Rainey sitting with them near the top. He was looking rather smug.

"Well genius, what have you discovered?" I asked.

"Come see for yourself My Lady." He said pleased as punch.

I shooed the dogs away and joined him. The step had swung out like it was on a swivel of some sort. We were staring into a black abyss. I hugged him. "Rainey, you did it, you found an entry."

He hugged me back. "Don't get too excited my dear…we have no idea what is down or up there. Stay put while I find a flashlight."

"I'll go get one from the pantry."

The back door opened just as I grabbed the lights. "Hey Mom, we're home. Where are you going with those?" It was Ava with the rest of the crew close behind.

"Come see what Rainey has found!" They followed me up the stairs and as we reached the last curvature I gasped. Rainey was nowhere in sight. Please Lord; don't let him have fallen into a cavernous pit. "**Rainey**!" I shrieked. "**Are you down there?**"

There was no answer. I got down on my hands and knees and with the help of a flashlight peered into the opening. All I could see was what appeared to be more steps.

"Mother, what is down there?" Ava asked.

"Is Dad down there Vienna?" Mason sounded concerned.

"I don't know,; I left him right here when I went for the flashlights."

"Hi kids, I see you're back. Was that you yelling Vienna?" Rainey appeared at the top of the steps.

"Rainey Quinn, I am going to shoot you! I thought you had fallen down the hole."

"Lucky for me then that there are no guns in the house. Sorry I worried you Babe, but I had to go to the loo."

"Obviously, you haven't seen Jeremy's gun collection have you Rainey?" Rosy queried.

"Oh, I have seen them and am thankful they are under lock and key." He winked at me.

"I suppose you don't know that Mama keeps a pistol behind the headboard of the bed do you?" Ava asked teasingly.

"Vienna, tell me she's joking?"

"I do, but it is not loaded. Up until now I have not had the need to use it but one never knows when it will come in handy. I have my honor to protect you know." Rainey's and my eyes met and mischievously he assured me that I had nothing to fear as long as he was here.

"What good would an unloaded gun do anyhow Vienna, and you can't shoot ghosts can you?" Mason asked.

"Good question Son…now let's see what we have behind this step."

I stood up and let Rainey take my spot telling him that the flashlights didn't help much.

"What's all the commotion about up there?" It was Duffy starting up the stairs.

"Duffy, old sport," Rainey called down. "We need more light… do you have a trouble light that will reach up here?"

"Right-O; send someone down for the extension and I'll fetch the light."

"I'll go Dad." Morgan offered and returned with the cord and plugged it into the receptacle at the top of the stairs.

A few minutes later Duffy arrived with the huge bulb and handed it to Rainey. "What have you discovered there Son?"

"Don't know yet Duff…have you ever seen this step open before?"

"Can't rightly say that I have. How did it happen to come apart?"

"I'll explain later. Well, I'll be danged…from what I can see there are two steps going down and then a flat area that leads to two or more stairs going up. Only one way to find out where they lead…"

Rainey turned around and was ready to descend when I grabbed onto him. "Don't do anything foolish… here, take this flashlight."

"I'm coming too Dad." Mason said.

"Wait here Mase, I won't be long. Keep them back Vienna."

He slid carefully into the small opening that the step had revealed. It was a tight squeeze and anyone larger than he would have difficulty gaining entrance into the cavity. He called back that he was on secure ground and crossing a plank floor to another set of steps.

In a few anxious minutes he was back looking like the cat that had swallowed the canary. He spoke to us from inside the hole.

"Well, I do believe that we have found one of the secret rooms and you are going to be very surprised to learn where it is. Vienna knows and it is because of her rational thinking that I was able to put 2 and 2 together and conclude the entrance was here."

I asked him if it was what he thought and he said I could see for myself. He offered me his hand but I insisted that the kids go first. He told us that two could come down at a time. Rosy nudged Mason and Morgan but they insisted that the girls go first.

"Just get going will you before I push you down!" Rosy said through gritted teeth.

They finally agreed and descended. Ava and Rosy went next. Duffy declined saying he was claustrophobic but was most curious as to what Rainey had discovered. The kids returned and didn't offer any insight into what they had seen. It was now my turn. I wasn't too happy about slipping into the narrow entrance. Ava said it was easier to go in backwards and so I did. Rainey's arms were around me before I even hit the floor. The light from the torches cast a multitude of eerie shadows onto the walls. Rainey took my hand as he guided me across the floor. We took an abrupt right and up four steps.

"Lady Vienna, are you ready to have a peak into the belfry? What we are in right now is the antechamber. There are four steps that open unto the bartizan. We cannot enter the little room as I do not know how sturdy it is, but it is as you said…see, the large hook in the ceiling and the pulley system that was used to secure the bell. Can you imagine the loud tolling that a bell that size would have emitted? No wonder it was dismantled. What do you think?"

"I guess I am a little astounded that Jeremy never told anyone about this area…you do think he knew don't you?"

"Perhaps it has more secrets to be revealed or perhaps he thought that it was insignificant. We will probably never know until we find the blueprints to the castle. Yes, I do believe he knew about this room as he did tell the girls that there were three secret rooms and I am sure this must be one of them. Come, I want to show you something."

I went back with him into what he called the antechamber. He gave me a flashlight to hold on one of the walls which I now noticed had knobs protruding from it. Rainey opened it to reveal very deep cupboards with shelves. I asked him what he thought they had been used for as they were certainly not of easy access.

"At this point I have no idea, but if this whole chamber was here antebellum, then I would imagine they housed stores in case the castle came under attack."

"Do you mean World War I or II or the Scottish Wars?"

"Again, I have no idea. If we had any indication as to how much of the original castle was left when remodeling started we would know a hell of a lot more. For now we'll have to be content with whatever we can piece together."

"My big question for the moment is how did you come to realize that the stairs would come apart and just how do they?"

"Let's join everyone in the kitchen where I will explain it all. Do you want to go back the way we came or do you want to take the scenic tour of which I am not entirely sure where it will take us to. I hardly doubt that this is the only way in here; do you?"

"Surely I do not know Rainey, but if you are suggesting we explore an alternative entrance may I suggest we postpone that for now and return at another time, maybe with Johnny?" I slowly crawled up the two steps with Rainey pushing me from behind. "Was that necessary Rainey?"

"Yeah, for my benefit it was, and I agree that asking Johnny to join us is a good idea."

We entered the kitchen to find everyone waiting patiently for us. Mason asked what took us so long. I think Rosy kicked him under the table as he said "Ow." and gave her a dirty look. Mrs. D poured us coffee.

"Sit here Rainey…this is so exciting that you have found a room that we did not know existed. This ole castle it holds many secrets still me thinks."

"Yes to be sure Mary. This one may have never been discovered had it not been for Vienna's suggestion that perhaps we were all looking in the wrong place for clues as how to gain entrance into the mysterious hidden rooms."

"Don't pay any attention to him…he is the one who noticed that the turret jotting out from the north wing was larger than any of the others. I had never given it any thought but then it appears that it is only noticeable from on top the hill behind the pavilion. How exactly it is that Rainey deduced the steps opening up is still baffling to me." I looked at him for the answer.

"As I said, Vienna alerted me to something that has been puzzling me for a while. Has no one else ever wondered why the numbers 4 and 7 are colored in red on the call box…but only in the kitchen and in the master suite?"

Everyone shook their heads. "Perhaps I asked Mr. Jeremy about it once but don't recall if he had an answer for me or not." Mary stated.

"Well when my darling wife pointed to the butler's box today it got me thinking about something else that I have found curious; that being the four lancet windows that are in the niches on the back stairs. They are very elaborately carved and I have wondered if they have a purpose other than to show different views of the estate. Perhaps it is just the architect in me working overtime but one day I investigated them thoroughly, and to my dismay found nothing out of the ordinary except that the first three finials could be maneuvered but appeared to do nothing. The finial on the fourth spire was a horse of a different color. When I fiddled with it I was sure that I heard a definite clicking noise but could not detect where it was coming from. I guess I put the whole matter in the back of my mind and forgot to even mention it to Vienna and then today something clicked. It was just a hunch but when she brought up the numbers on the call box I played a hunch and pushed 4 and 7 together and then ran down to the seventh step from the top which is opposite the last recessed window. I undid the finial and pushed on the spire and the clicking was followed by a whoosh and the steps opened up. I was quite amazed I can assure you…actually, I was dumfounded. It appears that the mechanism is released only when the two procedures have been activated consecutively. The stairs cannot be opened otherwise. Does everyone understand because if you do I would be surprised as I can not quite fathom the extent of the mind that created such a contraption?"

We were all captivated by Rainey's explanation and I for one was baffled by how he had reasoned the whole thing out. The only question now was who had developed such a system. It surely wasn't incorporated into the house merely as a way to access the bell I was sure. I was full of questions, but who could possibly answer them?"

"Perhaps the room once held a mad relative or a prisoner of war, or it was simply just another place to store provisions." I suggested looking at Rainey. "You believe that there is another entrance to the room don't you?"

Our eyes locked and I wondered if he had meant something else when he had asked me if I wanted to take the scenic route. Darn him…that smile, those piercing blue eyes… why do these feelings of passion erupt at such inopportune times. I choked back a lump in my throat and continued as if no other thoughts had entered my mind.

"Is everyone up to a little more investigating?"

Of course they were. I started to get up but my legs wouldn't hold me and I sank back unto the chair. Ava, who was next to me steadied me and asked me if I was all right. I said that I was but had just got up too fast. That didn't satisfy Rainey as he tipped his chair over trying to get to me…afraid I am sure that I might have another fainting spell.

"You're shaking Vienna; I think you should go and lay down."

"Nonsense, I am fine. I'm just a little weak in the knees…too much coffee perhaps." I gritted my teeth and whispered to him. "And you are not helping any."

He looked at me quizzically and finally caught on to what I was inferring. "Are you sure you don't want to take a break, we can continue our quest later?"

"No, we are all hyped up so let's do it now."

"Okay, if you are sure. You know what, I think I would like Johnny to accompany us; does anyone know where he is?"

"There's only one way to find out." I volunteered to phone Brackenshire Manor as I wanted to check on Tanny anyhow. Amma answered and I explained to her what was going on and she said her and Johnny would be up immediately and that Alexa would keep Tanny until we called for her.

Rainey had sent Mason to the den to retrieve the blueprints that he had made of the castle as he knew it. Every room and every floor had been depicted in detailed fashion.

He laid the drawing out on the table and with a red pen outlined the newly discovered rooms and with a blue pen drew where he thought another entrance was. His plan was for him and Johnny to pursue what he conceived as another set of stairs. Since he had no idea where they would come out he wanted the rest of us in the cellars listening for their movement. The boys knew the area the best as they had been with Rainey when they had discovered the hidden door in the wine vaults so they would be our guides. We armed ourselves with flashlights and lanterns. Duffy and Mary would remain vigilant on the main floor. As we waited for Amma and Johnny to join us Morgan asked if he could talk to me for a minute. I was very warmed at what he had to say to me.

"Vienna, I want to thank you for what you have done for Dad."

"I haven't really done anything Morgan."

"You have given him a new outlook on life. He is not the same man he was six months ago. He pretended to be happy for our sakes, but Mason and I knew he wasn't. He put on a brave front but we saw right through it, but there was nothing we could do. He always told us that we were all responsible for our own happiness and that we should always pursue our dreams. Before we knew about you he had told us that he had lost his dream many years ago and he wouldn't let that happen to us. We had no idea what he meant by that for as far as we knew being an architect was all he had ever wanted. We now know that he was referring to you. He is always happy now and it's all because of you."

I held back the tears and told him that it was I who was a happier kinder person now and that it was all because of his father. Rainey was watching the two of us and I am sure wondered what was going on. I smiled to let him know everything was okay and then Mason came over and asked his brother if he had told me yet.

"No, I haven't but I guess this as good a time as any. Mase and I want to tell you that we have come to think of you as …as a stepmother, I guess."

I was sure that is not what Morgan wanted to say and so I said it for him. "Oh poosh, stepmother is such an ugly word, can't I just be your second mum?"

"We already think of you that way. We never knew what a real mother was supposed to act like until we met you."

There was no holding back the tears anymore and I put my arms around the two of them and blubbered. "How did I ever get so lucky to have your father back in my life and that he also came with two handsome and very charming boys? I love you both as if you were my own flesh and blood."

The show of emotion was too much for Rainey and he sauntered over to us and asked if there was something he should know about. We said no in unison and started laughing.

"All righty then, but I want you boys to know that I saw her first so don't be getting any ideas of how you can steal her away from me. Can I get in on the hugs?"

"She's all yours Dad, but just so you know, we love her too." Mason told him.

They left us to join the girls waiting in the hall for them.

"What was that all about? I am not used to seeing such a display of emotion coming from my teenage boys…what have you done to them Vienna? Have you worked your magic on them as you have on me?"

"Oh yes, because we all know I have mystical powers! No silly, they just wanted me to know how they felt about me and wanted to thank me for making you happy."

"Oh, is that all?" Rainey enclosed me in his arms and whispered. "Thank you."

Johnny and Amma had arrived and they were being filled in on the day's discovery. Mason said he still didn't understand what made the steps open and was most curious as to know how the system all worked.

Rainey put his hand on Mason's shoulder. "We'd all like to know that Son. I have very limited knowledge involving the construction of castles, but do know that they were built originally as fortresses and as we have discovered have many hidden stairways that were probably used as escape routes. One can only wonder how much of the medieval castle was left standing for Avanloch to be built upon. There could be a vast labyrinth of tunnels running throughout the building. The entrance we found today could be one of dozens that are connected to one another. There could also be mazes that have dead ends to confuse the enemy. There appear to be walls within walls. I know Jeremy told the family that there were three hidden rooms and three secret stairways, but he never mentioned the stairs beneath the wine cellar. I've thought that he must have known of their existence, but now I wonder if he did. We came upon it purely by accident. What other imaginative marvels are there here just waiting to be discovered? My curiosity would be satisfied if the original plans would show up."

"I believe it was Alice in Wonderland who said, "Curiouser and Curiouser." I added.

"Only Mama would come up with that alliteration!" Rosy laughed.

I told the kids to start for the basement and that I would join them in a minute but I had no intention of doing so. Rainey asked me what was wrong. I clung to him and told him that I wanted to go with him.

"Honey, let Johnny and I do this okay? If we do stumble upon another stairway it will likely be dilapidated and infested with who knows what…I don't want you subject to that. Please go with Amma."

"All right, I will do as you wish. Please be careful."

He kissed me on my forehead. "Thank you; see you on the other side."

"Rainey!"

"I didn't mean it like that V. If we are lucky, we should meet up with you all shortly."

Why had he called me V? Johnny told me not to worry as he wouldn't let Rainey do anything fool hearty.

"Come on, let's go find the kids." Amma said taking my hand. "Vienna, you are so pale…your hands are clammy…oh no."

The next thing I remember was seeing Amma, Ava, Mary and Duffy hovering over me. I was on the floor, something was under my head and a blanket was covering me. I tried to sit up but met with resistance from all. "Please tell me I didn't faint again?"

"You did Honey. I braced you as best I could but you didn't give much warning. Your eyes seemed to rotate and then they went blank and you were falling. I hope you haven't hurt yourself."

"I think I am okay Amma. Where's Rainey?"

"Don't you remember Mama? He and Johnny went in search of another way into that strange little room? You were supposed to meet us in the cellars. Duffy came and told us about your "episode" and I came back. I sent the rest on to find Rainey." Ava explained.

"Help me sit up please. Yes, I remember. How long was I unconscious for?"

"Five minutes maybe." Amma guessed.

"What, that can't be!"

The cellar door burst open and Rainey came barreling in breathing as if he had just run a marathon. "Jesus, Mary, and Joseph, not again Vienna!" He cradled me in his arms. "I should have known something was wrong…damn it! Ava, get the lift, I'm taking her upstairs. Can you put your arms around my neck honey?"

"I'm all right, I can walk Rainey."

"No DAMN way! Now do as you're told."

Johnny and the rest of the family had arrived, all out of breath. I felt so humiliated to be causing so much trouble…again. I started to apologize. Rainey told me to be quiet and so I buried my head in his chest. The rest of the entourage was waiting for us at the top of the grand staircase.

Rainey lowered me to the bed and sat down beside me. "Ava, Rosy, I think you need to call the doctor." It wasn't a suggestion but more of an order.

"No need to, I already know what is wrong." I told them.

"What do you mean Vienna?" Rainey asked in a frustrated voice.

"Sorry, it has been so busy around here that I forgot to tell you that Dr. Mac called me last week. He informed me that all of my tests were negative as to anything serious. He said that I was only slightly anemic and that I should take an iron supplement, drink more water and avoid getting up suddenly, but above all I need to try and control my anxiety or else I am going to have to go back on my medication. Luckily, I have warning signs prior to my fainting spells."

"What the hell does that even mean Vienna and when were you going to share this information with us?" Rainey demanded.

Mason came to my defense. "Go easy on her Dad."

"It's okay Mase; your dad has every right to be annoyed with me. Preceding the fainting spells I experience symptoms like dizziness, blurry visions, lightheadedness or extreme apprehension. Apparently, if I was not having these warning symptoms it would be cause for alarm, but I do have them and I am powerless to control them. Dr. Mac also said that I may be experiencing low blood sugar at the time and so I should try and eat regularly and to supplement my diet with a multi vitamin."

"Thank you for clearing that up; is everyone still as confused as I am?" Rainey asked.

Rosy asked if I would like to get undressed and climb right into bed. I was going to decline but decided it might be a good idea and told her I would. The boys came over and hugged me and said they were glad I was all right. Amma and Johnny gave me pecks on my cheeks and started to leave.

"Wait!" I said. "What happened in the cellar?"

"Let us help you Mama then Rainey can fill you in." Ava suggested.

Johnny put his arm around Rainey's shoulder as they left the room. Rainey didn't look back at me. As soon as they were out of earshot I started to cry. The girls knew why and tried their best to comfort me.

"He's just worried Mama as we all are. I think he needs to confirm your diagnosis with the doctor. You are not shielding us from anything dire are you?"

"No Ava, it is just as I said."

"Okay." She said covering me up with the sheet. "We're going to go and help with supper. Oh, by the way do you know that Mrs. D has hired a new cook? Apparently, she is an old friend that has returned to the valley."

No, I did not know. What else was happening that I wasn't aware of?

I slid under the cool satin sheet and turned to face the wall. I heard the door close and anticipated what was coming next. As usual, I underestimated my husband. He said nothing as he lay down facing me. He wiped the tears from my face.

"Are you crying because you think I am angry with you, or are you hurting?"

I told him I had no pain but was sorry for my neglect to inform him of my condition.

"I am not angry with you Vienna, but I am at myself. I knew something was wrong with the way you were acting but I was too hyped up to acknowledge it. Please forgive me?"

"Forgive you…how could you have known I was going to pass out again?"

"Because you didn't want to let me go. There was a pleading in your voice and I ignored it…I won't make that mistake again. I will not ignore that fear in your eyes ever again."

"Are you getting tired of my childish episodes Rainey because I wouldn't blame you if you were."

"No, never, I know you have no control over what happens. To put your mind at rest, no one was in any danger at all today. The whole mission was a success."

I sat up and Rainey supported me with pillows. "Tell me Rainey, tell me what you and Johnny discovered."

"Well, while you were laying down on the job…"He stopped to check my reaction to his assertion, grinning as usual.

"Ha-ha, very funny; you know I would rather have been with you."

"Yes I know, and perhaps I should have let you come, but you could have passed out on us and fallen down those rickety stairs. I am thankful that you chose to collapse in the hallway and not while you were en route to the basement."

"Me too; go on with your account."

"Remember those cupboards that I showed you? Johnny thought we should investigate them further and lo and behold one of them opened up when we pushed on it! They did indeed conceal another set of steps and we followed them to the subterranean floor. They were quite solid even though we were sure they had not been used in many a year. We were knee deep in cobwebs and dust…I kid you not. Some semblance of a door barred our exit but with the help of the kids who heard our every movement from the other side we were all able to pry it open. Next time we go off on another quest we will be sure to take proper tools with us. When we pushed through I was greeted with the news of your latest black out and had no time to investigate. You'll never guess where we came out."

"In the tunnel that leads to the mausoleum?"

"How could you possibly know that?"

"Am I right?"

"Yes, you are right, but what made you guess that?"

"Because silly, all roads lead to Rome!"

"Now you are really confusing me…what?"

"You know how you are always saying that I have this uncanny memory…well you may not have noticed but all the windows on the kitchen stairs have a proverb, inscription or whatever you choose to call them engraved on the sill. The one above the step that opens reads: All roads lead to Rome."

"I still don't get the connection Hon."

"Then let me explain. Above the door of the family crypt is the inscription; All roads lead to Rome. I have also seen those exact words somewhere else but I can't bring them into focus right now. You said that you and Johnny could find no way out of the back room of the crypt but I believe there is one and that it provides a path to freedom in case of attack; some place far away from the castle."

"Somehow what you are saying makes sense, but we left no brick unturned searching for an exit out of the crypt."

"That's because you were looking in the wrong place! Tomorrow we will explore it further; you need a woman's hand."

"Oh I need a woman's hand all right but tomorrow we are seeing the doctor and then we have to meet with the Macleods."

"Who the hell are they Rainey?"

"They are friends of Evan's that he has recommended for positions here. Don't you remember him mentioning it at the barbeque?"

"This is the first I am hearing of it. Apparently Mrs. D has hired a new cook also."

"That will be a big help to Mary. Now all we need is for Johnny to find a decent helper and a housekeeper for Brackenshire, and so let's hope these people work out."

"And then just what am I supposed to do mister? Avanloch will be so overrun with people I will have no privacy or duties!"

"Quit pouting and learn to be a lady of leisure! I can assure you that I plan on keeping you very occupied. Now lay back down and rest until supper."

"I will but only if you rest with me."

"Rest…is that what we are calling it now?"

Just as I slipped into Rainey's arms came the all too familiar knock on the door.

"Are you two decent?"

"That would be your daughter." Rainey frowned. "Come in Rosy."

The serving cart preceded her into the room and right behind her was Ava holding a little hand that belonged to Tanny who broke loose and jumped on the bed between Rainey and me.

"Tia, Rainey I miss you. Guess what Ally and I did? Can you guess? Tell them Ava."

Laughing I said. "Yes, please tell us Ava."

"Fishin, we's went fishin and I got me a… what was it Ava?"

Ava smiled. "A minnow."

"Yeah a minnnnow. Can I have supper with you Tia?"

"I think not." Rosy told her but we insisted that she stay and so the big girls left us to enjoy the company of the sweet innocent child that we had come to love.

Rainey phoned Dr. Mac's office and he was able to see us at 11 a.m. the next morning. We strolled down to the garage hand in hand and met Winston backing out. "Does that mean that he is chauffeuring us? Will I ever get to drive again?" Rainey whined.

"Quit your bellyaching; he has to earn his pay somehow and wouldn't you rather sit back and enjoy the scenery and the company of your wife?"

"I like driving." He frowned.

Mac told Rainey exactly the same things he had me and I think that reassured him some. Then Rainey said something to him that flabbergasted me. I felt my face heat up and I am sure it had turned beet red.

"Just prior to and immediately after one of Vienna's episodes she becomes …how can I put this delicately…extremely sexually stimulated, is this usual?"

"RAINEY QUINN!" I exclaimed.

They both looked at me and Mac broke out in hilarious laughter. "I can't say that I have ever encountered this reaction before but I find it rather refreshing. Rainey, I am pleased to tell you that this is probably not a side effect but just her desire to be comforted." He stroked his chin. "A most pleasurable one I hope you pursue. Now run along you love birds and I will see you at your nuptials next week.' He rose and shook Rainey's hand and hugged me and said. "Don't you ever be embarrassed about your feelings. There would be less divorce if more women were open about their desires."

Rainey took my hand and we glanced into each other's eyes anxious to get home. After a quick stop at the pharmacy and the market we cuddled in the back seat. "Isn't this better than you driving?" He said if he was driving we'd probably be in the ditch already.

When we entered the gate at Avanloch he told Winston to let us off at the front steps. He gingerly opened the huge door and beckoned to me that it was all clear. We closed the door silently and proceeded up the grand staircase. We may have made it if we hadn't been giggling like school children. Johnny's thunderous voice caught us off guard.

"Ahem…and just where do you think the two of you are sneaking off to?"

"I'm feared the jig is up My Lady." Rainey turned me around to face the music.

Johnny said he had a couple he wanted us to meet and did we have the time. We both sighed and made our way back down the stairs amid the grins of Amma and Johnny. We followed them into the small reception room where a man and woman were standing.

"This is Vienna and Rainey Quinn, the proprietors of this great estate; otherwise known as the Lady and Laird of Avanloch."

Rainey snickered at the mention of the word 'laird'. I surmised that these were the friends that Evan had recommended. Johnny introduced them as Wesley and Nanette Macleod. Wesley stepped forward to shake Rainey's hand and took mine in his.

"I am so very pleased to meet you Mr. Quinn, Lady Vienna." He took a step back and the procedure was copied by his wife. I thought that she held on to Rainey's hand a little too long. I couldn't be done with them soon enough.

Amma sensed my annoyance and steered me aside. I said through gritted teeth, "Get me out of here…please."

She ignored my plea. "We have shown Nanette and Wesley around the premises and are going to sit down to a late lunch at Brackenshire. You will join us won't you Vienna?"

She was fooling with me and I intended to get even with her. I replied in my best superior tone that neither Mr. Quinn nor I were up to lunch; I wanted to add "with the peasants" but thought better of it. I took Rainey's arm and asked to be excused. He told Amma that she could check in with us later.

"Enjoy your lunch." He acknowledged the newcomers with a partial wave. "Nice to have met you."

This time we made it all the way up the stairs, trying not to be too obvious with our merriment. We heard Amma say that they must forgive us as we were newlyweds. At the top of the stairs Rainey kissed me long and passionately and bowed to the spectators. Once inside the privacy of our bedroom we broke out into laughter.

"I pray I never offend that 'holier than thou' woman I just came in contact with down there. What was that all about Lady Vienna?"

I was unbuttoning his shirt. "I didn't like the way that she looked at you."

"You're kidding right? How do you think she looked at me?"

"With lust in her eyes my dear."

"The only one I see around here with lust in her eyes is you and I have to say it is a most becoming look."

"She is your type Rainey…long black hair and legs that go on forever and bedroom eyes and a smile that says she is available."

"I believe the woman is married, and may I remind you that there is only one woman for me. No one can hold a candle to you and would only shame themselves if they tried."

"I'm just saying I don't like her and if it is up to me, I would not hire her."

"I have never known you to make a snap judgment before but you are the **one** that has the final say. Now will you shut up so that I might have my final say with you?"

Summer Solstice

It was mid-morning. I was sitting at my dressing table pinning my hair up. Rainey came up behind me and kissed my neck. I covered his hand with mine.

"I love you Vienna LaFontaine."

"You haven't called me that for a long time; it's usually Lady Vienna or Mrs. Quinn."

"You will always be Vienna LaFontaine to me."

"Thank you for supervising my bath Rain."

"It was my pleasure and if you are a good girl I may even take you swimming tonight."

"I would love that as I want to introduce Tanny to the pool."

"May I ask where you are off to now my pretty?"

"You may ask." I teased.

"In other words… it is none of my business."

"I am off to Brackenshire to tell Amma that if she likes "this Mrs. Macleod" woman she may hire her for the manor, but I do not need her here."

Rainey's eyes twinkled. "That is very self- sacrificing of you my dear."

"There is nothing noble about it; Johnny and Amma can have anything they want. I just hope it is not a mistake to hire them. I won't have to see much of them anyhow."

"They need not interfere with our lives. Do you remember that one of Johnny's first priorities is to remodel room six? Wesley seems to have all the qualifications required to assist him."

"No, I need no reminder. Perhaps once the Macleod's hear of the history of the room and the castle they will choose not to stay."

"Most people with any sense at all would not believe the exorcism anyhow."

"Excuse me; are you saying I have no sense?"

"I wouldn't dream of it; but even you have to admit that your events of what happened are right out of cloud-cuckoo-land?"

"I am sure stranger things have happened! Anyhow, I am off to have tea with Amma."

"She knows you hate tea, right?"

"Oh yes, but she will make it anyhow."

Rainey laughed and asked if he could accompany me as far as the stables. I told him yes and asked where the boys were today. He said they were investigating as usual and after he had told them about my theory that there must be an exit from the mausoleum they had decided to examine it from the outside.

"I hope they are successful. You know what Rain? Today is the summer solstice and I do believe that I heard there is to be a solar eclipse; the moon comes between the earth and sun right?"

"You are precisely right, only I believe I read that this is to be only a partial eclipse. There won't be as much fanfare as there would be if it was a total one. We may not witness much here."

"Well it is to be the longest day of the year and there is to be a new moon. I believe it is one of the most magical times of the year."

"You do, do you? Haven't we already had our share of the magic?"

"There is much more to come I promise. Now if we don't get going the day will be over and I will have accomplished nothing."

I met the new cook whose name was Lois when I returned from Brackenshire. She was a woman of small stature with thin graying hair who appeared to have the same rheumatic condition as Mary

McDuff. She was very amiable and I liked her immediately. Though she was a good fifteen or twenty years Mary's junior they had been friends before she had married and left the valley. She was a widow now and was hoping to find a residence or boarding house nearby. I invited her to stay with us as we had a room right across the hall from the kitchen and it was not in use. I told her she could stay until she made other arrangements, or perhaps she would chose to stay with us permanently.

Mrs. D nudged her and said. "There, did I not tell you that Miss Vela…sorry; I will get the hang of Vienna sooner or later. She be a fine mistress is what I be sayin."

There was a heavy rapping on the front door and no one appeared to be around to answer it. I shuffled off muttering to myself that perhaps I wasn't the lady of the house after all, but a butler. Where was everyone…was it already quitting time?

My heart did a little flutter as I opened the door unto a woman who could only be Mollie Magan's granddaughter. "You have finally arrived!" I blurted out.

"Ah, so you know who I be? And, you could only be Lady McAllister!"

"I am, and what a delight that you should arrive on just such a day! Come in, come in, you must be weary, where have you come from and did you have to hire a hack? Let me send someone down to fetch your things and even up with him. That is if I can find anyone in this house!"

"Be steady My Lady; he has been taken care of. I will just send him on his way."

As the driver backed out of the driveway I saw that he had deposited a number of trunks and boxes on the pavement.

"I do hope that I interpreted your letter correctly and that is to say that I am the inheritor of the estate of Granny Mary, or I guess you all knew her to be, Mollie Magan?"

"We only ever called her Mollie. Come, come and let me ring for tea." I sat her down on the red velveteen settee and entered the kitchen call number into the butler's box. Mrs. D answered. With excitement I requested that she come to the reception hall. She arrived promptly and was just as pleased to see Meggie as I was.

"Well, speak o' the devil! We was a blethering about your granny, me and Lois, and here you be! Ye must have taken the long way to get here."

I introduced Meggie to Mary stating that she and her grandmother had been good friends. They exchanged pleasantries. What little I knew about Meggie I had learned from Millie. No one knew who her father was or why she kept the name Magan.

I continued to tell her that the letter advising her of her grandmother's passing and the contents of the will was sent years ago. "Please tell me that it didn't take all this time to get to you?"

Her laugh was so much like I remembered Mollie's that I had to choke back a tear.

"I have been on my way for a very long time. It is not easy to come upon a good paying job when you are limited to fortune telling and scullery work. But I be here now and if it wouldn't be too much to ask I would most like to see the ole cabin."

"Mary, do you know where Rainey is?"

"I'm right behind you Love."

"Rainey, you near scared the living daylights out of me!"

"Sorry Darling, I see we have another guest." Rainey extended his hand as I introduced them and told him who Meggie was. "Vienna has told me many stories of her escapades with your grandmother. I can see how delighted she is that you have finally arrived. What can I do to help?"

"Can you load Meggie's things into the jeep and drive us to Gypsy Hollow? Mary, please gather enough provisions to last a few days until we can get to Waverly?"

"Please, I do not want to be of any trouble." Meggie tried to protest but we assured her it was no problem.

"Vienna, is it?" She asked as Rainey and Mary left us. "Am I mistaken that you are not the Lady Vela McAllister who sent the letter?"

"I was then. I have remarried and my real name is Vienna."

"You have a most fascinating aura. I have seen your halo change from pale blue to a purple hue to pink and then red. Your circle of light changed in density when your young man entered the room. You are very devoted to each other. I look forward to doing a complete reading for you…I can feel that you are most agreeable to this"

"Do I really have an aura?" I felt the top of my head and she laughed.

"You cannot feel it my dear. I sense that you are very intuitive yourself…have you had unexplained experiences, perhaps with the spirit world?"

"Yes, I fear that I am a receptacle for the paranormal."

"That is a quality many people try to achieve, but it is not available to everyone and that is a good thing. You already know that I have arrived on the eve of the summer solstice and that is no coincidence. I planned it just that way. I myself do not know exactly why but I believe it must have something to do with you. Tell me, what do you know about Midsummer's Eve?"

"Nothing much, just what I learned from your grandmother. She told me that it was a time for fairies and magic." I laughed. "She told me that we should gather fern seed as it would make us invisible to the fairies and we could watch their festivities without being detected. By the way, it didn't work."

Apparently I was a source of amusement for her as her hearty laugh indicated so. She relayed details of her long journey that had finally brought her to her destination. I also learned that her partner had passed away several years ago and that their two children had been abroad for many years. She revealed that she and Sergio had never married as he had been raised in the Catholic faith and the church did not recognize divorce and so he remained forever bound to his first wife. She had taken his surname but now went by Magan. That explained everything without me even having to ask. Mary returned with several hampers of provisions.

"I hesitate to ask, but would there be coffee among the goods?" Meggie inquired.

"And certainly there is; I thought to myself that you might like the dreadful stuff coming from Bulgaria and all."

"Thank you Mrs. McDuff. I can see that you may have the rheumatism; did my granny use to fix salves for you?"

"Oh she certainly did, me and half of Scotland! I have found none so soothing."

"I will be most pleased to see if my concoctions can stand next to hers."

Mary blessed her as Rainey came in and said all was loaded and picked up the supplies.

I jumped in the front seat of the jeep and announced to Rainey that I had an aura.

"I don't doubt that you do Darling but the question is what color is it?" He said smiling at me. "Is it white or black?"

I hit him and told him not to be rude and that black did not exist in auras.

"On the contrary Miss Vienna, people do cast a black aura, but it is a confusing color and it can mean unbalance or evasiveness. Your lady does not have any such aura. Hers is a rainbow of colors and she radiates happiness and peace."

"I would expect nothing less from her Meggie." Rainey acknowledged her in the mirror.

Johnny and I had been looking after the cabin ever since Mollie's passing. We had found homes for her stubborn old mule, cow and chickens. We left the power connected but shut off the main breaker and only turned it on in the winter months. There were several small electric wall heaters that kept the place from freezing up. The water was gravity fed from the glacial stream that flowed into Miller's Creek that was also the water source for Avanloch and the Village of Domne.

Meggie was most amazed at the immaculate condition inside and out of her new home.

"This is all your doing isn't it Lady Vienna?"

"Please, I am just Vienna. It was no trouble as I thought of your grandmother as my own. I never had a grandmother and so Mollie became part of my extended family."

"Bless you my child for being so kind to her for the good Lord knows her own family abandoned her."

"Oh no, she never thought that. She was invited to come and live with you and her mother countless times but chose to stay here, did you not know that."

"Perhaps I did, I cannot say for sure. Shall we fix some coffee?"

Rainey had turned the kitchen breaker on and climbed up the hillside to dislodge any debris that may have collected around the mouth of the intake pipe that fed the water to the house. I turned the tap on and let it run freely until all the buildup of sludge had run its course. I turned the little hot plate on and set the coffee pot on it to perk.

When he returned I asked if he would like to join us for coffee. He said that he had promised Johnny that he would help him with some broken down fences and would return for me in an hour or two if that was suitable. I believe that he sensed that I wanted to spend some time alone with Meggie. I gave him a peck and sent him on his way.

"Do you know about the dance of the fireflies Meggie?" I asked.

"Do they still come?"

"Oh yes, me and the girls come several times in the summer to see their antics. I am looking forward to bringing Rainey and Tanny to see them."

"Who is Tanny?"

I explained while Meggie ruffled through one of her cases intent upon finding something. "Aha, here they are!" She seemed pleased that she had found what she was looking for. "Come sit, I cannot wait any longer; I must do a reading for you!"

I was hesitant. "I don't know Meggie; reading my aura was one thing but tarot cards…"

"Have you never had your fortune told before Vienna? It doesn't hurt at all. Did Mollie not tell you of things to come?"

"Maybe, once. When I was very young, a carnival gypsy revealed my future to me."

"Like me. I have been referred to many times as a charlatan, but no matter, one either believes or they don't. Pray tell, what words of wisdom did this woman have for you?"

"She predicted that I would live in foreign lands and that I would have wealth and that I would find a great love, but there would be many obstacles in our way."

"Was it a good prediction?"

"If you mean did it come true…yes, it all did."

"Then shall we proceed? I believe the coffee is ready."

I got up to pour us each a cup while Meggie shuffled the cards in a particular strange fashion. She was swishing them around in frenzy like motions. I sat back down and told her that tarot cards scared me. She picked one up and asked if it scared me. I said "No."

She explained that the cards were known as The Zodiac Reading. They were divided into four suits that corresponded to the four astrological elements, fire, air, water and earth. Today they would be represented by Aries, the ram, Leo, the lion, Virgo, the maiden and Aquarius, the water bearer. I was still hesitant but I told her to go ahead. She gathered the cards up and cut them twice and then asked me to cut them once with my left hand. She asked me if I would like to choose a signnificator and did I have a question for the cards.

"Oh, surely I would if I knew what a signnificator was. My question would be, "Are Rainey and I going to find the rightful heir to the Infinity Bracelets?"

Of course she had no idea what I was talking about did she? She did not comment.

"You will choose the card on the top of the deck and it shall represent you. We can keep it off to the side and we will read it when it will be useful to us." She indicated for me to do so and so I did. I laid it face up and Meggie let out a little squeal of delight.

"My almost favorite card, The Queen of Aries …how appropriate!"

I smiled at her exuberance as she continued to lay the rest of the cards face down in a circular pattern. She told me that she was using the astrological spread and that it represented the twelve months of the coming year. She placed the Queen in the 12th position saying that she would draw her out if need be, whatever that meant.

"Take a breath my dear and relax." I told her that I was relaxed though if I drank too much of this potent brew I would become jittery. I leaned forward and tried to look interested. I had no idea what to expect.

Meggie turned the card closest to me up. It was the Ace of Aries. Apparently it represented love and fulfillment, partnership, marriage and the creation of a family. This was the Holy Grail of the zodiac cards and represented all that was good in life. I was elated as this certainly did pertain to my life and my astrological sign was Aries.

"What a divine start; shall we proceed?" With that she placed the second card face up; it was the Seven of Aries. So far she had turned up all rams in my reading; I wondered if this was a good sign as so far they seemed to be favorable.

"Ah, this card has an aura of mystery surrounding it. It suggests that all is not what it seems, your imagination may be playing tricks on you and you may very well have trouble sorting out the real from the unreal. You may be rewarded by a mystical presence." She looked at me to see how I was reacting.

"If you are asking if this is anything new to me then the answer is no."

"Very well."

The third card was the six from the sign of Leo. Meggie explained that it showed a time for great activity and that everything was appearing to happen all at once. She said that the right path was being taken and that opportunities needed to be explored and that there was travel in my future. I nodded in affirmation.

She turned over the Three of Virgo and I thought I seen her frown. "Do you see how this card is upside down? This suggests a loss of balance and difficulty deciding what is real and what is not. Someone may be trying to deceive you." She quickly moved on to the Five of Aries. "This shows that emotions are being turned inside out and are in a constant state of unrest, but do not fear as all is not lost and hard work will win out."

I wanted to tell her to stop but I was not a quitter and so let her carry on although I did not like the interpretation of the next card. It was the Eight of Aquarius and it was in the reverse position. It was a negative card that told of senseless efforts, a loss of energy, frustration and that a lack of achievement could lead to depression. Wonderful, was that what I had to look forward to? I reminded myself that I was the captain of my own ship.

The Seven of Virgo was more favorable. It suggested determination, victory, and a promise of success. Inner strength would win out. The Nine of the water bearer, Aquarius, was just the opposite. It foretold of deception, disappointment and failure. This was the card of the martyr. It suggested acceptance and servitude and great frustration. I thought that Meggie should bring in the Queen to save me although I knew not why or what the card could do.

She turned over the Nine in the suit of Leo, the lion; it was also reversed. It seemed to foretell that the present situation would not last as it had been achieved through devious means. There were forces around that created destruction. Oh boy, I was loving this. Thank goodness we had only two cards to go before the Queen.

The tenth card revealed was the Six from the maiden of Virgo. Its emphasis was on the past and an opportunity to appreciate the present. There would be new opportunities in the future. Harmony was taking hold although there was still conflict afoot. The last card that Meggie turned up was the King of the Lions. She smiled slightly.

"A dangerous situation might be on the horizon. There is strife but on the positive side this is necessary for there is a favorable resolution to the struggle. There will be three parties involved in this triangle and there will be much upheaval but eventually it will be resolved as the King will come for his Queen and the good will triumph!"

She let out a sigh of relief. "Pleases take all that I have told you with a grain of salt…it is just a hint of things to come and by no means is it gospel. Now, let's get to the piece de resistance…the Queen of Aries! She has been representing you through all." She took both my hands in hers. "I have a feeling that you have many of her traits. You have a natural beauty and kindness that radiates for all to see. You have a talent for the arts; you are a poet and an artist. You are very intuitive and may even be a visionary. Yes, you do have a mystical aura and it reaches out to all you come in contact with. People love you and you are inspired by romance and are a true friend and lover. You will have much happiness and will always win out against evil. You will live long and remember that you are indeed a queen." She fell back in her chair and released my hands. I thought that perhaps she had been in a trance of sorts. I waited for her to regain her composure.

"You're the third stranger and you have come to warn me haven't you Meggie?"

She asked me to explain and I told her about the messages that were mysteriously left for me. She told me to be vigilant, stalwart, and to be aware of a wolf in sheep's clothing.

Rainey's rapping at the door prevented me from questioning her any further. I said goodbye to my new friend and told her that I would look in on her the next day and to try and have her telephone reconnected immediately. She made me promise to pay attention to what the cards had told me. Rainey waved to her and we walked hand in hand to the jeep. He opened the door for me and I told him that I felt like he was picking me up for a date just like he used to do a hundred years ago.

"Then we shall have just that; will you do me the honor of coming out with me tomorrow evening My Lady?"

"Most certainly kind sir, and where will we go?"

"You will be the first to know, right after me." We both laughed.

I settled back to endure the rocky ride back to Avanloch. "I am glad that is over with."

"What…didn't you enjoy your visit?"

"Sort of; Meggie did a reading for me."

"Did she elaborate more on your colorful headlights?" He smirked.

"Rainey! No, she did a reading with cards."

"Please tell me that she didn't use tarot cards?"

"What's the difference? I have had my fortune told with a crystal ball and I have attended séances and played with a Ouija Board, had my palms read and oh yeah, I have consorted with a white witch and ghosts…the tarot cards seem to be right up my alley. Anyhow, half the reading was negative but Meggie felt compelled to the reading and so I went along."

He reached over and squeezed my hand. "Is there something that I should know about?"

"Meggie is the third stranger Rain…the one with a warning though I am not clear what it is. It appears as if I am going to have conflict in my life and will have to deal with deception. I will lose touch with reality and should be on my guard as all is not what it seems to be. But on the other hand, I will have a long life and love and be loved."

"The last part is certainly true and you should take everything else with a grain of salt."

"That is just what Meggie said and I intend to do just that. How did it go with the fencing and are the Macleod's' hired." I was hoping that they weren't.

"Johnny wanted my input on Wesley and so I sat in on the so called interview. He seems to require the skills that Johnny is looking for and so he is hired on a three month probation period and I guess Amma thinks that the Mrs. will work out for her…I don't remember her first name."

"Of course you don't Darling; you were too busy checking out her attributes."

"I don't think that was called for Vienna."

"You are right and I apologize. Is there something else you want to tell me?"

"How do you know?"

"Because you have this crease in your forehead that stands out when you are troubled and it is definitely refined right now."

"I told Johnny that I would approach you on this matter because I wasn't sure what your reaction would be and it was better to have you annoyed with me than him. There doesn't seem to be any places for rent in the Village so seeing that the apartment is vacant above the garages, would you consider letting the Macleod's stay there?" He pulled up to the front door and looked at me for reaction.

"Why not, but just so they know, this is not a bed and breakfast." I slammed the door and took off in a huff. I guess my reaction to their hiring was a little overboard, but I just didn't like them. I shouldn't doubt my husband's fidelity just because another woman looked too long at him? I despised Rainey's jealousy and now here was I. It wasn't even his idea, it was Johnny's, and if I had any misgivings I should take the matter up with him. I sat down in the vestibule and waited for Rainey. After a half hour he had not shown up and so I went looking for him. I found him in the kitchen.

"Where did you get to Vienna? I've been waiting for you."

"And I was waiting for you, sorry."

"No need to be Hon. I was just informing Mary and Lois that we would not be here for dinner tomorrow night and that we had new occupants for the garage apartment but that they were strictly on their own when it came to meals." He meant to placate me.

I nodded and asked if anyone knew where Tanny was. I could tell that dinner was almost ready and I wanted to make sure she was presentable. Rainey said that she was upstairs with Ava and should we collect her together?

We took the back stairs and I apologized for slamming the door in his face.

"If you were younger I would take you over my knee and spank you young lady… umm, that doesn't sound like a bad idea to me at all."

I kissed him and asked him to forgive me for being a brat.

"I'm happy to say you are my brat. Remember, you are the boss and you don't always have to be so obliging. If you are uncomfortable with these people Johnny and Amma will understand. Don't ever be embarrassed to exert your authority."

"Rainey, we are all in this together; we are a big family here. Perhaps I am a little touchy after the reading today. Everyone deserves a chance and I will be on my guard as heaven only knows I have no idea what I am supposed to be guarding against. I should warn you though that I will fight tooth and nail for you, and I will not hesitate to bring black magic into the equation."

He broke into laughter. "Lord, I pray it never comes to that! Vienna, what am I ever going to do with you?"

Ava and Tanny came out to meet us. Tanny ran straight to Rainey and Ava asked what all the laughter was about. "Ask you mother." Rainey said as he picked Tanny up and swung her around in the air.

"Your father thinks that I won't use magic to get what I want."

"Mama, when have you ever averted to trickery? I heard that Mollie's granddaughter arrived today. Don't tell me that she has been teaching you her brand of magic already?"

"She does have a certain je ne sais quoi, but no, I have my own powers and I am not ashamed to say that I will use them if necessary."

"I am sure I don't even want to know what that means." She arched her eyebrows.

"I told you Ava that your mother enchanted me from the moment I met her, and now it appears that she has indeed the power to cast a spell on me." Rainey winked at me. "I believe that she has already done that."

"I hope I will never have to conjure up anything more than a love potion."

"I think you two live in your own little world sometimes. I am happy to go along with your little games as long as things don't get too crazy."

"Ava Honey, we live in a story book castle, and things are always zany here. Rainey and I have spent too long apart and everything is new and mystical to us so we will learn as we go along. One thing is for sure and that is that we are very happy."

"Amen to that." Rainey concurred.

After dinner we all went for a walk around the grounds and then adjourned to the games room to play Rummoli. Tanny bounced between Rainey and me depending on who had the most chips in their possession. At 8:30 she could hardly keep her eyes open and so I took her up to bed. She fell asleep almost immediately and I decided to go to bed also. The next thing I remember was Rainey's arms around me and I turned over and thanked him for rescuing me.

"You're welcome Darling; but just what did I rescue you from?"

"Silly," I said with a slurred tongue, "from the Grandfather clock of course."

"I think you have been dreaming Sweetie; there is no Grandfather clock in here, and I doubt that it would be holding you hostage."

"Of course it isn't here, it is in the harem room as always, and if you hadn't found me I would still be wrestling with it trying to find my way home."

"I think you are still half asleep Vienna…do you want to try and wake up?"

"I'm awake. Is she gone?"

He got out of bed and walked around to my side and rolled me over and sat me up.

"There, now do you want to tell me what you have been dreaming about?"

I yawned. "The moon is still out."

"It's only midnight Hon; welcome to the first day of summer."

"Midnight, how can that be? The clock struck 12 when I was inside of it."

"How the dickens did you get inside the clock? You had a strange dream didn't you?"

"Was she gone when you found me?" I looked around the room.

"Who is *she* Vienna?"

"The Grey Lady."

"Is that the elusive specter you told me about the other day? Are you telling me that you dreamt that she locked you inside the Grandfather clock?"

"She didn't lock me inside of it; she just left me there trying to open it and get back up the stairs. I don't know what her purpose was other than to show me how to get into the stairwell. I should go back and see if it closed." I slid out of bed pushing him aside.

"I'll go with you if you tell me where we are going."

"To the bookcase of course!"

Rainey scratched his head. "Okay."

He followed me out into the hall and across to the little useless vestibule. "Damn it, it's closed! Maybe it was never open, maybe I was able to pass through it with her."

"You went through the bookcase and then what?"

"Well, we went down the stairs…oh yeah, there is another secret stairway that comes out in the harem room through the Grandfather clock. Look, she must have come back this way because there's the candelabra that she was carrying!"

Rainey turned around and saw what I was referring to. He felt the candles' wicks and examined the spent wax that had dripped down. He appeared perplexed. "Well, somebody did make use of these tapers and quite recently. I don't like the idea of you roaming around with lit candles in your hands."

"It wasn't me Rainey; it was the Grey Lady. She came to tell me something but I am unclear as to what it was."

"Let's go back to bed. We can talk about this in the morning okay?"

Chapter 4

The Calm Before the Storm

Rainey woke up to an empty bed. He could hear no signs of activity through the open door. He glanced at the clock; it was only 6:30. Hell, had he had any sleep at all? How long had he been up with Vienna last night? She must be in the bathroom, but why would she have left the bedroom door open. He struggled to arouse his body when she didn't return after a few minutes. He walked into the hall and a movement to his right alerted him. She was back in the foyer…no doubt still trying to get back inside the bookcase.

He walked over to her and casually asked what she was doing. Startled she spun around.

"Oh Darling, I am sorry if I awoke you. I'm trying to make some sense of that silly dream I had last night."

He was pleased that she acknowledged it as a dream. "Who knows why we dream Honey. Remember those dreams I used to have about you plunging over the cliff? It was all symbolism because I had indeed lost you but sometimes dreams have no meaning what so ever. You have an overactive mind and what with all the going ons…"

Vienna interrupted him. "Exactly Rainey, dreams represent something. They are our unconscious mind trying to tell us something. I just need to figure out what it all means. On the other hand, perhaps I wasn't dreaming, but my journey through the bookcase and down the mysterious passage actually happened…what then?"

How was he going to handle this newest fantasy of hers? With tact he told himself. He joined her in her plight to find a loose or jarred book.

"The girls and I have searched this along with every other book-case in the castle several times over and found nothing, so what makes me think that something is going to budge now? Am I crazy Rain?"

He pulled her away and into his arms. "You're not crazy Honey. I hope it was all a dream…like Alice being led by the white rabbit, only the grey lady was your guide. I cannot explain the candles, but I fully intend to have a talk with that Grandfather clock!"

"Oh Rainey, you can find humor in everything. I give up for today. Can we please go back to bed?" He told me that I took the words right out of his mouth.

The first chance Rainey had when Vienna was elsewhere occupied was to inspect the clock in the harem room. He found nothing unusual about the clock but found one of Vienna's pearl earrings lying on the floor in front of it. Strange because she was not careless with her jewelry and she had no use for this room so what was it doing here? He pocketed it with full intention of questioning her about its disappearance later.

It wasn't until they were getting ready for their date that he remembered the earring. She was sitting at her night table with Tanny beside her helping her decide what necklace and earrings she would wear.

"It would help if I knew where we were going wouldn't it Tanny? I don't know if I should wear slacks or a dress?" She looked at Rainey for a hint.

"I think you should wear whatever you like but make sure you bring a sweater. By the way, have you been missing this?" He passed her the earring.

"Rainey, where did you find it? I could swear that I put it right here last night."

He decided to tell a little white lie and not reveal where he really found the earring.

"Where is its mate?"

"Funny you should ask because I woke up with a sore ear and sure enough it was from the earring gouging into my skin. You know I always take everything off before I go to bed, even my rings. I tore the bed sheets apart trying to find the matching one. They are the ones that you bought for me in Vancouver Rainey."

"I know, but it has been found on the floor so no need to fret. If you don't get a move on we are going to be late for our dinner reservation. Help her will you Tanny?"

"Yes, come along Tanny, we will go and check out Miss Mary's closet."

"Can I play with the necklaces and shoes Tia?"

"Yes Dear, you certainly can."

Rainey dressed and went into the parlor to fix himself a small drink. He walked to the south window where there was just a hint of the mausoleum's doomed roof visible. He raised his glass as if in a toast. "Here's to you Avanloch and all the mystery surrounding your walls and to the ghosts that escape from the McAllister crypt to entice my wife…I will unlock all of your doors one day… I promise."

He heard the clip clopping of Tanny's oversized heels coming down the hall. Vienna was a vision in a pale yellow summer frock. It had short puffy sleeves and a revealing neckline. Tanny peeked out from under her huge purple hat.

"Rainey look how pretty Tia is. I want to be like her when I grow up."

"You are pretty already Honey. I do like your choice Vienna and as usual you light up anything you wear."

"It is a little too tight for me, my tummy is showing. Pretty soon I won't be able to fit into any of Miss Mary's clothes I fear."

"Vienna…are you…?"

"NO, I am just fat."

"No one thinks so but you. Now grab a sweater and oh yeah, shoes, and let's take this show on the road."

Rainey took Vienna to a newly opened seafood restaurant called Ale and Claws. Vienna beamed when she saw lobster on the menu. "I haven't had lobster since Vancouver! I hope they are not out."

"They are not my dear, I made sure of that. After dinner I thought we could go to a movie. There are two choices; "Alicn", which is a horror space movie starring Sigourney Weaver." Rainey was consulting notes which he had typed up. "Then there is "Indiana

Jones and the Raiders of the Lost Ark" which is an action adventure thriller starring Harrison Ford; it is a brand new release. The girls haven't even seen it yet."

"I think that you have done some research into this. They both sound good but," Vienna put her hand on Rainey's thigh, "You know how I hate horror movies so I think the other one. Is it an account of Noah's Ark?"

Rainey laughed. "You really are out of the loop aren't you? No, it is purely a work of fiction and the Ark in question is The Ark of the Covenant."

"You mean the Ark that held The Ten Commandments?"

"Yes Dear, that Ark."

"Sounds like marvelous fun, but it also sounds like you have already seen it?"

"No, I haven't; as I said it is a new release and I am surprised it's in Scotland already."

"It's been a very long time since we've been to a movie together isn't it?"

"I just hope you can keep your hands off me this time."

"Rainey Quinn! I seem to remember it as being the other way around."

He treated her as if they were on a first date; popcorn and chocolate and cokes though they were both still full from the magnificent meal. They held hands and he stole a kiss now and then whenever she was covering up her eyes in horror, especially at the snakes. When they emerged from the theater she thanked Rainey for taking her and exclaimed that she had a new favorite movie.

"You mean it has topped The Wizard of Oz? That's almost miraculous!"

"I wouldn't go that far but after I have seen it a few more times I am sure it will be right up there with my top ten. I hope there will be many more date nights for us Rainey."

"Oh, there will be my dear. We still have so many years to make up for."

Rosalyn left for London the next day to put in a weeks' worth of work at McAllister Shipping before she was needed at home to help with the upcoming wedding. Lois, the newly hired cook had arrived at the right time and was in her glory making the cakes. She iced the fruit cakes in a rich marzipan and one evening everyone joined in cutting the cakes into slices that were then wrapped in cellophane and frozen. There was enough for three hundred people as all the Village was invited to tea and champagne punch and typical English fare after the ceremony.

Rainey and Vienna had already decided to postpone the honeymoon to September again once the boys went back to Canada. Tanny's mother was being released from hospital on July the 6th and Vienna wanted to make sure she got settled in comfortably.

The Fourth of July was a glorious day. Vienna finally met Rainey's friends Stu and Daisy and she felt as though she had known them forever. Jannie and John, Ash and Gray, Evan and Roberge were the only out of town guests. Vienna was surprised as she walked down the aisle on Uncle John's arm to find Ava at the organ and Rosy with her harp at the front of the church playing their version of the wedding march. The bridal party had Amma as the Matron of Honor and Tanny and Delta O"Shea as the flower girls. Ava and Rosy did double duty as the bridesmaids again. Johnny was the best man and Mason and Morgan were groomsmen. Once again it was a beautiful ceremony and even more special than the first one for Vienna as words from the heart were spoken by her good friend, Reverend Peters. They were serenaded by a barrage of pipers when they exited the church which brought tears to everyone's eyes. For a brief second Vienna thought she saw a vision in white towering over the crowd. She squeezed Rainey's hand extra hard and he smiled at her and bent down and kissed her and they ran hand in hand up the castle walkway.

At the reception Stu and Daisy announced to Rainey and Vienna that were going to have a child in December. They had given up hope many years ago but now it had happened. Stu was worried because Daisy was forty four and the doctors had warned her that she must be diligent with her health. Vienna enclosed Daisy's hands in her own.

"There is no cause for worry; you will give birth to a bouncing, healthy, baby boy."

"We do not know the sex Vienna." Stu said.

"Oh, I am sorry if I spoiled the surprise." Vienna said apologetically. Later Rainey asked Vienna why she told Daisy and Stu that they were having a son.

"Well, because they are."

"Just why would you think that you know that Vienna?" Rainey questioned dubiously.

"It's as clear as the nose on your face; just like you and I will have a daughter."

"You are not even pregnant and you are already saying that if you do become pregnant that it will be a girl…I'm sorry; I don't get your logic, or is it …?"

She hugged him. "Witchcraft…you can say it, one isn't going to swoop down on her broom and ride off with you. Don't look so serious; it's just a fact … LaFontaine women don't give birth to boys. They can't be bothered with man children."

He grabbed hold of her as she started to dash away. "Not so fast young lady, explain yourself…what is wrong with male children?"

"They are no use to us as children Rain. They are troublesome and needy, but when they become men…well, that is a totally different story then."

"You know you are playing with fire don't you? Are you saying that I am only here to satisfy your lustful needs? If I wasn't a gentleman I would have you here and now!"

"My Lord, I have no need for a gentleman. Give me a rogue anytime."

"You're becoming more and more saucier with each marriage. Is this what I have to look forward to for the rest of my life?"

"Only if you are lucky my dear. Now, we really should make nice with the guests. If they are not gone by eight, you have my permission to kick them all off the grounds."

"That is going to prove a tad difficult my love since several of them have rooms booked in our illustrious inn."

"Drats, you're right."

Rosy met them coming up the pavilion steps. "Should I even ask what you two have been up to? It's time to cut your cake. Rainey, straighten out your clothes.'

He looked down and nothing was out of place. Rosy winked at him over her shoulder.

He shook his head and said under his breath. "And she isn't even a LaFontaine."

Vienna visited Meggie nearly every day but there were no more fortunes told. They visited the elfin pools with whoever wanted to watch the fireflies perform several times over the summer. Rainey had built a fire pit in the back yard adjacent to the pavilion and once a week they had a cookout over an open fire. It gave the cooks a night off and was the one night they all indulged in "junk food." That was the way they celebrated Rainey's birthday as he didn't want a big fuss made. Ava joined her parents when they took the boys to venues of the Highland Games throughout Scotland. They also spent two weeks touring the sites of England which included Buckingham Palace, the changing of the guards, the Tower of London, the ancient Roman Baths, the White Cliffs of Dover and Dover castle. Vienna's favorite was the World Heritage Site of Stonehenge. She felt at one with the mysterious stones and wondered why she had not visited them before in the twenty years that she had made Scotland her home. Tanny had returned to her home at her grandparents' along with her mother who seemed to have tolerated the treatments successfully. The castle was quiet without her and she was a frequent visitor whenever Vienna and Rainey were at home. It was time to make plans to visit Roberge's grandmother in Spain. Rainey phoned him and the date for departure was set.

The last bonfire was on a cool August 30th evening. Rainey and Vienna were leaving the next morning for London with the boys as their summer vacation had come to an end. They would be departing for Canada on September 1st. Ava had tried to book a flight at the same time but was not successful. Cam had phoned to tell her that he had a month off and did she think she would want to see him if he came to Scotland. She didn't want him to have to bear the expense of the trip and so decided that she would meet him in Hawthorne. She wanted to get to know her grandparents better anyhow and visit with Lara and her aunt Sissy. She was to leave on the 8th.

Everyone had left the fire except for Rainey and Vienna, Amma and Johnny. Rainey was adding another log to the fire when Amma asked him how he and Vienna had met.

"You don't know?" He looked at Amma and she shook her head "no".

He sat back down beside Vienna on the wooden bench and pulled a blanket around her.

"I guess you could say that I picked her up on the street in Bridge Falls."

"Rainey," Vienna protested, "you make it sound like I was a street walker!"

He laughed at her objection. "Okay, it wasn't like that. I hadn't been back from school for very long and it was the first time I had made it down to Bridge. It was June 11th. I wouldn't have remembered the date but Vienna knew and that is why we were first married on that day. Anyhow, I was with my buddy Jimmy who you have heard me talk about. We were probably looking to get into some old fashioned trouble…well I got into trouble all right, just not the kind I was expecting." He squeezed Vienna's hand. "No sir, I hadn't planned on meeting the love of my life. She was with my cousin Lara and they had to work at the restaurant which her mother owned until nine that night. Jimmy and I had dinner there and went to a movie to wait for them. Apparently, I watched her every move at the diner and was upset when she appeared to be flirting with other male customers. Jimmy said he knew then that I was smitten even though I had just met V a few hours ago. Well, he was right…I was completely enchanted by her. When I was in her company the outside world didn't exist. Unfortunately, what I was feeling also scared the hell out of me, and I was too stupid to acknowledge that I was in love with her. She was only sixteen and I had a lot of living to do and falling in love was not on my agenda. We went through some rough times over the next year and a half, all my fault I'm afraid. I denied my love for her and you know what that cost us. I went to Italy and Vienna came here to Scotland."

"How old were you Rainey?" Johnny asked.

"Twenty one when we first met…I know what you are thinking…you wouldn't want one of your young teenage daughters dating a guy in his twenties. I guess you think that I was a real jackass, but the age difference was not apparent; Vienna was very mature. Really guys, what did you think of the man who got a young girl pregnant and then abandoned her? You must have thought she was better off without me right?"

Amma didn't want Rainey to think anything of the sort. "None of us thought anything Rainey. We didn't know the whole story like we do now. I suppose we thought that something terrible must have happened that sent Vienna here. She would get this sad faraway look in her eyes and I know now that she was thinking of you. After Ava was born she told us that Ava's father had been killed in an accident in Italy."

"What about you Johnny? Did you think that I was a rotten son of a bitch?"

"Yes, I suppose I did. I never bought that story about Ava's father being killed in Italy. Unless Vienna hated him there was no reason to keep his identity a secret if he was really dead. I know the circumstances now, and all I can say is that it is a crying shame that two people who loved each other so much spent twenty years apart!"

"Rainey is not to blame Johnny. He never abandoned me; he didn't know. I was the one who was foolish. I was given a second chance and will never be so dim witted again. How many men would forgive what I did?"

"She likes to take all the blame as you can see. However, we both made mistakes and the past is just that; the past. The important thing is that we are together now and will never be apart again." Rainey was emphatic.

Totally unexpected Amma broke into tears. "I'm just as much to blame Rainey as the people back in Canada for keeping you from Vienna."

Vienna dropped the blanket and went to sit beside her dear friend. "Whatever are you talking about Amma?"

She directed her answer towards Rainey. "When Vienna came home from seeing you in 1972 and confided in me, I did nothing. I saw then that she still loved you and I should have tracked you down. I knew your name and I knew where you were from, but I was too afraid to take a chance and go behind my friend's back; I'm so very sorry."

Rainey knelt down beside Amma and took her hand. "You did what everyone else did and that was to obey Vienna's wishes. I have forgiven Lara and Jimmy and Vienna's parents and if you need me to forgive you then I do, but you are in no way to ever feel guilty. I should be thanking you for being the friend you are to her and accepting me into your family. Are we straight on this?"

Blubbering Amma said. "Yes, but you should know something. When I first got word that you and Vienna were together I was happy for her but I was prepared not to like you. I was worried that you would keep her all to yourself and that she would never come home again."

Johnny asked why she never told him any of this and she said because it made her sound selfish and he would think that she was daft. He laughed and said that he was going to take his Scottish lass home and that Rainey should take his too.

"You mean my little French lady, don't you Johnny? I have no idea what nationality Lane is. What is it Honey?"

"Lane is not my mother's surname; it is Gibson. Did you not know that Lily and Jannie are of Scottish heritage?"

"No, you never mentioned that you were of Scottish descent. Gibson doesn't sound Scottish. Faith and Begorrah, I learn more about you every day."

"Obviously, the subject never came up before. I see you do know some Irish after all."

"I must have picked it up from dad or one of the aunts; I'm not sure of its meaning."

"Faith and by God is its literal translation." Johnny told him.

"I shall remember that. So, I am married to Scottish lass after all. Tell me Vienna, do you partake in the haggis on Bobbie Burns Day?" Rainey asked.

"You will have to wait and see won't you? Johnny, we must take Rainey on the fox hunt in October and initiate him properly, don't you think?" Vienna teased.

"Fox hunt, you can count me in, but what is this about initiating me?"

Vienna smiled mischievously. "My lips are sealed."

"One more thing before we say goodnight…now that K and V will be leaving us there will be no housekeepers for Avanloch…have you thought of that Vienna?" Amma asked.

"No, not really; do you have someone in mind?"

"You know that I do not require Nanette eight hours every day and so she has been keeping herself busy in the gardens and has taken the care of the fowl under her wing. Don't worry; she knows to stay out of your rose garden. However, seeing that she is already in our employ, would you mind if she helped out at Avanloch?"

"I didn't realize that my distaste of Mrs. Macleod was so obvious, but no Amma, I would not mind if she was to help with the house while we are away. I will look for replacements for the girls when I return home."

"What am I missing here? Vienna, if you don't like Nanette why didn't you say so? We would never have hired her or Wesley. Am I the only one who is in the dark here?" Johnny looked at Rainey for confirmation but Vienna answered.

"It's a personal thing Johnny. She has worked out fine for you and Amma and that is all that is important, okay? Now come here you two and give me a big hug. We are leaving very early tomorrow morning and I don't expect you to see us off."

"I'm going to miss you so very much Vienna and you too Rainey." Amma sniffled.

Rainey reassured her that they would only be gone for two or three weeks.

I awoke at 5 a.m. the next morning, roused Rainey and went across the foyer and knocked on the boy's door. They were already up and ready to leave. I dressed quickly and told Rainey I'd make the coffee. He said that he would and handed me the phone. "What do you want me to do with this?" I asked.

"You've been putting off calling your father for some reason and so I would like you to do it before we go."

"You want me to ask him about the Novia thing don't you?"

"Yes, will you indulge me? I have a feeling we are going to discover more about that portrait that looks so much like you on our trip."

"I don't know why you would say that, but yes Darling, I will phone. I should tell my parents of our plans anyway. I'll make it quick, see you in the kitchen."

The bags had all been loaded into the sedan the day before, so by the time I joined them in the kitchen the boys had already had breakfast, and Rainey was holding a thermos of coffee and a picnic lunch that Lois had made for us. We had decided to drive to London as it would be just as fast as taking the train and Rainey loved to drive. He had driven from Vancouver to Hawthorne so many times in his lifetime that a few extra hours meant nothing. We'd leave the car with Rosy and Evan. I had no time to savor my morning ritual of two cups of coffee and opted to sip from a travel mug once we were on our way. We made it to the gate when I yelled at Rainey to stop.

"What did you forget Hon?" He asked me.

I got out and stood for a few minutes looking back at the castle. I heard Meggie's words cautioning me to be ever vigilant. Rainey closed his hand over mine when I got back into the car. "I'm sorry, I just needed to say goodbye."

"It's not going anywhere Honey and it will be right here when we get home."

Sadly, we watched the boys as they got on the plane for home. Before they left they made their dad promise to keep up the quest for the other hidden rooms. He said he would and told them to phone the apartment as soon as they were home safely. He double checked to make sure they had all the correct phone numbers.

Rosalyn and Evan had come to see them off as well and then the four of us went out to dinner. I expressed my concern that I might not have access to a phone in Andorra.

"Of course you will Mother! You're not going to Antarctica you know." Rosy stated.

"I know Dear, but we may end up in a remote village where there are no phones. I have to know that you girls will stay connected, so please stay in touch with your sister."

"I will Mama, I promise. Ava will be so busy with Cam that she won't have any time to be lonely."

"You'll look after my Rosy won't you Evan?"

"You can count on that Mrs. Q. This is yours and Rainey's opportunity to have your long awaited honeymoon, so don't be worrying about things over here okay?"

"Thanks Evan. I hope to keep your future mother in law very busy so she has no time to worry about anything." Rainey said with a twinkle in his eye.

Rosy blushed. "Rainey Quinn, how brazen of you!"

Evan laughed and said. "Is that so farfetched Rosy? I would like nothing more than to have these two as my in- laws."

"Now see what you have started Rainey?" Rosy scolded but was not annoyed at all.

Rainey climbed into bed and snuggled up to me. He ran his fingers through my hair.

"What are you doing?" I asked him.

"Nothing."

"Yes you are; you're playing with my hair and you know how I hate that."

"Oh, I know how you hate it all right."

"Rainey, do you believe in reincarnation?"

"To be honest I haven't given it any thought. What made you bring the subject up?"

"Don't you ever wonder why I fell head over heels in love with you the first time that we met? I mean, I was only sixteen, and I hadn't even thought about love. There was a connection there that was so magnetic that could only have happened if we had known each other in a previous life. Do you ever have sensations of déjà vu?"

"Yes I do, but I usually don't think anything of it."

"Doesn't it get you to wondering why you have seen yourself doing precisely the same thing before? I have had so many experiences that send shivers up my spine."

"Are you having one right now?"

"No. I'm being melodramatic aren't I? You know how I hate to fly and we are going into unchartered water. I think I am a little apprehensive and perhaps we should call the whole expedition off."

"If you are having second thoughts it is all right with me. Do you want to sleep on it?"

"Yes, perhaps I should. Things always look clearer in the light of day."

Rainey kissed my neck. I turned over to face him. "You're going to make me forget about crossing the sea aren't you?"

We spent the next evening with Stu and Daisy at their flat. After dinner Daisy invited Vienna to come and see the nursery.

"I see you have decided to go with a unisex theme…good idea. Everything is just lovely Daisy and your baby will be very contented here." I told her.

"I think about the day that you told us that we were having a boy…I like to think that is true as I would dearly love to give Stu a son."

"Daisy, please forgive me for sometimes things just pop out of my mouth without first clearing it with my brain. If you give birth to a boy very well, but I know a daughter will be welcomed and loved equally. At least there is a chance that you may have a son, but there will be no male children for Rainey and me."

"How do you know that Vienna?"

"I just do Daisy, but it is all right as he already has two sons and Rosalyn will give us a grandson. Ava will have daughters just as all LaFontaine women before her."

"But it is the man who determines the sex of the child isn't it?"

"It doesn't matter Daisy; that is just the way it is."

"You do have the sight don't you Vienna?"

"Heavens no; if I did I would know what is going to happen when we go to Andorra and I don't have an inkling except that things are not going to go according to plan."

"What do you mean by that?"

"I have absolutely no idea. Now show me the layette."

As soon as the ladies were out of the room Rainey took advantage of their absence. He pulled the little portrait from inside his jacket and gave it to Stu who studied it for a minute and then turned it over and read the inscription.

"It appears to be a very old picture…from the 1800's… am I right?"

"Don't rightly know Stu. Roberge Farradan, you met him at our wedding, found the portrait. He will be travelling with us to Spain as it is his grandmother who might have some important information for us regarding the bracelets. He discovered it in some shoppe somewhere and thought that the woman bore an uncanny resemblance to Vienna and presented it to her…actually, to us."

"I can see the likeness to a much younger Vienna. Does she want to find out who the girl in the photo is?"

"It is not so much her as it is for me. You're right; Vienna looked exactly like this when she was sixteen and seventeen. What is really strange is that Vienna's great grandmother's name was Novia, but Vienna says she knows nothing about the name."

"That is a very interesting fact indeed. Is the Novia name from her mother or father?"

"On her father's side and believe me, he does not speak of his ancestry. Nevertheless, I coaxed Vienna into calling her father before we left home. He told her very little and wanted to know why the sudden interest. She told him about the portrait of Angeliqua Novia. He did not show much interest, but asked her if she would care to see some other pictures of his long forgotten family. She was not aware that any existed and was mystified as to why he would keep them from his children. He offered no explanation but said he would send Sissy to his safety deposit box in Bridge and she could forward them to her. She didn't question him further as we were leaving, but she has said that she will delve into the matter when we get home. I intend to hold her to that promise as I am most curious as to why her father has kept his ancestry in the closet."

"It could prove to be very interesting .Why are you carrying the photo with you?"

"You know what Stu, I really don't know. Novia is a French name, and Roberge is French, as well as Spanish. I am hoping that his grandmother may have some insight into the name. I am more curious than Vienna…that is all it is, just curiosity. I take it you have never heard of the name Novia before?"

"Oh, I know the name as it is a common French last name, but I know nothing more than that."

"I figured that you might with your vast knowledge of historical data and names. I must comment on the new décor of your home… so much neater without the fifty thousand books. You didn't get rid of everything did you?"

Stu chuckled. "Hardly, I rent a basement from a colleague and anything that I deemed worthy is stored there. I am not ashamed to say that I am still collecting. Daisy does not object as long as I keep it out of her sight. I'm still doing research and so if you like I will see what I can come up with for you. I'm not promising, but I will need something to do this winter then pace the floor waiting for the baby's arrival."

"Thanks Stu. I am hoping that this trip will lessen Vienna's anxiety. Her fainting episodes seem to have diminished since she's been taking the vitamins and following the doctor's orders. There has been so much activity at the castle what with uncovering secret rooms and ghosts appearing out of nowhere and witches…no wonder she has been anxious."

"Whoa there Rainey, witches?"

"It's a long story and I will go into it another time…no harm, no foul though. The only worry right now is to get Vienna across the English Channel."

"Well I know Vienna is not afraid of water and you can't possibly expect me to believe that she is afraid of flying, so what is it?"

"Are you talking about me?" Vienna sat down beside Rainey. "Are you telling Stu all of my idiosyncrasies? What about yours Darling, did you show him the portrait?"

"How do you know that I brought it with me?" Rainey asked surprised that she knew.

"You do know that your wife is a little bit psychic don't you?" Daisy asked.

"I know she knows things that she shouldn't Daisy, but I don't think that I would go as far as to say that she is psychic." Rainey looked at Vienna for confirmation.

"Everyone knows things they shouldn't Rainey, but if you thought that I wouldn't notice that the portrait of Angeliqua was missing then you're wrong, and besides, I saw it in your jacket pocket. It is only natural that you would bring it to the most knowledgeable man you know. So, what do you think Stu…is it me from another lifetime?"

"You give me way too much credit Lady Vienna." Stu stammered.

"Somebody tell me what you are all talking about please." Daisy begged.

Stu handed her the picture. "Is this you when you were a young girl Vienna?" She turned it over and then said. "Who is Angeliqua Novia?"

"That is precisely what we want to know Daisy, and hopefully we will have some answers soon. I want to know who this beauty is who has my wife's face."

"There may be skeletons you know that are better left in the closet." Stu warned.

"I am sure every family has secrets that they would rather not have revealed. I think I can handle the past, but am most interested in finding out why my father has photos and mementos of his ancestry but never bothered to share any of them with us."

"I hope you find the answers to all of your questions Vienna, and hopefully Roberge's family will have the information that you are seeking regarding the Infinity Bracelets. I expect a full report when you get back from your excursion, and remember to have fun as after all, it is your honeymoon."

We said our goodbyes promising to do just that.

Chapter 5

Saragossa Spain
Sept 3 - 5

Roberge met them at the airport. They had a pleasant trip and landed in Saragossa at 8 P.M. Rainey asked Vienna if she was happy that she was on the ground again.

"You know the old saying: "A day to come seems longer than a year that's gone?"

"I can't say that I have heard that. Is it one of your proverbs?"

"I'm just saying that it takes longer for an anticipated event to happen and worrying about it only adds to the agony and length of the wait, understand?"

"Yup, it's clear as mud."

Roberge had a family car waiting for them at the airport. He dropped them off at the hotel which he had reserved for them. It was in the older section of town and close to his grandmother's residence where she lived with her daughter and family. The hotel was surrounded by a brick wall that was covered in bougainvillea. They entered unto a Spanish courtyard that housed an elaborate fountain. Their modern yet traditionally furnished room had a terrace from where they could view the city and the landscape.

They settled in and ordered room service before the kitchen closed for the night. Roberge was picking them up for an early lunch at the family home the next morning. After their light meal which they enjoyed on the terrace they phoned the children to inform them of their safe arrival. Vienna took one of her sleeping tablets to ensure that she would have a restful sleep. Rainey sat up and mulled over the maps which he had compiled of Andorra. He calculated the mileage to Andorra La Vella, Andorra's largest city. His plans were to make their headquarters there. He hoped the destination would be determined tomorrow.

After coffee the next morning Rainey went for a stroll around the courtyard while Vienna readied herself. Everyone he met was friendly and curious at the same time asking what had brought him here. Several times over he explained as briefly as possible never bringing the Infinity Bracelets into the conversation. He returned to the room and knocked and then let himself in with his key. Vienna was waiting for him. He whistled.

She looked like a Spanish senorita. She was wearing a ruffled high collared lacey ivory blouse tucked into a long flowing rust colored skirt. Around her neck she wore a white and sepia cameo that was on a black satin ribbon. Her earrings matched. She wore very little make-up but her coral lips matched the combs that were holding her hair in place atop her head. She asked Rainey if she looked all right.

"Darling, you are beautiful as usual. You could pass for a Spanish Queen!"

"Do they still have queens here? The last one I remember was Isabella."

"Don't know; we can ask Roberge. Shall we go and wait for him? How do I look?"

"Rainey, you always have the tailored look but it is your charm and manners and sexuality that will win Abella over."

"Really, have you ever considered that I am only that way in your eyes? You do know that Abella is ninety something and so I don't think she is going to be turned on by me."

"You underestimate yourself Dear, and I hope that when I am ninety I will still be stimulated by a handsome and suave gentleman."

"And my dear I hope that I will still be the one that arouses you." He helped her into her jacket that matched her skirt. "From Miss Mary's closet I presume?"

"She must have been with child as this ensemble is larger than her other costumes."

The home of Pilar and Diaz Paredes was in a state of disrepair. Pieces of the terra cotta roof had fallen off and lay broken on the ground. Shards of stucco from the walls were piled up in a heap on the parched lawn. The driveway pavement was cracked and heaved as was the walkway that led into the house. Well attended rose bushes of every color lined the sidewalk. Olive trees divided the house from the neighbors. A vegetable garden occupied the whole of the backyard. Vienna couldn't see a weed anywhere, unlike the front yard. Roberge apologized for the condition of the house and explained that the family had come upon hard times when his brother in law had lost his lifelong job at the food processing plant due to modernization. Things were looking up though as he had found work at the foundry. It hadn't helped any that a wind storm had wreaked havoc with the roof. Vienna knew that Roberge did not have the funds to aid his sister's family and she couldn't see his self-centered wife offering financial assistance. It was obvious that there was no royalty in this family. Roberge was only a Duke because his wife, the Duchess of Calendria, had bestowed the title on him.

Roberge escorted them through glass doors into a beautifully furnished dining room. The carpet was worn and the walls needed painting. Vienna scolded herself for even noticing. The table was set for eight and she wondered who all would be joining them. Colorful dinnerware adorned the lace tablecloth. The room was tastefully decorated with antiques and greenery. It was warm and Vienna felt at home.

Roberge called out that they had arrived. A petite salt and pepper haired woman emerged from a closed door. Right behind her were two teenage girls. Roberge had informed us on the ride over that his nieces Mayra and Shilane lived with his sister's family as their parents had been killed in a plane crash several years earlier. He introduced us to them and they did a little curtsey as their way of saying hello.

He put his arm around his mother's waist and said proudly. "May I present mi Madre Celesta?" She took Vienna's and Rainey's hand and welcomed them.

"Where is Pilar and Grandmamma?" Roberge asked.

"They will be here soon. Offer our guests some refreshments please."

"Rainey, what is your pleasure? May I suggest sangria sans alcohol Vienna?"

"It is a little early Roberge and so I will join Vienna and have the sangria thank you."

"Sangria all around then please girls?"

They nodded just as a door at the opposite end of the room opened and Pilar entered with Abella. Roberge set the pitcher of sangria down and went to help his grandmother to her chair. She kept her eyes on Vienna as she took her place at one end of the table.

Pilar greeted them in Spanish. "Bienvenido Lady Vienna and Lord Rainey."

"Please Senora Paredes, we are but Rainey and Vienna." Rainey accentuated.

"And I am Pilar and this is the woman you have come all this way to see, mi Abuela, Abella. She has been waiting for this day for a very long time."

Vienna took the worn and sun bleached hands of the matriarch in hers. "It is I who has been waiting to meet you."

Abella pointed to the chair to her right and said. "May I have the pleasure of your company my dear?" Her English was perfect.

Rainey held the chair for Vienna as he introduced himself.

"Will it please you sir to sit next to your beautiful wife?" Abella asked.

Rainey raised Abella's hand to his lips and bestowed a delicate kiss on it. "Rainey Quinn at your service Senora. Yes, it always pleases me to sit beside my wife."

Abella's eyes twinkled and she laughed faintly. "A gentleman of nobility I see."

"There is no aristocracy in my family I can assure you Abella. We cannot say the same for Vienna's ancestry."

"Perhaps I can shed some light on that subject for I have known her from a time so very long ago." She was still studying Vienna.

"Whatever do you mean by that Gramama?" Roberge asked.

"Don't look so indignant Robbie. Vienna has the countenance of my childhood friend Evangelina that is all I am saying. It sets an old heart to smiling to see that her likeness lives on."

Vienna sat back and peered at the aged woman wondering what she was actually saying.

Rainey reached into his jacket pocket and produced the portrait of Angeliqua Novia. Vienna put her hand on his to stop him, but Abella had already noticed.

"What is it you have there young man?"

He smiled at Vienna in a way that said it would be all right. She sighed.

Abella held the miniature portrait in her fragile hands for several minutes. The room was quiet waiting for her reaction. She asked Roberge to fetch her spectacles. She ran her fingers tentatively over the face that was peering out to her. A single tear slid down her cheek. Her eyes darted from Vienna to Rainey and back again to Vienna. She had not turned the picture over.

"Just how are you related to my beloved Evangelina? Indeed you must be for the resemblance is too great…I noticed it the second I saw your face."

Before Vienna could utter a response Roberge asked Rainey what had possessed him to bring the photo with him. He got up and walked over to his Grandmother.

"I don't know exactly why…I just had a hunch. I am sorry if I upset you Senora Abella. I didn't know that it would remind you of someone you once knew. Forgive me for I was only hoping that you might know the name Novia." Rainey apologized.

"I am not upset young man. How do you know of the Novia name?"

Roberge reached down and turned the picture over.

"Ah, tis Angeliqua, Evangeline's mother." Abella exclaimed. "They were a mirror image of each other. Robbie, how do you know of this?"

"It is I who found it Grammama. I came across it in a little Shoppe and saw the likeness to Vienna and thought that she and Rainey would be amused with it."

"Amused? How was your reaction Vienna…was it one of amusement?" Abella asked.

"More curiosity I suppose for my great grandmother's name was Novia."

Roberge was shocked but recovered quickly. "I am sure it means nothing as Novia is a common French name. Was your great grandmother's name Angeliqua?"

"I have no idea. My father never spoke of that side of the family but I have been in contact with him, and will hopefully have some answers soon."

"It makes no difference to an old woman. Except for the hair color you are the image of my dear Evangelina who died way before her time." Abella reminisced sadly.

Vienna placed her hand on Abella's. "Has this brought back sad memories for you?"

"My eyes and my heart already knew my dear and we shall talk further of this later."

Pilar declared that it was time to eat and the two young girls followed her into the kitchen. They emerged with a steaming tureen of corn soup and tortilla chips which they had made fresh that morning. It was followed by a delicious Spanish Frittata with several varieties of cheeses, grapes, pears and olives. A tray of chocolate fritters which were called conchurros and cream filled delicacies were served last with more coffee and cocoa for the girls.

Rainey sat back and said that he could be a Spaniard very easily if this was the way they ate every day. Pilar assured him that she hoped dinner would meet with his approval also.

"Please tell me that you have not made plans for dinner already Pilar?"

"It will be started soon but we do not sup until 6 P.M. or so. Diaz likes to unwind a bit before he eats. Will that be to your liking Mr. Quinn?"

"It would dear lady, but we cannot accept for it would please Vienna and myself if you would all be our guests tonight…I will need you to point us in the right direction of an establishment that serves the finest of cuisine."

"Grammama does not venture far out of the casa and so I am not sure if …"

Abella halted Roberge with a shaky hand. "I believe that I will make an exception for these delightful people and so on behalf of the family, I thank you and accept. So before I take leave for my rest we best get to the reason why you have come all this way."

Vienna asked Rainey to help her off with her jacket. She undid the tiny buttons on the sleeve of her blouse and slid the bracelets off. She passed them to Abella who donned her spectacles again and examined them one by one, inside and out. She snapped her fingers and asked Mayra, the eldest of her great grandchildren, to bring her the silver box from underneath the sideboard.

"Madre, would you please quit treating the girls like servants?" Celesta scolded.

Abella laughed. "They don't mind, do you girls?"

"Of course not Grammama; we are here to serve you." She set the box on the table in front of Abella who had cleared a place for it. The girls asked to be excused and giggling left with a handful of dirty plates and escaped from the adults.

"See you at supper girls." Rainey called after them.

Abella retrieved a key from deep inside one of her pockets and with Roberge's help opened the weather worn box that looked more like a small pirate's trunk. On top of the pile of memorabilia was a yellowed manila envelope. "This old drawing of what we believed was the Infinity Bracelets has been in the possession of the family for many years. The rest of the contents have only come to us recently. Yes Roberge, you do not even know what is in here. It will all become clear soon enough. Shall I tell you the story from the beginning as I know it?"

Vienna said. "Yes please, I always think that the beginning is a good place to start."

"Very well. You will forgive the lapses in my memory but I will do my best and Celesta will help. The year was early 1800's and France and Spain were at war…would that have been the Napoleonic War?"

"I believe so, but that seems way too early for the date on the bracelets is 1852 or 1853 or perhaps there is a mistake there?" Rainey answered.

Abella looked a little perplexed. "I don't recall another war that late."

"Madre, you are forgetting the Spanish Civil war and the Carlist Wars." Pilar said.

"You are right Cara Mia. I doubt that it would have been during the civil war so it must have been during the Carlist wars. Yes, that makes sense."

Rainey and Vienna both said they had never heard of them before.

"Celesta, we may need the help of the history book do you think?" Abella asked.

Pilar found the book and put it down between her mother and herself and started to leaf through it. "Here it is. The wars took place over a forty year period in the middle of the 19th century from 1833 to 1876. Does that fit the time frame better Rainey?"

"Yes it certainly does. What were the wars all about and where did the name Carlist come from?"

Pilar read from the Spanish History book. "A man called Carlos was the leader of the movement and his followers were known as Carlists. They were members of a political conservative group. They established a foothold in Basque Country, Valencia and Catalonia." She looked at Roberge when she said that and he acknowledged her with a nod. Vienna wondered what that meant. Celesta took up the reading.

"Spain was under the rule of Queen Isabella the 2nd. She had the support of France, Britain and Portugal. However, her reign was troubled by all of this political instability and the rule of military politicians. After thirty six years of political turmoil she abdicated or, as some believe, was deposed even before the Carlists were defeated. The story as we know it was that Anton Christoval was a valued member of the Queen's legion and was deemed one of the biggest threats to Carlos and his minions and was sent into hiding to devise a plot to overthrow them."

"I bow to my children; they should be telling this story." Abella said proudly.

"We have only relayed a little piece of history Cara. You are the one that has unraveled the mystery since receiving this chest from your brother that was left in care of his son."

"You are too… how do they say, modest? Without their help I would still be sorting through useless papers. Anyhow, this is the story that was passed down from mi Madre." Abella crossed herself and said a prayer. "Please to correct me if I make a mistake again. So Anton was whisked off to somewhere in the Pyrenees Mountains in Andorra. France and Spain had been fighting over that country also but the Queen was probably assured that he would be safe there in a monastery. Rumor has it that he may have been wounded and while out walking fell down an escarpment and was found there unconscious by Katarina. She managed to get him back to her village though one can only surmise how and care for him. She became his mistress and found herself with child after he had returned to Spain. She never saw him again, according to legend."

"I thought they were married and that Anton was of Spanish royalty." Vienna said.

"Perhaps he and Katarina were married; no one knows for sure. He did marry Castilla Vendelaze, however. It was an arranged marriage between the families. The Vendelaze was a name of wealth and the Christoval coffers had all been depleted in the wars. Anton probably married her to save his family from financial ruin, but no, he was not an heir to the Spanish throne. When he returned to Andorra he found his beloved Katarina and her daughter had been victims of masked terrorists, but the story is unclear…some accounts have Katarina tortured and dragged to her death while others say she and her daughter were taken alive and unharmed. Some witnesses say they saw blood gushing from her arm as the bracelets were ripped from her. Anton avowed revenge."

Abella stopped and let herself breathe for a few minutes. "Now this is where the facts become fiction and no one knew for sure what was truth and what was not…until now, but I get ahead of myself."

Rainey looked at Roberge but he only shook his head for he did not know what was coming. Vienna squeezed the old woman's hand and told her to take her time.

"Some say he found his daughter and Katarina, and other reports have him going to his grave never finding either of them. There is another cruel scenario that paints his wife Castilla as an evil and jealous creature who orchestrated the murder of Katrina and sentenced the child to life in an abominable orphanage. The bracelets never surfaced but of course it is believed that they were sold by the assassins. Many have taken up the quest to discover the truth but no one has succeeded because of unknown facts. My family of course were the primary searchers for after all, they were Christovals. I believe they were all unsuccessful because they did not have all the facts. There was never a mention of Katarina's last name or the village that she lived in. It seems that Anton did not reveal this to anyone except perhaps one trusted soul. Mind you, Andorra was not so populated back then that the whole of it could not have been questioned but at what expense and for what reason? How many do you think knew about the silver bracelets and there worth back then? We can only guess."

Abella sat back and closed her eyes. Only her daughter and granddaughter knew what was to come. Roberge was impatient and proceeded to lift the lid on the box. He was met by a sharp blow to the knuckles. His mother and sister chuckled.

Abella's eyes opened wide. "Have you not learned that good things come to those that sit and wait Roberge Farradan?"

"I don't want our guests to become bored Grammama." He said in his defense.

"Believe me, we are not bored." Rainey assured him.

"Is there more coffee Pilar?" Abella asked as she took her time opening the box again.

Pilar poured her grandmother another cup of coffee and asked Vienna and Rainey if they would care for a refill. Rainey laughed.

"You don't know my wife very well…coffee is her weakness and she has already asked me to find out the name of this aromatic blend for she plans on purchasing a crate of it."

"It is Saimaza, shall I write the name down for you?" Pilar asked.

"Yes please." Vienna replied and waited for Abella to continue her narrative.

"I shall not go into great detail with my family tree, but will start with my bisabuelo Darius who was a cousin to Anton."

Roberge explained that was Abella's great grandfather.

She continued. "He was his trusted friend and confidante. The year would have been in the 1850's as established. It appears that Darius may have accompanied Anton to search for his family; that fact is not completely clear, but what is, is that when Anton passed away around 1885 his possessions were passed on to Darius who passed away himself shortly after. Anton and Castilla were childless and so Darius's son, who was also called Darius, inherited this here chest. There is no way to tell if he ever opened it and eventually it passed on down the line to his son Cervantes, mi tio, who we shall say was the black sheep as you say in America. He had a very public affair with a French chanteuse who died giving birth to his illegitimate son Marchant named for his lover."

At the mention of the name Marchant and that his mother was a French singer Vienna whispered to Rainey that perhaps they were related to Gizelle. He squeezed her hand and mouthed "Perhaps."

"Is there a question Vienna?" Abella asked.

"It is not important. I am sorry to have interrupted you."

"Why not let me be the judge if your question is of importance my dear?"

Rainey rescued Vienna. "We know of a French songstress with the last name of Marchant and are curious if there is a possibility the families are related."

"If you mean Gizelle Marchant, yes, we know her very well and she is a distant cousin. Do you know of her music?" Pilar inquired.

"I discovered her when I was in Europe many years ago and at the same time or shortly after, Vienna wrote a song that Gizelle recorded, "Mademoiselle"; have you heard it?" Rainey looked at his wife proudly and was surprised to see her blushing.

"This is a rare moment to meet someone who also knows Gizelle!" Pilar exclaimed. "Yes, we know the song and might I add is a favorite. Vienna, you are most talented."

"It was just a whim that I sent it off to her, and believe me no one was more shocked than me that she chose to record it. Sadly though we have never met…talked on the phone, but that is all. I did not mean to distract us from the subject of the bracelets. Please excuse the interruption Abella." Vienna apologized.

"You have done no such thing. It is a small world indeed that we have a connection to Gizelle. Where was I?"

"You were just about to tell us about Marchant I believe Grammama and to reveal what is in the chest." Roberge stated.

"So I was. Cervantes, much to the amazement of the family formed a bond with the child and became his sole caregiver. Everyone thought that he would blame the child for the death of his lover but he only blamed himself. He retreated to an island off the coast of France where he stayed until his death in 1960. He was eighty two years old. Marchant himself was a recluse, but did marry a woman from Corsica. They had no children and he passed away in 1980 of a drug overdose. That is the story that was relayed to us by his wife who only informed us of his death a month ago. The chest arrived shortly after. Pilar and Celesta and the young girls have worked long hours going through all the papers. Most all was useless information and had no interest to us. However, hidden among the rubbish was a journal." Abella paused and she looked at Roberge and then Vienna and Rainey. "I think you will be most interested to know who the journal belongs to."

"Yes we would Gramama." Roberge said anxiously. "You have teased us enough."

Abella grinned. "Anton Christoval…the diary is that of Anton Christoval."

"And you didn't feel the need to tell me earlier?" Roberge questioned.

His mother told him that they had only discovered it in the past week so there was no need for accusation as they were not keeping anything from him. He apologized

Abella lifted the diary from the little trunk and passed it to Vienna. "It is yours to extract what information you can from it and perhaps find an heir to the Infinity bracelets. We did not find any mention as to whether Anton found Katarina or little Catalina."

Vienna thanked her and said it was a most unexpected pleasure. She said her and Rainey would examine it carefully for any clues that might help them in their search. She delicately opened the fragile leather journal. She turned several pages over with the utmost sensitivity. She could feel everyone's eyes waiting for her reaction. She put her hand over her mouth and burst out laughing. Rainey asked her what was wrong.

"It's in Chinese." She said through her laughter passing it to him.

"Is that the Scottish way of saying 'it's all Greek to me?'" Pilar asked with amusement.

"Oh yes," Rainey grinned, "we are going to be able to translate this with five or ten years of Spanish lessons."

"And even then," Pilar told them, "it will not be easy for most of it is in code. That is why it has taken so long to try and decipher Anton's mixed up words and we were not very successful I am afraid."

"Were you not able to translate anything Pilar?" Roberge inquired.

"It will take a lot more study but the two things we feel will be important to Vienna and Rainey is that Katarina's family name was Carvarra and her village was Nazeth. He did not want these facts to be discovered by the wrong people and he was most tricky as to how he hid the names."

"This journal will be no benefit to us Pilar and so it shall remain in your hands to further explore if you so desire. The two facts you have given us are a big help because we had no clue as to where we were going but now we have something to work with. Thank you for your diligence in perusing the writings." Vienna acknowledged the tiresome work the ladies had done.

Rainey agreed. "Yes, Vienna is right. We will see what we can accomplish with the information you have given us." He passed the diary back to Abella who thanked them for gracing the family table.

"I must take my rest now if I am to be alert for tonight. Until then, dear friends."

Rainey rose to help her with her chair and Pilar led her out of the room.

"I suppose that we should be leaving Vienna as there is the little matter of finding a vehicle for our trip. What can we help you with Senora Farradan?"

"Nada, you are the guests. Surely you do not do your own clean up at the castle? How many servants do you have?" Celesta asked.

Roberge was quick to point out to his mother that Vienna did not have servants. She was very surprised. "How do you manage such a structure by yourselves?"

"We could not Senora and have many employees but they are not servants. We do not have upstairs and downstairs maids nor do we have separate quarters on one floor that the staff resides in. We have no hand maidens or a butler or valets. There is a suite of rooms on the main floor that our cherished cook and her husband occupy. Mr. and Mrs. McDuff have been with the family for over twenty five years. I am sad to say that Mary will be retiring soon but she has already found a replacement that is staying at the castle in what used to be called the maids room. We just call it the guest staff room now. This past summer we had two young ladies with us as housekeepers and aids to Mrs. D in the kitchen. Neither girl had ever been away from home before and so it was a great learning experience for all. Our table is always open to all the staff and we so enjoy the company of the young people. I do not know if the early McAllister's functioned any differently. I assume that they were more aristocratic and employed a much larger staff. We are only a stones throw away from a small village but help is not always easy to find."

Pilar had returned and took a seat beside her brother. "It sounds as if you run a very friendly household Vienna. This is much different than your home isn't it Roberge?"

"I am not sure one would refer to Calendria as a home Pilar. It is more like Lauren's Ice Palace… cold and unfriendly." He answered.

"You make it sound dreadful Roberge; surely it can't be all that bad?" Rainey asked.

Roberge laughed harshly. "You haven't met my wife Rainey, but Vienna has, and my family has and I don't think any of them would ever want to meet up with her again. Her whole attitude towards the staff is one of servitude. No matter how hard they try they cannot please her. It is a most inhospitable place to live. Thankfully though I have my own quarters and only have to be present when she deems me a necessity. I have adapted and find her whole lifestyle amusing and tolerate her manipulation so that I may enjoy the pithy allowance that she doles out to me. It was a condition of me marrying her. However for her snobbish friends benefit I am a Duke waiting for a very substantial inheritance that is in arbitration. How long she can keep this fabrication going is beyond me. You tell Rainey what you think of my dear wife Vienna."

"We did not get off to a friendly start I must admit. She does not like me that is certain, but I cannot speak unkindly of her as I do not know the circumstances that may have attributed to her aloofness. Roberge, you are not chained to her and there are no children to consider and so if you are so unhappy why don't you just leave?"

"Who says I am unhappy…maybe I like playing the role of martyr and oh, did I mention the allowance I receive for being her whipping boy?" Roberge laughed.

"It is no use Vienna; we have told him over and over that he is welcome to come and live with us until another rich woman who will treat him better comes along, but no, he does not come. Ay Ay Ay. Tell us more about Avanloch Vienna." Pilar encouraged.

"Our Avanloch family is not complete without my dearest and most trusted friends, Amma and Johnny O'Shea. They are the backbone of the whole estate. Lord Jeremy first hired Johnny as a carpenter, but his responsibilities are so much more than that. Not only does he oversee the lands and the castle, he is also instrumental in keeping the mill and dairy in the village running efficiently. Amma helps me with the finances and operations of the house. They have three lovely daughters and live at Brackenshire Manor which is a stones throw away. I leave the most important people in my life to last although they will always come first. Rosalyn is the true McAllister and will inherit Avanloch. Right now she is going to college and helping to run McAllister Enterprises. I adopted her when she was but a small child. Rainey's and my daughter is Ava. I do not know if you are familiar with our story but I will make it brief and tell you that we have been apart for twenty years. I left Canada and fled to Scotland where my aunt was. She was residing at Brackenshire then but was mistress to Avanloch. Rainey had no part in my running away and did not know where I had gone and did not know that I was pregnant with his child. I am afraid that I made my family lie for me. But we are together now and I do not know how I managed without him. He has taken on many challenges and has cut Johnny's work down immensely." Vienna beamed as she smiled at Rainey.

"She gives me far too much credit. Believe me it was just as much my fault as hers that we were apart for two decades. I cannot imagine Avanloch or me existing without her."

Celesta said. "Thank you for sharing; I only wish my Robbie had such love in his life."

Pilar and her mother walked them to the car. Vienna and Rainey expressed their gratitude and said they were looking forward to the evening. Rainey had made reservations at the Hacienda, a family favorite restaurant. When they were in the car Vienna asked Roberge when his father had passed away.

"Do you know something that I don't?" He asked lightheartedly.

"I just assumed that he was no longer alive…am I wrong?"

"He may be and he may not be. The last any of us heard of him was from a family friend who ran into him somewhere in France five or six years ago. Apparently he has gone back to his Castilian family."

"But your father was French; aren't the Castilians Spanish?" Vienna queried.

"We cannot speak of any of this without mentioning the Basque. The Basque language was spoken in northern Spain and south France. The people inhabited adjacent areas of both countries. My father's family were either Basque or Castilian or both. Remember the reference to the Carlist Wars and the defeat of the Basques and the Catalonians?"

"Yes, and I noticed that Pilar looked at you when she mentioned that."

"For a reason and that being that the Basques were exiled several times after losing the wars. The second time they went to Catalonia and the third time they went to France and then some to America. You think that my father was French…you will probably not find the name in France for it is a combination of Farre, heavy accent on the 'e' and Dani which is a Catalan surname and it has an alternate spelling of Ferrani. How far back it goes I cannot tell you for we know very little of the history since my father left us when I was a young lad. Does this answer your question Vienna?"

"It really is none of my business but thank you for the history lesson. I really know very little of the Basque culture but I think it could prove to be very interesting."

"Might I say that your search for Katarina's ancestors has got me to thinking that perhaps it is time that I did some digging into my own?"

"Then you and Vienna have something in common for after we return from our trip to Andorra she plans on doing the same with her family tree and who knows, I may just catch the bug and investigate my own Irish ancestry." Rainey pronounced.

Vienna returned to the hotel to rest while Roberge drove Rainey around to the car rental dealers. There was not a jeep or four wheel drive to be had, so in desperation Rainey ended up purchasing a used land rover. Luckily, all the pertinent paperwork could be done at the dealership. Roberge accompanied him to a store that sold recreation equipment. Fully outfitted with everything that Rainey thought they might require for their trip into the unknown country he thanked Roberge and returned to Vienna.

She was not surprised to find out that he had to buy the jeep and was impressed with the supplies that he had jammed into the back. He drove her to the grocerteria where they furnished themselves with mostly nonperishable goods. Of course 24 coffee packages of 900 grams each was among the necessities and a case of the Sangria that Rainey liked.

They continued on to the restaurant where they had a pleasant evening with Roberge's family and their new found friends. There were hugs and promises to come back again.

"Vaya Condios." Vienna echoed the family's sentiment as she waved farewell. She smiled at Rainey and said. "I'm ready to say adios to Spain and Hola to Andorra."

Chapter 6

Portentous Destiny

Vienna and Rainey arrived in Andorra La Vella, the largest city and capital of Andorra early in the evening on the 5th of September. They spent the night and set out for Nazeth early the next morning. When Rainey inquired about the road conditions he was told that some wash-outs had occurred after the heavy rains of the week prior and they would encounter rough gravel roads, but it was all passable.

The sun was on its way and the temperature was to be 15C which was average for September. It would be predominately cooler in the mountains. There was no rain or snow forecast for the see-able future. Rainey informed Vienna of the road conditions but she was too excited to be concerned over washouts and gravel roads. Her feelings changed drastically after they left the pavement and climbed rapidly unto a winding, narrow and steep patch of mountainous road.

"Are you sure you didn't take a wrong turn Rainey? This hardly seems like it is traveled much. Perhaps we should turn around?"

"I will if you want me to though I don't know where but I assure you that we are on the right road. It will probably straighten out soon. Sit back and try and relax.'

"Easy for you to say…you're not looking down at a five hundred foot drop!"

"I am nowhere near the edge Vienna. Since when have you been afraid of heights?"

"Always…why do you think I don't like to fly? Can you hug the bank a little more…I would rather run into another car than plunge off the road and into the canyon."

"We are not going to slide off the road Vienna…maybe you would be more comfortable driving." Rainey was mildly argumentative.

"Don't be absurd!"

"All right then, please sit still and quit worrying."

Vienna sat quietly and didn't complain anymore. A few minutes went by.

"Are you playing with your gum Vienna" Rainey asked in an accusing voice.

"Quit looking at me and keep your eyes on the road!"

"Well it is very distracting. I have never known you to do such a thing before."

"That's because you know very well that I don't chew gum." She rolled her window down and threw it out. "You don't have to be so testy with me. I'm sorry for being such a bother. I'll just sit here and try not to annoy you."

"If we ever come to a wide spot I am going to pull over. You're not a bother and you know that Vienna. I think it is more than just this rocky road that is bothering you…would you care to share with me?"

"This isn't a road Rain; it's a goat trail! I wish we were on horseback. There isn't anything bothering me, I am just anxious. I know you're a good driver and I trust you with our lives. Perhaps I should get out and walk for a while?"

"I don't think so Babe. We are over half way there now and I promise you'll laugh when you recall your trepidation of this so called road to everyone back home."

"You are not succeeding at relieving my anxiety, but thanks for trying. I should have taken a pill, but who thought the road would be this bad or I would have a meltdown. Just get **us** there safely Rain. I think I will find another way out of this country."

"You think so eh? I'll get us there safe and sound; no need to worry about that."

"I wish I was back home in Scotland. My angst is most disturbing; I'm sorry Darling."

"If it's any consolation I wasn't expecting the road to be so steep and rough myself. I guess I should have paid more attention to the elevation on the map… not that it would have made any difference anyhow; we are, in the heart of the Pyrenees after all."

"Maybe if you went a little slower I would feel better."

"If I went any slower we'd be stopped."

Vienna sighed in resignation. She sat in silence. Rainey decided it was best not to try and engage her in conversation. Half an hour later he checked the mileage and realized they were within twelve kilometers of Nazeth. He pulled over assuming that they would be able to see Nazeth from atop the hill. He told her they were stopping for a minute.

"Why, is something wrong with the car?"

"No, I need a break. Sit tight and I will come and open your door."

"I'm perfectly capable of opening my own door." She said irritably.

By the time he got around to her side she was already out standing with her hands clutching her stomach. "Do you feel ill, or are you just angry with me?"

"Angry with you…of course I am for it is your fault that we are here in the first place and you're to blame for the state of the road. How small minded do you think I am?"

He told her she wasn't and he had broad shoulders so if she wanted to vent she could.

He took her hand and coaxed her to walk with him to the crest of the hill.

"Oh Rainey, we're here! Tell me that is Nazeth down there? It's beautiful!"

The small hamlet nestled comfortably in the arms of the Pyrenees was before them.

"I surely hope it is Nazeth because I don't think I can stand another minute of your ire."

"Do I exasperate you Rain?"

"Who…you? I would be lying if I said no. You are a force to contend with at times but I wouldn't have it any other way for then I get to hold you like this and you're all teary and apologetic." He pushed the hair back off her face and kissed her. "Now there's the girl that I love all safe and sound."

"Safe but I am not too sure how sound. We are very grateful Rainey."

"Oh we are, are we? Since when do you refer to yourself as 'we' Missy?"

"Since there are two of us."

He held her a little away from him and looked beseeching into her eyes. She smiled.

"I wanted to tell you at home but I can't wait any longer…it's happened Rain, we are going to have a baby."

"You little minx! Now I know why you were so apprehensive. I wish you would have told me before…I wouldn't have been so hard on you. How long have you known?"

"You weren't hard on me Sweetheart and I'm sorry I was such a worry wart. I only found out a few days before we left. If I had of told you then chances are that we wouldn't be here today, am I right?"

"Yes, we definitely would not have made this arduous trek. Did the rough road upset you and the baby…do you feel nauseous?"

"No, I am not. Are you happy Rainey?"

"Do you have to ask? I know how much you want to have another child and I get to go through this pregnancy with you is somewhat of a miracle. I get to raise our daughter with you right from the get go…it will be a girl right? Yes my darling, I am very happy."

"Not any child Rainey…yours and mine, and yes, I'm pretty sure it will be a girl."

"I already have two boys and so a little girl will be wonderful and especially if she looks like her mother. I warn you though that I am going to dote on you. There will be no stair climbing or horseback riding or hanky panky." He said grinning.

"We'll see about the stairs and horseback riding, but the other, I hardly doubt it." "Oh really…but I am going to pamper you my lady and you are going to enjoy it and so am I. Have I told you how much I love you?"

"Not in the past two hours but as soon as we get bunked down I'll let you show me." Vienna promised. "Now let's get off this mountaintop."

At the bottom of the hill they encountered a number of small farms on each side of the road. The houses appeared to be built up against the hillsides. They all had steep slate roofs and were constructed of brick and logs. Most of them had sheep and cattle grazing in the fields. The fences were made of rough timbers. Chickens, ducks and geese ran wildly in front of them.

"Have you been here before Rainey?" Vienna asked unexpectedly.

Rainey looked at her and asked why she would ask such a bizarre question.

"Because I have been here before and I was hoping that it had been with you." She said.

Rainey sucked in his breath. Here we go again he thought to himself. "Is this one of your déjà vu moments hon?"

They passed by a very old church standing all alone on a hill just before they entered Nazeth. It added to the tranquility and peacefulness of the old world village.

"Yes," Vienna repeated. "I have definitely been here before."

Rainey didn't comment.

"Here is the Pyrenees' Inn that was in the brochure; shall we see if they have a room?"

"Sounds good to me. I would just as soon get settled before we wander around."

He parked on the side of the building on a pebbled lot. The Pyrenees's Inn was rustic which suited Vienna fine as she wasn't looking for anything fancy. A young girl was sitting on a chesterfield reading a magazine and looked up as the cowbell over the door alerted her to customers. She got up and welcomed them saying she certainly hadn't been expecting anyone today.

"Oh, I am jumping to conclusions; pardon me. Perhaps you don't want a room at all?"

Her name tag read "Althea". Rainey laughed and told her they indeed wanted a room if there was vacancy. He was pleased that she spoke English.

"To be sure Sir, we have rooms. Tourist season is all but over for the time being and except for a few rooms rented out to a road crew, we are empty."

"Did you say road crew Althea? Well we certainly didn't encounter any on our trip!"

"You must have come from La Vella did you? Yes, that road is a sorry mess. They are working on the west this week and then I suppose they will get to the east; one can only hope before the snows fly. I imagine your trip wasn't very pleasant?"

Vienna smiled slightly. "It wasn't that bad was it Rainey?"

"My wife jests…she hated it. Now what do you have to offer us? We will probably be here for a few days depending on how much luck we have finding what we came for."

"If you want to view the mountains and the village I have the perfect room for you."

They followed her up to the second floor where she showed them to a comely room.

"This is just perfect Althea. I will rest while you retrieve the luggage Rainey."

"Good idea Hon. I'll just see to the bill and be right back."

On the way down the stairs Rainey asked Althea if she had ever heard the name Carvarra. She said she hadn't but it didn't mean anything as she didn't live here and that this was the first year that she had come to work for her aunt at the inn. She could ask around if he liked because her aunt wouldn't be back for a few days. Rainey told her it wasn't necessary as they could do that themselves.

Vienna greeted him with a big hug when he returned. "I feel so at home here Rainey. This room is furnished almost exactly like the way we did LizBeth's old room right down to the brass bed and vintage rocking chair. Come look." She pulled him into the bathroom. "An antique claw footed tub just like the one at the Palace in Bridge! I can hardly wait to climb into it and get this dust off me."

"Go ahead then Honey and I will be only too delighted to shampoo your hair."

"I think that is best left for later for I won't want to leave afterwards. I will try and make myself presentable for now as I am absolutely famished."

"I must admit I am rather hungry myself. Althea told me that we might like to try the FrenSpai restaurant as it is the best one open right now. Apparently, this is the time of year when the town closes up for a while. The summer crowd is gone and the snow people won't arrive for several months."

"Fren what…that's an unusual name?"

"Not wanting to offend the French or the Spanish, the owner named it after both countries and the fare is of both countries plus local cuisine. I'm not too sure how politically involved France and Spain are in Andorra's government or if they are at all anymore. This small state is governed by an Executive Council; each parish, and I think the principality has seven and each has their own mayor."

"And you know this because…?"

"I did a little research for I wanted to make sure I wasn't bringing you to an uncivilized country. So far so good except for the road but we have our own share of bad roadways back home as I am sure every country does. It was just our luck to arrive after a torrential rain storm."

"You are right as usual Rainey. Do I look presentable enough to go out on the town?"

"Are you trying to impress anyone else besides me?"

"Don't be silly. Let's go before I fade away…yeah, like that is ever going to happen. Pretty soon I am going to get really fat. Last time I lost weight because of my depression, but that won't be happening this time because you'll be with me won't you Rainey? My God, I actually said the D word and didn't have a conniption fit."

"Yes, you did, and I look forward to every pound you might gain for it would mean that you and the baby are healthy. I will never be very far from your side you can be assured of that. What did Dr. Mac have to say about your pregnancy?"

"He said that many women who are much older than me give birth without any complications and if I keep eating healthy and exercise I should have no problem. I need to pick up my vitamins as soon as we get home. Do you think I should take a jacket?"

"Yes, my little mother you should. It probably cools off here very quickly."

"This is going to be so much fun having you around to take care of me. I am so lucky."

As they exited the Inn they noted that there was a small health clinic and Laundromat across the street. The lawn alongside of the Inn was in dire need of a manicure. Colorful geraniums and petunias cascaded out of old wine barrels. Rainey asked Vienna if she had the energy to take a little stroll around the town. She said she thought that she could manage. They took a right and climbed up a few steps unto a wooden sidewalk that went down one side of Alpine Avenue. The narrow roadway was a mix of cobblestones and paving bricks and looked very rough. Rustic flower boxes overflowing with pansies, marigolds, nasturtiums and trailing vines stood outside the storefronts. Most of the businesses had signs displaying their hours of operation but were closed until November or December. They passed by Kellian's Bar and Grill that advertised a games room. A sporting goods store, a boutique and a variety store were next in line. At the end of the avenue was a small bank that was only open on Thursdays and Fridays. The Town Park and school stood atop Castilian hill at the south end of town. There appeared to be a dozen or so homes behind the school grounds. They crossed over to the other side and peeked around the corner of the Cotillion Hotel to see another street. A boarding house, hostel, tiny library and community hall ran the length of the gravel road which bore the name Nazeth Drive. They could barely make out a service station and grocery market half way down Castilian Hill. They continued past the hotel, a coffee shop, barber shop, bakery and liquor outlet…all closed. Next to the FrenSpai restaurant was a hardware and general store. It was a grey structure created out of large brick blocks. All of the stores appeared to have residences above them. Nazeth Drive continued down another cobblestone road and disappeared over an embankment. Alpine Avenue came to a halt at the intersection between the hardware store and the inn. Spent wildflowers covered a steep bank that led into a forested area. They could hear the sound of running water.

"This is an odd little town isn't it Rainey? It appears as if it just sprung up between the mountains. They certainly made good use of the little area of flat land. I wonder what is over the bank next to the community hall and do you think Castilian Hill leads out of town… it must be the way west. You know, in a way Nazeth reminds me of home."

"You mean Scotland? I really don't see any resemblance Honey."

"No, not Scotland…Canada. I've been in many mountainous small towns over there."

"I didn't know you still considered Canada your home."

"I do Rainey, and someday, when Rosy or Ava, but I suspect it will be Rosy, decides to become the true mistress of Avanloch, I want to grow old in Bridge at the Palace. Would you like that Rainey?"

"I would, but as long as I am with you it doesn't matter where I hang my hat. Now what do you say we have that long awaited meal?"

They were greeted by a tall slim young man who told them they could sit wherever they wanted. They choose a table by the window and sat down together on one side.

"Good afternoon, I suppose I should say evening. What brings such a charming couple to our little hamlet so late in the season if I may be so bold to inquire?"

His name tag stated that his name was James and Rainey addressed him as such.

"Yes you may James. Vienna, my beautiful wife, and I are combining our honeymoon with a mission to find a beneficiary to an inheritance and that has led us here to your quaint little village. Are you familiar with the name Carvarra?"

"No Sir, the name does not ring any bells for me, but then I only work here during the summer and so most of the people I meet are tourists. My uncle will be in tomorrow morning and so I am sure he can help you as he has lived here his whole life."

"Call me Rainey, and this is Vienna."

"Very pleased to meet you Vienna; what an enchanting name. Were you named for the Austrian city or Vienne, France? I am of French heritage and so hope it is Vienne."

Vienna laughed. "Thank you James. Funny that you should ask as my husband thinks so also, but I am pretty sure that my mother named me after the Austrian city."

"Do I detect a Scottish accent?"

"Rainey and I are both Canadian but I have been living in Scotland for twenty years. I suppose I have picked up some of their inflections."

"Ah Canada, I hope to travel there someday. I hear it is most friendly and beautiful."

"Not any more so than right here. Where do you hail from James? Your English is impeccable." Rainey remarked.

"I have been attending Cambridge College in London for three years as someday I will hopefully become a translator for the United Nations. I speak several other languages as well as French and Castilian. I am from a small town in France called Muret."

"I am sure you will James and may we convey our best wishes for your success. We have something in common as our daughters also attend college in London." Rainey remarked with pride.

"It's a small world isn't it sir? Perhaps we have even met…your daughters and me? But now I must bring you a celebration complimentary bottle of wine. What would be your pleasure?" James asked.

He either didn't notice or was too polite to comment on the fact that if they were on their honeymoon, how they could have daughters of college age. Rainey stated that Vienna didn't drink and so he would just have one glass of wine and she would have coffee. She reminded him that it was time for her to give up caffeine and so she would have a club soda.

"Sorry Darling, I guess the coffee we bought in Spain will have to wait awhile."

James brought them menus with their drinks. They ordered the house specialty which was a savory stew made from local game. It was accompanied by a garden salad and fresh biscuits and cheesecake for dessert. Vienna wanted to start with dessert.

After James left with their orders Rainey said' "See, even James, who is a stranger had asked if you were named after the city Vienne in France."

"And again I say, I don't think so, and what would it matter? Remember, I have an "a" at the end of my name?"

"Well your dad is French and for all we know he or his family was from Vienne. Your mother may have added the 'a' for she didn't want it to be French. Just saying, it is possible and you will ask your dad right?"

"I will if only to satisfy your curiosity. Would you rather that my name be Vienne?"

"No, of course not; I love your name. Here's James …let's ask him about the town."

James was able to answer all their questions. Yes, Castilian Hill led out of town to several more farms, past the supermarket and garage and to Verdarra which was the town to the west. It also led to the ranger station, ski hill, lodge and hot springs. The granite road beyond Nazeth Drive curved down and around and ended at an old monastery.

"Hot springs…we must go there Rainey!" Vienna exclaimed.

"We will if we have time. I am more interested in the old monastery right now. What can you tell us about it James? Surely it is not in operation as such?"

"Hardly, the residence was demolished many years ago. Time and weather had taken its toll on the hand hewn log building. The foundation had all but sunk into the ground. For the safety of the public it was torn down and burned sometime around the turn of the century. Only the church survived due to the fact that it was made of stone and only connected to the rectory by a covered walkway. However, it has been out of bounds to all for quite some time I am told. Several years ago the Catholic Diocese decided that it was of some importance in history and that it should be resurrected. A team arrived last summer and shored the place up so it was deemed safe. A caretaker was assigned but the public was still not allowed entrance. Recently, a priest by the name of Father Bissette was sent to oversee further renovations and to conduct services. The only other church in town is the Lady of Peace and it is Protestant. I am certain that most of the inhabitants are of the Catholic faith and were happy to see the church offering mass again. That is about all I can tell you. I have met the priest and his lackey, Sandez. He is a regular here partaking of drink almost daily."

"Thank you James, you are a good ambassador for the town. We are interested in the early history as it may hold a key to our quest. Would you know off hand if there are any archives around?" Rainey inquired.

"There are no city offices so to speak, but the community center houses any information that is pertinent to the town. I would suggest you visit with the priest for I have heard through the gossip mongers that ancient manuscripts have been uncovered. Makes for a little intrigue wouldn't you say?"

"Yes indeedy. We have taken up enough of your time and should let you get back to other things."

Vienna had gone to the ladies room and Rainey jokingly told James that he would love a cup of coffee but it wouldn't be fair to her so he had better not have one.

"I have just the thing for her Sir and I don't think she would begrudge you one cup." He hurried off and returned with two steaming cups and set one down in front of Vienna. "Chamomile and lavender tea for the lady and a nightcap for you sir."

Rainey tried not to laugh but couldn't help it. Seeing the stunned look on James's face he explained that Vienna hated tea.

"This is no ordinary tea and I guarantee you will like it Vienna."

Politely, she took a sip and then another and smiled. "You are right James; this is not that horrible tasting stuff I am usually subjected to. Lavender…did I not taste it in the cheesecake also?"

"You did. The people of Andorra eat healthy and live long and lavender is baked into most goods. It is supposed to help with digestion and of course is known for its aid in sleeping. Be sure to take some buds and dried petals home with you."

"We grow it in Scotland but I have not had it in tea before. It is quite lovely. Thank you and please excuse Rainey's rudeness."

"There is no need as he was only looking out for your wellbeing."

They said goodnight and Rainey left a huge tip which James protested was far too much.

Rainey woke up the next morning to Vienna jumping up and down on the bed and jubilantly enticing him to wake up. "Get up, get up Rainey! It's time to get going!"

He reached for her managing to get hold of her nightie and pulled her down on the bed.

"Really, what's the hurry?" He looked at her and grinned.

"Don't look at me! No, it serves you right for making me come to bed last night with wet hair. Do I remind you of the wicked witches from your childhood nightmares?"

"Oh yes, you are very wicked. How about showing me just how much?"

"Later Darling; you said you want to get me home as soon as possible right? Well, the sooner we get going the sooner we'll be home. You shower while I try to do something with my hair okay?"

"Can't you just lie with me for a few minutes?"

"All right, a few minutes and that's all, my spoiled baby." Vienna nestled in with her back to him.

He put his hands on her stomach and gently caressed it. "So this is where you are keeping our little bundle of joy is it?"

"Yes it is my darling and I promise that I will keep her safe."

"I know you will. When you first told me that you wanted to have a child with me I wasn't very enthused and doubted that it would happen anyhow. But now, and especially from having Tanny around, I am truly delighted. I am going to take very good care of the two of you. I love you Vienna LaFontaine and have never been so happy."

"I love you Rainey Quinn. I will never love anyone the way that I love you."

Jokingly he said. "Well I certainly hope not for that would mean that I would be gone and I am not going anywhere, not ever."

"Promise? Rainey, you don't think that we are tempting the fates do you?"

"I promise, but what's this about the fates? You're not having feelings of uneasiness again are you?"

"No. I am so contented that it scares me a little. We better get a move on Rain."

After a quick European breakfast of fruit and croissants with blackberry preserves that Althea had set out for them, they left the inn for the village. They didn't get very far when Vienna asked Rainey where the camera was. He asked her if they really needed it and she said they might.

"All right, I'll go back for it. You wait right here for me okay?"

She said she would. Rainey ran up the stairs and grabbed the camera. For some reason he looked out the window that stared down at Alpine Avenue. Vienna was crossing the cobblestone street. He shook his head and said out loud that he should have known better than to believe she was going to stay put and wait for him. She turned and gazed directly at the window and waved to him and then she turned and he watched her walk away. He smiled and then a visualization from years ago flooded his senses and he started for the door crying "Vienna… no, no!"

He was stopped momentarily by a thunderous blast that rocked the building. "What the hell was that? Must be the road crew blasting." He attempted to reach the stairs but another explosion halted him again. This one was louder and sounded like a hundred gas tanks exploding. The walls seemed to be closing in on him. He managed to stay erect fighting off queasiness as the steps rose up to greet him. "Vienna, Vienna, I'm coming."

He had no idea how much time had elapsed since he had seen Vienna at the window until he reached the bottom of the stairs. He glanced at his watch; it was 9 A.M. That was crazy…where had the last twenty minutes gone? He was perplexed, but a whimpering snapped him back to reality. Where was Althea? He had past her on the stairs when he went to retrieve the camera. He found her cowering in the corner of the lobby among broken glass and odds and ends from the curio cabinet. He coaxed her to get up.

She was trembling. "What was **that** Mr. Quinn?"

"I think it was an earthquake." He stammered. "Is there anyone else in the hotel?"

She told him that there wasn't.

He convinced her to come out into the yard. He took her far away from the inn and told her to stay there until someone came for her. She had a vacant look in her eyes and he followed her stare as she pointed down the street. A cloud of dust hung over the once serene village. The big grey building was gone. It appeared to have collapsed in on itself. He had last seen Vienna by the store before she rounded the corner and disappeared out of sight. A deafening siren was sounding. His feet felt like lead as he made his way down the street. He tried to pick up the pace, but he couldn't. He heard the sound of gushing water and looked up to see where a fissure had appeared atop the wall of wild flowers and a trickle of water was streaming down unto Alpine Avenue and into a gaping hole that had opened up in the cobblestones. People were screaming and running around furiously. Half the buildings were in shambles; debris was still filtering down. Rainey saw two people in an upstairs apartment clinging to the rafters of the floor below them. He noticed smoke spewing out from the back of the FrenSpai restaurant. He rushed to Nazeth Drive just as the road crew arrived with a back hoe, dump truck and front end loader. He told them of possible flooding of the whole town if the creek was not diverted. James arrived and was visually stunned at the carnage. Rainey shook him and told him to get it together and get the fire under control. He couldn't stay to help because he had to find Vienna. He left James asking questions but had no time to answer them.

He ran frantically from building to building calling out her name. He overturned everything that he came into contact with. All the structures on Nazeth Drive seemed to be intact, but he stumbled through them in case Vienna had taken refuge in one of them. She was nowhere. This was crazy…why had she scurried off without waiting for him?

A sickening feeling came over him as he rounded the corner. Was it possible that she lay beneath the rubble of the grey building?

He started to claw at the bricks and picking them up threw them as far as he could. Soon others were taking up the plight with him. The whole population of the area came to pitch in. Farmers arrived with their tractors and trucks and loaded up the bricks and debris. Rainey enlisted someone to shut off the ear-piercing siren. James came to work beside him and Rainey asked him to go and find Althea. He had told her not to leave and she was probably still there, alone and scared.

Six hours later a search and rescue team arrived, but they were ultimately too late. The townspeople had the job done. They had worked relentlessly until every brick was discarded. Among the rubble the bodies of Shelly and Ames Credence were found. Three others lost their lives when the buildings they were in collapsed; Six others sustained non-life threatening injuries and two had been air lifted out. Vienna was not among the injured or the deceased. She had simply vanished. Rainey at long last sat down and wept.

A huge forestry tent had been erected for temporary shelter for those who required assistance. An outdoor kitchen had been set up and a steady stream of food began arriving from the locals. Water was not a problem as the town well had not been damaged. It appeared as though the earthquake had only wrecked havoc with north Alpine Avenue. The businesses and the school at the south end of town had no substantial damage. Homeowners and farmers also reported no damage. The old monastery had not fared as well.

Rainey lifted his heavy head as he heard a commotion coming from behind him. James sat down beside him and explained that the bodies of Father Bissette and Sandez had been brought down from the Catholic Church. Sandez's crushed body had been found in a pool of blood on the seat of his truck that had come to rest against a tree part way up the hill. The old priest had been found on the steps of the rectory with no apparent injuries. The consensus was that he may have suffered a fatal heart attack. James assured Rainey that the ruins and the forests had been searched thoroughly and there was no sign of Vienna anywhere. Rainey wanted to check the area out for himself and James said he would go with him. Franklin, the junior ranger offered to accompany them.

Rainey was surprised to see how steep the bank was and had a vision of Vienna falling down the precipice…just like in his dreams of long ago. There was a slow, narrow body of water flowing at the bottom. He stopped and peered over the rock face. Franklin told him that although the banks had been searched a team of sniffer dogs was arriving in the morning. He asked if Rainey was contemplating the idea that Mrs. Quinn may have drowned even though the river was very shallow and slow moving.

"No, Vienna is incapable of drowning." Rainey said soberly. "I do welcome the idea of the dogs and I will supply their handlers with whatever they require."

James wondered what Rainey meant by the statement of drowning but said nothing.

After searching the grounds around the church and finding nothing, Rainey ventured into the building itself. He was warned that it may be unstable but he didn't care. He entered calling out Vienna's name. James decided to join him as he was sure his new friend was not thinking straight and may take unnecessary chances. They left no stone unturned, but came up cold. She was not in the church, cellars or sleeping quarters.

Down trodden they returned to the town site. Althea was waiting for them and convinced Rainey and James to come back to the inn with her as there was nothing more to be done today. It was 6 P.M. He agreed saying that he had to get hold of his daughter.

Ava was humming as she strolled through her mother's rose garden. She was picking a fresh bouquet to take to Rosalyn in London. She had all her bags packed and had decided to leave a day early to spend it with her sister. She was still in a quandary over the phone call she had received earlier in the day. Dr. Mac had mistaken her for her mother informing her that her pre natal vitamins were ready for her and would she pick them up or should he courier them to her. Ava neglected to tell him who she was but thanked him and said she would pick them up. Mama and Rainey are going to have a baby…I'm going to have another sister. She smiled at the prospect wondering if she should tell anyone.

The day was seasonally warm with nary a breeze. She had taken Barrett and Browning and the two new pups, Bronte and Austen for a long walk winding through the meadows.

She remembered how pleased her mother had been when she learned that Johnny had named the new dogs after two of her favorite authors. They had a huge reputation to live up to if they were going to follow in the paw prints of Shelley and Keats. She and Rosy had grown up with the dogs that had once belonged to Maveryn. Her mother had taken a page from Rosy's mother and called the new additions Barrett and Browning after famous poets. Now there were two new dogs to carry on the legacy.

She had just returned the shears to the garden shed when a strong gust of wind bore down on her. "Now where did that come from?" She had no sooner passed through the arbor when she heard a crash. She turned and found the "V" from "Vienna's Garden" plaque had fallen to the ground. She picked it up and placed it with the shears reminding herself to inform Johnny of the mishap.

She was too excited to be hungry but to appease the cooks she ate a small dinner. Lois and Mary were already complaining that there would be no one to cook for and the house was going to be empty. Ava reminded them that they were supposed to be on holidays but they both scoffed at the notion. Ava shook her head and thanked them for dinner.

She wandered aimlessly through the castle smiling as she reminded herself of her mother's midnight jaunts. She encountered Johnny in the grand reception hall and asked him what he was doing working so late. He explained that the women of the house were watching some tear jerker movie on the telly and he had been feeling restless and decided to return and repair a damaged door jamb. Ava told him she was feeling the same way. She continued on down the hall. The telephone rang and she answered the one that was on the wall between the formal dining room and the games room.

"Hello."

"Ava, is that you Honey?"

The voice on the other end of the line was Rainey, but he sounded funny.

"Hi Rainey, I think we have a bad connection. Is there any news? Where's Mama?"

"She's gone Ava…I'm so sorry…I lost her." Rainey was sobbing.

Ava couldn't breathe. What was he saying? "What's wrong with you Rainey? Put Mama on the phone."

"I can't Ava; she's not here. I can't find her. There was an earthquake…."

Ava screamed and fell to the floor.

Johnny heard the piercing scream. "What the hell?" He dropped the chisel and ran down the hall and found Ava sitting on the floor crying hysterically; the phone was dangling off its hook. Mrs.D arrived at the doorway.

"Get Amma here right away Mary. I don't know what has happened but it can't be anything good to have Ava in such a state."

He put one hand on her quivering shoulder and picked up the receiver with the other.

"Who is this?" He yelled into the mouthpiece.

"Johnny, its Rainey…where's Ava, is she all right?"

"No, she is not all right. What the hell did you say to her?"

"Vienna's gone Johnny. She's disappeared."

It was difficult to understand what Rainey was saying. There was static on the line and Rainey sounded as if he had been drinking. Ava was sobbing relentlessly. Mrs.D had set off the main alarm alerting the estate and the village to disaster. The sound was ominous.

"Rainey, what the hell are you saying?"

"There was an earthquake…I let her out of my sight for two minutes and I lost her Johnny. She's gone; she's gone." Rainey was sobbing.

"Rainey, are you saying that Vienna is dead?"

Ava screamed. Damn it, why did I have to say dead? Johnny asked himself while trying to comfort Ava. He wasn't having any luck.

Rainey sounded a bit more composed. "There are bodies, but hers is not among them. I've searched…we've all searched. She's not here, she's just gone."

Johnny was suddenly hopeful. "You mean she's missing?"

"Yes, she just disappeared…the angels have her."

"The angels? You're not making any sense Rainey."

"Nothing makes any sense. I can't lose her again Johnny. I don't know what to do."

Johnny tried to reason with him saying that she had to be somewhere. They must have overlooked something. He heard the door slam and footsteps running down the hall. He didn't have time to ask Amma how she got there so fast but explained to her briefly what had happened and went back on the line with Rainey. He got his exact location and the number where he could be reached. He scribbled it on the message board hanging beside the phone. He told Rainey that as soon as he got off the phone he was going to contact Evan and they would all fly out tomorrow.

Rainey told him that they couldn't land the plane in Nazeth and Johnny said he would let Evan worry about that.

"I need to talk to Ava Johnny."

"Rainey wants to talk to you Ava… can you manage?"

Amma helped her up and said through her own tears. "Your dad needs you Honey."

Ava nodded and said she would try. "Rainey, can you hold on 'til tomorrow? We'll be there as soon as we can."

"I'm so sorry Ava…I'm so sorry."

"It's not your fault Daddy. We'll find her; we have to. I love you Daddy."

"I love you Ava. I can't lose her Ava…I just can't."

Amma caught Ava before she collapsed again. Mrs.D arrived with a pitcher of water and the two of them led the grief stricken girl into the den. Amma told Mary that she didn't have all of the facts but told her what little she had surmised. Mary told her there was a mob of villagers in the yard and they would have to be told something. She left sobbing and mumbling and wringing her hands as she shuffled down the hall.

Johnny made sure that Ava was all right and went into the office to find Evan's number. Rosy answered and Johnny cursed. He decided to give the bare facts to Evan and let him deal with Rosy. He couldn't do it right now. He heard Evan gasp and Rosy asking what was wrong. Johnny said that he and Ava would drive straight through to London and could Evan make the flight plans. Evan told him that they would do no such thing and that he would pick them up in Waverly at first light the next morning and then they would fly straight to Andorra. He would handle all the details, but make sure they brought their papers.

Johnny dialed the number in Nazeth; a female voice answered. "It's for you Mr. Quinn."

As soon as he hung up Rosy called. He passed the phone to Ava and he and Amma left. Arm and arm they went out to greet the mob of villagers who had gathered in the driveway wondering why the general alarm had sounded. Johnny told them the bare facts as that was all he had and hopefully he would know more when he met up with Rainey. He explained that he and the girls were flying out to Nazeth tomorrow morning. No one uttered a word but the cries and hang dog faces said it all. There wasn't a soul among them that didn't love Vienna. Johnny beckoned Reverend Peters to lead them in a prayer for her safe return. The crowd reluctantly dispersed with Jacob Peters promising to hold prayer services for however long it took and pledged that updates would be posted daily.

Amma and Johnny found Ava still in the den talking to Rosalyn.

"I love you Rosy. I'm so glad you have Evan. Are you sure you can handle talking to Ash and Jannie? I'll try and get through to Lily and Papa Joe. Until tomorrow my darling sister…I don't know how I am going to get through the night."

"The same way we all will Ava…with great difficulty." Amma put her arms around Ava and said she would help her pack.

Ava laughed coldly. "I'm already packed Amma… I was going to go and see Cam."

"I know Sweetie, I know. Let me help you repack for you won't be needing all those clothes you were going to take to Canada."

The two left and Johnny went in to talk to the McDuffs and Lois before he went home to pack a few things for himself. His three girls were sitting at the kitchen table. They came running to him crying. He enclosed them in his arms and apologized for neglecting them at such a sorrowful time. He reiterated what he knew trying to sound hopeful.

Amma offered to stay the night with Ava but she refused saying that her girls would need her. "I'm going to sleep in Mama's room and I have to make a few more phone calls. I will be all right Amma, please don't worry. Tomorrow I will be with Rosy and Rainey. It's not going to be easy and I will try and be brave."

Amma offered to call her grandparents and Ava agreed to that. She thanked Amma and asked her to look after the McDuffs for her mom was like a daughter to them. She made her way slowly to her parent's bedroom where she flung herself down and cried into her mother's pillow. "Don't leave us Mama …please don't leave us."

After she calmed down she reached for the telephone and dialed a number. A sleepy voice answered. "Jimmy, its Ava. Oh Jimmy, something terrible has happened."

At 5 A.M. Johnny and Ava were ready to leave for Waverly. Mary McDuff saw Ava to the car and made her promise to call as soon as she arrived in Andorra. Amma was clinging to Johnny and trying not to cry.

He held her away from him. "Look at me Amma. I need you to keep it together here. Can you do that for me Honey? I need to know that you are going to be able to handle things; you have the girls to think about. Leave the rest up to Wesley and Nannette; it's time they proved their worth. I love her too you know."

"I know you do Johnny. I'll be good, I promise."

An hour and a half later they were seated in the Cessna Skywagon. This was the model 180J that held five passengers. Evan had cut his teeth on the Cessna 180, a high wing light aircraft in Australia when he was employed as a bush pilot. Johnny sat next to him in the cockpit. The girls huddled in the back and said a prayer as they took off.

Chapter 7

Verde El Mar Spain
September 7th

Antonio glanced at the clock and wondered how it was only 2 P.M. He continued to pace back and forth in the little visitor's room at Verde El Mar Hospital waiting for some news of the woman's condition. He sat down and put his head in his hands whispering "Dulce Madre de Dios" over and over again. "Sweet Mother of God, what have I done?"

He tried to piece together the ill-fated events that led up to his being here and anxiously awaiting word on his loyal friend and employee Constantine and this unknown woman.

He had been summoned the day before to a small town in Andorra by his great uncle, Father Joseph Bissette. The priest had been appointed to supervise renovations to a century old church that had once been a house of worship to a long forgotten order of Monks. The monastery had been demolished many years before but it had been decided by the hierarchy that the church was still worth saving. Father Bissette was his French mother's uncle and had taken Antonio under his wing when he was a rebellious adolescent. The old Priest and his devoted assistant had uncovered some scrolls in an underground tunnel that they thought would be of great interest to Antonio in his never-ending quest. Anton had been in the dank cellars of the church examining the fragile parchment rolls when the first tremor brought him to his knees.

"Sacre bleu, what is this?" He staggered to his feet and blindly headed for the steps just as the lights flickered and went out. He heard his uncle calling for him. "I am in the basement Father; bring a lamp s'il vous plait."

The door opened as another tremor rocked the old cathedral. He crawled up the rickety stairs to the sound of his uncle's voice directing him. The priest grabbed him and steered him towards the outside door. Anton was not satisfied with the documents he had saved and tried to retrieve the rest from the vestibule.

"Leave them, leave them my Son. There is no time; we must leave before the walls collapse on us." Father Bissette cried. "Come quickly."

Antonio grabbed what he could manage and ran out the door and down the steps. He realized his uncle was not with him and turned and seen the old man clutching his chest just before he fell to the ground. Anton tried to coax him to get up but it was too late; he was gone. Somner, his pilot and friend, begged Anton to leave the priest as there was nothing they could do. Anton said a somber prayer and started for the helicopter that was already fired up for take off.

"Constantine… where is Constantine?" He asked.

"He has not returned from the village. He and the priest's helper Sandez went to get supplies and have not returned. We cannot wait Sir…if there is another shock wave we may not make it out of here. You do not want to risk being seen do you?"

"We can not leave without Connie…listen, I hear a vehicle. Yes, here it comes. What is that fool Sandez doing?"

They watched in horror as the truck sputtered and weaved its way over the rough cobblestones. It came to a stop and then rolled backwards coming to rest up against a tree. They ran down the road and found a bleeding Sandez lying across the body of Constantine. Sandez was dead. Anton pulled the semi conscious Connie up and was startled to see that he had been shielding a woman. "Save her Sir…save Katarina."

"Anton, are you all right? Is there any word of Constantine or the woman?" Somner was at the door and had startled Anton who was still in a daze.

"Yes, Connie is stable; I do not know about the woman yet. Are you cleared with the airport officials…did they ask why you didn't follow procedures?"

"No, they let the condition of the patients speak for themselves."

"Were they not curious as to where they had sustained their injuries?"

"They did not keep me as they knew that I wanted to get to the hospital. I am sure there will be questions. Have you come up with a plausible answer yet?"

"I am working on it." Anton stood up as a young nurse entered the room.

"Senor DeMarco, would you like to see your wife?"

Somner looked at Anton in bewilderment. Had the nurse said "wife?" Anton asked him to go and sit with Connie while he accompanied the nurse to Katarina's room. Had Anton told the hospital that the woman was his wife…that didn't make any sense? Maybe Connie had some answers for him…

Anton stood gazing down at the still woman's body. Her small hands were lying on top of the bedding; they were cut and dried blood still clung to them. She was not wearing a wedding ring or any other jewelry. He couldn't remember if she had any on before. Her face was drained of any color; her eyes were closed. Someone had attempted to wash the blood from her face and in doing so had exposed the many abrasions she had suffered. Her long copper hair lay matted and tangled on the pillow. Even so, she looked peaceful. He leaned close to her and felt a faint breath escape from her lips. He looked at the nurse for assurance that she was indeed breathing.

"I will leave you Sir to be alone with your wife. The doctor will be with you soon."

When he heard the nurse close the door he ran his fingers gently down the sleeping woman's face. He was taken aback by the tingling he felt when he touched her. He sat in the chair next to her bed and took her hand in his and leaned his head down to kiss it. "Are you the one I have been searching for? Are you my Katarina, beautiful lady? Is it possible that you have found your way back to me after all these years? Are we the star-crossed lovers of yesteryear? If it be so, I pledge that it will end much differently for I shall not leave you…not ever."

"Anton, have you taken leave of your senses? This is not Katarina and you are not Anton Christoval! No good will come of this…have you had a knock on the head?"

"I thought I told you to sit with Connie! I am quite sane and I believe I was destined to find this lovely creature and to save her. You will see, she will awaken and know me."

They were interrupted by the doctor. He walked over to Anton and shook his hand. "You are one lucky man Senor DeMarco that you got your wife here so quickly. I am feared that if it had of been much longer she would have succumbed to her bodily injuries and loss of blood. We were able to stop the bleeding but she did lose a substantial amount and will require more transfusions. Are you up to recounting the accident now?"

"She was in a horrific car accident on the Isle of Rose. Luckily, I had access to a helicopter and rushed her here immediately as I am sure you are well aware that there is no hospital there. How soon will she regain consciousness?"

"We must remain vigilant. The first 72 hours are crucial. You must take care yourself."

"I will stay at her bedside for I have nowhere of any importance that I need to be."

Somner asked Dr. Mendez if Constantine would make a full recovery.

"He is not my patient but from what I understand his injuries were minimal and will be released in a day or two. We are still cautious as he may have suffered a concussion."

Anton asked if Katarina had also.

"In her case there is no way to tell and we have done limited x-rays due to her condition. Senor DeMarco. You are aware that your wife is pregnant, yes?"

There was no way that Anton could hide his shock. He stuttered. "No, I did not. Are the x-rays not a danger to the baby?"

"No, there is little risk of radiation as the fetus is only 3-4 weeks old. The pregnancy was discovered through a blood test but had we had the results prior to the discovery x-rays would still have been necessary. We will not deal with her hip and leg injury at the present time."

"Are there fractures there?" Anton asked worriedly.

"No, but we recovered pieces of unidentified slivers from her wounds. She will require surgery if the wounds don't heal on their own, but at a much later date. As I said all her vitals are acceptable for the trauma that she sustained and the only thing we can do now is to watch and wait. Perhaps it would be a good idea if you were to inform her family of her condition?"

"I am her only family. Thank you Dr. Mendez. I am somewhat assured and I am certain that Kat is in the best of hands. There is to be no expense spared do you understand?"

"You can be comforted to know that this is the most advanced and caring facility in the region. With your permission I should like to consult a colleague who leads the pack when it comes to head trauma. His name is Zinc Zaccaris and I can promise you that he will be most interested in this case."

With that Dr. Mendez took his leave and Anton returned to his vigil at Katarina's bed.

Somner walked over to the other side and confronted his friend again. "Anton, what is going on with you? For God's sake the woman has a husband; she is going to have his baby. Why, I ask you, why?"

"We do not know that she is married. She has no wedding ring and even if she is, where was he when the earth shook? No, I think she is alone and she is my responsibility now!"

"I talked to Connie and he had no answers only that she approached him and Sandez and said something about Katarina. That does not mean that **her** name is Katarina and even if it did, perhaps it is a very common name in Andorra. Think Anton…she is not **the** Kat that you think she is! That is just preposterous!"

"Look at her Somner, really look and then tell me that she does not resemble the photo."

Somner sighed. "Her face is battered and bruised…I see no resemblance what so ever."

"Does it not seem ominous to you that we went to that little hamlet to examine the scrolls father Bissette had found and we find this damsel who claims to be Katarina?"

"We know no such thing and perhaps never will as she may never wake up."

"How can you say such a cruel thing?"

"I am sorry Anton, but I am just facing facts. Where are the scrolls anyway? They were not on the plane. How had you the time to retrieve them?"

"They are safe; that is all you need to know. But now, I need you to return to Nazeth and find out what you can about this beautiful lady but be very secretive...I warn you."

Nazeth

James met the helicopter at the park that was carrying Rainey's family. It was almost noon. He identified himself and escorted them down Alpine Avenue to where his friend was waiting. Ava broke free from the pack as soon as she spotted her father sitting on a bench with several other people in front of a huge tent. He tried to muster a smile as she threw her arms around him and clung to him. Rosy caught up to them and encircled them both in her embrace. He tears flowed freely.

He hugged them as tightly as he could. "My girls, my darling girls... I am so sorry."

"You must not blame yourself Daddy. We know Mama is compulsive. It is not your fault she didn't wait for you. Please don't think we blame you." Ava sobbed.

Rainey patted her to comfort her but said. "I'll never forgive myself for going back for that damn camera! What did I think was going to become of this weekend? It was Labor day after all; nothing good ever happens then, nothing. It wasn't supposed to be this way. We were supposed to be together forever."

"You will be Rainey; we will all be together again. What crazy twist of fate led you two here on the precise day of an earthquake? We are to understand that there has never been one before, is that right?

It doesn't matter, it happened and we are going to find Mama…that is all there is to it!" Rosy stated emphatically more to assure herself then anyone else.

Rainey kept his hold on the girls but reached out and shook hands with Johnny and Evan and told them how much he appreciated them coming and that there were no words to say what it meant to him.

"You know we wouldn't be anywhere else Rain. It's lucky for us that Evan could fly us here and make all the arrangements with the airport in Andorra La Vella for a copter to drop us off here. James tells me that we are to follow him to the Pyrenees Inn where lunch is waiting and that we will be boarding there also. We can talk over a meal and coffee. I do say that you look like you could use some fortitude." Johnny stated.

"I suppose I look like hell." Rainey said feebly.

The girls walked arm and arm with him to the Inn not wanting to let go. They entered the lobby and were greeted by a lovely young girl. She told them her name was Althea and that she had made their rooms ready for them. She escorted them into a charming sitting room. Rosy commented that it looked like it was somebody's living room.

"It is." Althea told them. "The Inn belongs to my Auntie Chantel. It was once her home but once her husband passed away and the children moved off she turned it into a boarding house and now it is a hotel. The kind folks of the valley have been keeping those less fortunate fed and bedded. They knew you were all arriving today and have dropped buckets of home cooking off for you here. Take as much time as you need. Rainey, bring them in when you are ready."

"I think they have all had a long trip already and perhaps some nourishment is what we all need. It is going to be another long night waiting for the policia to report back to us on their findings or lack there of." Rainey led the pack into the dining room off the kitchen. Ava and Rosy sat on either side of him. Evan led the prayer for Vienna's safe return.

Althea and James had set the table with a variety of casseroles and breads that had been left by the people of Nazeth. Steaming cups of coffee were poured for everyone. Rainey took a sip of the hot brew and commented that Vienna would love it. He didn't eat much but pushed the food around on his plate just as a child might do.

Johnny pumped James and Althea for information about the vicinity around Nazeth. It did appear that there was no other way out except the one road to the west and the one to the east. The valley was indeed hemmed in by mountains and the only other way out would be by helicopter or by foot over the treacherous peaks. James assured them that the latter would be almost impossible as the few passable trails did not lead anywhere and were fit only for a mountain goat. Dessert was laid out just as several men dressed in blue uniforms entered the premises. They removed their hats and one asked if he could have a word with Mr. Quinn.

"Whatever you have to tell us, you can say to us all." Rainey said.

The Police Corps of Andorra had dispatched five law enforcement officers to conduct a thorough search of the area to locate survivors and to tend to any emergencies that may have arisen due to the unprecedented event. The officer in a charge, a Captain Albain, informed them that he and his officers along with the forest rangers had completed their door to door search. They assured the solemn group that nothing was left unturned. Every house and barn and vacant dwelling had been searched. The school, churches, apartments and businesses and even the Pyre Lodge and all of the chalets at the ski hill have been combed. No one was harboring Mrs. Quinn. There is no sign of her whatsoever. The dogs picked up her scent outside the inn but it ended at the corner or Alpine and Nazeth. We thought they found it again on the road to the old church where the caretaker's truck was found but that proved to be false."

"Why do you say that Captain? Did they pick up her scent or not?" Johnny questioned.

"It was a mistake. One of the rangers accidentally dropped Mrs. Quinn's scarf on the floor of the truck before the dogs arrived and that set them off. I have just now spoken to a scientist, a Monsieur Clarneau, from the Institute of Seismology in France, and he has no explanation to her disappearance either. He stated that the ground did not swallow anyone up as there are no fissures more than half a meter deep. I am sorry that we have failed at providing you with a solution but we will remain here for several more days and if there is something or someone to be found then we will do so. Good evening."

Johnny got up and said he would walk them to the door. He walked outside with them and said. "So, where do we go from here Captain?"

"As I said before, we will leave a team here for a few more days until every inch has been covered once again. We are not hopeful that we will find her; Mrs. Quinn has simply disappeared. If she had not been seen by several people I would be of the belief that she was never even here."

"She was here all right and there is only one other explanation and that is that Vienna Quinn has been abducted…wouldn't you agree Sir?"

"Do you think that we have not considered that possibility, but for what reason? Who would do such a thing and then there is the question *again*; how? The road crew ascertains that no vehicle or person passed them prior to the quake. The road to the east was compromised and so that lets that road off the hook."

"Surely, a four wheel drive could maneuver up and around the hillsides?" Johnny wasn't going to be put off that easily.

"No Sir, that is not possible. There would have been fresh signs and there just aren't any. No fences have been disturbed behind the farms and the residents have all assured us that there was no traffic on the day in question. There is no conspiracy; they all tell the same story. This is a very secluded valley Mr. O'Shea. I am afraid we have exhausted the possibilities." Captain Albain asserted.

"Then there is only one possibility isn't there Captain…Vienna was flown out?"

"We have considered that, but there was no helicopter stationed here and surely it would have been noticed landing and taking off."

"But yet, she has vanished, has she not? She has not been found anywhere; you say she could not have fallen down the embankment for it has been searched by both man and dog and she couldn't have drowned for the river is shallow and is damned and so nobody could have passed by. Perhaps the copter had been here prior to the earthquake, have you considered that? And, I doubt that anyone would have heard it taking off amongst all the commotion. No, that is the only plausible explanation…Vienna was airlifted out." Johnny stated emphatically.

Captain Albain continued to doubt. "Mr. O'Shea, you make a good argument; but to what gain? Does Mrs. Quinn have enemies? Has there been an attempt on her life before? Who would benefit from her disappearance and why on earth would they chose to kidnap her in this remote part of the world? Someone would have had to know the Quinn's plans and followed them here. According to the locals, they were the only visitors to arrive in Nazeth in the past few days. You're theory does not wash Sir."

"Please call me Johnny. You ask who would stand to gain from her disappearance and I must admit I know of no one who would do such a thing. Vienna has no enemies; in fact just the opposite…she is loved by everyone. You are aware that she is a very wealthy woman are you not?"

"A woman of means, yes, I have ascertained. How are you acquainted with the Quinn's, may I enquire, and what do you know of her assets?"

"I have known Lady Vienna for twenty years. She is my dear friend and is like a sister to me. I became an employee of Avanloch properties the same time as Vienna became Mistress of Avanloch. If you do not know already Captain, Avanloch is a castle in northern Scotland. Vienna and her two daughters, along with a sister- in-law are the sole legatees of the properties. They also own McAllister Enterprises which consist of a shipping business with its headquarters in London and a flour mill and dairy in the village of Domne which is situated on Avanloch lands. Many people are indebted to the family for their livelihood and hold Vienna in great esteem and she treats them all with respect. I say, without a shadow of a doubt that the family would pay anything for her safe return."

"I see your point Johnny…I was not aware of her affluence. What can you tell me of the sister-in-law and correct me if I am wrong, but Mr. and Mrs. Quinn are newlyweds are they not? Would it be to his advantage if his wife were to disappear?"

Johnny snickered. "If you knew the story of Rainey and Vienna, you would know how ludicrous that question is. They have known each other since the early sixties but have only recently been reunited. Without going into great detail, I will tell you the bare facts. They had a relationship back then and conceived a child. For reasons of her own Vienna fled to Scotland where she had family, and did not inform Rainey of her whereabouts or the child. She consequently married Lord Jeremy McAllister and took her place as Mistress of Avanloch. He has since passed away and she and Rainey are at long last together again. He would lay down his life for her as she would for him. No Sir, I assure you Rainey is not suspect in her disappearance. As for Ash, the sister-in-law, she has nothing to gain. Only if she were the last survivor of the McAllister family would she stand to inherit the whole empire and she could care less. She has no need for anything."

Captain Albain nodded. "I suppose that explains the haunted look in Mr. Quinn's eyes…he has only recently found her and now she is gone again. Thank you for enlightening me but it still does not explain what they were doing here?"

"They are in possession of what they believe to be a family heirloom and their search for the rightful owner has led them here. It is as simple as that Sir. So what say, we give this abduction theory of mine a shot?"

"As you wish Johnny O'Shea. They are two fortunate people, despite the circumstances, to have such a concerned friend. Shall we meet at 0800 hours tomorrow at the community center? We will once again explore the road towards and around the old church for that is the only place left that I, myself, have not investigated. You will inform Mr. Quinn and the others of our quest?"

"I will indeed and thank you Sir. I hope I haven't overstepped the boundaries between a stranger from another country and your fine police corp.?"

"You have not. Goodnight Mr. O'Shea."

Johnny re-entered the inn to find everyone except Rainey in the living room. He asked where Rainey was and Ava said she thought her father had been with him as he left right after Johnny walked the police to the door. James said that he was sure he knew where Rainey was and that was on Nazeth Avenue…the last place he had seen Vienna. Ava stood up and said that she had better go to him but Johnny said that he needed to talk to Rainey man to man and would she mind?

Ava hugged him. "Of course not Johnny. He probably needs a friend more than a distraught daughter right now."

Johnny found his friend sitting on a bench overlooking the river which was now only a stream, trickling over a bed of rocks. He sat down along side of him.

Rainey acknowledged him. "John."

"Do you want to talk Buddy?" Johnny was surprised by Rainey's answer.

"I wish I had never found those damn bracelets Johnny. They are cursed, you know. A young woman may have been slain for them over a century ago. Who knows what tragedies befell anyone else who possessed them? I sure as hell know what happened to me…I bought them for Vienna for Christmas but arrived home to find that she had left me and now because of them, I have lost her again. I am going to throw them in the deepest and darkest crevasse of the ocean so that they will never be found to bring anyone else misery ever again!"

"The circumstances are different this time Rainey. Vienna didn't leave you on her own accord; I am sure of that. There has to be a plausible reason for her disappearance."

"You would be amazed if you knew just how similar the two events are John."

"Are you saying that Vienna orchestrated her own disappearance? Do you know how ridiculous that sounds Rainey?"

"Yes, I do. I'm not sure I know what the hell I am saying at this point. In my heart, I know she wouldn't leave me or the girls. We had so many plans…our life was just beginning. I have no idea how I can carry on without her." Rainey had decided that he would tell no one that Vienna was pregnant. It would only add to everyone's anguish and he was going to have to deal with that pain all on his own.

"We are going to find her Rain. No one vanishes just like that. I believe that she had to be flown out, though for what reason, I cannot comprehend. Captain Albain says they have exhausted every possibility and have come up empty. I think he was reluctant to consider my theory but has agreed to meet us tomorrow morning to canvass the area between here and the church. He admitted that he had not been with the squad that searched that region originally. Tell me Rainey, have you considered the possibility that she was kidnapped?"

"Oh, it has been foremost in my mind Johnny, but why? Why now and why here? As far as I know there has never been an attempt before and if money is the reason why has there been no ransom notice? No one could have known that there was going to be an earthquake and that Vienna would wander off by herself. Of course, that was the perfect diversion but that supposition doesn't wash with me. Do you know something that I don't…has there been an attempt to abduct her before?" Rainey looked pleadingly at Johnny hoping the answer would be *no*.

"No, there never has been, but what other conclusion is there? With all the commotion going on who would have noticed a helicopter taking off and especially if it came from an area away from the village? You were here right away Rain, would you have heard one taking off?"

"I wasn't here immediately Johnny. I was on my way down stairs when the first tremor hit. I was only stunned for a second but the next jolt was stronger and it took me a few seconds to gain my equilibrium. If I am to be totally honest, I cannot account for almost fifteen minutes. Anything could have transpired in that time. Do you know how heavy that weighs on me? The last time I saw her she was waving to me from the street and then in a flash she was gone…just like in my dreams. I can't get that image out of my mind…I failed her Johnny and God help me, I don't see how I can live with that."

"Rainey, you are grieving right now and brother I sympathize with your feelings of guilt but you are not to blame. You are a very rational man and in time you will come to see that it was not your fault. The whole event is too fresh in your mind right now and you wanting to blame yourself is only human, but you need to know that

no one blames you. We will find some clue tomorrow, I am sure of it. Now, do you agree with me that the copter thing is a possibility?"

"Johnny, at this point, I am open to the idea that she could have been beamed aboard the Starship Enterprise…actually, I hope Captain Kirk and the crew do have my beloved."

"I'm glad to see that you still have your sense of humor Buddy."

"You are the first person to insinuate that I even have a sense of humor. So, we are seriously considering the thought that Vienna was kidnapped are we? Have you discussed this theory of yours with the girls yet? I can only imagine what their reaction was."

September 8th

Storm clouds were threatening the Nazeth Valley as the search party set out to comb the road that led to the church and its grounds. The girls had been very enthused when Rainey and Johnny had told them of their plans the night before. Evan expressed his opinion that the possibility of Vienna being flown out was a distinct possibility. Rainey had taken him aside and asked how much time in advance the pilot of the helicopter needed before he could fly in for them. Evan told him that the plane and pilot were on retainer and at their disposal so all he had to do was make a phone call. Rainey instructed Evan to make the call for pick-up in three hours. He said that he was positive that they would not discover any new evidence as he had already searched the area in question.

"We need to do this for the girls and Johnny. I don't want to subject Ava and Rosy to any more of this futility; it's time to go home. I am going to hire a private investigator and hopefully, he will be able to look at things with a fresh perspective. He can delve into the possibility that Vienna was kidnapped, and why and by whom. I cannot deal with the fact that I may have played into somebody's plans by bringing her here."

"Correct me if I am wrong Rainey, but wasn't it Vienna's idea to come here, not yours? You are not to blame for wanting to satisfy her curiosity about there being a living ancestor to those mysterious bangles."

Rainey touched Evan's arm and said. "Thanks Evan for trying to absolve me but there will be no redemption for me until I have Vienna back."

Ava held her father's hand as they walked up the hill to the church. Johnny had stopped with Captain Albain where the old truck still rested against the tree.

"This is an enormous amount of blood to have come from only one person is it not Captain?" Johnny questioned.

"Let me assure you Johnny, it is not. We believe by the huge wound in Sandez's skull that he was hit by falling debris. A very large shard of glass was found protruding from his head…it is amazing that he was able to drive at all. However, an autopsy will reveal the extent of all of his injuries and that will be forthcoming. A full report of all of the findings whether they pertain to Mrs. Quinn's disappearance or not will be forwarded to the family."

"What about the possibility that there was another passenger in the truck?"

"And, who would that be Mr. O'Shea? The priest was found dead and everyone else is accounted for…except Mrs. Quinn, of course."

"Exactly."

"But then, we would have found her if she had wandered off wouldn't we? I do understand where you are coming from as you want to find your friend, and I hope and pray that somewhere, something will turn up. Shall we join the others?"

They found Rosy and Ava with Althea and one police officer combing the grounds and steps by the church for any sign of their mother. Johnny and Captain Albain trekked up the stone steps that led to a level field to join Rainey and Evan. Rain had been falling steadily for the past half hour. Evan had been examining the soil for any fuel residue that could have been left by an aircraft. He said that it was definitely a landing site for helicopters but there was no way he could tell how recent the last departure was.

"Of course it is;" Captain Albain asserted. "that is how the priest came and went."

"Do you know when the priest's last arrival was?" Johnny asked.

"According to the locals it was several days before the earthquake…how unfortunate for the priest and his companion."

"Would the helicopter have remained?" Evan questioned Captain Albain.

"Perhaps, but I see no reason for it to have remained. From what I understand, Father Bissette would telephone when he required transportation and that was only once a month or so. So here would be no sense for the pilot to hang around and tie up the plane and pilot now would there?"

"I am certain you are right Captain, but you can't blame us for pursuing any little detail, no matter how remote, that my wife was airlifted out of the valley. Surely, aviation control would have records of every flight in and out, would they not?"

"You would think so wouldn't you Mr. Quinn, and that is certainly on my list to confirm. Being the Church, I would suspect that everything was legal. I am leaving several officers behind but I must take my leave today. I will be in touch with any new findings but please feel free to call me at any time. You have all of the numbers where I can be reached, do you not Mr. Quinn?"

"I do Sir." Rainey shook Captain Albain's hand. "Thank you for your promptness and courtesy in addressing our concerns."

"I did nothing out of the ordinary. I am sorry to have met you all under such trying circumstances. Mrs. Quinn's picture will be circulating throughout Andorra and to the surrounding precincts in Spain and France. Somebody always knows something and it is just a matter of time before we stumble on that one crucial clue. We will leave no stone unturned. I bid you adieu gentlemen."

The girls were waiting for them on what was left of the rectory steps. No one had any findings to report. Evan told them that Captain Albain had confirmed his supposition that there was indeed a heli landing site at the top of the hill, but that it proved nothing. They were all in agreement that Vienna had definitely been flown out, but the how, where and why was yet to be discovered.

"Mama is safe then isn't she Dad?" Ava implored.

"Yes, we have to believe that and she will come back to us just as soon as she can. Now, it is time for us to go home." Rainey put his arms around the girls trying to put on a brave face for them but his heart wasn't in it.

"Are you sure you don't want to stay another day or two Rainey?" Rosy asked.

"There is nothing more we can do here girls. The good people of Nazeth will be ever vigilant and the policia will be canvassing the valley again. Evan has already notified the pilot and he should be arriving shortly. Will you girls pack up Vienna's things please?"

"Yes, of course." Ava answered. "I noticed that Mama's rings were in her jewelry case. Why wasn't she wearing them Dad?"

Rainey smiled at his daughter. She had been calling him "dad" ever since he had to inform her of Vienna's disappearance and he had been too preoccupied to give it much thought. He would tell her that it pleased him once they were back at Avanloch.

"You know she never wore any jewelry to bed…she always said she felt like she was being strangled. I guess she was so excited that morning that she forgot to put them on."

"That doesn't sound like Mama." Ava said.

"Well…what can I say? I don't pretend to know everything that goes on inside your mother's head. I am sure that when we find her she will have a very plausible explanation as to why she didn't wait for me at the inn. Do you know that when we first entered the valley, she said that she had been here before and asked me if I had too? I suppose she was playing out one of her fantasies and meant in another lifetime. She always believed that we were star crossed lovers…whatever that means."

"It's a romantic concept Rainey and I think she thought if fit into her life. You don't really want to get rid of the Infinity Bracelets do you?" Rosy asked.

"So Johnny told you did he? I don't care what happens to them…they are jinxed."

"Rainey, Mama loves them and that is because you bought them for her so long ago and held on to them hoping you would find her one day."

"Well, I did, didn't I, but only to lose her again and all because of those damn trinkets! We wouldn't all be here if it wasn't for them." Rainey said emotionally.

"You may be right Dad but it was Mama's wish to try and locate the rightful heir and I don't think you could deny her that." Ava said with tears in her eyes.

"You're right Ava and I apologize if I have upset you. Now, I have to go and say my goodbyes and meet with James's uncle who is steering me in the direction of a private detective who specializes in finding lost people. He has his office in France not far from Andorra's border. Apparently, he knows this area very well and has connections with the constabulary of both France and Spain which should come in handy."

"I was going to suggest that Uncle John would know someone who could help, but hiring a detective who knows the area is a much better idea. Thank you Rainey."

"No need to thank me Rosy; I want her back just as much as you do and I will go to the ends of the earth to do so."

"We know you will Dad. You're right; there is no reason to stay here any longer for Mama is gone from this place." Ava hugged her father and left for the inn with Rosy.

The helicopter arrived on time and as they were flying back to Andorra La Vela, Evan relayed what information Pierre, the pilot, had uncovered for them. No aircraft had registered a flight plan with the airport a week prior to or after the earthquake that wasn't official. His flight in and out was the exception.

"However," Evan explained, "that didn't mean that an aircraft didn't fly in under the radar. Apparently, the air control officers are constantly picking up blips which are not accounted for. As in any country, there is always a need for outlaw pilots who are capable of flying without detection and will go anywhere for the right amount of money. I would wager my pilot's license that all the signs at the church landing field indicate that a craft had definitely been there within the last few days. I was hoping that Pierre would have uncovered some useful information, but unfortunately that was not to be. Sorry."

"We are all sorry Evan, but thank you for finding out what you did. It is in the hands of the authorities for now." Rainey said half heartily.

An hour later they were saying good bye to Andorra. Johnny was occupying the seat next to Evan in the jet. He turned and said. "I think I am ready to entertain Rainey's idea that Vienna was beamed aboard the Starship Enterprise…what do you say girls?"

"Did you really say that Dad? Mama would be impressed to hear that you even know the name of the starship on Star Trek. Periodically, we would watch re-runs of the television series and I think Mama had a crush on Mr. Spock."

"Really Ava…I wouldn't think he was her type."

"I think it was the pointy ears Rainey; probably reminded her of you." Rosy teased.

"You think so do you Rosy?" Rainey attempted a smile. "I guess we will have to spend the night in London as it will be too late to drive to Avanloch when we touch down."

"Oh no Rainey, Evan has already made arrangements to fly us home tonight."

"You mean into Waverly, don't you Rosy?"

Johnny informed them that Land's End Air had offered a helicopter and a pilot so they would all be home tonight.

Rainey said loud enough for Evan to hear. "Is this so Evan and what did you have to do or promise to do for the airline in return?"

"Nothing Sir; it is their way of contributing to the cause. Before the family purchased this jet, they flew with Land's End for a good many years and so I guess they are just helping out in a way that they can." Evan stated.

"What's with this "sir"? I think we have progressed way beyond that Evan. Anyhow, I am most grateful as I would really like to get the girls home. Apparently, I still have a lot to learn about the McAllister influence."

"No one who knows Vienna or the girls would have a reason to kidnap her so it has to be for the money. The question still remains as to why hasn't there been a ransom demand?" Johnny questioned. "What are they waiting for?"

"Don't know John…maybe something will turn up at Avanloch. If not, then we will hope that the private detective will turn up something. You can be sure that everyone who has ever known Vienna will be investigated. I am sure that you have all been thinking that it is someone who holds a vendetta against me, and that the best way to get back at me would be to take the woman I love from me…well, I can only think of one person who hates me that much and that is my ex-wife. To be totally honest, I wouldn't put anything past that woman but kidnapping is even beyond her. I don't believe that I have made any enemies through my business dealings and so I am at a loss to come up with any suspects. Yet if no attempt has ever been made before on Vienna…why now? It would seem plausible that I am the catalyst." Rainey said flatly.

"Please don't think that way Rainey…none of us does." Rosy said.

"Thanks honey, but I think we all know where the blame lies." Rainey turned his head and stared out the window. Ava squeezed his hand and the tears that fell down her cheek were just as much for her father as they were for her mother.

Dusk was rapidly approaching as the pilot landed and deposited his passengers at the gates of Avanloch. He was invited to spend the night but chose to head back to London. A throng of people, having heard the helicopter, had amassed hoping that Vienna was aboard. Johnny said that he would deal with them and sent the rest into the house where they were greeted by Amma and the McDuffs. Rainey excused himself and said that he needed some fresh air. No one objected. He walked around the side of the castle and said. "I'm here at your castle Vienna. Shall I wait for you or are you never coming back?"

He thought that a walk through the gardens that Vienna so loved would lighten his mood but it only added to his despondency. He stopped at the rose named for her and was not surprised to find nothing but dead flowers on the stems. It, as well as the rest of the garden was shedding its leaves and getting ready to retire for the season. He remembered Vienna saying that it was always a sad time of year for her when she had to prepare the plants for winter. The ivies and creeping vines that covered the castle walls were turning gold and crimson. He picked a bouquet of late blooming daisies, asters and fragrant lilies. He smiled remembering how he had paid attention to Vienna as she gave him and Tanny a lesson in horticulture. He took a short cut through the back yard and unlocked the conservatory's door and found a vase and filled it with water for the flowers. He relocked the door and put the key back under the planter where Vienna could find it.

At the south side of Avanloch, he glanced up at Vienna's bedroom windows reminding himself to design her balcony so that it could be built before she returned. He rounded the corner and looked down upon the village. He remembered the day that they had left on their ill-fated trip. Vienna had asked him to stop the car and she had gotten out and looked sadly back at Avanloch…he had promised her that it would be there when she returned and it was, but it was *she* who had not returned. Did she know something was going to happen to her? No, he didn't believe that but he was sure going to talk to Meggie because she had read the cards for Vienna …damn it, why didn't they pay more attention to that dire warning? On the morning before the earthquake Vienna had asked him if they were tempting the fates…what had she had meant by that. Hopefully, Maveryn would have an answer.

Rainey swung the door to the mausoleum open and placed *the* rock against it. He knew that one could open the door from inside but he placed the rock just to humor Vienna. He flipped on the recessed wall light and found Maveryn's niche and placed the vase of flowers in her window. "I hope you are home Maveryn as I really need to talk to you. If you don't already know, Vienna did not come home with us. I lost her in Andorra. She simply vanished after an earthquake. We spent days looking for her, but to no avail. The consensus is that she may have been kidnapped. I don't have any idea how far you can travel but if you can see her, you must somehow tell me or the girls. I know what you are thinking… I don't even believe that your spirit exists, so why would I come to me? Well, I confess, I am not a true believer, but if there is any chance that you know where Vienna is, I will never doubt the spirit world again. I will do anything to bring Vienna back home and I do mean anything! I will give her up if that is what it takes because the girls need her, but Maveryn, she is going to have our baby and she wants it so badly. On the other hand, I will fight tooth and nail for her and I suppose I would even sell my soul to the devil. Don't make me do that Maveryn…I am begging you for help. I guess this is also a prayer to The Man above; someone hear me please."

Rainey hadn't even realized that he was kneeling. Trembling, he stood up and walked out of the crypt. He closed the door and gazed up at the sky. A few stars were twinkling down at him. He made a wish on the first one he saw. What else could he do? He had made a plea to a deceased woman, prayed to God, and now he had made a wish upon a star and he was going to enlist the aid of a physic…he was a desperate man. Tomorrow, he would go to the chapel and enlist the help of the Good Lord properly.

Rainey's plan was to sneak in the front entrance and make his way quietly to the second floor. On the third step of the grand staircase he heard music and muffled voices coming from the parlor. Wondering who was in Vienna's favorite room, he crept silently to the door and peeked in. Rosalyn and Ava were snuggled up in the high backed gold brocade Queen Anne chair that they referred to as Vienna's throne. The girls had once told Rainey that many nights had been spent huddled up with their mother in that very chair while she told them bedtime stories. It was their special time together. It was where they came when they were upset or ill and needed guidance or comforting.

The girls had one of Vienna's much loved tapes of Scottish Highland music playing. They were obviously leafing through photograph albums. Ava spotted him first and waved the colorful peacock plume that she was holding at him. Rosy beckoned him to join them from behind the elegant Spanish fan that she was wielding. Rainey knew that they referred to the fan and plume as their mother's scepters.

"Come in and join us Rainey; we were wondering where you had gotten to."

"Not very far; I was visiting with Maveryn." Rainey answered.

Rosy smiled and said they were going over to talk with her later.

Ava moved up to sit on the arm of the oversized chair. "Come join us Dad."

"I don't want to intrude on your private memories."

"Don't be a silly goose Dad! This is where Mama would tell us the stories of Emerald and Laddy, so you see you are in our memories too." Ava assured him.

"Thank you. Would you girls like a fire?"

"Why didn't we think of that Ava?" Rosy asked her sister. "Yes, we would love one."

Rainey laid the logs and lit a match and watched it roar to life. The heat felt good on his weary bones. He stood for a few minutes letting the flames die down before adding more fuel. He faced the girls and told them that he would like to replace the bronze mirror over the fireplace with the portrait of Vienna; what did they think?

"Mama will kill us when she sees it, but yes, let's! Her picture has graced the storage room long enough." Rosy said and Ava agreed.

Rosy made room for Rainey beside her. He knew that Vienna had labored over redecorating this room more so than any of the others. It was situated between the library and the informal drawing room. Next to her throne chair was a small oval mahogany table which held some of her cherished works of prose from Shakespeare, Elizabeth Barrett Browning, Lord Tennyson, Lord Bryon, Shelley and Keats. Other precious books were nearby in the library. A mirrored silver tray with an ivory treasure box which held trinkets that the girls had given her over the years, sat next to the books.

The rest of the room was furnished with period pieces that Vienna had found including a six seated maroon and gold roundabout footstool that Rainey rested his feet on. The big yellow throne chair Jeremy had found for Vienna in Paris and had it shipped home to her. It was rumored that it had once belonged to Josephine Bonaparte. Vienna had the chair remodeled so that it could swivel and rock. It sat close to the hearth but when rotated faced the large French doors which looked out on the edge of the gardens, and Brackenshire Manor. Rainey did not relay his feelings of utter desolation to the girls but promised himself that he would be strong for them until Vienna returned to Avanloch. Although he had viewed the photograph albums with Vienna when he first came to Avanloch, he sat quietly and let the girls relive the pictures with him again.

"Look at Rosy, Dad; doesn't she look every inch the fairy godmother?"

"Yes, she certainly does Ava. I have been meaning to thank you for the wishes you bestowed upon your mother Rosy. Without the last one, I may very well have never been reunited with her."

"Whatever do you mean Rainey?" Rosy asked inquisitively.

"I see; you do not know the story. After Vienna's and my brief encounter in Hawthorne last winter when she rebuffed me, I wasn't sure that I would ever see her again. I would not have given up so easy though, I want you to know. Anyhow, as we all know, she did let me back into her life. She asked me to take her to the Palace and I was surprised when we got there that she had a fire waiting to be lit and music on the phonograph player and wine and cheeses ready. I asked her how she knew I would come back to see her after the way she had ran out on me the day before and she said, "Because I wished you here." I asked her what she meant and she told me about the wishes you had granted her many years ago and that she had saved the last one for me. Well, needless to say, I was a little dubious. Apparently, I have a lot to learn about fairy godmothers. Please tell me you have one more wish up your sleeve Rosy?"

A tear filled Rosy's eye. She leaned her head on Rainey's shoulder. "Oh, I have tried, but I guess I was only allotted the three."

"Thank you for sharing the story Dad." Ava said solemnly reaching out to her sister and her father. "We will keep wishing and praying and whatever else it takes to get Mama back."

"Hey, what is going on in here?" Evan shouted from the doorway.

"Evan, I was wondering where you were." Rainey answered.

"I sent him for a nap as he could barely keep his eyes open through supper. Did you get a little rest Honey?" Rosy asked.

"I did and I showered and am refreshed. I put a pot of coffee on and I suspect you could use a little fortitude Rainey seeing you missed supper."

"I am not at all hungry but coffee sounds inviting. Speaking of which, where did Vienna's Spanish coffee get to?"

"Johnny stowed it away in one of the pantries in the cellar." Evan said.

"Good, I think that I will take a pound to Meggie Magan tomorrow."

"She would like that Dad. Is there a specific reason that you want to see her?"

"Yes, Ava, I need to find out what she knows about Vienna's disappearance."

No one said anything but they all wondered what Rainey meant by the statement.

It was almost midnight when Rainey climbed the stairs and lumbered down the hall to the bedroom. He opened the door and was confronted by a cold awareness that he was all alone. He walked around the bed touching the pillow where Vienna should be resting her head. He ran his hand over her chair where she would sit while he brushed her hair. He slid back the closet doors and stared at her clothes. "I won't be sleeping here without you Vienna." In her parlor, he randomly pulled out one of the letters she had written him. He read: *My darling Rainey ...how I miss you...*He could read no more.

Chapter 8

Antonio/Rainey

September 11th

At the request of Doctor Zaccaris, Antonio was at the hospital for another consultation regarding Katarina's condition. He wondered what more he could possibly learn about the unconscious state she was in. What he had been told was ingrained in his brain. Kat did not respond to pain, light, sound or other stimuli. Brain damage in comatose patients ranges from mild to moderate to severe. After four months in such a state, recovery was as low as 15%. On the positive side, although Kat had some swelling of the frontal lobe, there were no fractures or fluid buildup. Her respirations and other vital functions were stable. She would have to remain in the Intensive Care Unit as she would require constant monitoring for some time. No surgery was required which gave Anton hope.

Somner reminded him every day that she may never regain consciousness and if she did, what was he going to do then when she remembered who she was? Anton responded the same every time. "We will deal with that when the time comes."

Somner was deeply concerned for his friend's mental state. Constantine was no help. He still insisted that just before the shaking started the woman had approached him and Sandez and said that her name was Katarina and asked if they could help her. Then she was struck by falling bricks and while they were helping her into the vehicle they were all knocked down by the second tremor and bombarded by another onslaught of bricks. He remembered getting

Kat into the truck, but nothing after that. He hadn't been aware that Sandez had been killed until Somner told him at the hospital.

Doctor Zinc Zaccaris found Anton at Katarina's bedside holding her hand and talking to her. Anton had told him the same story that he told all the hospital staff and that was that he and Kat had fallen in love at first sight. They had been married for less than a month and had spent their honeymoon on Rose Island where they had met. He had gone to ready the plane while she packed up. The taxi she was riding in had been hit by an unoccupied run away truck. He had gone to see what was keeping her and came upon the accident. He had made the decision immediately to fly her to the hospital here in Verde El Mar as it was only a fifteen minute flight and he knew she would get the best care here. It was true; his decision had most assuredly saved her life. This was the simple lie he had fabricated and he would go to extreme measures if need be to substantiate it.

Doctor Z, as he preferred to be called, put his hand on Anton's shoulder. "Are you ready to take a break Son? Refreshments have been set up for us in the family room."

Anton followed him out. He knew Kat's condition had not changed and wondered again why the doctor had asked to see him. He soon found out.

"As I am sure you know Anton, I am most interested in your wife's case. She is a very stunning lady and I would hate for her condition to deteriorate further, so what I am going to propose to you is for her and the baby's wellbeing. We have no way of knowing when she will wake up or if she ever will. The fetus needs more nutrients and this can be supplied by tube feeding. The medical term for this is nasogastric. A tube is surgically inserted into her abdomen where intravenous fluids are fed which will restore hydration, electrolytes, vitamins, and all the necessary nutrients and will not only benefit the baby, but Katarina as well. If consciousness is not restored within three days, I believe this is the route we must take. There is no danger to either patient and it has been proven to be a life saver in many circumstances. Do you have a thousand questions for me Anton?"

"More concerns than questions Doctor. If you say that this procedure is the best thing for Kat and the baby I will not question your expertise. I want to know what to expect when Kat wakes up… will she know who she is and remember what happened?"

"That is hard to say Anton. After a coma, comebacks are usually slow and patchy. Consciousness generally happens little by little. Patients usually awake in a profound state of confusion; we call this diminished consciousness. They may be in a minimally conscious state and require a program that provides gentle stimulation that involves all the senses. The patient may be receiving information, but is unable to respond. However, they may communicate with a blinking of the eyes, a facial expression or even the movement of a toe. The mind is a mysterious and complicated instrument, and when it has been subjected to trauma that incited coma there is no sure way of predicting the outcome. There is still much research to be done on the affect and cause of comas and as you know, it is the field that I am most interested in, and so every case is a challenge and the results are always different. I have seen patients wake up and carry on as if nothing happened and others take years to recall their memories and then, there are the ones that have permanent amnesia or never regain consciousness at all. There is no way of telling what category your wife will fall into. The critical 72 hours is up and there has been no change in her condition. This may not seem important to you Anton, but I assure you it is a positive sign. Katarina is not running a fever and all of her vitals are encouraging."

"Thank you Doctor. Now, about the tube that is to be inserted into Kat's abdomen, will there be any discomfort to her?'

"Only minimal and in her state, I believe that she will not be aware of it. Of course, she will have constant monitoring as I told you before, and we will keep her on the I.C.U. ward for awhile yet."

"Then what; how long will she be permitted to remain in the hospital?"

"Eventually she will be moved to an institution that cares for just such persons on a permanent basis. There are very respectable establishments that cater to comatose and end of life patients throughout the country. We will find a suitable home for Katarina when the time comes."

"If I were to hire a full time nurse and whatever else it would take could I have her come and live at home with me? I already have a large staff and am willing to provide personal and loving care. I can't bear to have her alone and away from me."

"There is no reason whatsoever Anton and there are many qualified nurses who prefer private practice. If this is to pass, may I offer a suggestion?"

"Please, I have no idea what I am dealing with. Any suggestions will be greatly appreciated. I never thought I would be in such a predicament."

"No one expects to have to deal with serious health issues in their families. You are at an advantage as you have the financial resources to be your wife's best advocate. I would suggest that you find a young companion for her; one that will sit with her, read, and talk to her and be her friend when no one else can. There is a home for girls in Valencia that can provide you with a suitable young lady. For now, just keep talking to Katarina for we have no way of knowing if her subconscious is able to detect your presence. For all we know, she can hear you and can feel your love."

Avanloch

The produce from the gardens and fields had been harvested back at the castle. There had been a fall festival in the village marking the autumnal equinox. Halloween was the next event to be celebrated. Lady Vienna would not be home to preside over the masquerade party this year and no one had the heart to host one and so everyone agreed to cater to the children only.

Rainey had learned nothing new from Decamber LaSalle, the private investigator, whom he had hired. No new leads had turned up anywhere in Andorra and he had now extended his search to nearby regions in France and Spain. He was still conducting interviews via the telephone with acquaintances of both Rainey and Vienna. He assured Rainey that no one would be overlooked and if he felt that someone was hiding pertinent information, a thorough search of them would be imminent. Decamber was almost positive that Louise

Quinn, Rainey's ex-wife, had not been involved, but she was still a person of interest.

Meggie Magan had no insight into where Vienna was. Rainey had questioned her about the reading she had done for his wife the day after he returned from Nazeth.

"Mr. Quinn," she said, "I wish that I could tell you where Miss Vienna is, but alas, I cannot. Her reading was very complicated and I advised her to use precaution as someone was going to dupe her and perhaps take advantage of her generous nature. I feared that she was going to face many obstacles and I felt that there would be issues that she could not identify with. It was obvious that there was to be travel involved. At no time did the cards suggest her demise; just subterfuge. The cards do not have a timetable and that is why I am at a loss to be able to tell you when she will return, but, come home she will for her king will save her. I have no doubt that will be you Mr. Rainey. I barely had the pleasure of getting to know your wife and it is with a heavy heart that I lay my head down every night. I shall tell you this …the last day I saw Lady Vienna, I noticed that her aura was twinkling like Christmas tree lights; this can mean that one is going through some major changes in life and a pregnant woman will emanate these lights also. Is Vienna with child Mr. Rainey?"

He told Meggie that she was, but no one else was to know. Could she keep this just between him and her as he did not want the girls to have anything more to worry about? She promised him that it would remain their secret.

He hadn't expected anything more but had been somewhat comforted that Meggie thought that he was the one who would be Vienna's savior…if only he knew how.

On September the 29th, Antonio brought Katarina to his home, Casscadia Casa. She had not woken or shown any signs of ever doing so, but Anton was optimistic that she would. A room next to his that received the morning light was assembled for her. It overlooked the Genoaen Bay and had a fantastic view of the mountains, the gardens and the uninhabited tiny island of Sonnara. He had her room prepared exactly the way he had been instructed to do and it was every bit as sophisticated as her room in the hospital. All her needs could be met. He had hired two private nurses from a convent and had found a young girl to be Kat's companion. She was an orphan and had no family that could be accounted for; this fit perfectly into his plans. Dr. Z supervised the transfer as he was most fond of Kat and planned to check in on her progress every week.

Somner was still not pleased with Antonio's decision to bring the woman home. He had traveled to Nazeth as Anton had ordered. He did not like what he had learned there. A young man by the name of James Parent was his source of first hand information. James and a young lady were leaving Nazeth; he was having his vehicle serviced before journeying on to England. Somner had stopped for fuel and noticed the pair sitting on a bench. He had casually sauntered over and said "Hello." He told them he had been on his way to La Vella when he had heard about the earthquake in Nazeth and curiosity got the best of him and here he was. He asked them if either of them had witnessed the quake. They said they surely had and related the horrific events of that fateful day. He learned about the destruction of life and structures and the disturbing case of a woman who seemed to have just disappeared. Apparently, James had befriended Rainey and Vienna Quinn the night before the catastrophe. The couple were on their honeymoon and combining it with some business in the area. Somner did not ask what sort of business because he didn't want to appear too curious. The whole town, a rescue team with sniffer dogs and police from Andorra had all been involved in the intensive search for Mrs. Quinn, but she was not found. Somner said that he found it hard to believe that someone could simply vanish from such a small town and that she had to be somewhere. James informed him that it was the consensus that Vienna must have been flown out but that theory could not be proven as there was no record of any aircraft filing a flight plan that day. Somner asked if a plane could have landed or descended without being noticed. James stated that it would have had to be a helicopter and no one could recall seeing anything as they were too busy dealing with the aftermath of the quake. The last question Somner asked was what had happened to Mr. Quinn.

"His family and friends came over from Scotland to help in the search. They all went home devastated without any answers. The search continues though as Mr. Quinn has hired a private investigator and the police continue to investigate. Althea and I will be visiting with the family later this fall as they have offices in London where we both attend college. Rainey Quinn will never quit looking for his wife and I pray every day that he will find her and soon as I can not see him living without her. He handed me the keys to his jeep as he was leaving and said it was mine…I will never forget the look of anguish in his eyes. I am sorry if I went into too much detail but the whole sad affair is still etched in my mind." James and Althea both had tears in their eyes as they left.

Somner thanked them for the story and climbed into his car and left the way he had come. He was not happy with what he had learned and when he returned to Verde El Mar relayed the whole sad story to his friend and boss. Anton told him to forget what he had learned for it made no difference as this person by the name Vienna no longer existed. The search for her would not come this far south. Somner was not sure he could live with the knowledge of knowing who Katarina really was and doing nothing about it. For now, he would bide his time and see what happened when and if she woke up. How anyone could be so devoted to a woman who was barely alive was foreign to him and yet, he witnessed it everyday. Anton spent countless hours at Katarina's bedside talking to her as if they had really had a relationship. Somner was concerned for his friend's mindset.

Two months had passed since Rainey had last seen Vienna and his sorrow increased with each passing day. He had made up his mind that he had to leave Avanloch.

Chapter 9

Katarina

November 11th

My head hurt. Actually, I hurt all over. Hesitantly, I opened my eyes and felt such a pain in the back of my head that I shut them again. I lay still for a few more minutes and willed myself to forgo the throbbing and open my eyes again. I tried to focus on my surroundings and realized that I had no idea where I was. I tried to move my body but it did not co-operate. I appeared to be in a bed attached to strange instruments that hung from the wall. The room was large and sparsely furnished. The clock on the wall read 9 o'clock. I didn't know if that was morning or evening as the room was dark. There was a woman clad in white sleeping in a chair a few feet away from me.

"Hello!" I called to her.

She jumped up with a start. "Oh, Miss Katarina, you are awake! Don't move, don't do anything! I will fetch Mr. DeMarco…oh, he will be so very happy! Zoe, Miss Katarina, she is awake…she is awake…hurry, hurry!"

Katarina…who was Katarina and Zoe, and Mr. DeMarco? Again, I tried to sit up but could not. Where was I and why couldn't I move?

A slender dark haired girl with very dark eyes was suddenly beside me. She couldn't have been more than fifteen or sixteen. She put one hand on my left shoulder and held my hands with the other.

She had a soft soothing voice and she told me her name was Zoe. "Miss Katarina, please do not worry; Mr. DeMarco will be here right away." With tears streaming down her face, she turned and said to the woman in white. "Call the doctor Sister Margaret."

"It is his day to visit, so he should be here any minute." The woman answered.

A tall dark haired handsome man with eyes the same color as Zoe's entered the room. I wondered if he was her father, but why would she call him Mr. DeMarco?

"It is a miracle Sir, Miss Katarina has awoken!"

He ordered the drapes to be opened as he approached the side of my bed. His face was kind and he seemed to be genuinely jubilant that I was awake. He held my hand. "Kat, you have at long last come back to me!" He tried to take me in his arms but I protested.

"Who are you? Where am I? Why am I in this bed? What is wrong with me?"

"Do you not know me Katarina? It is Anton, your husband."

I was most alarmed. "I have never seen you before in my life! I have no idea who you are and I am not Katarina!" I cried.

"Who do you think you are then?" He asked hesitantly.

I looked at him and Zoe and the nurse and realized that I had no idea who I was. I was about to say something when another man entered the room. He was small and his head was covered in straggly long strands of white hair that stood straight up at all angles. He had more hair on his eyebrows than on his head and his moustache was bushy and almost covered his upper lip. I thought he looked a little like Albert Einstein and was glad that I knew who that was even if I didn't know who I was.

"Miss Katarina!" He bellowed. "It is about time that you decided to wake up." He turned and asked who had witnessed my arousal.

The nurse said that she hadn't seen me wake up but was very startled when I called out.

He stroked his mustache. "Very strange, I say, very strange."

He walked around the bed analyzing me all the time. Finally, he leaned over me and grinned. "This is most unusual to have someone so alert after such a long time asleep."

"What do you mean…just how long have I been sleeping?" I asked bewildered.

"Yes, yes, we shall discuss that. Now, I need to do a full evaluation and we can talk as we do so. Antonio, will you and the others please give us a little privacy?"

"I want Zoe to stay, please." I begged of him.

"Very well, you may assist me Zoe. By the way, I am Doctor Zaccaris." He extended his hand to me and I squeezed his hoping that he could give me some answers and I asked him if he knew who I was.

"Well, my dear, you are Katarina DeMarco and it is not surprising that you do not know who you are right now for you have been in a coma for two months."

I gasped. "What…how?"

"You were in a horrific car accident dear lady, and it is only because of your husband's quick decision making that you are alive today. Zoe, help hold her head up. Does it hurt when I move your head around?"

"Not so much, but I do have a monster of a headache."

"We will give you something for that." He asked me to open and close my eyes and shone a small light into them. I flinched. He asked if the brightness stung and I nodded.

"I would expect nothing more for they are not accustomed to light but they will adjust. I am going to suggest that you wear sun glasses for awhile as even the house lights may cause you distress. He maneuvered my shoulders and checked my throat inside and out. Satisfied, he pulled the blankets off me and asked me if I could wiggle my toes. I could. He asked me to try and turn over unto my side, but I could not. Zoe helped him and he examined my back. Satisfied, he told me to relax. I told him that when he had turned me over my left hip hurt and I felt something funny digging into my abdomen. He told me that was the feeding tube. I did not understand what he meant and he explained that it was a device that had been surgically implanted into my abdomen so that vital nutrients could be administered to me and the baby.

"Baby…what baby?" I stammered.

"I am going way too fast…excuse me Katarina. I should have taken into consideration that if you have no memory so you certainly wouldn't remember being pregnant. But, yes my dear you are expecting a child; you are approximately thirteen weeks along."

"How can this be if I have been in a coma and who is the father?" I was too flabbergasted to put two and two together.

"You had a life before the car accident my dear lady, and of course Antonio is the baby's father. It was a miracle that the baby came through unscathed. An ultra sound has shown that the fetus is remarkably healthy. Perhaps, in a day or so, you would like to see the pictures. How do you feel about this Katarina?"

"Dr. Zacc…" I stuttered as I had forgotten his name.

"Call me Dr. Z, everyone does."

"All right. You have just told me that I have been in an accident and have been in a coma for two months and now, you tell me I am pregnant by a man I don't even know…how do you think I feel? I am dumbfounded. My head is filled with cobwebs and though I don't have an inkling who I am, I am certain that I am not this Katarina person."

"What makes you so sure that you are not Katarina? Are you experiencing memories of another identity?" Dr. Z asked.

"No, it is just a feeling that I have; I can not explain. How long will it be until I have my memory back?" I was hoping for an immediate result.

"I wish I had an answer for you, but the truth of the matter is that I cannot give you a time frame. You may very well have full recall at any time or you may gradually start to experience little flashes of memories. However, I have to warn you that amnesia has many faces ranging from partial to total loss of memory. When amnesia is extensive, memories for facts are usually left intact. Retrograde amnesia is the loss of one's past and it varies from person to person. This seems to be what you are experiencing at the moment. Although you may retain facts such as having total recall of… let's say a poem or a mathematical fact, you may have lost all memory of a past life."

"I don't understand…wouldn't my identity be more important than being able to remember poetry?"

"One would think so wouldn't one? Loss of memory such as facts, information and experiences can be caused by damage to areas of the brain that are vital for memory processing. General knowledge and perceptual skills may be stored in a memory separate from the one used to store personal information. Research suggests that there is more than one area of the brain used to store memory."

"What can I do to restore the loss? Surely, familiar things and people should jog my memory?" I was becoming more and more agitated.

"Yes, it could be as simple as someone walking in the door that you knew that will shock your memory banks into full recall or it could be a song or a food…it may come in the most unusual of circumstances, or, and I hate to say this, but your amnesia may be with you for life." Dr. Z was apologetic for something that wasn't even his fault.

"Well," I said emphatically, "I refuse to accept that!"

"Good for you girl! I like a woman with spunk. You must be patient though my dear…you have only awoke a short time ago and who is to say that tomorrow you will not have full control of your past again. There is no specific treatment for amnesia but techniques for enhancing memory and psychological support can help."

"That's what I will do; I will get hypnotized!"

Dr. Z laughed. "That is certainly something that we will explore at another time. Now, if there are no more questions we will try to get you up if you like?"

"Yes, I certainly do!"

"Zoe, will you please ask Mr. DeMarco to join us and if you would be so kind, could you fetch the wheel chair as I am sure we will need it."

As Zoe left the room I told Dr. Z that I was not comfortable around the man who said that he was my husband.

He leaned close and whispered. "Give the man a chance Miss Kat…you have in your mind, just met him. He has been by your side for two months and there is no man more devoted to his wife than he; I assure you of that."

I sighed and reluctantly agreed to be civil to Antonio. I scrutinized him as he crossed the floor. In any other circumstances, I am sure that I would have found him a fine specimen of a man. He was tall and muscular and had wavy black hair and very dark eyes.

He smiled at me and asked how I was feeling. "I have just found out that I have been in a coma for two months due to a serious car accident and that I am expecting a child and that you are my husband…I have no idea who I am or where I am…how do you think I am feeling?" I somehow felt that it was entirely his fault and I am sure that my voice echoed that sentiment.

"I can not imagine what you are experiencing but will help you in any way that I can."

I told him that I had no idea of how he could help me. Dr. Z emphasized again that I must be patient and he and Antonio proceeded to sit me up. The room started spinning and I felt like I was going to black out. They held me and the doctor ordered me to breathe slowly and keep my eyes closed until the dizziness faded. He said if it was too much for me we could wait until tomorrow.

"No, I am all right now. Can we continue?" I asked.

"Yes." He said. "We are going to swing your legs over the side of the bed; tell me if you have any discomfort."

I did but I wasn't going to admit to it. I felt a slight pulling coming from between my legs. Dr. Z explained that it was a catheter and would have to stay in for awhile. After a few minutes when he was assured that I wasn't suffering any more dizziness he said that they were going to try and stand me up. Zoe had returned with the wheelchair and he suggested that I hold on to the arms of it to steady myself. The second my feet touched the floor a sharp pain shot up from my left hip and I cried out. I thought that perhaps I had broken a bone. Dr. Z reassured me that I hadn't, but that the pain was caused from an injury to my left side that I had incurred in the accident. It took several minutes for the throbbing to subside. I had no luck in getting my feet to move and took his advice and let him and Antonio swing me around into the chair. At least I was sitting up and out of bed. I asked if I could be wheeled to the window. I was hoping that the view would jog my memory. It did not.

Antonio swung open the glass doors that opened onto a veranda. The height suggested that we were on the second or third floor of the house. The view was breath taking. There were low rolling hills to my right abundantly flourishing with what I assumed were grape vines. Below the deck was a colorful garden that covered the slopes that ran down to the waters edge. Several small watercrafts were harbored along the shore. Some distance out into the bay was a small island. I asked about it. Antonio told me that it was uninhabited and was not used for anything. I squinted but was sure that I could see an imposing castle standing regally in the bright sunlight. I blinked and it was gone…just like my memory.

I asked where we were and Antonio said that we were at Casscadia Casa in Verde El Mar in Spain. I looked at him and stated that that was impossible.

"Why do you say that Kat?" he asked.

"Because," I answered him, "I do not live in Spain."

Doctor Z interceded. "Where do you believe it is that you live Katarina?"

"I do not know, just that it is not here. What is the name of that island out there and what is the waterway?"

Antonio informed me that his properties were on the Genoaen Bay, an inlet off the Mediterranean Sea. The island was called Sonnara. I told him that it was all very beautiful but I may as well have been in Timbuktu as far as I was concerned.

"Of course you do not recognize the house or the countryside Katarina as you have never seen it before. We met on Rose Island in August and were married a few days later. I was bringing you home to Casscadia when you had the horrific accident so it is no wonder that nothing looks familiar."

"Where is this Rose Island; is that where I am from? And, you are telling me that we married after only knowing each other for two days…that's preposterous!" I exclaimed.

"It's true Katarina…we fell in love immediately. I guess it is like that age old saying; love at first sight. I am sorry that you do not remember. I do not know where you were living before you came to Rose Island. You were very vague as to your previous residence. All you would say is that you were from North America and that you were never going back. I did not pressure you for details." Antonio explained.

I snapped back at him. "That makes no sense whatsoever! Are you trying to tell me that you married a girl with a questionable past and never sought answers as to why she wouldn't or couldn't go back to her homeland? By the size of this house, I assume that you are a wealthy man…am I correct? Did I know this when I married you? Perhaps I am a gold digger, or perhaps I am an axe murderer, or a black widow…did you consider any of these scenarios?"

Antonio and Dr. Z both found my rationalizing amusing. "None of those people are you my dear Kat. I am a much better judge of character than you give me credit for. The mystery of where you came from or what you may have done before we met is of little consequence to me…it only adds to your charm." Antonio declared.

I looked at Dr. Z but he only shrugged his shoulders. "I know nothing more about you than what Anton has told me. I must confess though that I am delighted that you are such a spitfire. Keep asking questions as that is the only way you will find answers or come to terms with the unknown. Now, I am going to take my leave but will check in on you later in the evening. I am going to ask the cook to prepare you some broth and custards and we will see how your system tolerates that before we introduce any solids orally. A nice cup of tea might be nice to get you started…what do you say?"

"I am pretty sure that I don't like tea. When will you remove this tube from me?"

He laughed. "You are pretty sure you don't like tea eh? The tube has to stay in until we are sure that you are getting enough nourishment…remember, there is a baby to consider. Sister Margaret will be monitoring you for that." He nodded at Antonio. "I trust you will make sure the patient doesn't over tax herself. She has probably been exposed to enough sunlight for one day. Please look into acquiring some decent sun glasses for her."

He took my hand and I asked him if he was going to remain my doctor and he said. "I have been with you since the beginning and I will be never more than a phone call away."

He kissed me lightly on the cheek. "I am glad to see you come to life and I don't want you worrying about who you are. You'll see, everything in due time."

I wasn't entirely sure what he meant by that but I did know I didn't want him to leave me alone with Antonio. Zoe had left to get the tea. I shivered and Antonio asked me if I would like to go back inside. I nodded and pulled the shawl tighter around my shoulders as I got a sudden chill. "How long were we married for Antonio? I must be very fertile if I got pregnant immediately. How do you know the baby is even yours?"

He wheeled me into *my* room and asked me if I felt like lying down. I glanced over at the bed and saw that it had been freshly made up. I told him "no." He said that I would probably be more comfortable in the big chair and he could move it closer to the window if I would like so that I could look outside. I told him I would like that but how was he going to get me into it?

Antonio proceeded to move the chair and placed me to one side of it. "I believe I am quite capable of lifting you for I have been doing it for a number of weeks. You barely weigh 50 kilograms."

"One thing is for sure, I am not Spanish for I have no idea what a kilogram is." I ran my hands over my arms and stomach. "Have I lost a lot of weight?"

"Initially yes, but you have started to pick up some of the weight you lost. I am sure you will be back to normal soon."

He coaxed me to trust him as he slide his arms around me and effortlessly deposited me in the big chair. He asked me if he hurt me. I told him that he had not. I was able to scoot myself to the back and discovered that the chair was also a rocker. I thanked him and told him that he still hadn't answered my question about the paternity of the child I was carrying. He kneeled down beside me and took my hands in his.

"It would not matter to me who the father of the baby is for I love you Katarina, and I would accept it no matter what. However, I promise you that I am the father."

I think he was going to say something further but was interrupted by Sister Margaret and Zoe entering the room. They were each carrying a tray and set them down on a small table that Anton had pulled close to me.

"Will you be joining Miss Katarina for tea Sir?" Sister Margaret asked.

"Thank you, but I must put in an appearance at the docks and I do need to purchase some tinted glasses for Kat." He smiled down at me. "This is one of the happiest days of my life dear lady. I have prayed everyday for you to wake up and my prayers have been answered." He kissed my fingertips and left the room telling the ladies not to tire me.

Sister Margaret said that she was helping the cook prepare some special food for me so would not be staying either. I was fine with that as I really wanted to talk with Zoe alone.

"What do you want to try Ma'am…hot tea or iced tea?" Zoe asked.

"What do you usually call me Zoe; surely, it is not ma'am."

"No, I call you Miss Katarina and sometimes Miss Kat if Mr. DeMarco does not hear."

"If that is my name…then that is how you need to address me. Mr. DeMarco calls me Kat, so why can't you?"

"I don't know but I think he likes us to say Katarina."

"All right then. Zoe, do you think that if I looked at myself in a mirror I might remember who I am?"

"Why didn't any of us think of that I wonder?" She questioned herself.

She went over to a dresser and returned with a hand mirror and a brush. I stared at the reflection in the glass as Zoe brushed my hair. Looking back at me was someone I did not know and I asked Zoe if that was indeed me and she smiled and said that it was.

"You have the softest eyes and your hair is the color of caramel." She pinched my cheeks ever so slightly. "See how beautiful you are with a little pink on your face."

A solitary tear slid down my face. "I do not know the woman in the mirror." I brushed the tear away and tried to muster a smile and asked her why she had brought both hot and cold tea.

"Sister Margaret only drinks hot tea and she made it for you, but I thought that iced tea would be more soothing for your first drink."

I took a sip of the icy beverage and savored the taste in my mouth before I swallowed it. It went down smoothly and I took a longer drink.

"How is it Miss Kat? Do you like it?" Zoe asked.

"It is the elixir of the Gods!" I proclaimed.

"I put lots of sugar in it as I like it very sweet; do you want some lemon with it?"

"No, I like it just the way it is, thank-you."

She was very pleased and jumped up saying that she had just remembered something. She started for the door but turned and asked me if I would be all right alone for a few minutes. I assured her that I would be. She returned carrying two books. She sat down close to me and passed me one.

"This is a diary that I have kept for you ever since you came home from the hospital. You will please excuse my writing and my spelling as I am not that good in English." She handed me the other book; it was Jane Eyre by Charlotte Bronte. "I have been reading this book to you every day. It is about a poor young woman of yesterday who becomes a governess to the child of a Mr. Rochester who was a strange and I fear, lonely man. There are many words which I do not know or understand their meaning, but I am learning."

I held the treasured book to my breast. "I know the story Zoe and it is one of my favorites though I cannot tell you why. Together we will continue to read it and I will help you with the words if I can." I placed the book down on the little table and asked her to tell me about herself.

"There is not much to tell Miss Kat. Mr. DeMarco brought me here from a school for girls where I had been for eight years. Before that I was in an orphanage for eight years. The Sir chose me from twenty other girls to be your companion. I am glad he chose me."

"Have you no family Zoe? Surely, there is an aunt or an uncle or cousin. What happened to your parents?"

"I have no memory of them but have been told that they were killed in a train crash. The orphanage and school is all I remember. This is my home and I do many things here like help Senora Cara, the cook, and clean house when I am not at your side. I hope you will want me to stay."

"I am very glad that Senor DeMarco chose you; he did not make a mistake. I have only known you for a few hours but already know that we are going to be very good friends. I want to thank you for everything that you have done for me while I was in my deep sleep. I am sure that I must have sensed your presence."

I asked her if I could hug her and her eyes lit up and as we embraced I felt her tears upon my face. I was quite sure that this beautiful young lady had never been loved or appreciated before. All of that was going to change, but I was most curious or perhaps even suspicious as to why Antonio had chosen a girl with no family to be my companion. If I was to stay here until I figured out who I really was, Zoe would not be treated as a servant. We finished our tea and reluctantly I brought up the subject of the baby I was carrying and I said that I didn't know if I would be a good mother.

"Oh, Miss Katarina, don't worry, you are going to be the best mother ever. I will help you to look after her."

"*Her*, what makes you think that the baby will be a girl?" I queried.

"Just a feeling I have. I talk to her you know because you couldn't, but now you can."

I thanked her again for looking after me and the baby and told her I would like to have a bath and get out of the hideous gown. She told me that she would have to ask Sister Margaret but was pretty sure that the answer would be no. I asked her to find the Sister so that I could discuss the matter with her. She was right; Sister Margaret said that it was not a good idea and she would have to get Dr. Zaccaris's permission. I would not take no for an answer and said that I was going to have a bath whether she approved or not and she could chose to help me get in and out of the tub or I would do it myself. She became very flustered and went into great detail as to why I should wait until Mr. DeMarco returned home. She did not want to be responsible if I fell.

"Fiddlesticks, I am not going to fall! If you won't help, then you can leave and Zoe and I will manage on our own."

"Oh, dear, dear…will you at least wait until the physical therapist arrives?"

"What? What physical therapist?"

Zoe explained that Helga Bjorn came every day to massage my arms and legs and neck to keep me from seizing up. She said that

Helga was very strong and could carry me herself down to the pool where she performed water exercises with me.

"Pool…there is a pool here in the house?" I asked hopefully though I knew not why.

"Yes, it is on the back terrace. I help Helga to hold you up. At first, I was very afraid of the water but we do not go deep so I am okay. Someday I will learn to swim." Zoe informed me.

"Yes, you will Zoe and I will teach you." I avowed and then I wondered if I even knew how to swim myself. "When will Helga be here?"

Sister Margaret checked her watch and said that Helga should be arriving momentarily. We heard her before we saw her.

"What's this," she bellowed as she strutted into the room, "Katarina is awake?"

My Lord, she was an Amazon of a woman! I sat back a little in my chair as she approached me. I thought that she must be at least six feet tall. She had the body of a very muscular athlete. She stooped down and peered into my eyes with a large grin and then placed her significantly large hands on my shoulders.

"How do you feel Mrs DeMarco? Do you have any pain?"

"Please call me Kat or Katarina, for that is my name… apparently. I have no pain at the moment except for a slight headache and my left hip hurt when I tried to stand. I think that will all go away when I get into a tub of warm water. Sister Margaret said that you would help me to do that."

The sister said she did not say that exactly and didn't think that it was a good idea.

Helga laughed and said. "Nonsense, a bath never killed anyone! Why don't you start the water running Zoe while I do a few simple maneuvers with Miss Katarina?"

Apparently, I passed her test and she wheeled me into the bathroom. She told Sister Margaret that we would not need her assistance. With great ease she stood me up and maneuvered me into the tub of frothy, warm, revitalizing water. I sighed deeply. I soaked until the water cooled off and then called Zoe in to help me rinse my hair. She drained the tub and wrapped me in a huge towel and Helga came and carried me to the bed where she did a few more stretching exercises with my legs. I told Zoe that I didn't want to wear a nightgown and could she please bring me one of my old outfits, preferably a dress. She said that all of my clothes had been lost in the accident but that Mr. DeMarco had already bought several dresses for me. I wondered how my clothes could have been lost but said nothing. Zoe went to the closet and brought me a hideous bright pink garment.

"I hate pink! The only thing that looks good in pink is flowers." I stammered.

Helga smirked and said she agreed. Zoe exchanged the dress for a lovely blue one.

"That's better; blue is the color of the sky and the sea and the color of my true loves' eyes!" I exclaimed.

"Miss Kat, you had a memory, did you not?" Zoe asked hopefully.

I said that it was probably just a general observation and it meant nothing, I was sure. As Helga was leaving, I asked her if I could go to the pool tomorrow.

"Shall we see how you feel tomorrow? I know that you are anxious to get your life back, but you don't want to rush into anything too quickly do you?"

I told her that I had no idea what my life was suppose to be like but that I was quite sure that I had an affinity to water.

"Yes, I believe you do for even when you were comatose I had no problem keeping you afloat. But, it is the middle of November now and the days are cooling off, so we will have to wait and see what the day brings. I suppose we can always raise the temperature of the water; shall we just play it by ear? I have a feeling you are going to be a force to contend with and that "no" is not in your vocabulary."

Antonio was delighted that I was still up and dressed in one of his purchases. I inquired how my clothes could have been lost and he said that at the time of the accident it had not been a priority to retrieve them and new things could always be bought. He said that he would bring me catalogues and I could order whatever I wanted. I did not comment as I fully expected to do my own shopping in person as soon as I was able. I inquired as to the outside temperature and he said that it was about 15 degrees. I commented that it had felt more like 60 or 70 when I had been outside. He smiled and said that I was probably right if we used the Fahrenheit scale but in Spain temperature was measured in Celsius. I guess I had a lot to learn. I was given a horrible tasting broth which I nearly choked on. The custard pudding went down smoothly. Sister Margaret insisted that she give me a tube feeding and I agreed stating that it would be the last one. Dr. Z made an appearance and was pleased with my progress and told Sister Margaret that tomorrow I could have porridge in the morning and cream soups throughout the day.

I was exhausted by seven in the evening and was helped into bed. Antonio said that he would exchange the hospital bed for a normal one tomorrow and would I like a television set brought in? I declined and made my first entry into the diary Zoe had started for me.

November 11, 1981

This is my first day as Katarina. I have no choice at the moment but to accept what I have been told and that is that I am Katarina. Apparently, I have been in a coma for two months brought on by injuries I acquired from a car accident. I suppose that it is a blessing that I remember nothing of the traumatic event. I am in Spain in a villa by the sea. I am married to a man I have no recollection of and I am three months pregnant...just what any amnesiac needs to be told when she awakens from a coma.

I have been introduced to five people so far; Antonio DeMarco is supposedly the man I am married to, Doctor Zaccaris is my physician and a young girl whose name is Zoe, is my companion. Sister Margaret is my live-in nurse and Helga is my physical therapist. I like the doctor and Helga. Zoe is a sweetheart and the Sister, I can take or leave. Antonio is another matter completely. I wonder how it is that I know certain things and yet know not who

I am. I can recall historic facts and recite lines of poetry, but I have no memory of the days or even years before the accident. Dr. Z has tried to explain all the medical reasons why and cannot guarantee as to whether I will ever regain my personal memories.

I have looked in the mirror and I do not know the pale soul who peers back at me. Dr. Z says that he believes me to be in my mid thir-ties. I have only been married to Antonio for a short time before the accident so who was I before? Where did I come from? He says he does not know…that sounds highly suspicious to me. Why would a man marry a woman whom he knows nothing about? Am I some sort of fugi-tive? How did I get to this Rose Island where we met and were married? A thousand questions are plaguing me. I need answers and I am going to work very hard to regain my mem-ory for one thing is sure in my mind…I am not Katarina.

A month has passed since I emerged from my coma; nothing much has changed. Oh, I have all of my faculties back…except my memory, of course. My hip bothers me now and then, but I can manage the stairs to the first floor and get myself in and out of the bathtub. It is too cold to make use of the pool. Initially I lost weight after the removal of the feeding tube but I have gained it all back plus more. I find myself constantly in the kitchen rummaging through the cupboards and refrigerator to find things to satisfy my cravings. Senora Cara, the cook, does not mind and will make me anything I want. Zoe is a Godsend. I do not know what I would do without her. Whatever the reasons, Antonio made a good choice in selecting her to be my companion. I have no feelings for Antonio. He is kind and thoughtful and asks nothing of me; his only concern is for the well being of the baby and me. Time will tell if I will ever be able to accept him as my husband.

Chapter 10

Avanloch Castle

Winter had come early to Avanloch, and with the weather turning dismal and bitter, Rainey was experiencing a growing concern for Vienna's welfare. Was she somewhere warm and safe, or was she alone and cold wondering why he hadn't found her? A new scenario played out for him every night in his sleepless imagination. No matter where he was or what he was doing, she would come wandering into his mind and he would have to pause to see if he could see where she was. He was convinced that she was trying to communicate with him telepathically, but so far they hadn't been able to connect. He wondered how long he could go on this way.

Ava was his one saving grace. She had not gone back to school; she said she wasn't ready yet. Rainey was all right with that. Amma and Johnny practically lived at Avanloch during the day. Their three girls were all in school in Waverly and didn't arrive back home until late afternoon. After a light snack at the castle that Mrs. D always had waiting for them, they would trudge off to Brackenshire to do their homework and help Mrs. Macleod with the preparations for supper.

Johnny tried to keep Rainey occupied but it was not an easy task. He knew that Rainey was always preoccupied with concerns for Vienna. He missed her too. She had been a part of his life for twenty years…those same years that Rainey had been without her. Avanloch was not the cheerful place that it had been when Vienna reigned. Amma tried to put on a happy face for Rainey, but she was not very good at hiding her own sadness.

One day Amma had informed Rainey that he had a visitor. Before he could tell her that he wasn't up to entertaining he heard a little voice calling out his name.

"Rainey, Rainey! I'm here, it's me Tanny."

He stepped outside the office door and opened his arms up to the little girl who had been such an important part of his and Vienna's life in the summer.

"I miss you Rainey and I miss Tia Vienna!" She cried. "When is she coming home?"

"Soon Honey, soon." He had tried to sound hopeful.

Tanny and her mother became regular visitors to Avanloch. They would all have tea with Amma and Mrs.D in the small parlor. Tanny always made them laugh when she told them of her adventures with Vienna. She never failed to inform them that Tia Vienna didn't like tea and that she only pretended to drink it for Mrs. D's sake.

"She liked it when you put ice in it or made her coffee you know Mrs.D?"

That always brought a chuckle and a tear to Mary McDuff.

Rainey was going to miss his "tea time" with her.

Rosy and Evan came up every weekend and Jannie and John came every other week. Vienna's disappearance was extremely strenuous for Jannie. Roberge had come to lend his support, but was grief stricken himself so was not much comfort. Ash considered Vienna to be her sister and was heartbroken. She knew that Vienna was the glue that held Avanloch together and wondered how the castle and village could survive without her guidance and passion. Vienna's family called every week as did his parents. It was difficult to talk to Jimmy and Lara as they had shared so much together but he tried to control his emotions. He knew without a doubt that he would break down completely when he came face to face with them and that would be soon as he was going home.

The day was unusually cold for so early in December Duffy had told Rainey. The darkness of the day only added to his melancholy. He found his daughter watching some inane show on the television in the games room. He sat down beside her on the worn sofa. "Honey," he said ruefully, "I'm sorry, but I've decided to go back to Canada. I can't stay here any longer, especially with the holiday season coming. I need to see the boys and Mom and Dad."

"Don't be sorry Dad; I've seen it coming. Would it be all right if I tagged along?"

"The only thing that would make me happier is if your mother walked through the door this second. What about Rosy? I don't want her to think that we are abandoning her."

"She has Evan and I don't want to be here for Christmas. Everyone will understand and if they don't, well, too bad! We need to go and I say the sooner the better!"

"That's my girl. Rosy and Evan will be here for supper and we'll spring it on everyone then. Amma's girls are spending the night with her mother and so I will ask her and Johnny to join us. I suppose I should clear it with Mary and Lois."

"Let me do that Dad. Why don't you see if you can book a flight for next week?"

"I think we should have a visit with Jannie and John and Ash before we leave. I would also like to see Stu and Daisy too as I am sure they are in a frenzy waiting for the birth of their baby."

Ava hugged her father. "Perhaps we could even sneak in a visit with James and Althea, what do you think? Have you told Morgan and Mason yet?"

"I would so like to see James and Althea again and touch base with them. As for the boys, I think we will surprise them."

After the dishes had all been cleared from the table and coffee and dessert was served, Rainey informed everyone that he and Ava were leaving for Canada on the 9th of December. No one appeared to be surprised that he was going but made a big fuss over Ava's decision to follow her dad. Rainey guaranteed them that he would be back in the spring and that Ava was an adult and free to come and go as she chose.

"Whatever will I do without you sis?" Rosy bemoaned.

"I'll tell you what you can do darling sister and that is to carry on Mama's Christmas traditions and to get busy and make me an auntie!" Ava mischievously answered.

Rosy gasped as everyone else broke out laughing, including Evan. "Did you just say what I think you did young lady?"

Ava smiled and said she had some packing to do. Rainey asked to be excused also and made his nightly lonely trek to Vienna's sitting room. He spent every evening there reading her letters over and over again. Tonight, it was his turn to write to her.

Well Vienna, my love, it is with a sad heart that I pen these words to you. You have been gone from me for three months now though it seems like an eternity. The days drag on, I find no solace anywhere. I wander this mansion of yours at night but I meet no one…not even Maveryn. My heart and soul are crying tears that nobody sees, but everyone feels.

I am absconding to Canada. I cannot bear to be here at Avanloch without you any longer. This was to be our very first Christmas together and our child that you were carrying…does she still exist? I pray that the two of you are safe and being cared for. Ava is coming with me. Thank you my darling for giving me such a wonderful daughter.

I know not when I will return, but I will…perhaps in May. I will come and say hello to Avanloch, and then I will search for you again. I will keep searching until I find you. I know that you are still of this world for my heart would not be beating if you were not. Why you cannot come home is a mystery. I will wait for you forever. I love you Vienna La Fontaine. I hope you can feel me reaching out for you…for infinity…Rainey.

He folded the note paper and lightly touched his lips to it and then wrapped a yellow ribbon around it and placed it in the drawer next to the letters that Vienna had written to him. He locked the drawer that only he and Vienna knew about. Despondently, he walked he walked to the window and peered out into the blackness of the night. There was a light tapping on the door. He called out that it was open and to come in expecting that it was Ava. He was rather stunned to find Nanette Macleod standing there. He asked her what she was doing at Avanloch so late in the evening.

"I just wanted to see if I could do anything for you Rainey… anything, anything at all. I want to ease your pain in any way I can.

Whenever you should need someone, please know that I am here for you."

There was no mistaking her implication, but he chose to ignore it. "There is absolutely nothing that you could possibly do for me Mrs. Macleod. The only want I have is for my wife's return. Please close the door behind you."

He turned back to the window and waited until he heard her leave. "Sorry Vienna, I suppose I was rather rude, but I don't think you would object. I fear your intuitions regarding her may have been right."

There it was again…a flickering light coming from Willowisp Manor. It was easy to spot the illusive glow that moved from room to room and from floor to floor. He decided that it was time that he investigated. He stopped by his room and threw on a coat as it was cold outside and probably a lot colder in the manor. He crept down the stairs and let himself out through the conservatory. Snow had been in the forecast, but so far none had materialized. The ground was heavy with frost and it wasn't long until Rainey found his loafers thoroughly soaked through. He wondered why he hadn't worn over-shoes. At least he had remembered to bring a flashlight and the key that was hanging in the conservatory. He inserted it into the lock… the door swung open before he could turn it. Startled, he called out. "Hello, is anyone here?"

He didn't want to turn the lights on, but instinctively reached for the switch. He called out again…did he hear sobbing? He walked cautiously through the main floor of the manor and finding nothing proceeded up the stairs to the second floor. He stopped at every other step and listened…nothing. He knew that he was letting his imagination play tricks on him but he had the distinct feeling that he was not alone. If there was an entity haunting Willowisp Vienna would have surely told him about it…no, she had told the girls that lived here last summer that it wasn't haunted and Amma had attested to that. Come on Rainey, buck up, and keep moving. There were four bedrooms on the second floor and one bathroom and several closets. Rainey checked each one but found nothing that would account for the twinkling candle-like glow that he had been seeing for the past week. Perhaps the eerie light was always there…he would have to ask the family tomorrow. He wondered what he had been expecting to find…Maveryn or another ghost…or Vienna. He shook his head and made sure the door shut tightly, locked it and quickly walked back down to Avanloch. The iciness of the night had penetrated into his body and he couldn't shake the feeling of utter desolation.

Rainey was the last one into breakfast the next morning. Ava commented that he must have had a decent night's sleep for a change as he looked rested.

"Not so much Honey." He attempted a laugh. "Apparently, I look better than I feel. Anyhow, I am glad you are all still here as I have something I want to ask. Have any of you ever noticed a pale candle-like light emanating from Willowisp at night?"

They all shook their heads. Johnny said that they couldn't see Willowisp from Brackenshire and no one had had ever reported a sighting to him. He asked Rainey when he had seen the light.

"I first became aware of it last week but didn't pay it any mind thinking it was a reflection from the yard lamps. The past few nights I started to pay more attention to it and realized that it wasn't stationary. It appeared to move from floor to floor and room to room; it flickers exactly as a candle would. Well, last night got the better of me and I went to investigate. I found nothing tangible, not even a burnt out taper or footprints in the dust."

"What did you expect to see Dad?" Ava asked.

"I don't know… perhaps Maveryn, or the Grey Lady, or even an intruder."

"Maveryn never carries a candle Rainey as she emits her own light. Who is this grey lady?" Rosy leaned forward and placed her hand on top of his. She was intrigued by his encounter with a mysterious illumination, but silently thought he was imagining things. She had never once seen anything of the sort and she always looked out her bedroom window every night before she went to bed. Of course, she was in her father's old suite now and couldn't see Willowisp from there, but who on earth was this "grey lady"?"

"Come on you guys, you must have heard of the Grey Lady?" Rainey waited for someone to say they had, but again they all shook their heads. "Really? Well, I guess she is only a friend of Vienna's then. She visits her now and then and has taken her on some pretty funny trips through the bookcase in the upstairs foyer and yes, she carries candlesticks." Rainey waited for their reaction, but they all just sat there waiting for him to elaborate more.

"Do you all think that I am becoming unhinged…could be, but the Grandfather clock knows more than he is chiming!" Now I have your attention, he thought. One by one, he looked at them; no one was laughing.

"Are you jesting with us Dad?" Ava questioned. "Mama has never mentioned anything of the sort, and believe me, we have tried numerous times to get that bookcase to open."

"Honest to God truth; do you think I would kid about such a thing? Remember earlier in the summer when I took Vienna to see "Raiders of the Lost Ark? Well, it was about that time that she first told me about her encounters with the Grey Lady. Apparently, she started visiting Vienna just before the trip to Canada last January. She told me that you girls thought that you had talked her into going, but in reality, she was glad to get away from the shadowy grey figure. Vienna felt that the apparition was trying to take her somewhere, but if she did, Vienna had no memory of it. Anyhow, there were no more visits from her; perhaps I scared her off. Anyhow, one night we were all playing cards and Tanny was falling asleep so your mother took her upstairs and fell asleep herself…remember girls?" They nodded that they did.

"She woke up when I joined her later and thanked me for res-cuing her from the Grandfather clock. She said the Grey Lady had taken her on a trip through the bookcase in the foyer, down some stairs and through the Grandfather clock. She thought that I had rescued her. I was sure that she had been dreaming but she showed me the candelabra and insisted that there was a secret door inside the bookcase. We searched, but found none, but strangely, I found one of her pearl earrings outside the clock the next day. I never told her where I found it as I did not want to encourage her fantasies of yet another nocturnal entity. Come on people; think…there must be some mention of a grey lady somewhere?"

"I have read all the history of Avanloch that I can find and I don't recall any mention of anyone with the name Grey. It is a very common last name though so it is quite possible that there was such a person who existed and had connections to this land and castle, but maybe she wasn't important enough to be remembered on paper. However, I am pretty sure that mama never mentioned the name to me." Rosy asserted and Ava agreed.

"Doesn't matter anyhow…it was just a passing thought that it was "*her*" roaming around Willowisp." Rainey shrugged his shoulders and thought he had ended the inquiry.

"Did you venture into the cellar Rainey?" Johnny asked light heartedly.

"You have to be kidding…alone? I may not be eight years old like Vienna was when she had her encounter with the bogeyman, but I can still be frightened. I felt reasonably safe in the main floors but the basement…no way!" Rainey said laughing.

"Dad, you are just a fountain of information; Mama never told us any story about a bogeyman!"

"Well then Ava, I guess I will just have to tell you the story. You all know that Vienna's dad moved the family around a lot due to his work…one such job seen them located in some remote farm house somewhere in Alberta…I think it was Wainwright…anyhow, according to Vienna, the house was way out in the sticks. They didn't have a freezer and so a lot of perishables were kept in the cellar and it was one of Vienna's chores to retrieve said goods as her mother needed. She always cried that she was scared to go down by herself but Lily always told her to quit being such a baby and would not listen to her stories about a bogeyman." Rainey looked sideways at Rosy and Ava who were sitting side by side next to him and smiled. They encouraged him to continue and he hoped he'd do her story justice. He continued.

"So this so- called fiend would taunt her mercilessly saying, "I'm going to get you Vienna," over and over again. She said she would be as quiet as possible so as not to waken the sleeping monster. She got pretty good at grabbing what she had been sent for and was making it up the stairs faster and faster every time until the day she tripped and fell." Rainey paused briefly. "Lily had sent her down to get a pound of butter from the tin ice chest. Vienna had it her hand and was running for the stairs when she lost her footing and the butter went flying. By the time she retrieved it and was on her way up the steps, she heard him coming after her."

Rainey lowered his voice and spoke gruffly. **"Vienna…I'm on the first step…Vienna…I'm on the second step."** She yelled back at him that she was not Vienna, but he kept coming and taunting her. **"I'm on the fourth step little girl…I'm on the sixth step little girl."** Rainey swore he heard Ava shiver. **"I'm on the seventh step little girl…I'm going to get you this time! I'm right behind you little girl…can you feel me breathing down your neck?"**

"Just as Vienna reached for the door she knew that he was going to get her and she screamed as the ogre whispered. **"I'm on the last step little girl…"** Without missing a beat Rainey reached out and grabbed a wide eyed Rosy by the shoulder and said evilly. **"Gottcha!"** She screamed and would have fallen off her chair had he not caught her.

"Rainey Quinn, you but scared us half to death! If Mama were here she would scold you something awful. Are you all right Rosy?" Ava scolded her father surprised by his act.

"I can't believe Vienna never told you that story? Well, apparently it has some truth to it and she just embellished it a little. It was her favourite scary tale to tell around the bonfires, and believe me… she did it a lot more justice than I ever could. Sorry Rosy, I couldn't resist; forgive me?" Rainey got up and hugged her and grinned widely at Ava.

"Oh, I'll get you back someday Rainey." Rosy promised laughing along with everyone.

"Yes, my dear Rosy, I'm sure you will."

"I can attest to the fact that she will Dad…believe me, I know. You just made that story up though didn't you?" Ava looked to her father for an answer. "It would be so out of character for Mama. She never once mentioned a bogeyman to us, not even when we pestered her about letting us explore the cellars when we were young."

"No, it's her story, honest. How do you think she became known as V?"

"Really Dad, do you expect us to believe that the bogeyman scared the Vienna out of her?"

"You can ask her when she gets home." Rainey said matter of factually.

"Oh, Mr. Rainey, do you really believe that Miss Vienna will be coming home? There is so much sorrow that has come knocking on these doors that ah dinnae kin if I can take anymore. First, the good Lord took bonnie LizBeth…or so we thought…anyhow, she be gone from us. Lady Audrey, well she find peace when she pass over, but it be grief for the house and then Lady Maveryn, bless her beloved soul, and then Mr. Jeremy. Now Miss Vienna, the light of Avanloch…no, it is too much. I cannot stay here anymore." Mary McDuff moaned.

"Mary, I think you're right, you and Duffy need to get away from Avanloch." Rainey agreed. He walked around the table and knelt beside Mary's chair. "You asked me if I believed that Vienna will be coming home…I do, with all my heart and soul, but for some reason she is unable to right now. We all have to learn to live without her for a while…I know not for how long but she would want us to and so, we must." Rainey took her hand. "It is hard for all of us to be here and that is why I need a change of scenery, but I will be back. I think if you and Duffy were to spend the winter in London or wherever you want Avanloch will not seem so depressing to you when you return in the spring. What do you say? Your sister just moved to the Oxford district didn't she, and Duffy, don't your old army buddies live around the same area?"

Rainey stood up and asked Rosy if she could help them find suitable accommodations. She said that she most definitely could and it would be nice to have them close to her.

"But, who would look after Avanloch? Surely you are not proposing that Lois stay here all by herself are you, and what about Christmas?" Mary asked.

Rosy said that she hoped they would stay until after Christmas as there was still much work to be done and Ash and Gray, Jannie and John were all coming for the holiday. She suggested that Lois could also take a little holiday also.

"Don't worry about the house Mary, you know Amma and I are always here and then there are the MacLeod's. I think we could ask Winston to spend more time here also. If no one is here at night then I am sure the friendly ghosts will look after the place." Johnny promised.

The mention of ghosts brought a smile to Mary's face. "Yes, Miss Maveryn will keep the house safe and maybe this grey lady can help?" She winked at Rainey.

Ava said that the holiday would be the family's present for all the years that she and Duffy had been looking after them all. Mary dried her eyes with the hem of her apron and told Rainey and Ava that she was going to miss them something terribly.

"You brought a light to our Vienna when you come home with her Mister Rainey, and now soon she will bring the light back into your eyes…I pray." Rainey kissed her on the cheek and told her to keep that thought.

Johnny walked Rainey to the back staircase and placed his hand on Rainey's shoulder. "We are going to miss you Rain, but we understand why you need a change of scenery for a while. It's going to be a sad affair at Christmas without our fair lady at the helm, but Amma and I will do our best to see that all her traditions are upheld. The preparations kept Vienna busy, but there was always a noticeable change in her behaviour come December, and after all the hullabaloo of the festivities were over and done with, she would become sadder and sadder with each passing day. I was hoping it would be different this year because she had you and now not knowing where she is, I can't help but be apprehensive about her state of mind."

"Yes Johnny, I am well aware of her winter doldrums for I am to blame for them. It has been foremost in my mind for some time now and I am most concerned for her physical wellbeing, and just like you, I am most feared for her delicate emotional state." Rainey couldn't hide his feelings of despair. "This will be the first time that she has ever been away from her Avanloch family at Christmas, and it is bound to play havoc with her no matter where she is. What can we do Johnny except to hope and pray that she is being cared for?"

"You know she will be in our prayers every day just as you and Ava will be. Do you want me to keep watch with you tonight for the mysterious light at Willowisp?"

"Thanks Johnny, another time perhaps. I have a few corrections to make on the plans for Vienna's balcony …I'll leave them on her desk for you and you can do what you want with them. I don't mean to sound pessimistic, but I have this inexplicable sense that Vienna won't be coming home any time soon."

Johnny felt the same way but had not voiced his feelings to anyone. He, like Rainey, was a very rational man, but the feeling of hopelessness regarding Vienna's disappearance would not go away. He felt the same as Rainey; they would not be seeing her anytime soon.

They shook hands and Johnny turned away quickly not wanting to add to Rainey's despondency by his own sadness.

Rainey shut the door behind him in Vienna's upstairs parlor. He made a few notations on the blueprints and rolled them up and set them aside. He retrieved the key to the locked drawer and pulled it out and reread several of Vienna's letters to him. They were cheerful ones of her life at Avanloch and they lifted his spirits for a while. He promised that he would be back to read them again and proceeded to return them to the drawer for safekeeping but something obstructed the drawer from sliding. He got down on his hands and knees to see what the problem was and found an envelope lodged in between the drawers. He pulled it out and was surprised to see that it was addressed to him at his offices in Vancouver. There was no return address, but the handwriting was unmistakably Vienna's. He opened it warily and found a letter to him dated December 31, 1980. It wasn't like any of the others…there was no Dear Rainey or My beloved. A chill enveloped him as he read her words.

Rainey, this will be my last letter to you. Of course, if you are reading this, it means that you will never read the countless love letters that I have written to you over the years. I have decided that it is long past time that I drive you from my heart.

I have kept your memory alive for too long and it is time I let you go. My girls have kept me from being lonely, but they are grown now and I need to find someone to love. I need a man's arms around me and his lips on mine. I need to be alive again. I have lived these many years thinking that only you could fulfill me as a woman…how laughable is that? You, who have had countless women in your bed must find it amusing that I have only had one lover. I have not even shared my husband's bed. I was so naïve that I believed that I would be with you forever. Oh, you have been with me but I am sure that you forgot me a long time ago.

You never loved me, you never came for me and you ruined me for ever having feelings for another man. Do I sound angry? Yes, I think I am and it is about time! Goodbye Rainey Quinn. Oh, perhaps I should inform you that you have a daughter, just in case she comes looking for you. Her name is Ava Lane and she has eyes the color of an azure sea. I told myself that I would tell her about you when she was 21 because by that time I plan on being gone from Avanloch and living a new life, and I never plan on ever seeing you again.

It is New Year's Eve…exactly 20 years from the night you came to Bridge and took me to the dance in Hawthorne. I had so much hope *for us that night, but we all know how that turned out...*

May the sun shine brightly on your joyous days and the rain refresh you through peaceful nights. I still think enough about you to hope that you never fall 'crazy' in love...it will only break your heart sooner or later, and all the king's horses and all the king's men can't ever put it back together again.

The Grey Lady beckons me to follow her.

V

She hadn't even signed it Vienna. Why had he found this now… was it some sort of omen? He shuttered at the finality of her words. Who was this Grey Lady really and why was she calling Vienna to follow her?

Ava waited until they had been in the air for half an hour and her father had put the newspaper aside before she confronted him. "Dad, besides the obvious, what has you so pensive? Rosy and James both commented on how preoccupied you were. Have you learned something new regarding Mama?"

Rainey patted her hand. "Sorry Honey, I didn't realize that my mood was so obvious; but yes, you might say that something new has come to my attention." He reached inside his blazer pocket and extracted an envelope and passed it to Ava.

"What's this? It's addressed to you in Vancouver and it is in Mama's handwriting…oh God, what does it mean?" Ava stammered.

"It's an old letter Ava. Please read it."

She read it quickly and looked at her father. He was smiling sadly. She reread the letter, folded it and placed it back in the envelope. "She wrote this just a month or so before we went to Bridge, and Hawthorne."

"Yes and thank God that she came with you or who knows what she would have done."

"What do you mean?"

"Isn't it obvious? She made her feelings pretty clear, but there was something she wasn't saying…she was going to follow this grey lady, but to where? Was she contemplating …?"

Ava cut him off boisterously. "Don't you dare suggest that mama was going to do harm to herself…she never would!" Ava realized that her voice had risen to a fierce pitch and lowered it to a whisper. "Is that what you got from that letter because I didn't?"

"To tell you the truth, I am not sure of anything. I think it is fairly clear that she was going to banish me from her heart and find someone to love her. I am almost positive that she agreed to go to Canada with you, despite the grey lady's influence to see if Jack still wanted her."

"Jack Jennings; that's just crazy! Why would you say that?"

"He still has feelings for her and I think she has unresolved emotions for him. She told me and I believe her that they were never intimate but that he was there for her when I wasn't. He phoned her when we were in Bridge you know."

"So what? I think you are forgetting that Jack is married and if she wouldn't break up *your* marriage, she certainly wouldn't his."

"You are probably right, but for all she knew, he could have divorced his wife just as I should have mine in 1972 when she came to see me. If she knew that I was free, we would not have wasted all these years being apart; another cross for me to bear. Tell me Ava, how was your mom's mood that winter before you came over?"

"She was no different than usual. She was always cheerful and outgoing, concerned for everyone's happiness and wellbeing. Rosy and I should have paid more intention to her melancholy, but we were told that it was a clinical problem and it wasn't that serious. It's not true that she was only despondent during the winter as it was more constant than I like to admit. Rosy and I should have pried more into her past and kept at her until she told us the truth. Why didn't we question her nightmares about her cries for you? What kind of daughters are we?"

Rainey tightened his grip on his daughter's hand. "We will have none of that. I think we have both admonished ourselves enough for one day. In your defense, you girls lived rather a sheltered life until you went off to college didn't you? Am I correct in assuming that neither Rosy nor you ever dated before then? I imagine that it would be hard for you to think that your mother fell in love when she was only sixteen."

"You are right Dad, Rosy and I were home bodies until our late teens. We had plenty of friends, but never had boyfriends, so to speak. Yeah, and look what happened when I had my first serious relationship…I jumped into it just because I was curious. Thank goodness you came into my life before I made a mistake and married Randy. But we did know about love among young people because Mama's adventure stories of Emerald and Laddy also were about their devotion and affection towards each other. Now I know they were remembrances of her life with you. Soon as we get back to Avanloch I intend to read all of her accounts of our early years. I'm sure you will be amused by them. My favorite story is where she rescues you from the evil witch Priscilla."

Rainey put his head back and laughed. Ava asked him what was so funny.

"There really was a witchy woman with the name of Priscilla and your mother put her in her place and sent her packing."

"Really…so she was one of your many girlfriends was she?"

"No, she was never that…just a stupid dalliance. I never had 'girlfriends' so to speak. Sure, I had many meaningless flings when I was in university, but I never had what you would call a romance until the summer I met your mother. Of course, I blew that all to hell, but she took me back and again I almost sank my boat for good. That's where 'the witch' comes into the picture, but thankfully I learned the errors of my ways and won your mother back. I can honestly say that I have never been in love with anyone but her."

"Did you not love Louise at one time?"

"I had feelings for her because she was a nicer, kinder person when she was trying to get me to marry her, but no; I was not in love with her. By then, I was resigned to the fact that love was no longer in the cards for me and I settled for companionship. It was a poor substitute and within a few years I knew that marriage for me was a myth. Vienna says that I ruined her for any hope of loving someone else…well…she did the same for me. In that letter she said that she hoped I would never be 'crazy' in love…too late, I already was and am. Even though I have a broken heart right now, it will be mended as soon as she comes back to me. I will not stop searching for her this time. I think you know that I will do **anything** to bring her home. Enough of this; do you want to hear something preposterous?"

"In a minute, but first I want you to tell me how you know if you are really in love?"

"That's easy…when you wake up in the morning and you can't wait for the day to be over because you know you are going to be with the one you love later, or you wake up and she is already with you and your heart sings. Her smile and laughter are with you constantly. You eat, sleep and breathe with her name on your lips. When she touches you it is like a bolt of electricity flowing through your body and when she leaves, you are scared to death that she won't return. The rapture you feel when she is with you is nothing compared to the anguish that encompasses you when she's gone and you don't know if you will ever see her again. Your mother once told me that she owned my soul and that we would never be free of each other… little did she know how true that is."

Ava leaned her head on her dad's shoulder. "Oh Dad, that is so sad."

"Maybe, but I hope you will someday experience the wonders of true love and never experience the heartache. On a lighter note I ended up calling the boys and I guess we are going to be staying at the house because Louise has put it up for sale and flown the coop back to her mother's."

"What…can she do that?"

"No, my dear, she cannot, and so I guess the fireworks are going to start again."

Chapter 11

Life at Casscadia Casa

August 11ᵗʰ, 1982

Yesterday I married Antonio DeMarco. According to him, it was our second wedding, but to me it was the first. Only recently had I chose to be Anton's wife and so I thought that a few words spoken over us would sanctify our union. I do not know what I was expecting to feel after we were pronounced man and wife, but it did nothing to relieve the fact that I did not know my real identity. I will be Katarina DeMarco for the time being...

Just before Christmas last year I discovered that Anton had a mother and sister living across town. Apparently, they had visited me in the hospital and at the casa while I was still in the coma. Anton had not invited them over because he knew I was already coping with enough. One day I had found him and Somner attempting to wrap the gifts that he had purchased for them. I asked who the presents were for and he had no choice but to tell me.

"Why have you not told me about them; they are your family aren't they? I would give anything to know if I have a family!" I said annoyed that he had kept this from me.

"I'm sorry Kat…I should have told you, but I didn't think you were ready to receive guests. Forgive my blunder as I was only thinking of your well-being."

"Are they aristocratic… did they want you to marry royalty?"

For some reason they found my questions amusing. Somner excused himself but not before he looked at me and grinned. Anton asked me to sit down. I opted to stand.

I relinquished when he said he was only thinking of my painful hip. He explained his family to me. His father had been a fisherman all his life until he became ill and could not deal with the sea anymore. He found a position with a trading company and procured a part time job there for Anton when he was fifteen. After he finished school he went to work for the company full time and it is that same business that he owns today, only on a much larger scale. His father has since passed away and his sister Celestria and her husband Gilberto live in the family home with his mother Anya. Tria and Gil as he refers to his sister and brother-in-law have two grown children that live in France. Gil works for Anton and the family is far from being highborn, and are certainly not well-to-do. His mother is of French ancestry. I do not know why but that rang a bell in my subconscious mind. Anton told me that his family was only waiting for me to feel better before they made an appearance. I told Anton that Christmas would be the perfect time and that he should invite them for dinner. He didn't ask me if I was sure that I was up to it but came around the table and took my hand and said that it was more than he could have hoped for. The tear in his eye was my reward. I told him to sit down and we would finish wrapping the gifts together. He asked what I would like for Christmas.

I told him that the only thing I wanted was to regain my memory. He said he wished that for me also. He asked my opinion on what to buy for the staff. I had no idea, but together we came up with some ideas. I told him I would like to buy an electronic device that I had seen in the catalogue that played recorded movies for Zoe as she was quite enthralled by whatever movie she could find on the television. He said he knew exactly what I meant and believed it was called a video recorder and that there were several shops in the area that rented movies. He thought that was an excellent idea and that we should purchase some new clothes for her also as she had a very scant wardrobe. I asked him why he had chosen her from all the other girls to be my companion. He said he really didn't know only that he had felt some connection to her but could not explain it. I wasn't sure if I believed him. He then told me that he had set a bank account up for me in my name that was for my own personal needs. I told him I had no needs but he suggested that I might like to start purchasing things for the baby.

Senora Cara prepared a lovely Christmas dinner and I insisted that she join us for the meal as she had no family living in the area. I was most apprehensive about meeting Anton's family though I knew not why. I needn't have worried; they were most gracious, and I liked them immediately. They all spoke English very well but would throw in some Spanish or French phrases and then apologize afterwards. I told them there was no need for apologies as I understood most of the French and hoped to learn Spanish someday which was not altogether true, but I was trying to be polite. Anton's mother said that I reminded her of someone and did I have a French heritage; I told her I had no idea. She blushed and said she was sorry to have asked, but Gilberto interjected and said that he was positive that he had met me before but couldn't place where or when.

"Gil, you know that Katarina has amnesia, but I can positively tell you that you have not met her before. She is from North America and when we first met she told me that she had never been out of the country before, and seeing that you have never been to the United States that pretty much makes it impossible doesn't it?" Anton said, a little too vehemently I thought.

"If there is any chance that we have met I would be most interested Gil. Perhaps I just remind you of someone or," I said light-heartedly, "we knew each other in another lifetime."

Everyone laughed with me and no more was said of the matter.

I am not sure when it started; sometime towards the end of January, I think. I began to experience strange sensations with my vision…at least that is what I thought the problem was. I was glad that I hadn't said anything to Zoe or Anton for one day I realized that it wasn't my eyesight at all but my mind playing tricks with me. Two or three times a day I would feel as if something or someone was trying to make contact with me. I would close my eyes and see nothing but a black tunnel. For a fleeting moment I would catch a glimpse of something passing across the void and I would reach out to capture it, but I couldn`t. It was frustrating, but on the other hand I was hopeful that I would soon have a breakthrough to total recall.

February and March passed and I was no closer to regaining my memory. I could not reach into the recesses of my mind to establish a connection to my past. I could not touch whatever it was that was teasing me…always, just out of my grasp. I knew when a memory was trying to break free as I would experience a ringing in my head… not unlike the buzz of a bee and I would close my eyes, but I was always too late to catch a glimpse into the elusive shadows.

Anton and Zoe expressed their concern for me as they caught me many times in my trances. I always explained them away as saying that my ears were humming and that someone must be talking about me. I told them that it was time for me to see a doctor who could hypnotize me. Anton told me that I must discuss it with Dr. Z and Dr. Verache, my obstetrician, first.

In April, I was to see Dr. Verache twice a month and so on my next appointment I approached the subject of hypnosis with her and she advised me to wait until after the birth of my baby. Dr. Z agreed. He said that he had already spoken to a respected psychoanalyst on my behalf and that as soon as I was ready he would set up an appointment. He also suggested that it should be after the baby was born. He hoped he hadn't overstepped. I told him he hadn't, and that I would wait although I didn't want to prolong the hypnosis any longer than was necessary.

Most afternoons I would spend resting on the daybed in the family room. Zoe would put a movie in the VCR and I would try and keep my eyes open while it played but I usually fell asleep within the first half hour. Zoe was always amazed that I knew most of the actors. I suppose that I must have been a regular at the movie theater. On one such occasion I sat straight up and said. "I know that man!"

Zoe only smiled and said that she wasn't surprized.

"No, no…I mean I **know** him!"

"What do you mean Katarina, have you met him?"

I lay back down and said that I had no idea. I asked her what the actor's name was and she said "Rod Taylor." I had no clue as to who he was or why I should think that I knew him. She asked me if he was related to Elizabeth Taylor who she knew was my favourite actress. Again I told her I did not know, but I stayed awake through the whole movie wondering why I had such a strong attraction to the actor…did he remind me of someone from my dubious past?

Antonio's home was called Casscadia Casa and it sat atop a tiered hill above an inlet off the Genoaen Bay. The house was constructed from local materials and was a typical Spanish dwelling that the more affluent resided in. Anton had purchased it five years ago. Before that he had lived in the family home with his mother. He had wanted her to move in with him but she did not want to leave the only home she ever known. It was then that Tria and Gil moved in to share the house with her upon his suggestion as he had not wanted her to be alone. Anton never talked about his personal life. I was sure that he must have had his share of Spanish senoritas for he was a very handsome and kind man. He had so far not mentioned any romantic relationship and I had not asked.

The house was quite large and I wondered what had possessed Anton to invest in it. His right hand man, Somner Stamas, had his own bungalow on the property as did Constantine Vazques, another employer. They both worked at the Empire Emporium of Antiquities which is what Anton's business was called. Anton's brother-in-law was also employed there. Somner and Connie never worked on the same days. If Anton wasn't at home, one of them always was. They shared duties around the casa and acted as my drivers and body guard. I hardly ever stepped foot off of the estate so really had no need for a driver and certainly not a body guard, but Anton insisted that I never go anywhere alone. I wondered if he had enemies and would address the matter when I started to go out more. Right now I had no desire to tour around and was content to order baby things from the catalogues.

However, I did so like to explore the grounds in the mornings. The weather was quite pleasant and I did enjoy puttering in the gardens. Zoe was always my constant companion and we would meet up with the gardener who was pleased to have the company and was more than willing to answer all our questions that we had about the plant life. His name was Fernando, and his English was very limited. However, Zoe translated as best as she could. He talked a lot with his hands and was very proud of his work. There were three levels of terraces that were connected by rugged steps and gravel paths. Most of them I could manoeuvre, but if I kept gaining weight it wouldn't be for much longer so I best enjoy the gardens while I still could.

The kitchen door led to the vegetable and herb patches. Lettuces, spinach and other early crops had already been seeded. Every day Fernando would plant something new. Apparently, we would be eating fresh vegetables all summer. The aroma coming from the herb garden which contained lavender, thyme, and rosemary was both stimulating and eye appealing. There was a three foot wall of rock surrounding the plot and we exited through a small stone door. Fernando explained that the rocks provided shelter from the winds and also helped to retain heat.

Alongside of the wall was a floating water garden that was enclosed in a cement cistern. The aquatic plants were coming to life and the fish expected a handout at every visit. We were more than happy to oblige and always carried a container of their food with us.

A pergola awaited us just before we descended down unto the next level. It was covered in grape vines which later in the season would provide needed shade from the sweltering sun. Zoe and I usually sat on one of the benches. One day Fernando had described the plant life that was native to the area. Most of Spain was covered in spontaneous vegetation, but only a small part was woodland and forest, especially in the north in the Pyrenees Mountains. I asked him to tell us more about the Pyrenees for some reason I couldn't explain, I wanted to know more about them. He said that he had never been to the highlands but that I should ask Antonio because he knew them well.

Fruit trees grew among the olive trees and were starting to blossom. At the bottom of the steps was the rose garden. There must have been several hundred shrubs and I was looking forward to seeing each and every one in bloom. I closed my eyes and envisioned their fragrant perfume.

On the next level we found vibrant bougainvillea doing its best to conceal the structure that it climbed upon. I hoped I wouldn't miss its bloom time. Fernando informed me that it had a very long season. He told us that along with the other trailing vines he had a full time job just keeping them from invading the walks. Small shrubs and what looked like stunted trees to me completed the landscape on every landing. Stone pillars appeared to rise out of the ground and the smaller ones supported huge pottery urns which would soon spill over with new flowers. A tiled path led the way to a greenhouse where seasonal plants were kept. Inside a rainbow of blooming orchids sat on benches reaching towards the sun. I had been somewhat surprized to learn that Somner was responsible for this amazing display. I had no idea that the pots of orchids that adorned the dining room windows were grown right here on the grounds. Fernando said that the light fuchsia blooms were a favourite of Mr. Stamas's wife. I did not know that Somner was married but intended to find out why no one had bothered to mention it.

Grasses grew among the spring flowers that were in full splendour along the waters' edge on the bottom level. A rock wall that ran the length of Anton's property kept the plant life from escaping into the bay. Several small dinghies were anchored to a wharf at the beach. From the shore one could see Casscadia Casa sitting on the bank, overlooking the bay. It was quite impressive with its arched doorways and terra cotta gables. The roof tops of other homes protruded through the masses of trees. Sailboats were always visible out in the inlet. It was a long way back up to the top and in mid-April I decided that my jaunts would have to be postponed until after the baby arrived. I would do my gardening on the back deck.

I had asked Anton about Somner's wife. I was very shocked to find out that he indeed was married and that his wife was incarcerated. Anton did not or would not go into any detail regarding the circumstances. I knew that it was not any of my business but vowed that I would ask Somner myself one day. I had often wondered why he didn't have a hoard of women chasing after him as he was a very attractive man. He was always polite and would ask me every day what he could do for me. I believed that he was of Greek heritage and was in his mid-forties.

While I was trying to pry information out of Antonio, I thought I may as well inquire about Constantine's status also. Connie, as Anton called him, was older and had a stocky build and did not talk much…at least not around me, was also married. His wife had left him taking their two children with her many years ago. Apparently, he had a huge gambling habit and had lost the house to a debt he could not repay. He still bet on anything and everything but managed to send money to his wife every month. He always called me Miss Katarina and treated me with respect.

I also asked Anton if he ever went boating and he said. "Never, and you must not ever consider doing so yourself!" He had never spoken to me in that tone of voice before so I was a little bewildered by his response to such a simple question. He apologized at once and said. "Sorry my sweet, but I would worry about you too much." I wish he wouldn't call me pet names.

My due date was May 28th but my little bundle of joy arrived one week early. I named her Liliana. I would have been at a complete loss for a name if she had been a boy.

Chapter 12

Rainey and Ava

It took Rainey all of five minutes to straighten the house mess up. Mason dialled his grandmother's number and passed the phone to his dad when his mother answered.

"Louise, what the hell were you thinking putting the house up for sale?"

"How lovely to hear from you Rainey," Louise said sarcastically. "I see the boys have already contacted you. We do not need that house when Mother is all alone over here and all the amenities one needs are right here."

"You mean cooks and maids because you can't be bothered to do menial tasks yourself. Did you actually believe that the boys would want to change schools and leave their friends behind?"

"It's not that complicated Rainey; they can still go to the same school and see their friends whenever they want. Morgan has a car and can drive you know."

"That is not the point Louise…it would mean a forty minute drive twice a day to and from school, and what about extra- curricular activities? Do you think Morgan wants to taxi his brother around? Anyhow, none of that is happening. The house is not for sale and so you can contact your realtor and take it off the market."

"I can't do that Rainey as I am locked into an agreement for three months and there is already someone interested in it."

"Oh, really, have you forgotten the divorce agreement that says the house cannot be sold as long as the boys have need for it?"

"You told me that I could have the house remember?"

"Yes, I did, but there is nothing in writing to back that up is there? Ownership is still in both our names so you cannot sell without my okay. Did you forge my name on the contract?"

"You are still a heartless son of a bitch aren't you? Do you really think that you know what is best for the boys while you sit haughtily in that castle of your lovers?"

"I'm not at the castle Louise and you know very well that Vienna isn't either. By the way, did you have a hand in her disappearance?" Rainey felt that it was the perfect time to see how she would react to the accusation.

"What are you insinuating? Do you think I care enough about the two of you to give you any thought, let alone orchestrate a kidnapping? Ha! She left on her own volition. I told you that it was only a matter of time before she would leave you for someone else and she has, hasn't she?"

"No, but I am sure it makes you happy thinking that. But, we have strayed off the subject haven't we? A moving truck will be here first thing in the morning and so I suggest that you be here bright and early to see that nothing of yours is left behind for there will be no reason for you to ever return to the house again. Have I made myself clear Louise?" Rainey said emphatically.

"What? Are you here?" Louise was dumbfounded. She stammered, "Why?"

"We came to spend the holidays with the boys and will probably stay a lot longer. We will be moving into the house with them and providing them with the necessities of life…love and family… something their own mother couldn't be bothered to do."

Louise exploded. "WE…just who the hell is we?"

"Just me and my lovely daughter Ava…you remember her don't you Louise? She's the one who you called my bastard child to her face and whom you kept from her brothers."

"How dare you bring her into my house?"

"It is no longer yours or mine as we are going to give it to the boys. Do you understand what I am saying Louise? I wouldn't suggest that you fight me on this because there are certain documents that may just come to life? How is your mother anyhow?"

"You bastard! I should have known you wouldn't keep your word about destroying those friggin papers …how dumb am I for taking you at your word!'

"I don't know, but obviously you thought you could get the upper hand on me…well, think again. You really don't want to mess with me, so see you tomorrow then?"

Louise slammed the phone down hard. Rainey turned away rubbing his ear and smiled.

She stormed into the house the next morning, ignoring him and went in search of Mason and Morgan. Her disposition did not become any more amiable when Rainey informed her that they weren't home. He had them take Ava on a tour of the neighbourhood and shopping district as he didn't want his ex-wife anywhere near his daughter. He told her to take whatever she wanted as she would not be coming back ever.

"Just try and stop me!" Louise barked at him.

"The locks will all be changed and if you want to be charged with breaking and entering then that's fine by me." Rainey let her draw her own conclusion.

"You can't keep me from seeing the boys!" She retorted.

"That is entirely up to them, but you will not be visiting them here. Don't make me take out a restraining order on you Louise."

Hatred was in her eyes. "You righteous son of a bitch…hell is too good for you!"

Rainey went into his den and before shutting the door said. "Have a nice day." She threw a glass vase at the door barely missing him and cursed him again.

Monday morning Rainey phoned Quinn Enterprises and told his secretary Sylvie that he was back in town and asked her if she could arrange a meeting for him with the partners. She called him back immediately and said that everyone was in the office until early afternoon and were available anytime until then. He left Ava who was still rearranging the house after the mess that Louise had left in her tirade promising to be back as soon as possible. They needed to go shopping for furniture as he had sent his old bedroom suite and everything else he had no use for to a local charity. He had taken to sleeping in his den and hoped that new furnishings would change the cold atmosphere he seemed to encounter in the master bedroom. If not, he would swap with one of the boys as Ava was already settled in the guest room.

He was greeted warmly by everyone at his office and amidst the tears and grief that they all expressed over his loss; he assured them that Vienna was not dead…she was just away. He told the staff that he was planning on staying in Vancouver for a while and wondered if they could use an extra hand. The answer was a resounding 'yes'. The partners told him that they had more work than they could handle and had been contemplating hiring an apprentice architect so he had just solved the problem. He made sure they knew that he would be gone the moment that he had word that Vienna had been found. They understood. Sylvie escorted him into his old office; it was just as he had left it almost a year ago. No one had taken it over and he asked why.

"I really don't know Mr. Q; you will have to ask your partners. I kept a clipping for you from the Sun paper. I don't know if you care to read it as it is about the earthquake and might be a grim reminder of your pain …it's in your top drawer."

"Thank you Sylvie for your concern but my pain is always with me and I'm sure a newspaper article will not cause me any added grief. My daughter came with me and until she decides what she wants to do, I am hoping that we may find something to occupy her here…any suggestions?"

"Don't worry Mr.Q, we will find something for her. May I bring you coffee Sir?"

"I won't be staying today as Ava and I are going shopping for furniture. I hope to familiarize myself with the current operations and see how I fit in later in the week. I don't want to step on anyone's toes as I am no longer the boss, but I need something to do. I will be going to Hawthorne for the holiday so I hope that everyone will understand that my family comes first."

"We do Sir, and the offices will be closed from December 20th to January the 3rd so that we can all have a nice holiday. We will look forward to seeing you tomorrow Sir."

"Can you call me Rainey, Sylvie? Remind me to tell you the story about a real life witch that I met in Scotland."

"Are you foolin with me Sir…I mean Rainey?" She asked curiously.

"I assure you I am not. I could tell you stories about life in a castle that writers only dream about. You can't make this stuff up."

Sylvie smiled as she shut the door. "I can hardly wait to hear about life at Avanloch."

Rainey opened the drawer and took the newspaper article out and read.

From the World Wide Press September 10, 1981

Local connection to missing woman in European earthquake:
Well known architect, Rainey Quinn of Vancouver and wife Vienna LaFontaine, formerly of Bridge Falls B.C., were vacationing in Andorra when a 5.7 earthquake was centered in the village they were in. Several deaths have been reported even though damage was minimal. Mrs. Quinn has not been listed among the dead but has been reported as missing. The authorities have no explanation for her disappearance. Foul play has not been ruled out. Mr. Quinn and family remain abroad and are stalwart in their belief that Mrs. Quinn will be found unharmed. No one was available from Quinn Enterprises for comment.

He reached inside his jacket pocket and pulled out the last picture he had taken of Vienna and placed it on his desk. He had snapped it the night before the earthquake…she was laughing.

The months crept slowly by. It was time to return to the scene of the crime. On May 27th, Rainey penned a letter to Vienna.

My darling…I am writing this on the eve of my departure for Scotland. I am going to have a quick visit with our

Avanloch family and then I am off to Nazeth. Yes, I am returning to the very place that I lost you. I am living with the reality that it was my fault that you disappeared…just as it was in 1961. I am holding on to a thin thread that you are still alive. If it wasn't for Ava and the boys I don't know where I'd be without you.

We are all living in the house in Vancouver. Morgan is 17 and Mason 16. I arrived on the scene just in time to rescue them from being evicted by their evil witch of a mother. I am sad to say that we celebrated Ava's twentieth birthday without you. She tried very hard to be brave as this was her first birthday away from the only home she has ever known and without you or Rosy and everyone else at Avanloch. It was nothing compared to the tears she shed on your birthday. She and Rosy commiserated for an hour on the phone. When she hung up, she fell into my arms sobbing. "Where is she Dad…where is Mama?"

I am not making myself feel any better by writing this and so I will change direction. I am back at the firm because if I sat around the house I would go crazy. Ava has been working for a friend of mine who has offices just down the street from mine. We usually drive to work together unless I have appointments somewhere else. We, {the boys and you and me} bought her a little red sports car for her birthday. Mason is taking driving lessons. Oh, the facility that Ava works for is a wholesale pharmaceutical company. They supply medical clinics and pharmacies throughout the province. Once a week they send shipments to the far north via cargo planes. Ava does most of the paperwork and is contemplating taking some courses relating to the medical field. Because of her illustrative abilities I have enlisted her help several times with plans and perhaps someday she may decide to make architecture her vocation.

The hardest thing I have had to do in your absence was at Christmas when I had to come face to face with Mom and Dad and Jimmy, Lara and Sissy. It had to be done and through many tears we all got through it. Ava ended whatever it was with Cam. Oh, by the way, I met Jack Jennings. He came to see me at the Palace when Ava and I went to see Lara and your sister. His distress over your disappearance was most obvious and believe it or not, I was the one who tried to ease his pain. I got the distinct impression that Sissy and he are in some sort of a relationship. Would that bother you Vienna? He made it clear that you and he will always be friends. I found myself liking him. I know, wonders will never cease will they Sweetheart?

Something has changed in the way I picture you. What is different Vienna? Have you had our child? Oh, how I pray that you and she are well! I can't wait to meet her and I am so sorry that I wasn't able to be with you…I love you Vienna LaFontaine and I miss you with every breath that I take. Please be in Nazeth waiting for me.

Yours, until the end of time
Rainey

Chapter 13

Life as Mrs. DeMarco

Liliana was 4 months old when I found myself somewhat bored. She slept most of the day away and when she was awake I would just sit holding her and marvel at how she changed daily. She was born on May 21st, a beautiful spring morning at 9 a.m. I had not known what to expect when I went into labour at the casa but four hours later she arrived; I was pleasantly surprised that she had come into the world with very little effort on my part. She weighed 3.18 kilograms which was 7 pounds in English. I had gained so much weight that I had expected her to weigh at least 10 pounds. Dr. Verache said she was perfect and she was. She had a mass of blonde curls and blue eyes. I was told that would all change as she got older which I had assumed as Anton and I both had dark brown eyes. He had black hair whereas mine was a bronze color. However, here she is four months old and her hair is still blonde, and her eyes are bluer than they were at birth.

Anton was not concerned with her light coloring. He had wanted to be with me in the delivery room and was up until five minutes before Lili was born. Dr. Verache sent him out saying that his anxiety was not helping me to relax, and that he could return the minute the baby was born. I had not been exactly pleased that he had insisted being with me anyhow. He had tears in his eyes when the nurse showed him his new daughter. He had kissed me gently on the forehead and said. "Gracias Mi Querido for our bella daughter, Te amo." I knew that he was thanking me for giving him a beautiful daughter and that he loved me.

One of my nurses said something strange to me after Anton had left to inform his mother that she had a new granddaughter. "I have heard some pretty strange things when women are in the throes of labour but never have I heard a woman cry for rain to help her before. Do you remember saying that?" I had no idea why I would say such a thing.

Now here it was September and I needed something to occupy my mind. I was tired of watching movies in the afternoon when Lili was napping and I couldn't seem to concentrate on the plot or characters in a novel. I had not made any friends except for Anton's family who visited often. Of course, I had Zoe. She had asked me if I would help her read and speak English more fluently and so I would tutor her every day for an hour or so. She was a very quick learner and I enjoyed our time together. She also helped me with my Spanish although I was not that eager to learn anything except the basics, but surprisingly the language came quite easy to me. I often wondered how much education I had. Had I attended a college? I must have had a job or had I been married and dependent on my husband? Dr. Z had told me that I had not given birth before so at least I hadn't left any children behind. I was not so certain about a husband or lover though. Was he the "something" that was plaguing my subconscious? I was sure there was someone and I decided to write him a letter. I did not know whom to address the letter to or even what I should say, so I guessed I'd just speak from my heart.

To the unknown entity that lives in the shadows of my mind.

I do not know who or what you are to me, but I feel you are trying to make contact with me. Are you real or just a figment of my imagination? Were you my lover, did we have a tumultuous relationship, did I do you unspeakable harm? I fear that something dreadful must have happened and that I have chosen to erase you from my memory.

If this is so then I am sorry for whatever hurt I caused you. I have nothing more to say for the records of my yesterdays have all been obliterated and I am blank. If I am meant to recall my previous life then I will; If not, I am fairly content with my new existence. I have my dear friend and companion, Zoe, and my cherished daughter, Liliana. I have a man who loves me and yet, I find myself searching for you...

I had no idea what the night of August the fourth had in store for me when I lay my muddled head down on the icy cold pillow. My headaches were always worse when there was a full moon, and tonight was no exception. I was reluctant to take any medications as I was nursing Lili and I didn't want any drugs to enter her body. The only thing that helped to alleviate the throbbing was a cold pillow that I would cradle around my neck and so I always kept one in the freezer. As soon as I was settled, Zoe brought me a cold pack for my head and said she would check in on me in an hour to see if I had any luck falling asleep. I was still awake when I heard faint footsteps outside my room. "You can come in Zoe, I am awake." I called.

"It's not Zoe, Kat. Are you ready for another cold pack?" Anton approached my bedside and asked if there was anything else he could do for me.

I thanked him and told him 'no' and to go to bed. He kissed me lightly on my cheek and told me to ring for him if I needed anything. He said he hated to see me in such discomfort. I assured him that I would survive. Anton pinned the call-bell that had been installed when I was brought here from the hospital to my pillow.

I had been experiencing some pretty scary dreams lately but I always managed to wake myself up before they engulfed me. That night I found myself entangled in the thorns of a bramble bush.

My hands and feet were cut and bleeding from the barbs that were assaulting me from all angles. I was wearing a long white gown and it was soaked in bright red droplets of blood. I was exhausted from struggling with the prickly foul smelling devil claws; there was no way out. Just as I had coiled myself into a ball and was awaiting the final crucifixion I heard the voice of an angel calling me. "Come to me, come to me, come, and let me take you home." He was calling me by a name that I did not recognize. I reached out to take his hand but something grasped me from behind, and I screamed and screamed and screamed.

"Katarina, Katarina, wake up, wake up Cara mia."

I opened my eyes to see Anton and Zoe standing over me.

"Are you all right Katarina? You were screaming so…oh, I best to check on Liliana." Zoe ran out of the room as soon as she was sure I was okay.

Anton sat down on the bed and took my hand in his and asked me to tell him what my nightmare had been about. As I was telling him about the thorny bushes, I suddenly realized that I'd had the same horrendous dream before but knew not where or when.

Zoe returned and said that Lili was still sleeping soundly. I told her to go back to bed.

"Thank you for waking me Anton. Now I think that you should go back to bed too."

He asked me if I was going to be able to go back to sleep. I told him not for a while and that I was going to go and sit out on the terrace. He asked if he could join me and I told him that I would appreciate the company. He asked me if I wanted a dressing gown and slippers.

I smiled at him. "Do you really think I want something on my feet?"

He laughed. "Of course not my barefoot Cherie."

He draped the kimono over my shoulders and led me to the settee that overlooked the bay. He did not sit down beside me but took up a position behind me and proceeded to massage my shoulders and my neck.

I surrendered to the touch of his comforting masculine hands. "That feels wonderful Anton." I murmured.

"Then it is time that you have massage therapy every day. Perhaps it will alleviate your headaches. I will look into it tomorrow."

I placed a hand over his. "Why are you so good to me Anton?"

"I think you know the answer to that Katarina… it is because I love you."

"I don't know how you can keep saying that. I am not very nice to you; in fact some days, I am barely civil."

"It is all tolerable because I get to sit across from you at the dinner table and listen to you and Zoe talk about your day with Liliana and I get to see how your eyes light up when you are holding our little daughter. I cannot thank you enough for giving her to me. I will never be able to understand fully what you are going through in trying to regain your memory, but I hope one day that Lili and I will be enough for you."

His voice had become unusually deep, yet soft. My defences were down.

"Come and sit with me Anton."

He did and rested his arm on the back of the settee. I leaned into his body and he dropped his arm and his hand travelled up and down my face as he murmured my name over and over. I leaned into him and we kissed, gently at first, then with a pent up fervour that built and built until I could barely breathe. Anton picked me up and carried me to my bed. He leaned over me and thanked me. Still gasping to regain my breath I whispered. "What are you thanking me for?"

"For giving me hope." He said and stood up.

"Where are you going?" I asked him.

"I think I best take my leave from you while I still have my senses."

"Suppose if I don't want you to go?" I stuttered.

"Kat… are you sure?"

I reached out to him. "Oh yes, I don't want to be alone anymore."

I automatically woke up at a quarter to six. I had trained myself to wake up before Liliana so that I could be somewhat alert. I climbed out of bed quietly so as not to disturb Anton. I retrieved my night clothes from the floor and tip toed into the bathroom. I washed my face and peered into the mirror. Was that me? I suppose it was. Did I expect to look differently after spending the night with Antonio? This wasn't the first time that I had slept with him…we had Lili to attest to that. It was just the first time that I remembered.

Zoe already had Lili changed and ready for me. I sat in the rocking chair and Zoe handed her to me. I thanked her and apologized for startling her with my screams. She asked me if I was able to sleep peacefully for the rest of the night.

"Anton stayed with me."

"I'm glad he could help you forget your nightmare."

"That's not what I meant Zoe; I slept with him." I didn't want her to misunderstand.

She knew perfectly well what I meant. "You shouldn't be telling me this Miss Kat."

She hardly ever called me "Miss Kat" anymore. "Who else do I have to talk to?"

She pulled up a chair and sat beside me. "Do you love him Katarina?"

"I honestly don't know Zoe, but he loves me and perhaps in time, I will come to love him as a wife should love her husband. It doesn't help any that I cannot remember our wedding, or anything else for the matter."

"Perhaps you should get married again. I am sure Mr. Antonio would not object because you are right; he loves you very much and would do anything for you."

"Zoe, you are so wise for such a young girl! It is a marvellous idea and I shall discuss it with Anton later today." I reached out with my free hand to touch her. "One thing I do know for sure and that is that I love you!"

"And, I love you Katarina…you and little Lili are my family."

Anton did not go into work that day. It just so happened that the cook had asked for the day off and Anton had breakfast all ready for us when we made our way down to the kitchen. He asked if I was drinking coffee yet and I said. "I know Lili doesn't need the caffeine, but I surely do."

He smiled and said that he was sure it would be out of my body before her next feeding. He had made us a Spanish omelette sans the onion and peppers for mine and Liliana's benefit. The table was laden with freshs fruit, chocolate conchurros, and a variety of breads. I told him that I didn't usually eat this early and certainly never this much. I asked him if he was trying to fatten me up. He replied that I was a lot thinner than when he had first met me and that a few more kilograms wouldn't hurt. I had no idea what I had once looked like so had to take his word for it. I believe that Spanish men like their women a bit on the plump side.

True to his word, Anton arranged for me to have massages every day. Either Angelica or Sophia would arrive at two in the afternoon and I would enjoy their services for an hour or more. Lili was usually napping at this time of day so we were very seldom interrupted. The girls were both in their early twenties and spoke English quite well though we did not chat much during my treatments as I was supposed to concentrate on complete relaxation. I guess it worked as my headaches were becoming less and less bothersome. I was no longer tense and moody…but maybe my acceptance of Anton was the true reason. He certainly was a happy man and surely the day would come when I would love him as much as he did me after our wedding.

The ceremony had been a simple rite performed by a court official. Zoe, Somner and Connie were our only witnesses and Liliana, of course. Somner had fashioned a bouquet of orchids for me. I thanked him with a hug and said that I hoped his wife wouldn't mind. At once I wished that I could take my words back but it was too late. He looked at me with a grin and said: "You know about Lelani do you?"

"Only that you are married and take a special orchid to her every time you visit. Do you think that I could meet her one day?" I asked anticipating his answer.

"That day will never come my lady. Prison is not a place for a woman of your stature."

I wondered at the time what he had meant by that but didn't question him on it.

We did not inform Anton's mother or sister of our nuptials until after they had taken place. His mother had not been happy with us when we didn't have Liliana christened at her church. She and Celestria were devout Catholics, but Anton was no longer a practicing Catholic. We had discussed the matter at great lengths. Anton told me that he had lost faith with the church when he was a teenager. He was a rebellious teenager and at fourteen his parents had sent him to a summer camp for religious instruction. They had hoped that he would come around to the Catholic doctrine of belief. Instead, it had the opposite effect, and he ran away from the encampment and spent the rest of the year trekking through Spain and France picking up the odd job here and there. There was hell to pay when he returned home, but his parents wanted him to finish school and so they established a few ground rules and he agreed to them but was adamant that he wasn't returning to the church. His mother's uncle was a priest by the name of Father Bissette. He had been Anton's biggest advocate, but sadly, he had died recently under unusual circumstances that Anton would not elaborate on. Anton said that his influence had helped him to become the successful businessman that he was. Because I had no idea of my faith, we decided to put Liliana's christening off for the time being.

In October I met Armand Démodé. Thanks to Antonio's influence as a contributor to the Palacio de Verde El Mar Museo de Arte, {Palacio Vemma} I had been offered a position on the board of directors at the gallery. I readily accepted. We were scheduled to meet twice a month. The curator, Senora Elaina Bolivar, and I became immediate friends and she would often enlist my help with any number of tasks that needed attending to. I found myself at the museum that was housed in a beautiful old remodelled palace several days a week. Mostly, I did the cataloguing for the travelling canvasses and sculptures that were on loan from other galleries. Many masterpieces including works by Spanish artists Picasso and Dali graced the walls. Local artists abounded and Armand Démodé was my favourite.

One day I arrived at the museum to find a new work of his in preparation to be displayed. It was of a castle in Austria and I had to have it. I purchased it immediately agreeing to let it hang on the entrance wall of the museum for two weeks. A few days later I opened the casa door to a stranger carrying a large parcel.

"Are you Senora Katarina DeMarco?" He asked me.

I answered that I was and he said that he was Armand Démodé, and was here to deliver the painting I had bought. I was astounded that the man whose works I so admired was standing on my front steps. I implored him to come in and led him into the living room.

"Where would you like me to hang it Mrs. DeMarco?"

"Please just call me Vienna. You certainly don't have to hang it though!" I told him.

"Vienna?" He said. "Why would I call you that?"

"What?" I was confused.

"I'm sorry; I think I misunderstood you Senora." He proceeded to unwrap the painting. "Are you under the impression that this is a Viennese castle? It is from a region outside of the city."

"It doesn't matter where it's from. I fell in love with it the moment I saw it. I am deeply honoured that you have delivered it." I offered my hand to him and he took it and said that the honour was all his. I asked him to stay for refreshments and suggested that we let my husband look after the hanging of the canvass.

We engaged in idle conversation for a while and then I asked him if he ever gave art instruction. He asked me why and I told him that I wanted to learn how to paint.

"I will pay you handsomely if you would give me lessons."

"It would be my pleasure Mrs. Demarco, but I do not wish to be compensated. I have taught the basic techniques in several classes before but have never given private lessons, but would be honoured to be your personal instructor. How much schooling have you in the medium?"

I laughed. "I would not have expected you to know this, but I have amnesia and have no idea if I have ever had art lessons before let alone anything else. I am a clean slate I am sorry to say."

"I am sorry to hear of your dilemma, but for us, I think it will be an advantage to start from scratch. When would you like to begin Mrs. DeMarco?"

"I am Katarina and I would like to start as soon as you have the time."

"So be it Katarina! I shall arrive tomorrow and we will begin at once."

I am sure that Armand was a wonderful teacher, but I did not take to instruction easily. I just wanted to paint… I wanted to paint the castle that I visualized on the isle of Somara. I didn't need to know the basics or different techniques or the characteristics of the different mediums. I was very impatient and I know that Armand must have been disappointed with my lack of discipline, but he did not show it. Reluctantly, I agreed to listen to him and start at the beginning. The moment he was out the door I would put a new canvass up and frantically cover it with brushstrokes hoping that some semblance of the fortress would materialize, but it never did. I only succeeded in becoming more and more frustrated because I could not accomplish what I thought was an important clue to regaining my memory.

For two months I painted, if one could call it that. Armand said that I was making progress but he was only being polite. He knew that I wanted to put what was in my head onto canvass, but I had never told him what it was exactly. In early December he asked me to describe my visualization to him. He sketched as I explained it in great detail but he did not let me see it. Christmas was rapidly approaching and we adjourned our lessons until after the holiday.

Liliana was seven months old at Christmas. We had Anton's family over for the day again. There was much laughter and merriment, but I felt that something was missing…or was it someone? Anton had given me a multitude of gifts but one saddened me. It was a set of three silver bracelets held together by a fine chain. They were in a tiny silver box that had been wrapped in glimmering silver paper. I had a moment of trepidation as I opened the box. I fondled the bracelets and when I read the inscription I cried and cried and cried. Anton had taken me in his arms and begged me to tell him what was wrong…did I not like them?

I apologized to him and everyone else saying that I was overcome by their beauty and Anton's generosity. I was not known for making such a public display of my emotions and Zoe knew that something had upset me. She came over and hugged me and I showed her the inscription.

For My Beloved Kat…For Infinity, Anton

Somehow I was able to get through the rest of the day. The excitement was too much for Lili and she refused to let anyone hold her except me. By eight o'clock she had become unruly and I made our excuses and took her upstairs to her room. After getting her into her night clothes, I stripped down to my slip and brought her to to lie with me in her little bed. We cuddled and she immediately fell to sleep. I whispered as she drifted off. "I am so sad Lili. I know not why but it has something to do with those bracelets. Why, oh why can't I remember anything? I love you my little blue eyed doll." I kissed her and let the tear drops fall.

I carried on the next day as usual. Anton told me that he missed me in bed but understood that Lili needed me more. I left the bracelets under the tree.

As we were getting ready to go to a New Years' Eve party that Anton was throwing for his employees and acquaintances at his warehouse at the docks, the doorbell rang. Somner answered it and presented me with a large package. It appeared to be a canvass and it was. There was a note that said: 'Sorry this didn't make it for Christmas. Is this it? Cheers, Armand.'

I enlisted Somner's help to rip the heavy brown paper away from the canvass as he was the only person in the room with me. I couldn't remember being this excited ever. I stood back and laughed and laughed. "This is it Somner; this is it! This is my castle!"

He stammered. "What do you mean "your" castle Katarina?"

"The one I see when I look at Somara Isle, you know about it don't you? Well, here it is. I couldn't paint what I was seeing and so Armand did it for me." I was so happy that I grabbed Somner by the arm and proceeded to dance around him. My merriness was contagious as he swung me around rejoicing with me.

"Well, well, well, I must say that this is not a sight one sees everyday…what's the occasion?" Anton questioned us as he entered the living room.

I pulled him beside me and pointed to the canvass. "Look Anton…it's my castle!"

He looked over at Somner and said curtly. "What's the meaning of this?" The expression on his face was one of ire which was out of character for him.

"Why are you asking Somner? He has nothing to do with it; Armand painted it for me and I would think that you would be happy that my vision is now a reality for me! You need not worry as I will hang it in my room and you never have to see what you have always called my 'silly folly' again. Somner, will you help me take it upstairs please." I was hurt and I wanted Anton to know it.

"Katarina, Cara mia, I am sorry." He tried to take me in his arms but I backed away. "It just took me by surprise is all that another man has given my wife what I could not. If it makes you happy, then I am happy and we will hang it in the entrance, what do you say? Can I have a little kiss? I don't want to start the evening with you angry with me?"

Zoe saved me entering the room saying that Anton's Madre and Tria had arrived to babysit. We visited with them for a few minutes and then left for the party. I was in no mood for the festivities, but it was Zoe's first social event and I would not spoil it for her. I was a little amazed that I had acted so fervently to Anton's reaction over the painting, but the way that he had looked at Somner was puzzling, and almost accusingly that had shocked me.

I had been at the Import-Export Emporium several times before. Anton had wanted me to come and chose some new, which really meant 'old', pieces for the casa. The first time I had been awe struck by the enormity of the building and its' contents. I had walked around touching century old pieces that had been set up for display for customers Anton proudly described what each piece was made of and where it had come from. There were bespoke cabinets richly decorated with panels of silver, tortoiseshell, ebony and woods like rosewood and chestnut. He explained to me that at the end of the 16th century an edict had been issued that prohibited the making and selling of "silver" merchandise. Now anything from before that period was very hard to come by. Museums housed the majority of those treasures, but there were still individuals who needed the monies and would sell their inheritances to the highest bidders such as himself.

I couldn't explain why I felt so at home with all of the antiquities. I chose six high backed Portuguese dark brown leather chairs that had numerous figures of birds and floral scrolls inlaid in them. The dining room chairs at the casa needed repair and so these would replace them. They would go nicely with the large Spanish chestnut table and credenza and other furnishings in the room. I also picked out several highly decorated Chinese bamboo screens, one for me and one for Zoe. Anton wanted me to make the casa homier and I told him I would take stock and chose more furnishings at another time as it was all too overwhelming for me. Several weeks later I returned and selected embroidered velveteen covered chairs and settees, colourful tapestries and ornamental pieces and mirrors decorated with gold leaf and bronze gilt for the sitting room. Perhaps I would do some more decorating next autumn.

Anton and his band of merry helpers had turned the display area in the warehouse into a dance floor. The vintage furniture had all been replaced with everyday inexpensive pieces. There was a buffet table laden with traditional Spanish fare and a fully stocked bar. A local band had been hired to entertain us. Anton had spared no expense. Much to my dismay, I had hurt my hip in my little dance with Somner and was only able to manage several waltzes. I enjoyed watching Zoe as she was whirled and twirled around the room. Somner had taught her the basics of waltz and bop. She was a very fast learner and was never without a partner.

Anton did not dance much but wanted me on his arm as we strolled around talking to the guests. Just before midnight, he excused himself and said he seen someone he needed to speak to. I was not invited to attend him. I did not want to appear as if I was spying on him so I went and stood beside a door and watched his encounter with an older woman who was standing in a far corner of the room. At first it appeared to be amiable, but soon it seemed to turn into an argument. Anton threw his arms in the air and the woman raised her hand as if she was going to slap him but Somner miraculously appeared and caught her hand. He abruptly escorted her out of the building. Anton waited for Somner to return and the two of them returned to the folds of the party deep in conversation. They stopped talking as soon as they saw me. The top of the hour was approaching and Anton asked me if I was up to a slow dance. I told him I was, but when the band started playing I was overwhelmed with a sadness that I could not comprehend. The song they were playing was in Spanish, but I recognized the melody and it was what had brought me to tears.

"What is it Cara mia…you never cry. Are you hurting that much?" Anton lifted my head up and looked into my eyes but they weren't his eyes staring back at me…they were eyes the color of an azure sea and I felt myself slipping into another world. The last thing I remember was the castle doors opening up and engulfing me.

I awoke on the sofa in Anton's office with everyone standing over me. I asked what had happened and was told that I had fainted. Anton ordered Somner to get the car as he needed to take me home. I objected vehemently stating that he needed to stay at his party and that Somner could drive me home. Zoe insisted on coming with me and only then would Anton allow me to go without him. In the car I asked Somner who the woman was that he had escorted out the door.

"Another time Katarina…it is not my business to be telling." He answered me.

I laughed. "What you are really saying is that it is none of *my* business isn't it?

"No my lady, I am not saying that. It's Anton's story to tell and he will in time."

"Ah, I see, she is his mistress."

"That's complete nonsense for you to think that…he only has eyes for you!"

"And, if he doesn't tell me, will you? There is something going on with Anton, but he denies that there is. You know what; don't tell me…I don't care one way or the other."

"Katarina, I promise that you will know all someday."

"All…what else is there? When is someday, the same day you tell me about Lelani?"

Somner didn't answer me but I knew he was grinning.

Anton telephoned several times to check in on me. The last time I told Zoe to tell him that I was sleeping. I did not want him fussing over me when he came home. We discussed my little fainting spell the next day. I laughed it off contributing it to exhaustion and being overheated. Anton was not convinced and wanted me to see Dr. Z. I told him that I was going to see a doctor all right but that it would be another psychoanalyst as I wanted to try hypnosis again.

"Why do you want to put yourself through that again? The results are bound to be the same…you are one of the rare people who cannot be hypnotized. I was hoping that you had come to terms with who you are, but I see that you have not." His tone was condescending.

"I will never give up trying to uncover my past. If you cannot live with that, then so be it." I walked out of the room and phoned Somner and asked him if he could please come over and help me. Anton followed me and asked me what I needed Somner for and I told him I needed help to hang my painting. Then I said something that was utterly callous.

"Perhaps you would prefer that I don't hang the canvass of the castle at all? In that case, I will just take it and Liliana and Zoe and be out of your hair!"

I had stunned Anton. He stood with his hands at his side and the look on his face was heart-breaking. "What have I done to ire you Katarina? Please enlighten me for I am at a loss…is it all over my initial reaction to the painting? I want you to have it for I see it is important to you. Please, let's hang it in the entry hall or closer to you if you like?"

Seeing the castle as I had imagined it a hundred times had unearthed something in me that I couldn't explain to Anton or even myself. The tune from last night was still playing in my head though I had yet to put a name to it. The two things were connected but how?

Somner arrived and we hung the painting where Anton had suggested…in the entry hall. Somner asked if he could do anything else for me and before I could answer Anton told him that he was home all day and we would not need his assistance anymore. I thanked Somner and he bowed to me, winked and said, "Anything for you my lady." I smiled.

As soon as he was out of sight Anton asked me what that was all about.

"Do you object to my friendship with your best friend?" I asked.

"Not at all, but I sense that the two of you share something that I am not privy to."

"You can relax Anton, we share nothing except laughter. You designated him to be my driver and bodyguard…though I know not why I would need one. Do you resent him for befriending me? I hope not for I have so very few friends."

"Of course I don't Cara mia. There is no one in the world I trust more than Somner. You scared me Kat when you said you would leave…please don't ever say that again. I couldn't lose you too." He took me in his arms. "I love you so Kat, I'm sorry, please forgive my ignorance?"

"There is nothing to forgive you for Anton; you didn't do anything wrong. I feel that I have been a little off kilter lately and so it is I who needs to ask for your forgiveness."

"I may not always appear sympathetic to your plight but believe me, I am. I know you live in pain, not only from your hip but with the amnesia. Sometimes I am so afraid that you will remember someone from your past…"

He did not finish the sentence so I did. "There is no one in my past…didn't you tell me that I told you that when we first met? I do want to regain my memory even if I may regret it. Do you understand Anton?"

"Yes and I will help you find a new analyst for I only want you to be happy, and I will do anything to make you love me."

"I do love you Anton."

He held me away from him. "Oh, how I have longed to hear you say that."

"Yes, I love you." I repeated.

It was true, I did love him, but I was most assuredly not "in love" with him. I knew that because in my heart I knew that I had been "in love" before and I was sure that it had been so profound that I had suffered deeply because of it. Perhaps it was better that I had lost all sense of it.

I did undergo therapy again and with the same results; I did not surrender to hypnosis. I decided to give up and live without a past. I wanted for nothing and I should be thankful that I had what most women would be perfectly happy with. I thought that I would like to have another child but it didn't happen and maybe it was because I was older than anyone thought. Anton's mother told me that I couldn't conceive while I was still nursing. I was weaning Liliana gradually and so then we would see if I could get pregnant again. If not, there was always adoption. I discussed the option with Anton and he said we would talk about it after I had the hip surgery which was scheduled for early September.

Lili had her first birthday. She had been walking for two months; thank goodness I had Zoe for I would not have been able to keep up with her. She still had blonde ringlets and her eyes seemed to get bluer and bluer with each passing day. She called both me and Zoe, Mama, and she was working hard at Papa. She loved Somner and he returned her affections threefold. I wondered why he and Lelani never had children, or perhaps they did. Something else I would ask him.

I had put my painting instructions on hold for the time being. I was busy with Liliana and the house and gardens and helping out at the art gallery, but there was still an emptiness in me that I could not explain.

I had scheduled a trip to Cairo, Egypt with Anton at the beginning of June. He had invited me to accompany him on other trips abroad before, but I had always declined. I had debated about taking Lili, but I wouldn't go without her, and Anton assured us that we would have the best accommodations available and she would be safe, and so I relinquished and agreed to go. However, two days before we were to leave Lili came down with a cold and I thought that might deter us from flying. I had left her favourite stuffed giraffe in the playroom and went to retrieve it. Anton and Somner were in the kitchen talking discreetly. I heard the name "Lelani" and wondered what was up. I listened from behind the open door.

"Do you think that she will even know that it is your weekend to visit Somner?"

"Oh, she will know all right. She keeps track of everything on her calendar and will be waiting for me at precisely eleven a.m. Saturday morning. She may be irrational, but she is not stupid… you know that Anton."

"Would you rather skip this trip Somner because Connie can go in your place?"

Somner laughed. "I don't think so Anton; you need me to translate. Thanks anyhow, but I will phone Balacalva Prision and tell them I am under quarantine and cannot leave the house. That sounds like a good excuse don't you think?"

I made up my mind right then and there that I would use Lili's cold as my reason for forgoing the trip and that I would take Somner's place at the prison.

Anton agreed that it was probably best if Liliana didn't fly. He said that he was sorry that I would not be going with him and would phone me often. I asked that he only call me on Friday evening and give me a number at which he could be reached and I would call him instead. He did call and I told him that Lili was no worse and so he shouldn't worry as it was only a cold. He made me promise to take her to the hospital if she grew worse and I said I would.

Zoe was most concerned with my plans for visiting Lelani. She wanted me to ask Connie to drive me but I vetoed that immediately; no one from the house could know where I was going. I had contacted the Penitenciaria Federal de Balacalva and requested permission to visit Lelani Stamas. I explained the circumstances stating that her husband was ill and that I would like to take his place. I had no idea what the requirements were for prison visitations in Spain or anywhere else for the matter. I was surprised to learn that the penitentiary was not a maximum security lockup and all they required from me was my name and address and relationship to the inmate. I replied that I was a family friend {not so much a lie} and asked if I was allowed to bring gifts. Yes, I was but would be subjected to a search if deemed necessary. I had no problem with that as I was only going to take toilette articles and a fruit basket.

At 8:30 Saturday morning, I was ready to go. Zoe said that she would watch for the limousine. I told her there was no car coming for me and that I was driving myself.

"What…what are you saying Kat, you don't even know how to drive!" She was horrified at what I was proposing to do.

"Who says I can't drive? Somner has been giving me lessons and he says that I must have driven before as I took to it right away."

"Do you have a license and why didn't you tell me before? I don't want you going alone; you must let me and Lili come with you…please Kat." She begged me crying.

I hugged her. "I am sorry I didn't tell you before …I suppose I wanted to surprise you and Anton. You know that you can't come with me Zoe…suppose Anton calls and Lili is still under the weather. I need you here. Tell me you understand."

"No, I don't understand! I don't even know why you are doing this. Anton and Somner are going to be furious! I've never known you to be so compulsive before."

"Perhaps I don't even know myself Zoe, but I feel compelled to meet the mysterious Lelani. Don't worry about me; it's only an hour and a half trip. I will be home before you have time to miss me."

"I doubt that and what do I tell Mr. DeMarco if he calls?"

"Tell him I'm sleeping." I kissed her and walked out the back door to the garage.

The prison was most intimidating. It was a dirty slate brick building with high barbed fences…it didn't look like a minimum security establishment to me. I pulled the sedan into the visitors' parking lot and grabbed the gifts and my handbag and gingerly made my way to the front door. For the first time since I had put my plan in motion, I was fearful.

I was ushered into a waiting room where all my articles were searched. I myself had passed through some sort of scanner. A guard whose name was Hannah collected me and took me to the visitor's room. She inquired as to how long I had known Lelani for. I explained the circumstances of my visit and admitted that I had never met Lelani before. She stopped and looked at me quizzically.

"You're not her lawyer or relative or friend and you have never met her before… really? Well, I certainly hope that you have a strong constitution for you are in for a very unpleasant ride."

Her words set my knees to knocking. I hadn't a clue as to what this lady looked like. If her name was any clue then I thought that she might be from some south sea country. Hannah motioned for me to take a seat at one side of a table. A side door opened and in walked a dishevelled woman. She was of medium build though it was hard to make out her figure in her drab prison garb. Her red shoulder length hair was matted and appeared as though it hadn't been combed in days. Her complexion was pallid which wasn't unusual considering her locale. Hannah pushed her into the chair across from me.

Lelani laughed maliciously at her. "And you have a nice day too, bitch." Then she leaned forward and said. "Just who the hell are you?"

She had the eyes of a mad woman. I wanted to recoil but I summoned up every bit of fortitude I had and smiled. "I am Anton DeMarco's wife and a friend of your husband's."

"Yeah, I just bet you are!" She laughed brazenly. I knew what she was insinuating but I did not take the bait and she practically spit at me. "I don't know who you think you are bamboozling here LADY because you sure as hell aren't Delaney DeMarco!"

I was a bit stunned by her declaration but managed to conceal it and smiled and said. "And, just who the HELL is Delaney DeMarco?"

Lelani stood up and leaned across the table and heckled. "I see you have been duped into thinking that you are Antonio the Great's wife!"

Hannah was across the room in a flash and ordered Lelani to sit back down. "I won't warn you again! Now answer the lady's question!"

Lelani sneered. "I forgot the question…oh yeah, who is Delaney DeMarco? She is my dear friend and Antonio's wife…someone you sure as hell ain't. Now I would like to go back to my room and away from this imposter." She stood up again.

Hannah approached her once more. This time she grabbed Lelani's arm roughly. "Are we forgetting our manners? This lady and I do mean **lady**, came all this way to pay you a visit and I think you can show her the decency to be civil…do you understand what I am saying Lela?"

Lelani saluted her and smiled sarcastically. "Yes ma'am, mia captain, I get the picture."

She winked at me. "I don't want *them* to take away my gruel so whatever you want…"

"I don't want you to get into trouble, and if you don't want to talk about Delaney, then it is okay with me. I'm sorry to have upset you Lelani." I rose to leave.

"Call me Lela; that was her name for me and I called her Laney. She was my only friend and Antonio had to go and spoil it all by marrying her. It was his fault that she drowned you know."

Her demeanour had changed drastically. A solitary tear filled the corners of her grey/blue eyes. Her features had softened and I was sure that beneath that tough exterior was a woman who could be kind and compliant. I sat back down as I definitely wanted to hear what she had to say.

"Thank you Lela and I am Katarina. I too, have only one female friend and would be very sad if anything happened to her. I am at a loss here for no one told me that Anton was married before or that his wife died. Why would everyone keep it a secret from me? There has never been any hint dropped in my direction, not by Anton, Somner or Connie…not even his mother or sister. Why do you think they haven't told me Lela?"

She reached across the table to take my hand but Hannah yelled at her. "NO TOUCHING!!"

I smiled to acknowledge the gesture. Again, Lela surprised me.

"I know about you." She stated bluntly. "Somner told me that Anton had remarried, and do you know what I said to him when he told me? I said I hoped that you were a horrible person and would cause him nothing but grief! He never mentioned you again. But, you are not vile are you…so why did you let yourself be fooled by Antonio's charisma? It's all hollow you know."

"Please tell me what you have against Anton. Why do you think he is responsible for Delaney's death? He has been nothing but kind and respectful towards me."

"How long have you known him and when and how did the two of you meet?"

"That is a loaded question Lela and I will tell you why. I have knowingly been Anton's wife since last August, but according to him, we were married a year before that. You see, I was in a car accident and was in a coma for two months. I have no memory prior to November 1982."

Lelani sat back in her chair and a smug look came over her face. "And, the plot thickens."

"What do you mean?" I asked.

"You have amnesia right? You have no family I presume, and you have no idea where you came from or what your real name is, and nobody else does either, right?"

I nodded and asked her what she was insinuating.

"He gave you the name Katarina didn't he? Do you know that he had the nerve to ask Delaney if she would change her name to Katarina?"

"Why…why would he do that?" I was curious as to why she would say such a thing.

"Because my dear, he believes that he is the reincarnation of Anton Christoval and he needs a lady to play the part of Katarina Carvarra. Delaney would not participate in his obsession and so he did away with her."

She had stated it so emphatically that I got goose bumps and shivered. I felt like someone had just walked on my grave. Why did this nonsensical story sound familiar to me? Had I just experienced déjà vu? I pretended not to be upset by what she had said.

"Lela, I do not know who these people are, but I can assure you that Anton and I live a perfectly normal life…there is no role playing. We have a beautiful daughter and I cannot even begin to conceive that Anton could do anyone harm let alone take a life. Perhaps it is your grief for your departed friend that you have come to believe that he had a part in her death."

"Is your daughter's name Catalina?"

"No, it is Liliana."

"Good…but will you promise me that you will ask Somner about Delaney because if you question Antonio he will tell you that I am delusional and that you can't take the word from some mad woman who killed her husband's lover and that I have promised to do the same thing to him when I am free."

"What?" I demanded. "You plan on killing Anton when you are released from prison?"

"NO, silly…Somner, I am going to plunge a dagger into Somner's heart!"

I stood up and this time I was really leaving. "I was starting to like you, and then you go and make such a ghastly threat …I can't…"

She started to laugh and interrupted me before I could finish my sentence. "Don't excite yourself Katarina, it's no secret; Somner knows what I am planning on doing. We do have conjugal visits you know and much is said in the heat of passion. If you could only see your face right now…"

I did not share in her laughter but turned around and told Hannah that I was done.

"It's Somner's birthday on June the ninth… I made him a card. Can I get it from my room Hannah? Will you deliver it to him Katarina?" Lelani was almost begging.

"Will you guarantee me that you have not laced it with hemlock?" I asked and I wasn't joking.

Both Hannah and Lelani smirked as they left to collect the card. On returning, Lelani handed me the envelope and said. "Will you come back and see me soon Katarina?"

"Why would I Lelani? Do you really think I have nothing better to do then listen to your accusations? Somner is my friend and I was hoping that I could also befriend his wife. He warned me not to come and I should have listened to him. I will pass your card along to him but I see no reason for me to return here. Goodbye Lelani." I handed her the gifts that I had brought.

"Wait," She struggled with the guard so she could say one last thing to me. "just talk to Somner and ask Anton about the infinity bracelets."

"What?" I yelled at her but the door had already closed behind her.

"What did she say Hannah, you heard her didn't you?"

"I think she said something about some infinite bracelet, but I wouldn't take anything she says seriously Mrs. DeMarco."

I sat in the car for several minutes and took some deep breaths to calm myself before I turned the key in the ignition. I thought of stopping for coffee before I started for home but decided that it might only add to my frayed nerves. I replayed every word that Lelani had spoken over and over again in my head, and I always came to the same conclusion that she was right, and that Anton was keeping things from me. Why had he not told me that he had been married before? Was it because she had died a violent death? Surely, he was not responsible. Had he really asked Delaney to change her name to Katarina…that made no sense what so ever? And, what about the bracelets…were they the ones he had given me at Christmas…and why did they upset me so?

I pulled into the driveway and realized that I must have been on auto-pilot for I couldn't remember anything since I had left the prison parking lot. Thank God that Anton wouldn't be home for another five days.

Zoe met me outside the garage with Liliana in her arms. "I am so glad you are home Kat; I have been so worried about you."

"I am fine Zoe." I hugged them both. "Now, let's go and have some of your delicious ice tea and I could do with a sandwich. I can hardly wait to tell you of my visit with Somner's strange wife, and then I have some strategic planning to do before he and Anton get home."

I slept restlessly and when I awoke my head felt as if it was filled with cobwebs. I reached for the clock on the night table to see if I had overslept. It was lying on its side, and next to it was a half spent candlestick in a brass candleholder. Mystified as to why it would be there, I picked it up and went to the highboy in the hall where all the candle paraphernalia was stored. I pulled open a metal bin and found at least four dozen more burned candles all of the same length. I needed to question the household staff about my findings. I made Senora Cara come with me so that she could translate my concerns to the maids. They knew of the stash of burned out candles, but thought that Senor DeMarco and I liked to have candlelight. We didn't. They had not been instructed to empty the bin. Did that mean that I was the one lighting candles at night…why, and where did I go with them? I shivered as a black cat ominously crossed in front of me.

It was disturbing that I was sleep walking and endangering everyone's' lives by carrying a lit torch throughout the house. Zoe knew nothing of my nightly strolls. I needed to come up with a plan that would alert her to my dangerous ramblings. Perhaps Somner could help. I was angry with Antonio so would not ask for his help. Subconsciously, I must have left the candle on my night table to warn me to what I was up to in the middle of the night. Most of the time I went to bed in Anton's room but would wake up in my own bed not remembering leaving his. I wondered if that was when I wandered the house. Was I searching for something …or someone?

I asked Senora Cara how long she had worked for Mr. DeMarco and she told me ever since he had bought the house and so that was almost five years ago. I asked her if she knew who owned the property before, and had anyone ever died in the house. She did not know and that it was a question for my husband.

"Yes, of course. By the way, did you know Mr. DeMarco's first wife?"

By her answer I assumed she thought that I knew about Delaney. "That was before I came to work for Mr. DeMarco so I did not know her. Of course I knew about the horrible accident. It was so awful as Mr. DeMarco had bought this house for her and they hadn't even moved in yet. We never speak of it though. It is like she never existed. How is he when he talks about it to you? Oh, I am sorry, it is not my business."

"It is quite all right Cara. It is still too painful for Anton to talk about her. I wish he would as I would give anything to have someone to talk about…"

"Perhaps you try too much to remember Mrs. DeMarco."

"Yes, maybe I do. I recently heard of some silly story about some bracelets. I believe they were called the infinity bracelets…do you know of them?"

"I have not. Do you not think that the person to ask would be Senora Bolivar from the gallery?"

"Of course, why didn't I think of that?"

The next day I had Connie drive me to the Palacio Vemma. On the way there I casually asked him when his and Somner's birthdays were. His was November 1st and he knew Somner's was this month some time but didn't know the exact date. He asked me why I wanted to know and I said because I felt like having a party and a birthday was a good excuse. I then told him that we would have it on Thursday when the men got home and so don't make other plans for dinner.

Elaina Bolivar was only too happy to answer my questions. She knew about the horrifying accident that had taken Delaney's life. She was surprised that Antonio had discussed it with me, and I did not tell her that he hadn't. Apparently, Delaney had ventured out in a small rowboat and a storm came up before she could make it back to shore. Witnesses from another vessel said that she stood up to retrieve an oar and fell overboard. She did not resurface and the people from the other craft could not find her. Her body was recovered later the same day.

I tried to hide my shock and I lied and said I knew all that and asked her if she knew Anton back then. She said she didn't.

"Elaina, I wonder if you know of the infinity bracelets? I am most curious about them."

"Heavens Katarina, I haven't heard mention of them since I was in college. Do tell how you unearthed such an old Spanish folklore?"

"An acquaintance asked me if Antonio had told me their story." Well, Lelani was an acquaintance so it wasn't another falsehood.

Elaina laughed. "Oh, I see. Because he has the same name as the fictional Anton and your name is Katarina, his lover, this friend thought that he must know if the fabled bracelets were real. Well, they weren't, not to my knowledge anyhow. It was a romantic tale that dated back to some forgotten time in the eighteen hundreds. According to legend, Anton and Katarina met in Andorra where he had been whisked away to some monastery by Queen Isabella. Katarina and her child were supposedly killed or kidnapped by enemies of the Queen. Anton supposedly had some silver bracelets made for Kat and they disappeared also. He searched for her but never found her and the bracelets, so named The Infinity Bracelets because of some dedication he had engraved on them, have also not surfaced. As far as I am concerned it is all speculation that they ever existed, but on the other hand…" She paused.

"What, do you know something no one else does?"

"I wish I did. No, I just wanted to say that I have heard that there is a family in Northern Spain that is the keeper of a diary that can authenticate that these bracelets did exist and may have knowledge of their whereabouts. Myself, I doubt it, but one never knows. Have I only added to your confusion Katarina?"

"Oh no, I am most interested in fables. You have just whet my appetite and finding out that these two people had the same names as Anton and me only adds to the intrigue. Where could I find out more about the tale? I have never been to Andorra, and yet I feel some strange connection to it every time someone mentions the name."

"Then you should ask Antonio about the country as he has visited there several times." Elaina laughed again. "Perhaps he is searching for the bracelets."

"You are the second person to tell me of Anton's visits to Andorra. Your theory may not be as farfetched as you may think." Those bracelets had some significance I was sure.

I thanked her as she handed me a piece of paper with the names of several books of Spanish folklore. I had no idea when I would have the time to visit the library as I had much more on my troubled mind then pursuing what may very well be a fairy tale. I needed to confront Anton and the birthday supper for Somner would be the perfect time. I would no doubt be in trouble with my prison escapade, but I could justify it with the knowledge that I had gained. I had no idea how Anton would react to my accusations that he had been lying to me. What other secrets was he keeping from me? Did he know more about me than he had told me and was Somner and Connie in on the deception? Suddenly, I wasn't sure that I wanted to know…yes, I did, I needed to know about Delaney and what was making me walk the halls at the wee hours. Sometimes in the night I would hear sobbing…was her ghost haunting the casa?

The day started cheerful enough. Liliana was completely over her cold. I had taken her to her pediatrician on Monday where she had a complete check-up and was told that she had no ear, eye or nose infection. The doctor took a throat culture and I was still awaiting the results but the doctor assured me that there was no inflammation that she could see. The real proof was that Lili was once again alert and playing and trying to carry on a conversation with Zoe and me.

Senora Cara helped me plan the menu for Somner's birthday dinner. We decided on a cool Gazpacho tomato soup, a Spanish cucumber salad and garlic shrimp for starters. The main course would be Somner's favourite roasted rack of lamb and a vegetable-chicken rice dish called paella. For dessert Cara made an orange flan and just to divert from all the Spanish fare, I decided to make a chocolate layer cake. I had no idea if I had ever made one before but managed to find a recipe that was to my liking and I hoped it would be edible.

The kitchen was where Antonio found me when he arrived home. I knew precisely what time he would be arriving from the airport and planned to be very busy when he walked through the door. I had sent Liliana with Zoe to the playroom so that Anton would have to go looking for his daughter. He shouted from the entrance that he was home and where were his girls. I pretended not to hear him.

"Katarina, didn't you hear me calling for you? Whatever are you doing?" He put his arms around me and kissed the back of my neck. "Leave whatever it is that you are doing and turn around. I have missed you so."

I turned to face him brandishing my knife that was covered with chocolate frosting. I held my arms out so as not to drip any on him. I tried not to sound too annoyed.

"Hello Anton, I hope you had a pleasant flight. I really wasn't expecting you home so soon." Lying was coming far too easy. "I thought that you might want to go by the docks to see if any of your acquisitions had arrived yet."

"I told you I would come directly home Cara mia. I wanted to see you and Liliana…where is she? And, you still haven't told me what you are doing?"

I let him kiss me lightly. "Haven't you ever seen anyone ice a cake before? It's for Somner as I am sure you are aware that it is his birthday today?"

"No, I have been far too busy to think about such things. How would you know anyhow?"

"I asked Connie. Of course, he wasn't sure of the date so I just decided to have a little celebration dinner tonight. Now you should probably call him and invite him to dinner; it will be at 7 p.m. Connie already knows."

"Tonight…why tonight? I wanted to spend it with you and Lili and besides, we have no present." Anton groaned,

"Of course we have presents! Now go and call, get freshened up and play with Lili until dinner. I really need to finish icing this cake." Just like that I had dismissed him.

He didn't say another word and stormed off. If he only knew what was coming next…

Chapter 14

Rainey

September 7th 1982

Ava found her dad in his study staring into nothingness. She often found him like this, but his brooding was increasing day by day since his uneventful trip overseas last spring. Today, he had some heartbreaking music playing on the stereo. He looked up and attempted a smile.

"Hi Dad. Who does that soulful voice belong to? I don't think I've heard him before."

"His name is Steve Young. I discovered him some time ago… long after your mother left me the first time. His songs seem to echo my sentiments."

Ava couldn't stop the flow of tears. She walked over and put her arms around her father. "Oh Daddy, Mama didn't leave you this time; you know that don't you? Tell me you believe that it wasn't her choice?"

Rainey patted his daughter's hand. "I do Honey; I just can't help comparing the two."

"Well, that doesn't make any sense at all. Mama isn't seventeen and she didn't run away because she was pregnant and unsure of your feelings for her!"

Rainey wanted so badly to tell her that her mother had indeed been with child last September and she may now have a baby sister. He had promised himself that he wouldn't burden the girls then, and so he wouldn't now; he would continue to keep the secret. He sniffled.

"Where is she Ava? Where is my barefoot lady? Do you know what today is?"

"Yes, I do Daddy…it's one year ago that Mama disappeared."

Rainey had only spent two nights at Avanloch last May. He couldn't even bring himself to reread Vienna's love letters. The elusive light was still haunting Willowisp though no one else had seen it in his absence. He spent a night in London with Rosalyn and Evan and had a quick visit with Jannie and John, Stu and Daisy and their new son. He decided to skip Andorra but met up with the detective, Decamber LaSalle, in Bordeaux, France. The two had been corresponding regularly but Rainey wanted to talk to him face to face. They met at the Hotel Lyon for drinks and dinner. Decamber had nothing to offer him that he didn't already know. Rainey had information that he decided to share with the detective that hadn't seemed important before.

"I know that every time a body is discovered and not identified you have been notified and you have verified that it is not Vienna, and I thank you for your diligence. I have resisted to come running whenever you have informed me of a new finding because I believe that with modern forensics there wouldn't be a mistake. However, there is a small bit of information about Vienna that I neglected to tell you and that is that she has a faint birthmark on her left thigh. It is in the shape of a teardrop. Did I consciously keep this from you? I honestly don't know, but she has been gone almost nine months now and she may be hard to identify and this might help."

Decamber put his drink down and leaned in and looked hard at Rainey. "Mr. Quinn, have you given up finding your wife alive?"

"I'll never give up until she is found one way or the other; but hope is fading."

"There is always hope Mr. Quinn, but I sense a futility in your voice that I have not detected in our telephone conversations. Have you been entertaining the thought that perhaps Mrs. Quinn orchestrated her own disappearance?"

"I suppose it has crossed my mind once or twice but only for a fleeting moment for I know Vienna would never leave me again.

Even if she had fallen out of love with me, there is no way in Hell that she would ever desert her girls. But, that is not the case and I will tell you why. Vienna and I were more in love than ever and we had never been happier. I am going to tell you something that I have kept from the family as it would only bring them more heartache. The day before Vienna went missing she told me that we were going to have a baby. She had just found out before we left Scotland and knew that I would not have ventured to take her to Spain and Andorra if she told me, and she was right. Can you imagine how many times I wish that I had of known about her pregnancy before going on our ill-fated quest? She was like a little child the night before the disaster and I must admit that I was pretty giddy myself. So, no Mr. LaSalle, Vienna had no hand in whatever happened to her in Nazeth."

"I see, and so we may very well be searching for two people. I will alert my aides-de camp of the possibility. Your agony is two-fold and I sympathize with your despair. We will not let up on the hunt… you can be assured of that."

"Thank you. I know you are doing everything possible to find her. A word, any word that she and the baby are well and being looked after is all I want at this point." Rainey lamented.

But, there had been no word and another year had passed. Rainey went through the motions of everyday living for Ava, Morgan and Mason, but he was dead inside. He had no interest in anything and could no longer concentrate on the company business. He went to the office only because it was better than being alone at home. His parents and Jimmy came to visit often and he was constantly in touch with Vienna's family and Avanloch, but no one or any words could ease his despondency. He hardly slept, had no appetite, and had lost a considerable amount of weight. The kids feared that he was endangering his physical health and wanted him to see a grief counsellor but he refused promising that he would start looking after himself better.

He had been postponing booking his trip to Avanloch for weeks. His excuse had been that he wanted to wait until after Morgan's graduation on the 10th of June. Now he told Ava that he wanted to wait until the boys were settled in with their summer jobs. He usually retired to his bedroom every evening around 10 o'clock. He would put several long play albums on the stereo hoping the music would lull him to sleep but not before he wrote a letter to Vienna. He would sit back and stare at the words he had written until his eyes stung. He always ended with 'I'll love you forever Vienna LaFontaine' and climb into bed and say his prayer for her and his new daughter.

He had considered himself lucky in one way, and that was that he didn't dream… but that had all changed on June the 9th when he had woke at midnight and wondered where he was. He sat straight up and gazed into the darkness. He reached for the lamp on the night table and clicked it on. Everything was normal except he had the strange sensation that he had been engaged in some sort of conflict. Deciding that he must have been dreaming he got out of bed feeling like he had been drugged, and staggered into the kitchen. He poured himself a glass of milk and realizing that he was hungry cut a piece of

Ava's coconut cream pie that he had refused at dinner. He sat reminiscing about the first piece of pie that he had eaten of hers. That was the day Vienna came back to him and he surprised himself that he could smile at the memory.

The next night he dreamt again. This time he knew that he was engaged in a game of chess and he was the white knight. Wherever he landed he was able to conquer an opponent and no rook or Bishop or rival knight could bring him down, and then suddenly, he was face to face with the black queen and she was laughing...

Night after night he had the same recurring dream always waking up just as the black queen was bearing down on him. Before he went to sleep on the fifth night he talked to himself like Vienna had taught him. She would tell him that when he had disturbing dreams he could control them somewhat by telling himself that he was the captain of his ship and the master of his own fate. Believing that if he could lead the black queen into a trap and destroy her, the senseless dreams would stop, and so he envisioned what he had to do. The scene was the same and he broke the rules and set the queen up for destruction. At the last second he moved out of her way, but he had miscalculated her strength and by saving himself he had put his own queen into jeopardy. He watched in horror as the malevolent queen set her sights on his regal lady. He realized that this dark creature was not a queen at all but a witch. She steered her broom in his direction for a second and screeched, "I'll get you later horseman, but first your lily white queen!" He turned and looked into the eyes of the woman he had sacrificed… into the eyes of Vienna…and he screamed and screamed.

"Dad, Dad wake up!" Morgan was shouting.

Rainey woke up to find his son's hands shaking him. Mason and Ava were standing near looking worried. He assured them that he was all right and reluctantly upon their insistence revealed the dreams he had been having admitting that the last one was no dream, but a ghastly nightmare.

"I'm scared kids." He said.

Ava put her arms around him. "It was only a dream Dad; only a dream."

"I'm afraid of its implications."

"You didn't actually see anything happen to Mama did you Dad? Do you know what I think it might mean? Maybe Mama is in some danger but we can save her Dad…**you can** save her. She is waiting for you Dad. I think this is a sign." Ava didn't believe a word of what she was saying.

"Are you saying that I have to go back and make the dream end differently?"

"Can you do that Dad?" Mason asked curiously.

"I'll never know unless I try Son, but not tonight. I'm going to talk to Sylvie tomorrow."

Rainey arrived at work to find a note on his desk from Sylvie reminding him that she had a dental appointment and wouldn't be in until 10. It had completely skipped his mind, but what he wanted to discuss with her could last until then. He decided to do something useful for a change and wandered into Clive's office tapping lightly on the door before entering. Clive was finishing up a phone conversation and beckoned for Rainey to come in.

"You're just the person I want to see Rainey." He opened a drawer and retrieved a file. "I can't make heads or tails out of this proposal; would you mind reading it over for me?" Rainey knew that nothing could be further from the truth as Cliff had the keenest mind of all the partners and this was only an attempt to try to get him to take an interest in the affairs of the company again. Rainey played along.

"Sure thing as I was running out of things to do anyhow. Say, how is the Converse project going? Let me know if I can be of any assistance there."

They chatted for a while until they were interrupted by the ringing of the telephone. Rainey picked up the file and headed back to his office. He opened it and placed it in front of him. He had to read every line over and over again before anything made any sense to him. "Damn it!" He cursed out loud. "Why can't I concentrate?"

He felt something on the back of his neck and brushed it off, but the tickling sensation would not go away. He slapped his neck hard and for a minute there was nothing, but then he felt it again… it was like someone was breathing down his neck. He jumped up and in doing so knocked his chair over. At the same time Vienna's picture that had been standing on his file cabinet went careening across the floor. The hairs on his arms were standing straight up. He was sure that if he turned around he'd see Vienna and he heard her in his head. "Stop trying to brush me off Rainey Quinn!"

"Mr. Q, are you all right?" Sylvie asked flinging open the door. "I heard a crash…what is Vienna's picture doing on the floor? She bent down to pick it up.

"I didn't do it Sylvie. It's like it had a mind of its own…it just flew off the shelf."

"I'm afraid the glass is broken Sir." Sylvie scraped the shards into the waste basket.

"I can always get another frame Sylvie; I just can't get another Vienna. I felt that she was here…is that crazy?"

Rainey motioned his secretary to take a seat and explained to her what had transpired before her picture fell and then he told her about his dreams and asked her what she made of it all.

"Well, I cannot explain what went on in here as there is no open window that would allow for the wind to enter and the air conditioner is off so…but I will take a stab at your dreams, but I am no expert. First, tell me what all the symbols and characters that you saw mean to you."

"There is a giant chess board at the castle and Vienna has referred to me as her white knight more than once. The white queen is her of course and as for the witch…well, she was always making jokes about witches and there was the time that she brought one into Avanloch, but that was a proclaimed white witch, not a black one."

"How strange that she would knowingly invite a witch, never mind the color, into the castle."

"What's so strange about that…your own niece practices witch-craft doesn't she? I'm sure she has been in your house a number of times." Rainey reasoned.

"That is different Mr. Q. Surely you know that Gretchen only plays at being a witch and though she may follow their doctrine, she and her friends have no actual powers. May I ask what this so called 'white witch' did for Vienna?"

Rainey laughed. "Oops, I told everyone that my secretary's niece was a real witch."

"No harm done. I'm sure Gretchen would be flattered, but getting back to **your** witch…"

"That's a story for another time Sylvie. I will just tell you that her coming rid us of a menace and no damage was done."

"All right for now, but I want to hear more about this mystifying white witch. Now, about your dreams…I think you already have concluded that the white queen represents Vienna, and to you she is pure and faithful and you, as a knight means you are loyal and protective. The witch is the catalyst that is trying to manipulate you into believing that you have failed in your duties and because of that you must die or suffer the consequences. Does this make any sense?"

"Yes, but Vienna taught me that I can change the outcome of my dreams and if I have it tonight, I fully intend to change the ending."

"Good for you Rainey for I believe that too. Now, I have something to confess to you. I hope you won't be angry with me or think that I have delved too far into the occult for I have asked Sibyl if she knows anything of Vienna."

"I have no idea who Sybil is Sylvie and as for the occult…are you forgetting that I have lived in a castle that embraces ghosts and have seen fairies frolicking in the mist, albeit that they were fireflies. I became captivated in the fantasy that they were the real thing and I have consulted with a genuine gypsy…not to mention having supper with a witch."

"You are just too funny Rainey. Sibyl, spelled SIBYL is the name of Gretchen's Ouija Board."

"Really? Tell me Sylvie, do all Ouijas' have a name? The one at Avanloch answers only to Mama… so I am told."

"I honestly don't know Rainey as most boards are used as parlour games by people who have no idea what they are doing. I doubt those people know they may be flirting with danger, for if by accident, they do conjure up an unfriendly spirit, there may be serious consequences. Most believe that the 'planchette', the little board you put your fingers on, is manipulated by force from their hands and it probably is in most cases. However, the true believers know that is not so. Sibyl means Prophetess …don't quote me, but I think it's Egyptian. Anyhow, to get to the point, I asked her if she knew Vienna LaFontaine Quinn and the answer was 'yes'. She did not know where she was. When asked if Vienna was alive, the answer was 'yes' again. Automatically, with no questions asked, the planchette spelled out water-green-lily. Do those words have any meaning to you?"

"Only that Vienna loves water and grows water lilies. I like the color green on her. Lily is also her mother's name. Thanks Sylvie. Now I need to book a flight to Scotland."

Ava was home studying for her exams. She had already completed and passed her First Aide and Medical Records courses. For the past six months she had been enrolled in classes at Truman Career Institute in the medical program. The company she worked for had opened a free walk-in clinic recently, and so she took the training which would allow her to take blood and administer injections so that she could donate her free time to working there. She had been banking all her wages until she found a suitable charitable foundation that was not only humanitarian but in deep need of monetary aid. Now, with the opening of the treatment centre, she could not only donate her services but help to finance it. She knew her mother would be pleased.

She put aside her papers to answer the phone. "Hello, Quinn residence."

"It's only me Honey; how is the studying going?" It was her father.

"Okay, but I could use you to quiz me."

"You'll have to get one of the boys to help you as I am going to Scotland on the first flight I can book. That's why I am calling, I left my wallet at home and I need a credit card. Can you go into the den and find it for me? I'm not certain where it is."

"On my way there Dad…give me a minute." Ava laid the phone down and started looking. It wasn't anywhere on the desk and so she started opening drawers but couldn't find it. Instead she found a piece of paper that was titled "The Game." I wonder what this is." She said to herself.

"It doesn't seem to be here Dad; could you have left it in your room?"

"Anything is possible after last night."

"Okay, walking again. How did you make out with Sylvie? Was she any help?"

"I'll tell you all about it when I get home."

Ava found the wallet lying on the floor almost under the bed. "Found it! What card do you want to use?"

"Doesn't matter."

Ava rattled off a number and expiry date. "I'm glad you are going to Avanloch Dad, but you know I can't come with you."

"I know, but I just **have** to go now. I'll explain when I see you. Thanks Honey."

Ava hung up and went back into the den. She was curious about the paper she had found. "I hope I'm not snooping." She said out loud but knew that she was. She sat down and began to read the words that her father had written in bold print.

Vienna, you introduced me to the game.
It was one I had never played before.
I didn't even know if it had a name.
To play it you had to give your heart and soul.
I did, and my life was never the same again.
But then one day you changed the rules.
You took the prize and left me cold.
I tried to play the game with others
But I failed pathetically as a lover.
I wandered in and out of heartless schemes
Never finding an answer to my dreams.
But then one day I rolled the dice
And found again my love, my life
She had returned, my beautiful brown eyed girl.
It was Vienna, my destiny, my reason, my world.
We lived, we loved, we played and vowed to be
Together until the end of days.
But alas, I followed her across the sea to play another game
Twists and turns and disaster was its name.
Little did I know that our destiny had already been cast
It was written in the cards, our future and our past.
I made a grave error and gambled on her behalf;
The joker raised his ugly head and held up his staff.
He laughed out loud and took my queen...
How could anyone be so mean?
He took my love to a land I know not where.
But I shall find her one day I swear
I will not rest until she is by my side
I will cross every bridge and fight the tides
I will bring her home never to leave again
And never again will we play this futile game.

Ava had a lump in her throat and tears in her eyes. She carefully folded the paper up and replaced it just as she had found it. She sat for a long time going over the last few years in her mind. How could this have happened? They were all so happy…especially her mother and father. It was the ever after in a fairy tale but unfortunately, it was not the end. Perhaps Rainey was right; those bracelets were cursed. She was sure that if he didn't find her mother this time, he would lose himself completely and she would not be able to bring him back. Her gloomy trance was interrupted by the front door slamming.

"Ava, where are you Ava?" Did her father sound excited?

She met him in the hall outside of the den. He picked her up and swung her around and around. He was downright giddy. "This is it Ava! Your mother's coming home!"

Ava gulped. "What's happened? Has there been word…tell me Dad, what?"

"It's nothing I can put into words Honey but more a feeling. She touched me this morning."

Ava led her father into the living room and sat him down and took a chair opposite him. She took his hands in hers. "Dad, I know you want to believe this but it is just not possible…I think you are still shook up from the nightmare last night."

Rainey smiled. "I love you Ava. From the moment I looked into your eyes at the house in Bridge, I knew you were mine. Never in my wildest dreams did I ever think that you would be my saving grace, but then I never thought that I would ever lose your mother again. It has always been at the back of my mind that I lost her for twenty years because I was so gullible and believed that she had stopped loving me. I know that nobody blames me, but I blame myself just as I live with the guilt of losing her in Andorra, but something has changed."

Ava listened quietly as Rainey told her about the events of the day. She wanted to believe that it was true and that her mother had somehow sent a sign. She hugged him with tears in her eyes.

"I love you too Rainey. No girl could ever ask for a better father and no man has ever loved a woman the way you love Mama. Now, let's get you packed so that you can bring Mama home!"

Rainey paid the driver and sent him on his way. He stopped at the top of the stately steps to say hello to Rosalyn's lions. He was about to drop the oversize brass door knocker into its holder when a loud noise startled him. He placed the knocker down gently and went in the direction of the ruckus. He rounded the side of the castle that ran parallel to the harem room. It was directly under Vienna's suites. Rainey laughed out loud and lost no time running up the newly constructed stairway two steps at a time. When he reached the top he spotted Johnny and two other men noisily pounding slate stones together on the floor. They all had their backs to him.

"You've done it Johnny O'Shea, you've done it! You've built Vienna's balcony!"

Johnny dropped his tools and rushed over to greet his friend. He hugged him and patted him on the back. "What a welcoming sight you are? Why didn't you tell us you were arriving today? How did you get here and is Ava here too? How long are you staying?"

Rainey hugged him back. "What question do you want answered first Buddy?"

"All of them. Take a half hour break guys; I need to catch up with my brother here."

Rainey was touched by the reference. He walked over to the nearly completed decorative railing and surveyed the view. "Vienna will love it Johnny; good job!"

"You feel it too Rain…Vienna's vibes are getting stronger?"

Rainey put his hand on Johnny's shoulder. "She's coming home John…I've had an epiphany."

"Amma feels it too. She feels Vienna struggling to find her way and believes that it is only a matter of time. Meggie Magan keeps doing readings for Vienna; water keeps showing up in the cards and there is something about lilies and a tall dark man."

Rainey told him about his dream and Sylvie and the Ouija and the event in his office.

"You know me Rainey, both feet planted firmly on the ground. Maybe I have been living among the ghosts of Avanloch for too long for I have been having uncanny sensations myself…hence the necessity to get the balcony built, and oh yeah, I've seen the mysterious light at Willowisp."

Chapter 11

The Confrontation

I was putting the finishing touches on the birthday dinner when Somner arrived. He stood at the kitchen door and watched me.

"This is a side of you I have never seen before Katarina, and I am honoured that you chose my birthday to try your hand at cooking."

I laughed. "Don't be too honoured as you haven't tasted anything yet. But, just to be on the safe side I had Senora Cara supervise the entire meal, and so I can say with some certainty that it will be edible. The cake is my own doing…so we will see."

"I haven't had a cake made especially for me since Lelani left and that one was…well; let's just say it was a baker's nightmare."

We laughed together at the reference and that was how Anton found us.

"Some private joke, I assume." He said sarcastically. "Am I intruding?"

"Don't be silly Antonio! Somner was only telling me about Lelani's expertise in the kitchen."

"Really, and why are you two discussing that mad woman?"

"Anton! How dare you speak of her that way!" I was ashamed of him but Somner was not offended and laughed it off.

"Anton has never hid his animosity towards my wife, and might I add that it is mutual."

Yes, I knew that from my brief conversation with Lelani, but now was not the time for me to let the cat out of the bag.

"Please take your seats at the dining table for everything is ready. Anton, if you will watch Lili then Zoe can help me serve."

The meal was perfecto, and I was very pleased that it had turned out so well. Anton was civil though I could feel him shooting daggers at me though for what reason I did not know. Perhaps he suspected something as I had been rather cool towards him. I pretended to be interested in the accounts that he and Somner related about their trip to Egypt when all I wanted was to see the look on Anton's face when he learned that I had been to the Penitenciaria.

Zoe and I cleared the table and we brought in the desserts and coffee. The men had emptied several bottles of wine at dinner as was their usual custom. I let Anton pour me a glass of chardonnay but I did not drink any and only raised my glass to toast Somner. Connie lit the single candle on the birthday cake.

"Only 1 candle my lady… what about the other 44?" Somner laughed.

"I didn't want to burn the house down." I quipped teasingly again wondering why he always addressed me as "my lady."

Zoe presented him with his gifts and he made a big fuss saying that we had gone to too much trouble. His eyes lit up when he opened the new volume on rare and endangered orchids that I had found for him. He said he had been looking for it and where had I found it. I told him that a girl had to have some secrets and his smile was my reward for haunting all the book stores. I reached into my dress pocket and retrieved Lelani's childish drawing and greeting. I passed the rumpled paper over the table to Somner. "One last thing…"

He unfolded it and read what his wife had written. He covered up his mouth with his hand to try and hide his amusement. He said to me. "I suppose you have read this?"

"I cannot tell a lie, I did."

"And, pray tell, how did you come upon this letter?"

"Oh, I think you know perfectly well where I got it from." I said matter of factually.

Anton was seething. "What the hell are you two talking about? What's in that letter Somner, and who wrote it?"

"It's just a simple drawing and a birthday wish." Somner turned it so Anton could see it. "It's from my darling wife."

Anton turned to me and said hostilely. "What does this have to do with you Katarina and why did Somner ask you where you got it? Didn't it come in the post?"

"Not exactly; Lelani gave it to me to deliver to Somner."

Just as I had expected Anton was incensed. He was on his feet and trembling. "So, this is what has been going on behind my back?" He directed his wrath at Somner. "So, you sent Kat to that deplorable prison to visit your crazy wife when you couldn't?"

Liliana was crying. I picked her up out of her high chair and handed her to Zoe who was only too glad to have an excuse to leave. Anton sputtered that he was sorry to have upset Lili and reached for her but Zoe darted past him and ran from the room. She knew what was coming.

"You can just leave Somner out of this Anton for he had no knowledge of my doings. I took it upon myself to go to the prison and visit with Lelani. I am a grown woman and I think I can make a few decisions on my own, contrary to your beliefs!" I raised my voice only so slightly.

"That is neither here nor now, but you did not do this on your own!" He glared at Connie. "You, you drove her to that…"

I didn't let him finish. "What part of "I did it **myself**" did you not understand? I gave Connie the day off. I drove myself."

"That's absurd! Do you take me for a fool? You can't drive and you certainly don't have a license!"

"Says who? How do you know I can't drive? I did have another life before you know."

A look of distress came over Anton's face and I was sure he thought that some part of my memory had returned. I continued. "The deed is done; I went, I met Lelani, I came home and I fully intend to visit her again!"

"Why are you being so obstinate Katarina? Did you not think that you were endangering your life when you ventured out on the highway alone and my God, you went to a prison full of raving lunatics…I don't understand you at all!"

"The inmates are not lunatics Anton, and I was perfectly safe there."

He stood up again and glared at Somner. "I know you conspired with her and I wonder just where your loyalties lie. I'm sick of this deceit! What else have you two been doing behind my back? I see the way you look at each other…"

I interrupted him again. "I think you have had a little too much wine Anton. The only thing Somner and I share is friendship and if you think anything else then you are delusional and you owe him and Connie an apology."

"I owe no one any apology and you have not heard the end of this!" He pushed his chair out of the way and was about to leave, but I was not finished with him and I boldly stood in front of him. He took my arm to push me out of the way, but I held fast. Somner came round the table to my defense.

"Anton, please don't do anything you'll regret! We both know how words can be misinterpreted and how situations can escalate don't we? Do I need to remind you of the consequences if certain truths were to be revealed?"

A look passed between the two of them that puzzled me. Anton's tone changed drastically and in that brief exchange I was certain that Somner was holding something over Anton.

"I'm sorry Kat, I shouldn't have bullied you. Will you accept my apologies boys?"

"There is no need Anton, but I will tell you this so that you don't blame Katarina solely. I have been giving her driving instructions and I have to say that she is one damn good driver. She wanted to surprise you. I'm sorry it had to come out this way. It is probably my fault also that she went to visit Lelani. She has been curious about her and I guess I didn't emphasise enough that my wife wasn't always in her right mind. I'm sorry Katarina; I imagine she was very rude."

"You certainly don't have to apologize to me for your wife's behaviour. Let's just say that we agreed to be civil to each other and I guess she trusts me as she asked me to visit her again. She did say a few things that troubled me though and I wonder if you know about her plans?"

"Can we talk about this another time? I think you and Anton need to clear the air. Thank you for the wonderful birthday. I shan't soon forget it and your kindness."

Connie added his sentiments and they left through the back door. Anton sat down and asked me if I had any more secrets that I wanted to reveal.

"That door swings both ways and I think that you should go first."

"I'm sure I have no idea what you are referring to Kat."

"Well, for starters, how about you tell me about Delaney, and then we can progress to what the infinity bracelets mean to you and why you have visited the Pyrenees so often in the past?"

He was mortified that I knew about Delaney and his hostility towards Lelani increased tenfold.

"That bitch! She had no right telling you things about my personal life! It was all a long, long time ago and I do not wish to discuss it with you now or ever!"

"That says it all then doesn't it Anton? You accused me of having secrets when in fact it is you who has a whole closet full. Apparently, I am not your personal life for if I was you would have told me about Delaney. I realize that it is probably very painful for you to talk about what happened to her, but I had a right to know. Don't for one moment put all the blame on Lelani. She is not the only one who knows and before you go jumping to conclusions again, I will tell you that Somner never mentioned her name to me. The ball is in your court; is it now or never?"

"I do not want to talk about any of this with you. It does not concern you; it all happened a long time before we met. I'm going to bed. You can come with me or not." He rose and turned his back to me and started for the door.

"Do you for one minute think that you can walk away from me without an explanation? I think I deserve some answers!" I was yelling, but I didn't care. "Is it Delaney's ghost who haunts this casa? Is it her I hear sobbing through the walls? Tell me Anton, tell me."

"You should be careful of the questions you ask for you may not like the answers Kat."

"Tell me tonight, or I will get the answers from Somner tomorrow! He knows all your secrets doesn't he?"

I swear he looked right through me as he spoke. "This casa is not haunted as Delaney never stepped foot in it. If you are talking about the moaning you hear when *you* roam the halls at night…well, it is not her you hear, but yourself. It is **you** who is crying."

"What are you talking about?" I was most appalled at what he was implying.

"I know all about your late night rendezvous throughout the house."

"You know that I am sleep walking with a lighted candle and you haven't stopped me? I could have set the house on fire! Why have you kept this from me? I have been endangering the life of our daughter!" I was extremely angry at his lack of concern for my recklessness.

"Dr. Z said that you were not putting us or yourself in jeopardy. I knew that one should not waken a sleep walker and he said I was right. He said that you were looking for your past and until you came to terms with yourself that you may never regain your memory you would always be searching. He told me to just let you be."

"Really? You have discussed this with him and yet did not feel the need to tell me! I find this totally unacceptable! How long have I been doing this and how do you know when I do?"

"I don't know how I know Kat, I just do. As far as I know, you have been sleep walking for a little over a year."

"That's just it Anton; you don't know for sure. Do you follow me and watch what I do and how many times have you not heard me? I only found out myself a few days ago when I found a burnt taper at my bedside. I then discovered all the other ones in the cupboard and I was mortified!"

"I can answer that with some certainty because I count the candles every morning."

"That makes me feel a whole lot better." I said sarcastically. I was blaming him for something that was entirely my fault but I was angry that he hadn't tried to put a stop to my wanderings. "Do you agree that we must try to keep me in bed at night? Can't we lock the doors or the cupboard or something?"

"I will not hold you prisoner and I don't think putting a lock on the cabinet will stop you. Now I am tired and would like to go to bed; are you coming?"

"You have to be kidding? We haven't even begun to discuss *your* secrets yet!"

"And we are not going to."

"Then, goodnight Anton." I brushed past him and made my way to my room.

I don't think I slept a wink all night worrying about my somnambulism. I lay in bed waiting to hear Anton's door open and close before I got out of bed. I heard him checking on Liliana and then descend the stairs and go out the back door. It was barely 6 a.m. Zoe and Lili were both still sleeping. I found two large garbage bags in a kitchen storeroom and proceeded to discard all of the candle paraphernalia. I attempted to engage a device that I assumed was what I had been lighting the candles with but could not get it to turn on, and wondered with what I had used as a lighter as there were no matches or anything else around. Perhaps in my dream state, I was much stronger. I failed to comprehend why Anton wouldn't have removed every candle and incendiary apparatus from the house. He could have left me a flashlight.

At 10 a.m. Somner arrived with several bags in hand and asked me if I would accompany him to the upstairs hallway. Zoe had just taken Lili outside to play before the heat of the day set in. I had been planning on joining them but felt I needed to deal with whatever Somner had in mind first. We stopped at the cabinet and Somner said that we should empty it out. I told him that I had already done so and how much did he know of my sleep walking escapades.

"Anton only informed me this morning and that you were very concerned for the welfare of Liliana and the casa. He asked me if I had any solutions and this is what I have come up with."

He opened the bag and produced two candle-like gadgets. As soon as he touched them, they lit up just like a candle.

I stood back a little in amazement for I had seen these substitutes before though I knew not where or when. "They are battery operated aren't they?" I asked.

"Yes, you have seen them before?"

"I don't know…maybe. Why didn't Anton think of them?"

"I don't know Kat; he has a lot on his mind."

"Oh, I am well aware of that and he plans on never telling me about Delaney. Do you know why Somner? I think you know why and a whole lot more…like about his trips to Andorra and those mysterious bracelets. What is it I cannot know?"

"I wish I could say, but I fear I have already said too much."

"You have told me nothing…nothing. I know you are loyal to Anton, but if I was in danger you would tell me wouldn't you? I felt that way last night."

"Katarina, my dear lady, you have nothing to fear from Anton. It is because of his great love for you that I must remain silent… at least for the time being."

"I have no idea what you mean Somner. I will only wait so long and if he doesn't confide in me…well, let's just leave it at that for now. But, there is something I want to warn you about. Lelani told me that when she gets out of prison she is going to put a knife in you and twist it until your blood runs cold."

Somner laughed. "I doubt if she was that descriptive, but you can rest easy as I know all about her rantings. She is still mad at me for cheating on her and she has every right to be. Now, I am going to install several cameras around the casa that will record your nightly wanderings."

"What good will that do?" I asked.

"Anton says you hear someone crying and that you believe that it is Delaney, right?"

"Yes, I suppose I told him that. He says that it is I who is doing the crying but I don't really believe him."

"Exactly, and now with the cameras, we will be able to see what you do and where you go and if indeed it is you who is sobbing."

"Wonderful! Now I will be able to see myself wandering the casa in the dark! This isn't some gothic novel where the heroine is seen weeping as she rambles through the castle searching for some lost soul, but it is *my* life we are talking about and I don't want to make a movie out of it."

"Are you saying you don't want to know? I think you have more gumption then that."

"Maybe I am just scared Somner. I don't know if I ever told you but I have this fear that I did something terrible in my unknown past and that is why I won't let myself remember. Suppose if I were to uncover what it is? Suppose I subconsciously know what it is and my sleep walking is how I deal with it and the crying is for regret?"

"No, you never told me that before and I sympathize with your plight even though I cannot fully understand your rationalizing. But, I will tell you one thing and that is that you did not do any harm to anyone, and so you have nothing to regret. Now, shall I install the cameras or not?"

"How could you possibly know that Somner? What is it you and Anton are hiding?"

He put his hands on my shoulders and said softly. "Katarina, you are possibly the sweetest lady I have ever had the pleasure of knowing, and it is just not possible that you could have ever done anything horrific, so put those thoughts out of your mind for nothing is further from the truth."

"Oh, and you are such a good judge of character aren't you? You married a woman who committed murder and plans on doing it again…need I say more?"

He laughed as always when discussing Lelani, but then he became dead serious. "You do know that it was self defense don't you? No, I can see by the look in your eyes that you do not. Well, I will enlighten you. Lelani found me with this other woman, Leda was her name. No, we were not in bed; we were sitting at her kitchen table, so you can wipe that look of horror off your face. Lelani knocked and Leda let her in. Apparently, Lelani suspected that we were having an affair and when she saw me she went berserk. You met her Kat, so you know she is not very big…well, she charged me and knocked me over and I hit my head against the counter. I guess I lost consciousness for a few seconds because I did not see Leda attack Lelani with a knife. They struggled and I came to just as Lelani pushed Leda through the open window and to her death. Lelani was bleeding profusely from the knife wound to her abdomen and was in intensive care for two weeks. I nearly lost her Kat, and it is me who should have gone to prison and not her. It is a millstone that I carry every day and yes, I admit Lelani is a little crazy at times, but it is because of me. She is my wife, and I will wait for her and hope that I can make amends for what my depraved lust cost her."

Tears stung my eyes. "But, it was self defense, so why did she not get off?"

"Who knows how the justice system thinks? We were lucky that she only got five years. She could have been out sooner but she hasn't exactly been a model prisoner. She only has a few more months to go providing she behaves herself."

"She will Somner and I will help her for I fully intend to keep visiting her and becoming a trusted friend. Tell me, why does Anton dislike her so?"

"Delaney was Lelani's dear friend and she and Anton just never saw eye to eye. Lelani has accused him of many things and she blames him for her death."

"Yes, she told me he was responsible but did not elaborate. Was she in prison when Delaney fell out of the boat and drowned?"

"Delaney was never in any boat." Somner said solemnly.

I was so dumbfounded that I couldn't speak. Somner realized he had spoken without thinking, but it was too late. I managed to stammer. "What?"

"I'm sorry Kat, I have said too much. Please forgive my slight of tongue. Shall we proceed with the mounting of the cameras?"

"Oh no you don't…you are not going to write me off like Anton did!"

We were interrupted by Zoe calling up the stairs to me that Lili had fallen down and scratched her knee and was crying for me. "Don't think that is the end of our conversation!" I yelled back at Somner as I ran down the stairs. "And yes, you can put up those dammed cameras!"

The only time Antonio and I saw each other was over the dinner table. Polite conversation was conducted for the sake of Zoe and Senora Cara. Liliana was always happy to see her father and would wait anxiously for his knock on the back door which he did every afternoon to announce to her that he was home. She and Gypsy, the German shepherd puppy that Somner had given her would run down the hall whenever Zoe would tell her that her papa was home.

Somner went to work every day and it was Connie who was left to handle the chauffeuring duties and anything else that might arise. I couldn't say for sure but was almost positive that Anton was deliberately keeping Somner and me apart. The only time I seen him was when he would arrive after the dinner hour to play the tapes from the previous night's baffling episodes of my disturbing sleep incidents.

Nothing showed up on film for almost a week and then one night, there I was coming out of my bedroom sauntering down the corridor wearing one of my white cotton night gowns. Now that I was aware of my sleep walking, I always put something on that wasn't transparent…just in case. I watched myself stop at the highboy and pick up the candle. I didn't seem to be aware that it didn't require lighting. I looked as if I was in a trance. With one hand on the railing and the other holding the candle I proceeded down the stairs. At the bottom, I pushed open the kitchen door and stood for a few seconds before turning and passing through the dining and living rooms. I crossed the hall, not bothering with the outside door and peered into the den and Lili's playroom where I stood and appeared to be looking for something. It was there that I always started crying. It was surreal to come face to face with myself and not have any understanding of what I was doing. It was most obvious that I was searching for something or someone when I undid the lock to the lower ground floor. I just stood on the top step and held the candle out and my crying turned into frenzied weeping. I did not wait for the tape to end but got up and said. "Well, that's that isn't it?"

I went to my room and prepared myself for the cameras again. Anton did knock on my door and ask if I was all right. I told him that I was fine which was a lie, but he may as well not be the only one hiding the truth.

Every day I went into the galleria for several hours to help prepare for the upcoming artist's exhibition. It was the only thing that took my mind off the situation at home. I did not plan on living my life in uncertainty for much longer. Once the gala event was over Anton was going to have to come clean or else…

Before long, my escapes of the night became commonplace. I never ventured from my routine of the first showing. Nothing else was ever revealed and yet, we watched the same movie over and over. The weeping of the lost woman on her endless quest did not upset me anymore. I had seen the same scenario seven times. Something changed though I know not what. It was July the thirteenth and the tapes had all been blank for a week. A month had gone by and Anton and I were still at an impasse.

The weather had been relentless with temperatures hovering over 37 Celsius for almost two weeks. It was too hot to take Liliana down to the beach, but thankfully, we had the pool and spent hours in it every day. Even though Anton knew that I was an excellent swimmer, he was still leery of the water, especially the sea. Why he hadn't got rid of the pool was beyond me. He never came in it with us but enjoyed watching Lili play in the shallow end. I was teaching her how to paddle and she could almost float. She never panicked if the water rose over her face. Zoe was finally comfortable in water over her head. She had made friends with several girls from the neighbourhood and they joined us in the afternoons for pool fun. A storm was brewing that afternoon of the 13th and I ordered the girls out of the water when the first bolt of lightning struck. It was one of the girl's birthdays and Zoe left with them for an overnight sleep over.

Anton was quiet during dinner and retired into the den immediately afterwards. I put Lili to bed early and sat out on the front sundeck to watch the brightly lit up skies. For a while it had appeared that the storm was going to pass us by as all had become quiet. But now, there was a new one erupting from the east. I couldn't explain my fascination with the weather phenomenon, but with every clap of thunder and streak of lightning, I felt exhilarated. We had so very few electrical storms here that I planned on enjoying every second of this one. I had brought the baby monitor with me so that I could hear Lili if she woke up.

Anton startled me. "Katarina, I wish that you would come in. It's dangerous out here."

"Thank you for your concern, but it is not warranted." I replied caustically.

"I can't do this any longer Kat. I'm ready to tell you everything you want to know."

I wasn't sure if I cared enough to hear his story. I had been secretly planning on taking Lili and Zoe and leaving Anton and Verde El Mar. I had a substantial bank account, thanks to Anton's generosity, so money was no problem. However, I owed it to myself to hear him out.

"The storm seems to be gathering momentum and the rain is not far off so we best go indoors. Do you mind if we go to your upstairs office as I want to be near Lili if the thunder wakes her?"

Anton took my arm to help me up. I welcomed the assistance as my hip had been wreaking havoc with my movements more so than usual lately. He handed me my cane and said that he would be glad when the surgery was done with and I was pain free. He sat me down on the divan in his office and pulled a chair up opposite me. He didn't make eye contact with me but took my hand and turned the rings on my fingers over and over.

"I have not spoken of this for a very long time and so I hope you will be patient with me and hear me out. I will start with the first day that I met Delaney. I was living at the family home and Somner and Lelani had a small apartment a few streets away. A late evening shipment had arrived at the docks and I stopped by their place to pick Somner up. He met me in the yard where he was waiting and talking with Lelani and a woman I had never seen before. He introduced me to Delaney saying that she was a school friend of Lelani's and had been living abroad but had just moved back to be with her mother after her father passed away. I was immediately drawn to her. She was not dark as most Spanish women are but had blue eyes and golden hair. I learned later that she was born in California. I hadn't been involved with anyone for years so perhaps I was gullible, but I fell in love with her as she did with me. We became engaged two months after we met and I bought this house as a wedding present for her. She loved the water just as you do. I kept the house a secret from her while it was undergoing repairs. I asked her to meet me here that fateful day. She arrived early and ventured down to the seaside where she found a skiff tied up at the docks and ventured out into the choppy waters. She fell overboard and although some fellow boaters tried to reach her they could not, and she drowned."

He quit talking as if that was the end of the story. So that was it, he was going to keep lying. I sat back and untangled my hand from his.

"Is that it Anton…is that the whole honest to God truth?"

"Pretty much so."

"It's all black and white then; there is no in between?"

"I fail to see what you are getting at Kat."

"Umm, suppose if I were to tell you that I know another version of the tragedy?"

He was adamant. "You can't possibly…"

"Really? And, if I was to tell you that I know there was no boat involved, what would you say then?"

He got up and walked over to the window and stared out into the night and the tempestuous sea. He turned to me and I could see the coldness in his eyes. "If you already know what really happened why are you putting me through this nightmare again?"

"I am not heartless Anton; I just want you to tell me the truth. I keep hearing bits and pieces of that horrible day but I can't make them fit. If you prefer not to confide in me, then so be it."

"There are only three, maybe four people who know what really happened and so, I can only conclude that you heard it from Somner. Am I right?"

"Somner only let it slip that there was no boat involved in Delaney's death."

"So, that bitch of a wife of his told you her sordid version?"

"No, to be fair to Lelani, she did not. All she said to me was that you were responsible for her dear friend's death."

Anton took a deep breath and turned his back on me again and muttered. "Yes, I am to blame."

I got up and walked over to him and laid my hand on his shoulder. He was quivering.

"I'm sorry Anton. I'm ashamed of myself for asking you to relive the most painful time of your life. You need say no more."

"Perhaps it's time I face what really happened that day." He took my hand and we walked back to the divan where he sat down next to me. "Delaney was unstable and I knew it. I thought that I could be her savoir and banish all the demons from her mind. You see Kat, her and Lelani were not schoolmates, but inmates…they had been in the same mental institution together. That's where they met and became friends. Delaney's parents had her committed because they could not help her. She was this beautiful girl, but she saw herself as an ugly duckling and was constantly doing harm to her body. She used sharp objects to cut and mutilate herself. I don't know for sure what Lelani's problems were back then, but I can guess. Anyhow, they formed a bond and stayed in touch. After Delaney was deemed not to be a harm to herself anymore her parents sent her to California for plastic surgery. She went to a beauty school and it boosted her confidence because she became a model and lived there for three years. I guess it is my fault that she never returned. She started having issues with her body soon after we met and was always saying that she wasn't worthy of my love. I should have paid more attention to her moods but I was sure that I could cure her once we were married. Her mother warned me that Delaney was on the doorstep to a breakdown, but I ignored her warnings. When I told her that I had a surprise for her and asked her to meet me here, she seemed perfectly fine and she said that she could hardly wait. She arrived before me and I was told by the gardener that she walked around the house and squealed in delight when she seen that the property extended to the Genoaen Bay and ran down the steps. He said he watched her throw off her sandals and walk into the water. He said she just kept walking and walking."

I was mortified. The lack of empathy in Anton's voice worried me. I wanted to ask more questions but couldn't find my voice. Anton continued unemotionally.

"You are probably wondering how and why I pulled this deception off. It was to protect her mother. I paid the gardener and a man in a boat, who never even seen her, to back my account up. That was how it was reported…a boat mishap. I put Delaney to rest and for three years I pretending it never happened and then you came into my life and you erased her memory."

A jagged bolt of lightning illuminated the sky and was followed by a thunderous clap of thunder. It startled both of us as we thought the storm was over. We listened for any sound coming from Lili's room but there was none. Anton was on edge. He went to the window and yanked the blinds down.

"It's time this damn storm was over and done with!" He growled.

I had been counting to myself…one hundred and one, one hundred and two, one hundred and three…"It's a new storm Anton; and it is almost upon us. It has been so unbearably hot, don't you find it a refreshing change?" I was still trying to process the whole sordid story that he had told.

"No, I hate thunderstorms! What else do you want to know Katarina?"

He didn't sound like a man who loved me. "Nothing." I said solemnly.

"Come on, there must be something…let's get it all out."

"All right, I am curious about a couple of things. One is did you ask Delaney to change her name to Katarina, and those bracelets that you gave me at Christmas…are they supposed to be a copy of the ones a man named Anton had made for his wife Katarina another lifetime ago?"

He laughed scathingly. "More rubbish that Lelani, the scallywag, concocted. Pray tell, why would I want anyone to change their name? That is pure rubbish. Yes, I must admit that I have been intrigued with the premise that the Infinity Bracelets exist and I have even tried to find them, but of course to no avail as they are pure fancy. Their legend does live on and they inspired me to have similar ones made for you. It is just that simple Kat. Finding a woman with the same name as the fabled one is purely a coincidence."

I started to speak but another barrage of lightning and thunder made me pause to listen for Lili. Sure enough, she was crying. I ran down the hall with Anton at my heels. We found her clinging to the crib rails wailing for me. I picked her up and started walking with her.

"Shh baby, mama is here. Look, your papa is here too."

After a few minutes she stopped crying but wouldn't let go of me. I took her into my bedroom and told her that she could sleep in my bed with me. Anton closed all the curtains and pulled the blinds saying he would sit with her while I changed into my night gown. Lili wanted nothing to do with him and started screaming again. Anton was disturbed with her rejection of him. I told him that she would be back to normal in the morning. He tucked me in and kissed me.

"I was hoping for a different outcome for the evening but I know Lili needs you more than me. I have missed you Kat. Please tell me you still love me."

I patted his hand and said. "I love you Anton." I knew not what else to say.

Lili fell asleep almost immediately and I was left to reflect on what Anton had told me of Delaney's demise and his other explanations which I didn't believe for one minute. I slept fitfully and it had nothing to do with the incessant rumblings outside.

Three times I had the same dream. The faceless man was calling me, but his words were carried away by the wind and every time he turned, I awoke, and he vanished into the ghostly mist. Who was this man who plagued my dreams and never let me see his face? What did it all mean?

Chapter 16

Happenings at the Castle

Rainey wasn't sure how he felt about Johnny seeing the puzzling light at Willowisp. On one hand, it proved that he wasn't imagining it, yet it took a little of the mystique away. He wondered if he had convinced himself that the illusive illumination had been meant for his eyes alone…that it was really Vienna's way of reaching out for him.

"The whole house is going to be delighted to see you Rain, but selfishly I have been hoping you would show up for my sake. I'm but a humble man living in a woman's world. It'll be good to have another man's take on things." Johnny confided on the way down the kitchen stairs.

"What about your man Wesley…is he not in your favour anymore?" Rainey asked.

Johnny laughed. "You are out of touch Son. The MacLeod's are no longer with us."

"Why is that, I thought you were quite pleased with their performance."

"Let's just say that they had more on their minds than employment."

"Ah, so you were also a gleam in Mrs. Macleod's eye?"

"She came on to you too? Why didn't you say anything?"

"It wasn't worth mentioning Johnny, and I think I warded off her advances without doing too much harm to her pride."

"I don't think the woman has any. I could have put up with her subtle innuendos because they were never going to go anywhere, but when Wesley made improper suggestions to Amma and Rosy…well, it was time to send them packing."

"It appears as if Vienna was right about them all along."

They entered the kitchen and found the women engaged in lively conversation over their afternoon tea. Amma jumped up so fast when she saw Rainey that she knocked her teacup over.

She ran to him and through her arms around him. "Rainey Quinn, you scoundrel; it's about time you showed up!"

"I love you too Darlin. Now, what's this I hear that you've been giving my boy here a hard time?"

Amma punched Johnny playfully. "Now, what's he been a tellin you dare I ask?"

Mary McDuff pushed her chair away from the table and struggled to right herself. Rainey and Johnny both took an arm and helped her to her feet. She accepted their help then held them off. "Ole Mary be not helpless yet boys. Lord loves a duck Mr. Rainey, 'tis be good to see ya."

Rainey returned her embrace and grinned broadly. That was one of Vienna's sayings. "It's good to see you too Mary dear. How's that old coot Duffy?"

"He be just fine and will be happy to see you."

Rainey glanced at the other three sitting at the table. "Nice to see you Lois."

"The same to you Sir. This here be Jeanette and Caren, new additions to the staff."

"Ah, good Irish names and where might you girls hail from?"

"We were both born and raised in Dublin but came to live with an aunt outside of Edinburgh. She knows Miss O'Shea and helped to get us this job. We love it here and hope that you will find our work to your liking Mr. Quinn." Kathleen said on behalf of her sister.

"I trust Miss O'Shea's judgement and far be it for me to interfere with her position as supervisor. This house and property could not manage without her and Johnny. I am but a guest in this mansion and have no say as how things are run so please do not think of me as your boss."

"Oh Rainey, you are a lot more than a guest! Don't be fooled girls as he is the Laird of Avanloch!" Amma giggled because she knew how much Rainey hated that ridiculous title. "By the way, we gave them the apartments over the carriage house because Johnny informed me that he is doing some remodelling at Willowisp and it is not available."

Johnny winked at Rainey and said. "Cuppa the witch's brew for you then Laddy?"

Mary smacked Johnny. "I dinnae mind that Lady Vienna call me tea that, but I dinnae have to take it from you Johnny Boy. Can I fix you some coffee then Mr. Rainey?"

Rainey was glad to be laughing again at the banter between the two of them. "God bless you Mary, but your rose hip tea will do. I am hoping you might have a piece of bramble pie for me?"

"If we's had known you was coming we would have baked up a storm wouldn't we have Lois? Will a sour cherry tartlet with some fresh cream do you Mr. Rainey?"

"It will indeed Mary. Now, what's with all this Mr. stuff? I thought we dispended with that talk a long time ago."

"Just tryin to set a good example for the new girls 'tis all."

Rainey addressed Jeanette and Caren. "No Mister, no sir, just Rainey, okay?"

They both nodded. "Yes Sir."

"Just a minute, I think that must be me girls." Mary went to the kitchen door. "Sure enough, those hungry girls will be wanting their snacks."

Amma and Johnny's youngest daughter entered with another smaller child in tow.

"How come everybody is here Mrs. D?" The little girl asked.

Mary smiled broadly. "Because we have a guest, child."

"We do?" Tanny looked around the people sitting at the table nodding at them all until she came to Rainey. Then with a hoop and a holler she ran straight for him. He stood up and swept her into his arms and twirled her around much to her delight.

"How comes no one told me you were coming? Did you bring Tia Vienna with you?" She could see that Vienna wasn't anywhere to be seen and her happiness faded.

"Tia can't be here right now Honey. Will I do for a little while?" Rainey asked.

Tanny kissed him. "Of course, you silly ole goose! I miss you Rainey, but guess what, you won't have to miss me much because I live here now. Well, only when Rosy is here or else I stay at Amma's and Johnny's with Alexa and Brie and Shannon."

Rainey was about to ask why but from the look on everyone's face he thought better. However, Tanny answered his unanswered question.

"My Mother is in Heaven now you know Rainey? Do you think she likes it there? Rosy says it is a nice place and that her mother has been there a long time and that she still watches out for her, and that my Mother can see me and looks after me because Heaven is very high in the sky."

"Rosy is absolutely right Honey. Heaven is a beautiful place, and I am sure your mother is happy there even if you can't be with her right now. She isn't sick and hurting anymore, so that is a good thing don't you think?"

"I know 'cause Rosy told me. Is Tia Vienna in Heaven Rainey and where is Ava?"

"Ava will be here in a few short weeks and no, Vienna is not in Heaven. We still have to say a prayer for her every day though so she can find her way home."

"Oh, yes, I remember Tia in my prayers every night and for you too Rainey and now you are here so that is good, right?"

"Time for your snack child or else you will be spoiling your supper." Mary said.

"Can I have supper here Mrs.D with Rainey?"

"Of course you can, everyone is coming."

"Is Rosy coming too?"

"Do as Mary tells you Tanny. After your snack we'll telephone Rosy and then we can ask her when she will be coming okay?" Rainey gently lifted her to the floor.

"Yeah, and then you can see how good I painted a flower for Tia Vienna."

Tanny ran off to the pantry with Mary and Shannon. Amma informed Rainey that Elsa McCracken had passed away in March. Vienna would have wanted Tanny here and so they applied for temporary custody.

"You did the right thing Amma, and I am sure when Vienna comes home we'll make her a permanent part of our family. What happened to the grandparents?"

"Mr. McCracken had a stroke and Mrs. McCracken can no longer care for him by herself so they went into a senior's home which provides 24 hour care. Apparently, no one else in the family would take Tanny in as they are all elderly also."

"Sorry to hear of their woes. I will make sure to visit them soon and let them know that Tanny is very much loved."

And so, life resumed at Avanloch for Rainey without Vienna. In his absence, Johnny and Evan had fashioned a helicopter pad off the gatehouse. Evan was still employed by Land's End Air, but his priority was flying for McAllister Enterprises. Rosy and Ash, as heads of the company, had sanctioned the purchase of a helicopter for the company and family's use. The commute from London to Avanloch was no longer a long day's journey. Every weekend, the house was a hubbub of activity with Rosy and Evan, Jannie and John and Ash and Grayson visiting. Rainey had missed everyone, especially Rosy, but they were no substitutes for his wife and he still felt alone. Ava arrived on July the 2nd with Rosy and Evan and they invited Meggie to sit down with them and tried to assemble the new clues as to Vienna's whereabouts. Water and lilies and the color green…they surely meant something as Meggie and Sylvia had both seen them. They gathered around the small table in the downstairs parlour feeling that if some clue was going to come to them that it would be in her favorite room.

Rosy was the first to speak up. "Perhaps green water means the green slough in the village, and there are lilies growing there also."

"Really Rosalyn, the green slough? And, I can't believe that you don't know the difference between a lily and an iris." Ava laughed at her sister."

"Oops, you're right. I know it sounds crazy but I can't think of any more green water."

"If indeed the Ouija board and the cards literally meant green water then our task of ever discovering the exact location is insurmountable. Lilies are of no help and then we have the tall, dark man that Meggie sees…we just don't have enough to go on." Rainey was despondent.

Ava patted his hand. "We're going to figure it out Dad, don't give up. Let's go back and revisit the ominous message that was left in Mama's sitting room."

Rainey smiled at his daughter. "I'll never give up Ava, you know that. Sorry, I didn't mean to sound so pessimistic. I've read those warnings over a thousand times and the only thing I take away from them is that none of us took the prediction seriously. We know that the first stranger to come to the doors of Avanloch was Roberge and he was the invited one. The second was that self-proclaimed witch Tathia because she was the one who had a mission to fulfill. The third stranger was you Meggie, and you were the welcomed one. When you read the cards for Vienna you warned her to be aware of her surroundings and be ever vigilant, right?"

"Yes, I remember that reading as if it was yesterday. I told her that all was not what it would seem to be and that she was going to have a difficult time deciding what was real and that her emotions would be in a constant state of unrest. She would encounter deception and failure. The cards warned of a wolf in sheep's clothing and I believe this is the tall dark man that I have seen every time I do another reading for her. He is always there, but then, so are you Rainey. You are personified as the king that saves her."

Meggie had sounded positive. "I pray you are right Meggie, but we are no further ahead in discovering where she has gone are we?"

"No, but I just remembered something else. Several times while I am thinking of Lady Vienna, I have had a vision of another man and he is dressed as a character right out of a Shakespearean play. He is holding books in his hands and beckoning an armoured knight to follow him. There is a message there but I have yet to decipher it. Does any of this make sense to any of you?"

They all nodded 'no' except Ava who said. "Mama does love to read and I am sure she has read all of Shakespeare's works. However, these characters could be the scholar and the knight from Chaucer's The Canterbury Tales which is one of her favorites, don't you think Rosy?"

"Of course, yes you are right Ava, and in one of her children's books, she wrote about a damsel in distress, which I am assuming was her, and that a Cavalier rode in on a majestic steed and rescued her. We know now that her knight in shining armour was you Rainey."

"Thanks girls, but I assure you that I am no hero even if I did play the role of a knight in my dreams and did save my queen from the black witch. It was just a fantasy that played out in my dreams and I can only hope that it comes to pass."

July 13th, The Grey Lady

"Damn those coyotes." Rainey cursed as he turned over to see what time it was. The clock was not there. "What?" He said out loud. He swung his feet over the side of the bed and the light from the fading moon told him that he was in Vienna's bedroom. He was still fully clothed. Shaking the cobwebs from his head he recapped the night's events. Nothing pertinent had taken place. Everyone had left for London the day before and once again it was just him and Ava. They had both retired early as they were exhausted after the busy weekend. Of course, he had come to Vienna's balcony to search for the light at Willowisp. He had not seen it for a week or more and for reasons he could not explain, the absence disturbed him. He remembered lying down on the bed he had shared with his love for seven months. He must have fallen asleep only to be woken by those howling coyotes. He decided to return to the room he had been sleeping in ever since Vienna's disappearance. He opened the door to find a shadowy figure standing there. She was dressed all in grey and a faded veil covered her face. She held a candelabrum aglow with flaming candles in one hand and beckoned him to follow her with the other. They crossed the hall that led into the foyer and Rainey watched in astonishment as the bookcase opened up before him.

"My God," he thought. "I am having Vienna's dream and this apparition is her Grey Lady." He trailed after her noticing that The History of Rome and Historic Greece were two novels on the shelf to his right of the teetering bookcase. He counted the stairs as they descended. He came to a halt on the 22nd step. The Grey Lady placed her candelabrum on a rickety old wooden table. He appeared to be in some sort of passageway that led to doors to his left and right. There was a mechanical device in front of him and he had no doubt that it was the backside of the Grandfather clock because he could hear a loud clunking. He turned around to see what the Grey Lady had in store for him, but she was nowhere to be seen. He approached the door to his right and found that it was overloaded with locks of every size and shape. One by one he unlatched them all and flung open the door to a room that looked like it belonged in another century. He couldn't decide whether the furnishings were of French or Spanish design as he had never taken much notice of period pieces. He had most assuredly stepped into a lady's boudoir.

Frilly lace and linen attire were scattered on the sofas and the bed and hung lopsided on the red toile wardrobe. Coverings that must have been intended to protect the delicate furnishings lay crumpled on the floor. Two high backed slipper chairs sat opposite a fireplace that still had the remains of burnt out logs in its grate. Rainey's eyes darted to the ceiling wondering which room was above the chimney. The bed was stately and he pictured a queen lounging on it in her royal gowns and crown jewels. In the corner of the room stood a small oval table and chair both engraved with some foreign insignia. A gold plated tea service sat waiting for its mistress. Among the clutter of knick-knacks and books on an oversized bureau were several small portraits of a child. Everything seemed to be in pristine condition. Rainey had the eerie feeling that he was being watched. He reminded himself that he was dreaming and continued his survey. He flung open a small door and found it contained the lavatory. He backed out and entered what he presumed was a closet. It was filled with dozens of costumes and he riffled through them not knowing why. Something dropped at his feet; it was a brass key. He bent down and picked it up wondering what it opened. He was about to turn and find his way out of the wardrobe when something shiny caught his eye. It was another lock on an almost invisible knee high door. He felt like Alice in Wonderland and bent down to insert the key. There was only one thing inside this crawl space and it was a richly decorated chest. There was a coat of arms richly engraved in red and gold on the top of the trunk. Under the heraldry was the name **NAVARRA** enclosed in a laurel. The crest consisted of crossed swords entangled with fleurs-de-lis. In each corner stood a battlement tower. Again Rainey was confused. The name sounded Spanish, but the fleur-de-lis was French. Hesitantly, he unfastened the clasp and was met with an array of gold and silver objects and sparkling jewels. The dazzling pieces caused him to take a step backwards. "What in the world have I uncovered?" He asked himself. He dug through the relics carefully until he came to a hard wooden cover that separated the trunk into two sections. He had to remove most of the artefacts before he could get inside the next level. He retreated back to the main room to retrieve a candle from the candelabrum as he needed more light. He extracted one of the candles and re-entered the little cubbyhole. Among more pieces of age old treasures, he found a bound journal. He removed it gently and carried it out to where the light was brighter. He laid it down on the divan and brushed the dust off. There in bold dark letters he read the title. It was **AVANLOCH.**

"What is this?" With great apprehension he opened the book to the inside cover and read the bone chilling words.

My name is Avaleena
I have been a prisoner in this dank castle for 22 years.

Rainey heard the Grandfather clock strike 12 times. He covered his ears and rolled over. He felt nauseous and thought he was going to be sick. He made a dash for the bathroom only to stub his toe on something hard lying on the floor. Foolishly, he bent down to see what it was. His whole head felt as though it were about to explode. He straightened up and wondered why he was experiencing symptoms much like a hangover. He knew he had not been drinking the night before so had no explanation for his light headiness. His alarm flashed 6:45…why in the world had the downstairs clock sounded 12?

He managed to fight off the queasy feeling in his stomach and picked up the book that he had almost fallen over. He blinked as he read the title: **AVANLOCH**

"Where the hell did this come from?" He asked himself. Something clicked inside his head. "No, it can't be."

He threw the book on the bed and ran out and into the little foyer. There was no opening in the bookcase. He walked over to it and scanned the shelves. His eyes sought out the history section. When he found what he was looking for he stood dumbfounded at what it all meant and cursed. He went back to his bedroom half expecting and also hoping that the Avanloch book would be gone. It wasn't. He went into the bathroom and splashed cold water on his face. He observed himself in the mirror not liking the haggard face that peered back at him. He frowned and told himself that he had better get his act together before Vienna came home. Sighing, he decided to take another gander at what Avaleena had written. He thought that he'd heard her name before but couldn't remember when. He placed the book on his desk top as it was too awkward and heavy to hold on his lap. He opened it only to find that it was not written in English.

Mystified, he skimmed through the hand written pages but they were all written in another language. He knew damn well that what he had read last night was in English. He decided that the writings were in Spanish and wondered if Ava was up yet.

He traipsed down the hall and the back stairs clutching the heavy tome and found Ava pouring a cup of coffee in the kitchen. "Good morning ladies." He said to Ava, Lois and Mary. "Pour one for me too will you Honey? Actually, bring the whole pot and join me in the study please."

He didn't wait for an answer. Ava shrugged her shoulders at the others wondering what was up with her father. With coffeepot in hand she trailed after him. He was sitting behind the desk looking as if he was in another world.

"Dad, is something wrong? You look a little bewildered."

"That's putting it mildly Ava. I need you to convince me that I am not going out of my mind …not that I haven't already worrying about your mother."

Ava handed him his coffee. "What's happened? What do you have in front of you?"

"To be sure, I do not know. Last night I could read this thing but today I find that it is in a foreign tongue."

"I don't understand." Ava said hoping that her father was joking.

He turned the book towards her. "Except for the cover, I think it is written in Spanish."

Ava was surprised to see **AVANLOCH** in bold print on the front cover.

"Open to the first page but don't tell me what the first few sentences say. You know I don't know Spanish, but this is what I read last night: "My name is Avaleena and I have been a prisoner in this dank castle for 22 years." Is that what it says Ava?"

"Yes, that is what I think it says. My Spanish is pretty rusty Dad, but I am pretty sure that is the translation. Now, I think you had better start at the beginning and tell me where you found this."

Rainey leaned back and cupped his hands together. "First, tell me who Avaleena is?"

"She was Jeremy's great, great and maybe another great Grandmother and Avanloch was renamed after her."

"I knew I had heard that name before. Well Honey, I was in her boudoir last night which just happens to be in an underground room whose entrance is through the bookcase in the little upstairs foyer. Oh, and I might add that my guide was the lady in grey."

Ava reached out and took Rainey's hand. "Well, it is too early for you to be drinking and you are not one to make up outlandish stories, so I guess I am just going to have to believe you. On the other hand, maybe you just had one fantastic dream, but that doesn't explain where you found the book does it?"

"No, it doesn't. There is no way that this could have happened… so the question is as you ask; where did the book come from? I nearly tripped over it when I got out of bed but have no recollection as to how it got there. As soon as I saw the title, I remembered the dream and that is where fact and fantasy have a parting of the way."

"Start at the beginning Dad, and don't leave anything out. No matter how farfetched your account is. I promise not to interrupt."

"No, interrupt me any time you've heard enough to convince you that your once rational dad has clearly gone off his rocker. For some reason I laid down on your mom's bed last night and I guess I fell asleep. I woke up, or at least I thought I did. I started for my room and found the Grey Lady waiting for me outside the door.…"

Rainey related the rest to his daughter as accurately as he could and ended with the words, "I woke up in my own bed just as the Grandfather clock struck 12. In actuality, it was 6:45. I have never heard the sounding of the hour before in my room… so explain that to me please."

Ava smiled at her father who was definitely having trouble believing that his dream wasn't a dream at all. "Dad, I have lived in this castle since I was two months old and I have never had an experience like you did, and as far as I know neither has Rosalyn. I cannot speak for Mama because as you know, she has kept many things from us. There must be some reason the Grey Lady choose you to find her journal and not one of us. I envy you Dad. Before I try and decipher Avaleena's writings, why don't we go and see if we can get through the bookcase?"

"I've already looked, and it is not open. Maybe we will try later, but first I want you to have a crack at the diary okay? Don't envy me because I am not comfortable with any of this at all."

"I know you're not, but remember Mama's words: 'Things happen for a reason.'"

"Yeah, well I wish she was here to explain the reason behind this absurdity."

She reminded him that her Spanish was not very good. She turned the page.

June 23, 1847

This is the happiest day of my life. Stewart and I were married at Trieste near the ponds. Father had seen to it that only the most polite swans could be in attendance! The day was most splendid and nary a breeze did blow. The sun shone gloriously upon us just as sure I am that it will in Scotland.

Stewart calls me his queen though in actuality I will only be a lady to the house of McAllister. What am I saying…it is no house at all, but a castle! A castle, can you imagine? I have been raised in luxury, but what can it compare to life in a castle? I swoon in anticipation.

"There is page after page here about the wedding Dad, who was there, what people wore, etc. etc. Do you want me to try and read it all?" Ava asked.

"No, why don't you skip ahead a few pages."

"Here, this page is dated July 2nd, and apparently, she is in Scotland now." Ava read on.

This has been the most harrowing ten days of my life. Stewart warned me that the trip was going to be long and arduous, but I didn't care as long as we were together. How foolish was I to think that love could conquer all!

We arrived at the gates of King's Down just before sunset. The castle had been in view for some distance and the closer we got the more intimidating it became. Surrounding the stronghold is a raging river and murky waters run under the drawbridge. From the minute the huge iron doors opened, a sinister feeling overwhelmed me. Stewart looked at me and said. "We are home my lady." He picked me up out of the brougham and carried me over the threshold laughing at my trepidation. I was at once introduced to a dozen house servants and escorted into a huge galley where tea of a hearty meal had been laid out for us. Hours of merriment was enjoyed by all except me. The toasting was unending and the mead flowed like water. Feigning exhaustion, I asked Stewart to show me to our quarters and then he could continue celebrating if he so wished.

It was July and yet the castle was an ice palace. The stairs were endless and hard to manoeuvre as they were only rough-hewn planks. The only things on the bleak grey walls were articles of heraldry.

Stewart picked me up again and kicked a wooden door open and carried me across a large expanse of a naked floor and deposited me on a colossal bed. He proceeded to undress me and through my protests he laughed and said that we must christen the wedding bed. This was not how I had envisioned my first night to be in my new home. My husband reeked of malt and sweat, and though his intentions may have been of the carnal nature, it was not to be so. He fell asleep in the act and I pushed him off me, thoroughly disgusted!

Ava snickered. "I guess nothing has changed much in a century has it Dad?"

Before he could respond, Mrs. D knocked on the door and asked if they would be coming for breakfast. "I have made all your favourites Mr. Rainey."

He answered her. "On our way Mary."

They followed her down the hall and into the kitchen where the aroma of sizzling bangers and pan roasted tomatoes awaited them. Rainey kissed Mary McDuff. "You shouldn't have gone to such trouble luv, but I'm mighty pleased that you did."

She blushed as she always did. "There will be none of that. Now what would Miss Vienna say if she…" Mary turned her back and muffled something.

"What was that Mary?" Rainey asked.

She turned around with frying pan in her hand. "Sunny side up right, and yours tossed, right Ava? I'm just sayin that she should be here. She should be sitting down to breaky with you, that's all I am sayin."

Rainey helped himself to potato scones or tatties as they were called in Scotland and toast and preserves. "We hear you Mary. Now sit yourself down and have some of this delicious fare."

"Me and the Duff, we ate a long while back. Must be on with the pie dough now as Lois will be back with the berries. Blackberry, it's *her* favourite too you know."

Rainey and Ava made small talk as they ate trying to be cheerful for Mary's sake. They returned to the study and Ava took up her perch in her mother's chair again. Rainey opted to stand and look over her shoulder as she translated more of Avaleena's despairing description of the castle. She definitely wasn't happy and described herself as being as grey as her surroundings were. She did love her husband though, and he was kind and generous, and she had carte blanche when it came to renovations. Her father-in-law was in very poor health and hardly ever made an appearance. Stewart had changed the name of the castle to Avanloch in honour of her.

Rainey left and went outside for a walk around the gardens. Ava kept reading as she was captivated. Her father returned to find her with a perplexing look on her face.

"I've read it over and over Dad…look here, see it's in French now, and I think the reason for that is so Stewart couldn't read it if he happened upon her diary. It appears as though he was away for months fighting some battle most of the time. Avaleena takes a lover and becomes pregnant by him. He is some distant cousin of her fathers. There are no other children Dad, only the one, Robert Bruce, and he was fathered by one Jacques Ferrani. Do you know what this means Dad?" She didn't wait for him to answer. "It means that there are no more McAllisters; the line ended with Stewart… Rosalyn is not a McAllister but a Ferrani!"

"Ava, that is preposterous! Surely, you misread?"

"I didn't Dad. Avaleena writes how lonely she was with Stewart gone and how tiresome it was to contend with her sick and cantankerous father-in-law. She goes into great detail to describe her affair with this Jacques person. She was pregnant when Stewart came home so she hid it from him for several months. Lucky for her I guess that the baby was born tiny and weak. He was not expected to live and Avaleena herself almost died. A wet nurse was brought in to take care of the ailing child and in time he and his mother both rallied. Stewart believed that the child had been born premature and as far as I have read, Avaleena never tells him that he is not the father."

"So why does she become a prisoner in her own home?"

"I don't know Dad. Something must have changed, but I haven't got to that part yet."

The phone rang. Rainey saw that Ava had no intention of answering it and so reached across the desk for it. "Hello, you've reached Avanloch. How may I help you?"

"Rainey, thank God you're there!"

"Stu, ole chap how are you? I've been trying to track you down…where are you?"

"I'm in Spain Rainey…Verde El Mar to be exact."

"Never heard of it. You sound a little off kilter Stu; what's wrong?"

"I'm not the only one here Rainey. She's here Rainey…Vienna is here."

Rainey sat down hard and motioned for Ava to pick up the other phone which she did because she knew something was wrong by the look on her father's face.

"Say it again Stu…"

"You heard me right Rain; Vienna is here, I've seen her." He said as he heard a sharp intake of breath. "Ava, is that you? I'm glad you're there with your father. It's true; I've seen your mother."

"How, where, is she all right? Oh Stu, this is the best news ever." Ava couldn't talk anymore because she could hardly breathe.

"Hold on Stu…I have to calm Ava down. I'm going to call for Amma." Rainey went out into the hall and with a voice that he had never used before yelled for Amma. She and Mrs. D both heard him and knew that something terrible must have happened. Amma ran down the long corridor with Mary limping along behind. She found Rainey on the phone smiling and wondered why Ava was in such a state.

Rainey covered the mouthpiece. "It's Vienna, she's alive! Stu has found her in Spain."

Amma broke out in jubilant laughing and pulled the tearful Ava into her arms. Mrs.D arrived out of breath and when she heard the news started crying also. She looked up and said, "Blessed be the Lord!" She crossed herself and took off out of the room at a run.

Rainey shook his head laughing and went back to quizzing Stu. "How in the world did you find her Stu? Never mind; how is she? Please tell me she's all right!"

"I have only seen her briefly once and she looked just fine, but she doesn't know that she's Vienna."

"What does that mean Stu? Have you talked to her? Just a sec Stu, I can't hear you. There is a loud siren going off here…Amma, what in tarnation is that deafening sound?"

Amma laughed. "It's Mrs. D; she sounded the alarm bell to alert everyone that something has happened at Avanloch."

"I wish she could have found a quieter way; can you turn it off please? Sorry Stu, I have just found out one more eccentric custom of the castle and that is to notify all of Scotland that an incident has taken place at Avanloch. I can barely talk right now. I am so excited and yet worried. You say she doesn't know who she is…what do you mean by that?"

"Sorry if I scared you Rain. I am down here doing a piece on unknown local artists. As I was walking in to the galleria a gust of wind came out of nowhere and blew the scarf off this woman coming towards me. I recovered it for her and imagine my shock when I looked into the eyes of Vienna! There was no hint of recognition of me on her part. Just as she was thanking me, two burly men came up beside her and ushered her into a waiting limo. It all happened so fast that I was caught off guard. I did call out her name, but it was too late as the car was already speeding away. I did get the licence plate… it read DeMarco. I went into the art gallery and introduced myself to the curator. I took a chance and said that I thought I had recognized the young woman who had just left. She asked me if I meant Mrs. DeMarco, and I said yes."

Rainey clutched his chest. "Dad, what's wrong?" Ava didn't wait for an answer but picked up the other phone again. "Stu, what did you say to Dad? He's scaring me."

Johnny burst into the room. "Is it true, Vienna's alive?"

Rainey nodded and put the phone on speaker. "Everyone's here Stu so please continue. You will have to forgive me but I have been waiting for this news for almost two years, and now here you are telling us that you have seen Vienna, but she's not Vienna?"

"Of course you are overwhelmed. Let me enlighten you a little. This curator, Elaina Bolivar, is a very good friend of Vienna's or as she knows her, Katarina." Stu heard a combined "What?"

"Go on Stu; we can't imagine what is coming next." Rainey said astounded to hear the name Katarina.

"I told Elaina that Mrs. DeMarco didn't appear to recognize me and she said. 'Oh, you must have known Katarina before her amnesia. Poor thing, she has no memory of anything before her car accident. Why, she doesn't even remember marrying Antonio.'" Stu stopped speaking and waited for a reaction from the castle. It was as he expected.

Rainey was on his feet once more. "That's because she's not married to anyone but me! Antonio, Katarina, what the hell is going on here? What car accident?"

Ava put her arms around her dad.. "It's okay Dad, Mama's alive, nothing else matters."

Johnny took command. "Is there anything else you can tell us Stu?"

"I've found the DeMarco compound…no, that's not correct. It's not a compound, just a gated community. I've already checked it out so there should be no problem there. Rainey, do you want to take me off speaker for a minute?"

"No, whatever, good or bad, you can tell us all." Rainey assured him.

"Okey dokey then. I want to give you a heads up before you get here…Vienna had a small child with her."

Amma covered her mouth with her hand to keep from crying out. Johnny held on to her but wondered why Rainey was not upset upon hearing this and neither was Ava. In fact, they both had big smiles on their faces.

"How old do you think she was Stu?" Rainey asked, praying for the right response.

"Well, according to Elaina, she's about a year and a half or so. Why would you assume that the child is a girl Rain?"

"Because Vienna told me the day before she disappeared that she was pregnant. I've been so worried that she may have lost the baby, but what you say fits the timeline. And, of course, if you remember, she always said the LaFontaine women only give birth to girls. This is such a relief Stu. I will never be able to thank you enough." Rainey was practically glowing.

"I do remember that Rain and when I see you two together again that will be all the thanks I need. And, I didn't do anything… just the right place, right time."

"Give me the number where I can reach you. I'm going to hang up and call Evan to pick us up and fly us to this Verde El Mar…is that right? Good, talk to you after we reach Rosy and Evan."

Rainey wrote the number down and grinning said. "Yeah, you heard me right, Vienna and I have a new daughter."

Ava walked over and hugged her father. "All this time you knew?"

"I must say you aren't shocked as are Amma and Johnny; why is that?"

"Because I knew too. Mac mistakenly took me for Mama on the phone when he called after you left for Spain and said my pre-natal vitamins were in. I didn't know if she told you before she disappeared and so I kept it to myself. I didn't want you to have an extra burden to carry."

"Thanks Honey. I wanted to tell you so many times, but for the same reason I couldn't. And, you know what, it wouldn't matter if the child was mine or not but it is, so Amma, you have nothing to worry about."

"I'm not worried Rainey, just amazed at how you and Ava kept it to yourselves. I'm so very happy and I can hardly wait to see them. Do you think I should tell the household?"

"They need to be told as does the village because I am sure everyone is wondering why the alarm was set off. Dial Evan's number for me pleases Ava, and after we have talked you can call your sister because I can see you are dying to do so."

"I'm coming with you Rainey." Johnny said.

"I know you are." Rainey said as he gave his friend a hug.

A few minutes passed before Evan was tracked down at the hangar. After hearing the amazing story he assured Rainey that he would arrange all the flight plans and that he would take the jet to Waverly as it had just been serviced and was ready to go. He could be there by noon if they could meet him at the airport. He thought the whole trip whole trip would take six or seven hours. He would know more when he picked them up.

"Evan, don't waste time phoning Rosy, we'll do that. Just get here as fast as you can."

Rainey took the phone off speaker and passed it to Ava. "Tell Rosy we love her."

Johnny put his arm around Rainey's shoulders. "Walk with me Rain. Amma, I'll meet you down at the gates in a few minutes."

Amma kissed Rainey and scurried off, bustling with excitement to relay the news about Vienna to the crowd who had gathered outside the gates.

"Are you at all worried about what we may run into? Stu made it sound like Vienna is well guarded though for what reason is a mystery. Her amnesia might pose a problem to our rescue plans. I don't want to be pessimistic Rain, but suppose Vienna doesn't want to come with us?"

"I'm not even going to go there Johnny. I'm hoping that she will regain her memory as soon as she sees us. We need to come up with a plan to get her out once we are all together on the plane."

"I think we should take a little reinforcement along, what do you think?"

"As much as I hate the thought I have to agree with you. I'll see what I can come up with. You run along with Amma and help her to quieten the people at the gate. I need a few words with the staff to prepare them for Vienna's home coming. If I know Evan he'll be here before noon. You know John, not many people get a second chance to repair their mistakes, and here I am with my third. Nothing can go wrong; we can't gamble that our rescue is going to go like clockwork."

"None of this was ever your fault Rain, but I see you are still punishing yourself. Well, I for one, are not coming home without Vienna! I don't care if we have to drag her out by her hair!"

"Right there with you Buddy." Rainey left Johnny at the kitchen door and after a short discussion with Mary and the staff went to collect Ava. She was still on the phone.

"Chop, chop, young lady, we have things to do before we have to meet Evan in Waverly." He tapped his watch.

"And Rosy." Her eyes were red from crying so much.

Rainey folded her into his arms. "It'll be hours before we pick your sister up. I guess I shouldn't have told Evan not to call her as we would."

"Of course he called her. I only talked to her for a minute because she had to get to the airport, so she's already in the air."

"That will save time then as we won't have to land in London. I should have known Evan would call her. Who were you talking to then?"

"Aunt Jannie. What about Joe and Lily, and your parents"

"Should we wait until tomorrow? You girls can decide later. Tomorrow we will have your mother home. Right now I know that tomorrow seems like an eternity away and I don't know how any of us are going to get through this night, but together we will."

He looked down at the Avanloch journal. Ava asked him what he was going to do with it and he said he'd just lock it in one of his drawers for now. He cautioned her about not mentioning any of their findings to Rosalyn.

"I'd never do that Dad, and you won't tell Mama, will you… at least not for a while?"

"I'll just see how things go. I won't confront her with anything that she can't handle."

As they passed by the kitchen, Rainey peeked in the door and asked Mary if she could phone Meggie and tell her the good news. She said it was already on her list of to dos.

Rainey packed quickly hoping that one change of clothes was all he would need. He deposited the journal in the bottom bureau drawer as it was the only one that locked though he had no idea why he felt he had to keep it under lock and key. Then he left his room and went to Vienna's sitting room scowling at the bookcase as he crossed through the foyer. He walked through the bedroom that they had shared almost two years ago and the newly constructed balcony. He decided to put a quick phone call into Roberge who was ecstatic at the news. Then he tried his cousin Lara and Jimmy; neither was home. He decided not to leave a message and call later.

He knocked lightly on Ava's open door. "Are you all packed Honey?"

"Almost, but I have to stop by Rosy's room and pick up a few things for her. She also asked me to bring a pair of shoes for Mama. Isn't that funny Dad that she thinks Mama won't have shoes on when we rescue her?"

Rainey smiled. "Not really. I'll go pick up a pair; any preference?"

"I think her little red slipper-like ones will be good, what do you think?"

"Sounds good to me." Rainey walked back to Vienna's bedroom and rifled through her closet until he found her favourite shoes. He thought of moving his clothes back but decided that he probably didn't have time. He returned to his daughter's room and plopped down in the rocker.

Ava thought her father looked troubled and pulled up a chair beside him. "What's wrong Dad?"

"I'd be lying if I said I wasn't worried. What if your mother's amnesia is permanent? Suppose she doesn't recognize us Ava, what then? I don't think my heart could take it."

"She will know us Dad. She loves us all too much not to remember us, but on the slight possibility that she doesn't, well, we will have to kidnap her just like this DeMarco person did! What do you think about that?"

Rainey squeezed Ava's hand and smiled. "I think that's the plan Honey. Now, let's go collect Rosalyn's stuff as I need to get a few things from there myself."

"Whatever could you want from Rosy's room?"

He put Vienna's shoes in his duffle and followed Ava down the hall to Rosy's suite. She watched as he pulled a key out of his pocket and walked over to the gun cabinet and unlocked it.

"Dad, tell me you're not seriously thinking of taking firearms?" Ava asked fearfully.

"We have no idea what or who we are going to encounter down there Ava. Stu said Vienna had what appeared to be bodyguards. It's better to be prepared than to be sorry that we weren't."

"I guess you are right, but you hate guns."

"I do, and I certainly hope there will be no call to use them, and if it makes you feel any better, we probably won't even load them. You know I will do anything in order to get your mother back and so will Johnny."

"I know Dad." Ava opened her purse and withdrew an envelope. "I was going to give you this tomorrow for your birthday, but I think today is a good day."

Rainey opened it and unfolded an official looking document. Ava would remember the expression on his face forever. He shook his head and enfolded his daughter into his arms. "How did I ever get so lucky as to have you as my daughter? This is without a doubt the second best present I will ever receive. I don't have to tell you what the first is. Thank you Ava; you have just made my day much brighter."

Proudly, he read the paper out loud.

Official name change: Ava Lane McAllister
to
Ava Lane McAllister Quinn

Chapter 17

Bringing Vienna Home

Casscadia Casa July 14th

Liliana and I had slept until 9. The house was empty. We entered the kitchen and I found two notes propped up on the table. One was from Senora Cara and it stated that her good friend Elvira had fallen last night in the power outage and that she was at the hospital with her but would be home in time to prepare dinner. Lili's porridge just needed warming. I put Lili in her highchair and gave her a banana while I read Anton's note.

Kat, my love,

I so wanted to be here when you awoke but something has come up at the docks that I must attend to. Have a pleasant morning and I will be home just as soon as I can be.

Love you Kat, Anton

I put the porridge in the microwave and gazed at the calendar hanging next to it. There was a big red circle around todays date. I wondered what was so special about July 14th. I tried to feed Lili her breakfast which turned out to be a total disaster as she wanted nothing to do with the gruel and spat it and the banana all over me. I poured myself a cup of old coffee and after one sip, dumped it down the sink and decided to do without.

Lili was content to sit and play with her toys on the floor in the family room. I felt a headache coming on as I recalled last night's events. I was not totally satisfied with Anton's account of Delaney's demise. When I had asked if he ever sees her mother, he had said only once, and that was New Year's Eve when she crashed the party. He had to ask her to leave as she planned on causing a commotion. I hadn't said anything but realized that she must have been the woman I had witnessed him having an altercation with. His trips to some little town in the Pyrenees were to collect some ancient scrolls his uncle had uncovered. When I had asked him what was on the scrolls he had said nothing I would be interested in. I asked if I might see them and he had replied that they were most delicate and were being authenticated and refurbished in Barcelona. Not once did he say that the scrolls were in any way connected to the bracelets. Something fishy was going on and I had every intention of finding out what it was.

Zoe interrupted my chain of thoughts when she came in complaining about the heat and cautioned me not to take Lili outside.

"It's not even ten yet, how can it be so hot?" I asked her.

"Must be because of the storm last night…it feels like the sky is going to fall in. It is most humid. Did the power go off here?"

I told her I didn't think so. We talked for a while about her sleepover and the storm before she left to make something to eat. I told her that I could use a pot of coffee and that Lili had refused breakfast so maybe she could get her to eat something..

The doorbell rang and Lili ran down the hall saying "Papa, Papa." I snatched her up as I knew it wasn't Anton as he never came in the front door. She struggled until I put her down. We never had company except for Anton's family and they always called first. I opened the door to find two lovely young ladies standing on the front step.

Verde El Mar, Spain July 13th, 8 P.M.

Stu had decided to kill time by visiting the gallery again as he had hours before the crew from Scotland would arrive. He learned that Antonio DeMarco owned an export/import business and drove down to the docks to check it out. There were half a dozen men unloading crates under the watchful eye of an overseer. Stu recognized him as one of the men whom he had seen with Vienna. He prayed they would all be here at work tomorrow. He was waiting at the airport when the small jet landed and the five animated passengers alit. Evan made arrangements for the plane to be refuelled and ready for their departure the next day. After checking in to their perspective rooms at an inn not far from The Demarco residence that Stu had reserved for them, they met for a much needed meal and to discuss the strategy for Vienna's liberation from captivity. As much as Rainey hated to admit it, he didn't think that Vienna was a prisoner, thanks to her amnesia. No one knew what to expect, but they all agreed caution was of the essence and because there was a child involved only heightened the need for concern.

In the end, they had all decided that the best thing to do was to send Ava and Rosalyn in first. No one should be suspicious of two young women and the men could survey the surroundings for any unforeseen obstacles. It all depended on who answered the door as to what the girls would say and what they would do.

Rainey paced the floor all night. At dawn, he finally dozed off for a few hours. He was awakened by a knocking on the door. His cohorts had arrived with much needed coffee and some breakfast goodies. Ava encouraged her dad to eat but he said that his stomach was full of butterflies and so there was no room for anything else. At 10 A.M. the girls exited the car for the DeMarco residence. Rainey watched but was not prepared for Vienna answering the door.

Johnny held him back. "Let's give them a few minutes Rain and then we'll all go in."

Rosy clutched her sister's hand as she rang the doorbell. "I wish you would quit shaking Ava. Let me do the talking just as we rehearsed, okay?"

Ava nodded. Seconds later a woman with dark brown eyes and short frosted caramel hair opened the door. She was wearing a long flowered blue summer dress that couldn't quite hide her bare feet. A little blue eyed girl was tugging at the woman's legs. Ava felt Rosy's grasp on her tighten just as she whispered "Mama" and felt herself swaying. Rosy held on to her tightly and their mother reached out and took hold of Ava's other arm.

"It must be this oppressive heat…let's bring her into the house. Lili, run and get Zoe!"

Rosy heard her mother speaking, but it was obvious that she did not know who Ava and she were. "This isn't like her to get so woozy; I apologize for my sister's behaviour."

"Think nothing of it, your sister is just a little lightheaded. The heat will do that to one, especially if they aren't used to it. Let's lie her down on the divan."

Ava protested saying that she was all right. Katarina looked from one girl to the other. They certainly didn't look as if they were related, yet there was something oddly familiar about them.

She was about to ask them if she knew them when Lili came running back with Zoe.

"What has happened Kat? Where did these young ladies come from?" She asked.

"Doesn't matter; please bring a pitcher of water. You were right, this heat is stifling."

Zoe rushed off. Lili walked over to Ava and said. "Up."

"No Sweetie, the lady needs to rest a minute. Sorry, she always wants to be picked up."

Ava smiled at her new sister and started to raise herself despite Rosy telling her not to. Lili surprised her and touched her cheeks almost sticking her fingers in her eyes and then she pointed to her own eyes, and turning to her mother, she said. "Mama, see."

The sisters watched as their mother sat back in the chair she had pulled up next to Ava. She gripped the arms of the chair with such force that her knuckles were turning white. She pushed herself up and the look in her eyes was frightening. She slowly backed up towards the entrance saying, "No…no…no." She covered her ears to try and block out the strange voices in her head. Wispy shadows faded in and out of her vision. She fought to keep herself from blacking out.

Zoe returned with the water pitcher but quickly put it down seeing the state that Kat was in. She rushed to her as did Rosy. "Kat, what's wrong? Oh God, what has happened?" She looked accusingly at Rosy. "What have you done, who are you?"

They both took hold of Kat as she was sinking to the floor. Lili was crying. Ava picked her up and tried to comfort her. Zoe was still questioning them as to who they were.

Rosy said point blank. "She's our mother and we have come to take her home."

Zoe gasped but said nothing as there was a commotion at the door which drew her attention to the man who had burst in and was struggling with Somner and Connie to break free from the hold they had on him. His voice was most woeful as he cried out.

"Vienna, oh God, Vienna!" He was reaching out for her. "Vienna, Vienna…"

Someone was calling her name. She knew his voice…it was the man from her dreams.

"Rainey? Is it you Rainey?" Tears were rolling down her face as she tried to reach him but Somner and Connie held him back from her.

"Let him go Somner! For God's sake let him go!" She ordered.

Somner released his hold on Rainey. "You heard the lady Connie, let him go."

In two steps Rainey was across the floor and kneeling beside his love. He took her in his arms and cried her name over and over. Her sobs were agonizing as she clung to him.

"Rainey, you came for me." She managed to mumble.

He held her back a little and said emotionally, "I'll always come for you my darling. I would have been here a lot sooner but I didn't know where you were. We have searched and searched."

"I don't even know where I am, and until two minutes ago, I didn't even know who I was. I'm Vienna, aren't I?" She pleaded.

Rainey kissed her tear soaked face. "Yes, my darling, you are Vienna."

"I told you I wasn't Katarina, didn't I Zoe?"

Zoe was crying too as she squeezed Vienna's hand. "Yes, you did, over and over again."

"Look Rainey, Rosy and Ava are here…it's been so long since I've seen any of you. Where have you been? Why am I here?" Vienna was struggling with her memory, but one thing was sure, the faceless man of her dreams now had a face and it was of the man she loved…Rainey.

The girls were crying and laughing and saying how much they had missed her when the slamming of a door and loud footsteps broke up their reunion. Everyone but Vienna turned and looked at the tall, dark man stomping down the hall. Somner stopped him from reaching Vienna.

"What's going on here? Who are these people who have invaded my house? What are you doing with them Katarina? What is the meaning of this? Let me go Somner!" He demanded.

Vienna sighed and asked to be helped to her feet. She winced in pain when she stood.

"What is it Honey, are you hurt?"

"She must have hurt herself when she collapsed." Ava said.

"It's an old injury and nothing to worry about." She assured them. "Zoe, take Rosy and go and collect the "bags" and don't forget Gypsy! Is there a car outside Rainey?" He told her there was. "Go out the back door girls, and Ava, take Liliana to the car. I need to talk to Anton. Rainey, will you wait for me?"

"I'm not going anywhere without you Vienna. Are you sure you want to do this?"

She stroked his face. "Yes, I need to, not for him, but for me."

Rainey felt helpless as Vienna limped her way to the man who had stolen his wife from him. He hated this man, but also felt sorry for him because Vienna was going to break his heart. He had lived without her for almost two years and couldn't imagine a lifetime deprived of her love.

Rainey watched as the man held out his arms for Vienna, but she stopped short of them.

"Who are these people Katarina, why have you let them into our house?" The man lamented.

Vienna's voice was accusing as she lashed out at him. "You know perfectly well who these people are; they are my family, and you have kept me away from them. How could you Anton? How could you do this to me?"

"I'm your family Kat, me and Liliana, **we** are your family; you're my wife!"

He reached out for her again, and again, she pushed him away. "Stop it Anton, stop it! I'm not Katarina; I'm not your wife! I'm Vienna, I'm Vienna LaFontaine Quinn!"

Rainey watched as she cruelly tore the rings off her finger and threw them at him.

"No Kat, no, I love you; you can't leave me. I won't let you go."

"That's not love Anton, that's possession. You tried to make me into someone I wasn't. You took advantage of my amnesia and forced me to be this imaginary Kat person. How long would you have perpetuated this travesty? You would never have told me would you? You married me all the while knowing that I was already married; what kind of a man does that? I thought that I was a fugitive from some crime and you let me go right on believing that so that you could tighten your unholy control over me. Tell me, did you pay everybody off who tried to help me regain my memory just as you did in Delaney's death? Did you do that Anton? How could you be so heartless?"

Anton fell to his knees wrapping himself around Vienna crying over and over of how much he loved her. She protested and Rainey took a step to rescue her from his grasp. The man she had called Somner held up his hand and firmly seized Anton by his arms.

"It's time Anton... it's time. You must let her go." He insisted.

"Never, never, I will never let you go Katarina." He tried to fight Somner off but wasn't successful.

"Go my lady, go." Somner commanded.

Rainey could swear that he saw a tear form in the bodyguard's eye as Vienna said to him. "And, you too Somner, you too."

Rainey helped to free her and she collapsed into his arms. She buried her head in his chest and the sobs wracking her body were heart-breaking. He picked her up and ran with her out the door. Anton's pleading and cries echoed behind them. Johnny held the car door open for them. Rainey told Vienna that he was going to have to let her down for a second while he put her in the car, but she would not relax her hold on him. Ava reached out to her mother.

"Come on Mama, come sit with us. Look, we are all here, Rosy and Lili and Zoe."

She let go of Rainey just long enough for the girls to pull her in beside them but the moment Rainey was in the car she clung to him again. He pulled her unto his lap and tried to reassure her that she was safe but she was still weeping uncontrollably.

"I love you Vienna, I love you." He whispered. "We're going home, we're going home. Get this show on the road Stu!"

"Stu?" Vienna said through her sobs. "Stu is here?"

"At your service Mrs. Quinn." He turned and saluted her before he pulled away from the curb.

"Stu found you Sweetheart and look, Johnny is here too, and Evan."

"Johnny," Vienna bubbled as she lifted her head, "you came for me too?"

He reached behind and took her hand and smiled. "I wouldn't have missed this for the world my lady."

"Amma, how is Amma and the girls Johnny, and, Mrs. D?" Vienna probed.

"They will all be a lot better when they see your beautiful face later today, I can promise you that." Johnny squeezed her hand.

"How can that be? We are so very far from home, we have an ocean to cross and…" Vienna couldn't go on.

Rosy reached out for her mother. "Evan is flying us home Mama. You have nothing to worry about because you'll be back at Avanloch before you know it."

"Evan, you came too. You flew all this way just for me?" Vienna was sobbing again.

"I have been in this quest to find you from the beginning, so there was no way I wasn't going to do my part to reunite you with your family. The castle just isn't the same without you Mrs. Quinn; welcome back."

"Can you relax a little now Honey? There, that's my girl." Rainey coaxed a small smile out of his wife.

"But, something is wrong, I am all mixed up. I don't know where I am or how I got here. Have I been here a long time because I don't remember when I last saw you."

"Twenty two months Honey."

"Oh! Why do I think I saw Stu just the other day?"

"Because you did Vienna. We ran into each other at the gallery. Do you remember me rescuing your scarf for you? You didn't recognize me though." Stu answered.

"Yes, I do remember you giving me my scarf, but you're right, I didn't know who you were. Why are you here?"

"Doing an article on local artists and thank the good Lord I accepted the invitation!"

"Do you mean the event at the Gallery? I would have been the one who sent you the invitation." Vienna leaned back into Rainey's arms again and shivered.

Zoe reached into one of the bags and pulled out a sweater. She kneeled on the floor and wrapped it around Vienna.

Rainey thanked her and asked what else was in the bags.

"Clothes and money and our papers…Katarina, I mean Vienna, was always prepared."

"Prepared for what Zoe?" Rainey was curious.

Zoe hesitated; Vienna told her it was okay to tell. "In case we had to leave in a hurry, in case the authorities came for her… we had to be always ready."

"What?" Ava said. "What authorities?"

"Your mother thought that she had fled the Americas because she had committed a crime but had no knowledge as to what it was."

"That bastard! Is that what he was holding over your head Vienna? He made you believe that you were a fugitive from justice?" Rainey was incensed.

She started to cry again. "He said he didn't know why I had run away and that I wouldn't talk about it. That was before I was in the car accident that took my memory."

Rainey hugged her, "Sorry Honey, I didn't mean to upset you. What car accident?"

"You tell him Zoe."

"That's how I came to know Katarina as that is who Mr. DeMarco told me she was. He came for me at the girl's school and home I was at and picked me out from all the girls to be his wife's companion. She needed someone besides the nurses to sit with her and be her friend."

"Why do you think he chose you Zoe?" Ava asked.

"Because she was an orphan and had no family what so ever." Vienna said flatly.

"Where did this so-called accident take place?" Rainey prodded Zoe for more information.

"On Rose Island just after they were married. Mr. DeMarco had Kat flown here as there is no hospital there. The doctors all said he saved her life by acting so quickly."

Rainey wanted to curse but thanked Zoe and said they would talk more later. He asked Vienna if Zoe was coming home with them.

"Yes, for Liliana and I are her family and she is ours."

"Good enough for me. Speaking of Liliana… I see you have gone and had another child without me and don't you think it's time that I have a formal introduction to my new daughter?"

"Oh Rainey, I didn't mean to and I am so sorry but Lili is not your daughter." Vienna said with tears falling again.

Rainey wiped them away and laughed. "I beg to differ with you my dear, but she is definitely my daughter. What do you think girls?"

"Yes Dad, she is undeniably ours. She has our eyes you know Mama." Ava beamed.

Vienna reached for her little girl. "Come here baby, come sit with mama. Is it true Rainey, is she our daughter. How can this be?"

Liliana went into Rainey's arms as if she had been doing it all her young life. "What's the last thing you remember Vienna? Do you recall going to Spain with Roberge and then to Andorra?"

"Sort of…yes, yes. The road was horrible wasn't it?"

"Yes Darling, it was. At the top of the hill looking down on Nazeth, you told me we were expecting a baby in May…when was Liliana born?"

"May the 21st last year. Oh, my God!" Vienna clasped her hands over her mouth. "All this time Anton made be believe he was her father and I was so gullible I believed him."

"Don't blame yourself Honey…you had no idea; remember, you had amnesia. Here, sit back and together we will hold our little miracle. You've been through enough for one day…actually a lifetime. Soon we'll be at the airport and on our way home."

"Sure as shottin; is that how you blokes say it; turning into the strip right now." Stu confirmed.

"By the way Rainey, Happy Birthday!" Rosy exclaimed.

"Is it your birthday, is it July the 14th? I saw that it was circled on the calendar this morning and didn't know why. I wonder if I did it sub-consciously. I have nothing to give you Rainey." Vienna said sadly.

"Honey, you are my present, you and Liliana. There is nothing more in life I want or need."

"Did you give Rainey your gift Ava?" Rosy asked her sister.

"She did indeed." Rainey answered for his daughter. "She is now officially a Quinn!"

Vienna smiled. "It has not been lost on my befuddled brain that you call Rainey, Dad. I am very pleased that you have taken his name. When did all of this happen? I am so sorry that I have missed almost two years of your lives. I fear I will never catch up."

Ava moved closer to her mother and tearfully said. "Mama, we never gave up hope that we would find you. There were times when we felt that you may be lost to us forever, but we had each other to lean on and get us through the next day."

"Did you think I was dead?"

Rosy sniffled and reached across and took her mother's hands in hers. "In our darkest hours, yes, there were times when we did; but like Ava said, we had each other. Even though Ava and Rainey were a continent away, I had Evan and all our Avanloch family. Because there was no physical evidence that you had perished in the earthquake…"

Vienna interrupted. "What? What earthquake?" She was shaking.

Rainey tightened his hold on her. "Honey, relax. Yes, there was an earthquake in Nazeth. It did minimal damage to the town, but unfortunately several people were killed. We searched for you for days, but there was sign of you. I'm afraid I was too distraught to reason what had happened to you. It was Johnny who rationalised that the only plausible explanation for your disappearance was that you had to be flown out. Evan pretty well confirmed that when we discovered a landing pad at the church. In all of the commotion no one would have noticed a helicopter in the air. We had to believe that you were in that chopper and that you were alive. However, the days went on and we were never contacted. There was no ransom demand so we were left in the dark as to "why" someone would have abducted you. Of course, we still do not know "why." I was going to tell you all this later."

"I'm sorry Rainey; I should never have blurted it out." Rosy apologized.

"It's all right Red. Your mother is going to have a lot of questions as we all do, and the sooner we address them, the closer we will be to discovering the truth. I can see you are mulling something over...what is it Vienna?"

"The church, you mentioned a church; Anton had an uncle who was the priest at a church in the Pyrenees...could this be the same one? I knew from some people that Anton visited a small village in the mountains there. Just last night I asked him what was there and he told me that his uncle, Father Bissette...I think that was his name, was resurrecting a church and had unearthed some lost scrolls. He wanted Anton to have them. I asked to see them but he told me they were being refurbished and were of no great importance. Do you think Anton was there in Nazeth the day of the earthquake, the day I disappeared? Could they be connected to our mission there?"

"We don't know Honey, but it certainly seems plausible. A Father Bissette did lose his life that day so I am sure they are one and the same. It doesn't explain why Anton took you though."

Zoe voiced her opinion. "Maybe Mr. DeMarco did find her and she was badly injured as we know she was, and he did fly her out, and maybe he did save her life, but it wasn't from a car accident but from the earthquake. I think that maybe Somner knows."

"Why do you say that Zoe?" Rainey asked

"Because one day I heard him and Anton arguing in a hushed voice outside of Kat's room. I couldn't make out the whole conversation but he warned Somner about revealing the truth. He said that Katarina would come to love him and that was the way it was."

"Do you remember when this was Zoe?"

"Yes, I do Mr. Quinn; it was only days after Kat woke up from her coma."

"I knew it! I always suspected that Somner had something he wanted to tell me. It all makes perfect sense now. Somner is a pilot and it was he who flew me from the island after the accident. Only we know now that I was never on Rose Island and there was no car accident. Yes, Somner knows, and he will damn well tell us everything!"

"In due time Vienna, in due time." Rainey smiled as he was glad to see his wife showing some tenacity. He started to open the door saying that he and Evan had a little business to conduct before they all went through customs.

"What could you possibly have to do, is something wrong?" Vienna questioned.

Evan didn't want to have her worrying. "I have to see to the plane as we have an extra passenger and I need to deploy the jump seat. Sorry Johnny, but it's not going to be too comfortable sitting back there."

"No problem Evan. You and Rain do whatever you have to and Stu and I will keep the ladies company. Is that all right with you Vienna?"

"Yes, hurry back Rainey."

He kissed her and winked at Rosy. "Why don't you tell your mother your news Rosy?"

For a second Rosy had no idea what her step father was asking of her, but Evan did. "I hope we have your blessings Mrs. Quinn." He squeezed Rosy's hand as he exited the car.

"Really Evan, you're still going to call me that even after you marry my daughter? Get out of here you two! Well, are you going to show me the ring around your neck or not Rosalyn Anne?"

"How do you know it's around my neck Mama?"

"Oh, for heaven's sake child, do you think I haven't noticed you fidgeting with whatever is on the chain? What else could it be but a ring? When is the big day?"

"Mama, we are not even officially engaged yet."

"And, why not?"

Ava answered for her sister. "She wouldn't announce it until you came home Mama."

"Well, if that isn't the silliest thing I have ever heard! Suppose if I…"

"Don't say it Mama, don't say it."

Vienna passed Lili to Zoe and gathered Rosy in her arms. "We are going to have one heck of a celebration! Is there going to be two weddings Ava?"

"I'm so sorry to disappoint you Mama, but there is no wedding in my future. Things did not work out for Cam and I, and I have been too busy to even consider a love life."

"Is my disappearance the cause you and he parted ways; it's my fault isn't it?"

"You are not to blame Mama, and please don't ever think that you were! If it had of been true love, we would have survived anything, just like you and Dad."

"Correct me if I am wrong as my memory is still a little foggy, but weren't you going to meet up with Cam about the time Rainey and I went to Spain?"

Ava didn't want to answer her mother and Rosy sensing her discomfort spoke up. "We were all thrown into a state of despair when you went missing Mama, but I can assure you that you were not the cause of their breakup."

"I contributed to it though didn't I?" Vienna was holding back tears again.

Ava decided to be truthful. "I don't think so Mama. Cam came to see me in Vancouver that first Christmas and he confessed to me that he had been seeing someone else but would end it with her if I thought there was still a chance for us. I was surprised that I didn't care one way or the other and told him that I had moved on also. Our brief romance was not strong enough to survive the distance between us. Uncle Jimmy told us that Cam is engaged and I am happy for him. Is this settled now?" Ava wished her father would return.

Vienna sighed. "I will let it rest for now. I feel so guilty; I haven't even asked about Jimmy and Lara or Lily and Papa Joe or Rainey's parents or Sissy and Addy. Is everyone all right?"

"Yes, they are all well. Addy is experiencing some sort of remission and has a new love interest." Rosy pulled Liliana up off the floor where she had been sitting with her puppy. "I don't suppose you knew that you had named this beautiful child after your mother did you Mama?"

"I don't know, maybe subconsciously I did. Is Sissy still at the Palace in Bridge?"

Thankfully, the girls didn't have to answer as Rainey opened the door and said it was time to go. "Ava, where are the shoes you brought for your mother?"

"You brought me shoes? Why?" Vienna said teasingly.

"Because we know you Mama." Ava passed the red slippers to Rainey and he slid them on and asked her if she could walk and she assured him that she could. He told the girls to go ahead with Johnny while he said goodbye to Stu.

"What?" Vienna questioned. "Why aren't you coming with us Stu?"

"I'll be along in a few days Vienna. Remember the reason I was here originally was to do an article on little known artists? I will be following through with that as I have an obligation to do so, but just as soon as I get back to London, I will bring Daisy and Devon to Avanloch to visit."

"Thank you so very much for reuniting me with my family Stu. The artist you need to interview is Armand Démodé." Vienna hugged him and said she could hardly wait to meet his son.

"It was nothing I did my Lady. I just had the good fortune to be here at the right time."

Rainey and Stu shook hands and he and Vienna waved until Stu was out of sight.

"Well my darling, are you ready to go home?" Rainey asked.

"Oh yes, how long will it take and is Evan flying us to Waverly, or will we be taking the train? I fear it will be morning before we get home." Vienna lamented.

"Don't you worry your pretty little head as we'll be home in time for supper."

They passed through customs without any confrontation. The officer in charge didn't even ask to see the puppy's papers. Evan ushered everyone into the Cessna Skywagon and took his place at the cock-pit with Rosy as his co-pilot. He turned and made sure they were all buckled in.

"You should know Vienna that your daughter can fly and land this plane just like a pro. She doesn't have her license yet, but will very soon. I'm sorry that there is no proper seat for Liliana; I'm afraid we neglected to see to that."

"It doesn't surprise me one little bit that Rosy has learned to fly. It's just one more accomplishment to add to her resume. And, you don't have to worry about Lili for her father and I will guard her with our lives."

Rainey flipped the arm rests up between him and Vienna so that she could be closer to him and Lili. He placed his daughter on his lap and snugly buckled her up with him. She seemed to be perfectly content in his arms holding on to her blue eyed doll.

"I think she likes the smell of you Rainey." Vienna remarked.

He smiled amorously. "I hope that is a mother-daughter trait."

She didn't answer him as she suddenly had a wave of uncertainty wash over her. Instead, she asked Zoe and Ava how they were doing with Gypsy.

"She's sleeping at our feet Mama. I think Zoe is a little apprehensive of flying."

"No, I am okay." Zoe said. "I just don't know what to expect when we get to Avanloch. I can't believe that you all live in a castle. What will everyone there think of me for I am not like you?"

Vienna turned. "They will all love you just as Lili and I do. And, whatever do you mean that you are not like us? Heavens, we are all of different nationalities and we all get along just fine. By the way, I am not American, but was born in Canada and didn't come to Scotland until I was seventeen. Rainey is also Canadian and Johnny is Irish and Evan is from Australia. You may have a little trouble understanding our Mrs. D. as she has a very strong Scottish tongue, but you will adapt quickly just as I did. Don't even think of Avanloch as a castle for it is just a large home and you already know what it looks like on the outside, right?"

Zoe nodded. "If Avanloch is the castle that you saw in your visions, than yes, I do."

"How could you possibly know what Avanloch looks like?" Rainey asked curiously.

"Because there is a picture of it hanging on the wall at the casa that Armand Démodé painted for Katarina…I mean Vienna."

"I'm confused; you're telling me this man painted a castle and it just happens to look like Avanloch?"

"I can't explain it Rainey, but I would visualize this castle in the Genoaen Bay on this little island called Somara. I could see it and then I would blink and it would be gone. I took art lessons from Armand for the sole purpose of hoping that I could recreate my vision, but I never could. One day Armand asked me to describe it to him and I did, and it is his rendition that hangs in the entrance at the casa, so I guess it was etched in my subconscious."

"I see." Rainey said flatly. "I wonder why that is the only thing you remembered."

"I don't understand it myself and so I can't explain it to you."

"And who named Lili's puppy, Gypsy? Was it you Vienna?"

"Are you suggesting that I remember more, but chose not to?" Vienna said testily.

"I'm not saying anything like that at all. I have no idea how amnesia works."

"Apparently, an amnesiac recalls certain things and there is no rhyme or reason to it. At least that is how I had it explained to me. I'm sorry that I didn't remember you." Vienna apologized and felt tears sting her eyes as she turned away from Rainey.

An awkward silence filled the plane. Lili had fallen asleep in Rainey's arms, but he chanced waking her as he reached over and put his arm around Vienna and attempted to pull her closer. He felt her stiffen at his touch and knew he had stepped over the line. "I'm sorry Babe; I didn't mean it to sound accusing. I have no idea what you went through. I have never been very tactful have I? You have only been back in my life for an hour and I am already asking you to forgive my stupidity. Please Honey; don't turn your back on me."

"You know how I hate that 'stupid' word Rainey. I don't need to forgive you because you have done nothing wrong. I am the one who needs to ask for forgiveness."

Ava undid her restraint and stood up. "Pass Lili to me Dad; you need to see to Mama."

Vienna sniffled. "I'm all right Ava; I want Rainey to keep hold of Lili. Sit down and quit worrying about me. I'm a big girl you know, and I will warn you all right now that there is going to be a big blow up between the two of us and it probably won't be pretty. I hope none of you will witness it."

"What do you mean by that Vienna? I assure you that I will not be arguing with you, but if you want to rant and rave, then I'm your man. Now, can I have a little kiss?"

"The question is, may I?"

"You're already correcting my English? Does she do that with you too Zoe?"

"My English is as good as it is because Kat… Vienna has been my teacher and she never scolds me." Zoe spoke out in defense of the woman who was like a mother to her.

"I think that the two of you are very lucky to have found each other. I am very glad that you have been at her side for all the time she has been lost to us." Rainey said gratefully. "Now, why don't you all try to get a little rest; you too, my love."

"I'm never going to sleep again; I have too much to catch up on. You first Rosy…I want to hear all about you and Evan and Jannie and Uncle John and Ash and Gray and you girls never told me how Sissy is managing."

There was silence again. "Oh God, something has happened to her…what is it, someone tell me please, please." Vienna begged.

"Your sister is just fine Honey. I see no reason for putting it off any longer. Sissy and your old friend Jack have become close since your disappearance. Tragedy has a way of uniting people."

"Is that it, you were afraid that I would be upset because Sissy and Jack were seeing each other? Oh no, I am delighted that two of my favourite people have made a connection. I think Sissy always had a thing for Jack. Apparently, the LaFontaine women all like bad boys."

"Am I included in that depiction?"

"Are you kidding? You were the cream of the crop as far as bad boys go!"

Rainey grinned. "I did give you a lot of grief didn't I? Well, through no fault of yours, you got me back in Spades! But getting back to Jack and Sissy… I met him the first Christmas you were gone and I must say that I liked him immediately. He seems to be very sensitive and conscientious. Lara says that their friendship blossomed and Sissy is planning on moving to Alberta to be near Jack. I guess our house will be empty again."

"I hope Jack is planning on making an honest woman out of my sister. Now, is there anything else I should know about?"

Rosy spoke up. "Yes, LizBeth passed away last spring. She had a bad bout with a virus and ended up on a ventilator but succumbed soon afterwards. We had a lovely service for her and she is at rest alongside her parents and Jeremy now. Tanny's mother also passed away and her grandparents are in a care facility. I will let Rainey tell you the rest."

"The rest…what else is there and where is Tanny?" Vienna demanded.

"She's at Avanloch Honey. She lived with Amma and Johnny and the girls until I came back. How would you feel about adopting her?"

"Us, you mean we can legally adopt her? Do you want to?"

Ava laughed from the backseat. "Are you kidding, Rainey has already filed the papers!"

"Really Rainey; you were going to adopt her even if I never came home?"

"I never doubted for a minute that you would be coming home Vienna. Everyday Tanny asks me when Tia Vienna is coming home, and every day I tell her "soon." I'm so very happy to be answering her prayers." Rainey had to quit talking as he was losing control of his emotions.

"Dad never ever gave up on you Mama. He wrote letters to you almost every day." Ava knew she was telling a little white lie remembering the days of her father's deep depression fearing that Vienna was forever lost, but she felt no guilt at doing so.

Vienna smiled at Rainey with tears in her eyes. "Thank you. I am so sorry for what I have put you all through. I wrote you a letter too Rainey; I didn't know who I was writing to at the time, but I knew it was someone I had loved and I was so afraid of what I may have done to him."

Johnny piped up from the rumble-seat. "It's getting mighty fogged up in here. Enough with the remorse Lady Vienna…now, would you care to hear about the mysterious visitor at Willowisp?" Without waiting for a reply, he recounted the eerie sightings of a strange light at the manor house. "Rainey witnessed the illumination shortly after you went missing. We all thought that he was hallucinating and that it was his way of dealing with his sorrow of losing you. He investigated the whole house for any signs of an intruder, but found nothing. He would sit and watch the evasive wispy glow from your upstairs parlour for hours. It was there every time he came home and he was convinced it was you trying to find your way home. This past spring, I witnessed the candle-like beam for the first time, and then Rainey came back and we tried to find the source, but could not. Then, a few weeks ago it disappeared and has never been seen again."

Zoe whispered something under her breath.

"What was that Zoe, what did you say?" Ava asked.

"Nothing; I don't know about castles or what goes on in them, but when Johnny told that story I got goose bumps." Zoe said softly.

Rainey turned and smiled at her and promised that she had nothing to fear at Avanloch. If he could contend with its eccentricities, then anyone could.

"Zoe thinks that **it** was **me** roaming the halls at Willowisp." Vienna said casually.

"Why do you say that Mama; she didn't even know about the manor until Johnny mentioned it. Surely, you wouldn't have remembered it?" Ava queried.

"I used to walk the floors of the casa in the midnight hours with a lighted candle, so strangely it appears as though the sightings at Willowisp were mimicking my movements. I don't know how that is even possible, but I learned long ago to never doubt the unexplained as there is always an answer somewhere just waiting to be discovered."

Rainey asked her if she was sleep -walking or was she conscious of her actions.

"No, I wasn't aware of anything, but Anton knew. I only made the discovery a month or so ago, and was very upset that I had put the household in danger. Anton said that he always watched me. I was very angry with him as I didn't believe that he could possibly know of every one of my night-time wanderings. Somner set up cameras so that I could witness them for myself. A battery operated candle was substituted for the real thing. It was very uncanny to view myself in a trance roaming around the house. I appeared to be searching for something and I always stopped at the basement stairs and started to weep before returning to my room. There have been no more midnight trysts for weeks now."

"It sounds as if they quit the same time as the light at Willowisp ceased. Now, I am sure that it was you trying to find your way home. I don't know how this is possible either Sweetheart, but I am no longer a sceptic in matters of the unexplainable. Now you can take your little sister Ava as I need to hold your mother." Rainey passed Lili to Ava and Zoe and took Vienna in his arms.

"I'm all right Rainey; you don't have to baby me."

"Suppose if I want to…this is for me as much as it is for you."

"I'm so afraid Rainey, so afraid." Vienna whimpered.

"There is nothing to fear Hon; we are all here and we are going home."

"You don't understand, none of you do. I am not your Vienna anymore."

Rainey held her tighter. Rosy turned around reaching for her mother. "Don't say that Mama; of course you're Vienna. We all love you so much. You'll feel so much better when we get home."

Johnny silently cursed Anton for what he had done and vowed to himself that the man would pay. Right now he had to help console his dearest friend. "Do I have to come up there and talk some sense into you Lady Vienna?"

"Yes, but I am afraid you will rock the boat." Vienna managed to say through her sobs.

Johnny didn't need any more encouragement. He left his seat and squeezed in beside Vienna. Rainey realized that she needed her old friend more than him and surrendered her to him. There were things that the two of them shared that he would never be a part of. He didn't want anyone else to be her hero, but it wasn't about him, and so he selfishly relinquished his seat to Johnny.

He made his way to the back and picking up the wandering puppy slouched into the seat made vacant by Johnny. He placed her on his lap and stroked her until she accepted him. "You're a mite too big for anyone's lap aren't you Gypsy? Are German Shepherds a common breed in Spain Zoe?"

"I don't know Mr. Rainey as I have never had a dog before. I don't think getting a dog was ever mentioned, but then Somner rescued three puppies from this old Gypsy lady whom he knew. She couldn't afford to feed them and so he brought them all home. Kat fell in love with them and insisted we have one for Liliana. She and Somner found good homes for the other two. I think that she called the puppy after that Gypsy woman."

"Perhaps you are right Zoe." He placed the pup on a blanket at his feet.

Zoe faced Rainey and said in a whisper. "I am much worried about Kat…I mean Vienna."

"It's okay Zoe, we understand. Now, why are you so worried about her?"

Zoe explained how vulnerable Kat had been when she emerged from her coma. "But, I have never seen her like this Mr. Rainey. She never cries, not even at sad movies. She is always in full control of her emotions. She is always so confident in what she does and says. I have not seen her afraid of anything… not even when she drove out to the penitentiary by herself to visit that wild woman." Zoe wondered if Rainey knew of his resemblance to the actor Rod Taylor.

Rainey leaned forward and Ava choked back her astonishment. "What? What wild woman and are you saying that Mama went to a prison all alone? Why?"

"Oh, I fear my foot has been in my mouth…is that how you say it? There was no harm done and it turned out to be a good thing because that is how she found out that Mr. DeMarco had been keeping many things from her. She confronted him and he lied to her some more. She has barely been able to be in his company for a long time now. I think she was thinking about leaving him, but then you all came. I think it is very good that you came for her when you did."

Rainey patted her hand. "Believe me Zoe; we would have come for her a lot sooner if we had of known where she was. But, tell me who is this 'wild woman' that Vienna went to see in prison?"

"I do not know her and neither did Vienna, but she is Somner's wife, and Vienna was most curious. Antonio always called Lelani, that is her name, a crazy woman. He was furious that Kat had gone to see her and he was very angry with Somner too. She didn't care and told Anton that Somner had not known of her plans and that she had full intentions of visiting Lelani again."

"So it appears that Lelani told Vienna things that Antonio wouldn't."

"Yes Sir, that is exactly right." Zoe opened up one of the bags and produced a vial of pills. "I think you should get your wife to take one of these Mr. Rainey."

"I am just Rainey, Zoe. Are these pain pills?"

"Yes, and they have a light sedative in them so she is going to refuse, but I think her hip must be causing her great discomfort for she finds it difficult to sit for very long."

"I'll see what I can do and thanks for the insight into Vienna's life in Verde El Mar."

Rainey rumpled Zoe's hair as he walked by her. She smiled warmly at him.

"I think you're husband wants his wife back." Johnny said jokingly to Vienna. He noticed the pill bottle in Rainey's hand and nodded. "I'll get you some water and a blanket and pillow."

"Thanks Johnny." Rainey sat down beside Vienna again. "Zoe thinks it might be a good idea if you take one of these Honey."

"Well, I don't want to; they make me sleepy." Vienna said firmly.

"Are you hurting? Are there after-affects from being in a coma or from the accident?"

"I'm all right Rainey. Zoe told you…well, that was a long time ago. I am not hurting."

"Really; you wouldn't lie to me now would you?"

"I might be hurting just a little, but I can cope with it. I want to hold my baby for a while, okay? Then I promise you I will take one of those damn pills!"

Rainey retrieved Lili from Ava again. He placed the little cherub in Vienna's arms and put the seat belt around the two of them. "She's beautiful Vienna." He said beaming.

She smiled. "Do you think so Rainey? Do you like her because I know she likes you?"

"What a silly question; I fell in love with her the second I saw her… just as I did her mother. She is every bit as beautiful as you and I am going to spoil her rotten."

"A wise woman once said to me that you can only spoil a child with love."

"Makes perfect sense to me. It must have been very traumatic to wake up and not know who you were or recognize anything or anyone. Why don't you tell us about that?"

"Well, for one thing, I don't have any recollection of it of course. But, I will tell you what I was told." Fifteen minutes later she said she was ready for her pill and relinquished Lili to Ava and Zoe. She curled up with her head on Rainey's lap. "I think she needs changing girls and she may be hungry. Can you manage?"

"Of course we can Mama." Ava answered.

"Are you all through playing musical chairs with the baby? This is your captain speaking and he would be very relieved if his passengers would stay seated and buckled in." Evan chided.

Vienna mumbled from her pillow. "Sorry Evan, this isn't an ideal playground for a child, or a dog for that matter. I promise we'll be good."

"I didn't mean anything by that remark Vienna, just concerned for everyone's safety. How you are all keeping Lili amused is beyond me. We haven't heard her cry once."

"She is a very good girl, and has no reason to cry Evan, and especially now as she has a brand new daddy and family."

Rosy turned and smiled at her mother. "She sure does Mama and we are so blessed to have you and her. There is finally going to be music at Avanloch again. Try and get a little rest Mama because before you know it we will be in London and Aunt Jannie will be waiting. Evan, do you think it would be possible for me to change places with Ava because I would really like to spend some time with Liliana…that is if she will let me."

"Of course you can Honey. I know you are getting saddle sore. Perhaps when you come back I will have a little break and you can take the con."

"Let's not do anything rash. I will tell you one thing though; we are going to get a bigger plane! This is the last time I am flying in this tin can. It's time to dig into the McAllister coffers!"

Vienna Awakens

Anton was standing over me with a dagger in his hand. "You belong to me Katarina, and if I can't have you… no one else will!"

I screamed and screamed and awoke just before the blade pierced my heart. Rainey was smiling down at me. "Hello gorgeous; did you have a good sleep?"

"Rainey," I stammered, "was I screaming?"

"No, you weren't, but you were thrashing around a little. Are you okay?"

I sat up and saw that Lili was asleep in Rosy's arms. "I want one of these Mama… she's so precious."

"I heard that Rosy." Evan teased from the captain's chair.

"I've been asking for a niece, but ." Ava asserted.

Rainey winked at me. "I have a feeling we are going to have a rash of grandchildren one day my darling. We'll be landing at Land's End in a few minutes;

I nodded. For some unknown reason I couldn't find my voice. I was reunited with my family and I should have been elated, but Anton was coming for me and I was terrified.

I spent a tearful twenty minutes with Aunt Jannie and Ash before we boarded the helicopter and headed for Avanloch. They both promised they would be out for a visit in a few days.

When we landed on the castle's grounds I was given instructions by both Rainey and Johnny. They would escort me, Ava, Zoe and Lili up the driveway. Evan and Rosy would address the crowd that had gathered at the gate. Did they think I was made of glass?

Of course I disobeyed them. As soon as I disembarked, I heard the throng of people singing "For she's our jolly good Lady!" Reverend Peters was leading the chant. I waved to them all and broke free of Rainey's grasp and ran down to the gate. The cheering stopped as I spoke.

"I am home everyone! Thank you for coming. God bless you all for I know you have been praying for me. See you all soon."

There was more cheering and rejoicing as Rainey and Johnny led me away.

"Well, one thing is certain, she hasn't lost her charisma has she Rainey?" Johnny quipped.

"No, she can still wow a crowd. I guess I should say her **people**."

"Tia, Tia!" Tanny was coming down the drive as fast as her little legs could carry her.

"You two are very funny…now, let go of me." I ordered. They did, and I gathered the little girl in my arms. "Who has been feeding you? Have you been into Bully Beefy's food again?" I teased her.

"Oh Tia, you are so silly. I missed you so much. You won't go away again will you?"

"Not if I have anything to say about it. Now, did you know I brought you a little sister?"

"A sister…you mean that baby Ava is holding is going to be my sister?" Tanny muttered.

"Yes my darling…that is if you want to be Rainey's and my little girl too. Do you?"

Rainey unwound her arms from around my neck as she was saying, "Yes, yes, yes."

"Vienna has had a long day Sweetie. How about you come with me and let her visit with Amma and Mrs. D for they have missed her too?"

"Okay, but I want to stay where I can see Tia."

My reunion with Amma and Mary McDuff was long and tearful. They both held me tightly with Alexa, Brie and Shannon O'Shea sneaking in between them. After, I was embraced by Duffy, Winston and Lois, and had introduced them all to Liliana and Zoe, I exclaimed that I was famished and wondered if there was anything to eat in the kitchen.

"What do you think child?" Mrs. D laughed and led the way walking faster than I remembered that she could.

"Are you overdosing on Meggie's tonics Mary, and how is the dear soul?" I asked.

"Never you mind my Lady. You can see for yourself tomoree as she be here to see you."

We all piled into the family dining room and were served a seven course meal by two young ladies. Someone had placed a high-chair in between me and Rainey. I laughed when he tried to place Lili in it. She pulled up her little legs and reached for me squealing in defiance.

"What's this all about?" Rainey asked with a grin. "Have we just witnessed a temper tantrum?"

"I'm afraid so." I replied placing Lili on my lap. "She hates to sit alone and usually takes turns sitting with Zoe and then me. Oh, and I should warn you…she likes to throw her food."

"Of course she does, she be just a bairn." Mary had helped not only in raising my girls, but all the O'Shea girls so nothing a child did would phase her. "It's 'bout time we had a little fun in this ole castle. It has been much too quiet around here. Now put your head down and hold hands and pray with me for we have much to be thankful for this Christmas day in July."

Rainey had removed the dreaded highchair and put his arm around me and Lili.

After the prayer Mary picked up her glass of sparkling water and said. "To you Lady Vienna and Happy Birthday Mr. Rainey!"

There was much laughter and stories told before coffee and tea was served with chocolate cake. It was my recipe; the same one I had made for Rainey so many, many years ago when we picnicked at Hudson's Crossing in Bridge Falls. I could tell that he was reminiscing also by the look he gave me. He then excused himself saying he had something to take care of. Half an hour later he returned and scooped Lili out of my lap. Ava and Rosy were at my side to help me up smiling mischievously.

"I didn't eat that much girls that I can't get up by myself. Thank-you for the wonderful meal Mary and Lois. I am so happy to be home with all of you." I hugged them as I let the girls pull me into the hallway and into the elevator. I asked them what the hurry was.

"We just want to show you something Mama." Rosy said.

I knew the second I stepped off the lift that things were different. For one thing, the old cold flooring had been replaced with plush colorful carpeting. My feet sank into it and I instinctively reached down and picked up Gypsy.

"Winston just had her out for a romp Mama, so don't worry." Ava assured me.

We stopped at the old room 6. It had been turned into a delightful living area. Tanny informed me that the room had a television and Rainey and her watched Disney before bed every night.

"Johnny and Dad did all the work Mama." Ava informed me. I turned to smile at Rainey, but he was too busy amusing Lili that he didn't notice.

We wandered on down towards my rooms. Tanny ran ahead and seemed to be very excited about something. I stopped and looked back at Rainey again. This time, his head was up and he flashed me his crooked little grin. Out of the corner of my eye I saw a black cat cross in front of me. I knew it was an illusion, but I shivered anyhow.

"What's the matter Mama?" Rosy asked.

The words were out of my mouth before I knew they were coming. "He won't be able to forgive me this time; it'll all be over soon."

"Mama, are you talking about Rainey? Why would you say that?" Ava said alarmed.

Before I could answer Tanny opened the bedroom door and ran across the floor and pulled the drapes back. "Look Tia, look what Johnny made you!" She came back and took my hand. "Come on Tia, come and see all the ladies Rainey got you."

Ladies, what was she talking about? I was at a loss for words. Never in a thousand years would I have dreamt that the balcony I had hinted at would actually be built. It was incredible. I felt like I could reach out and touch Willowisp and I now had a clear view of the meadows and the mausoleum. I didn't have time to absorb the whole panorama before Tanny was pulling at me again insisting I check out the ladies.

"I forget their names but Rainey knows them all don't you Rainey? I think this one is Venus…is that right Rainey? She's beautiful isn't she Tia? Do you like her?"

"Every day she brings us out here and quizzes us about their names so that she could tell you all about them when you came home." Rosy laughed.

"Did I remember right about Venus?" Tanny asked.

"Yes, you did. She is the Goddess of love and beauty just like Tia." Rainey answered.

She pulled me on to the next corner where a statue of Aphrodite stood on the balustrade. She appeared to be rising out of a churning sea. The statuette in the middle brought tears to my eyes. It was an amazing replica of the Three Graces; the three inseparable sisters. In their sheer gowns, they danced and frolicked with the muses at their feet. I had once made up a poem about their antics and recited it to Rainey…had he remembered I wondered.

Tanny was tugging at me again. "Here is Diana, is that right? See how she dances with the moon? Rainey says she is a little wild just like you." She giggled.

"Oh, he does, does he? Now, who is this on the cornerstone?"

"I forget her whole name, but it sounds like Is Is. It is Rainey's favourite because he says she is the Queen of all the ladies and that is just like you."

I think my heart broke a little right then because I realized that the image Rainey had of me had died in Verde El Mar. He had been silent allowing Tanny to do the commentary, but I could feel his eyes following my movements. "I don't know where you found all these delightful statuettes Rainey, but they are exquisite and I thank-you." I rescued a squirming Lili from him.

"It pleases me that you like them Vienna, but it is Johnny who deserves the credit for it was he who suggested I add the finishing touches, and Amma helped me chose them."

"Rainey is too modest Mama for he is the one who designed the balcony, and he went to great lengths to track down these specific sculptures." Rosy informed me.

"I am well aware of everyone's role in creating this magnificent structure, but I am not worthy of all the time and labour that went into it."

Rainey shook his head. "It was our pleasure Vienna and it was a labour of love."

I smiled, but I wanted to cry.

Ava took my hand. "Of course you're worthy Mama. You have always given so much of yourself and we are all so grateful that you are back where you belong and we just want you to be happy."

"I am happy and I don't know how I survived without any of you. Thank-you all for keeping me alive and in your hearts. I have a worry though as Lili is in her climbing phase, and she may find her way out here alone…"

Rainey was on his feet. "That is never going to happen Honey as there is one more rail to go up, and it will be virtually unreachable, especially to a toddler. But, we will make sure the patio doors are always locked and I don't think that Lili will ever be left alone and we do have monitors for when she is sleeping. You must be tired; come, and I will run a bath for you."

"Good idea Dad. Rosy and I will take Lili and get her and Zoe settled in." Ava agreed.

The girls left me to be alone with Rainey. I opened the wardrobe as he went in to start the tub. The illusory black cat jumped out at me. I stood back and stared at the empty closet that confronted me.

"Did you find something to wear Hon?"

"When did you move out on me Rainey? Was it when you found out I was alive or was it today when you disappeared from the dinner table? Did you rush up here and take all of your belongings away because you suddenly realized that it wasn't your saintly Vienna who had come home? Was today all an act for the girl's sakes? Why did you tell me that you loved me?"

He looked perplexed and I saw his shoulders droop. "Let me turn the water off."

I was still staring at his empty closet when he came up behind me and tried to turn me around to face him. I remained steadfast and petulant.

He sighed. "Why are you so angry with me Vienna?"

"I'm not angry with you Rainey, it's me…I'm angry at myself. I know you will never be able to forgive me and I don't blame you."

"Just a minute, just a damn minute! I have no idea what you are even talking about. Forgive you, for what? I have only been gone long enough to turn the taps on, so what could you have possibly done in that short time to warrant my forgiveness?"

"Don't be flippant Rainey. You know perfectly well what I've done. I've been with another man. I let him touch me, I've slept with him… I have been unfaithful."

He took a firm hold on me and spoke in a very calm voice. "First, I do love you and you know it! Nothing I said was for the girl's sakes…nothing, it was all for you. I'm sorry if I am not relaying my feelings for you strong enough. I'm still reeling from the fact that you are here and I haven't wanted to overload you, but damn-it Vienna, you are not making any sense. That wasn't you with Anton; that was some fictional dame that he invented for his own selfish needs.

You are in no way responsible for what Kat did. I'm mad as hell for what that egotistical mad man did to you, but he looked after you and I am grateful for that. The marriage, everything…that was Kat and you are not responsible for what she did. Look at me Vienna… you are no longer that woman, you are Vienna, my Vienna and the woman I love."

"I don't think you have had the time to properly analyze this sordid mess Rainey. How can you ever be sure that it wasn't me just pretending to be Katarina? You always said that I had two personalities didn't you."

Rainey made an attempt at laughter. "Yes, two personalities, but not two different identities. Anyhow, if you had of known who you were, you would have found a way to come home to us."

"How can you be sure of that?"

"Simple, you would never deliberately stay away from me and the girls because you love us. But, to be perfectly truthful, if you had of returned as Katarina, I would have loved you anyway."

"How can you possibly know that Rainey?"

"I think that she was a remarkable woman to survive everything that she went through. She never stopped questioning her identity but made the best of her life for herself and Zoe and Lili. You never fully lost your true self; it was always there just waiting to break out. I am thankful that you came back as Vienna though, but will there always be a bit of Kat in you won't there?"

"I don't know Rainey. I have been Vienna ever since you called my name, but I am not afraid of Kat, and if a little of her lives in me…will you be able to live with that?"

"Yes, more than ever my darling. Now, will you come with me?"

He took my hand and led me out the bedroom door and across the hall and into the little foyer. I stopped and asked him what was different about the room. He said he would tell me later and pulled me along stopping at room 1. He opened the door, let go of my hand, and walked ahead of me to the wardrobe. He flung it open and pulled open the drawers.

"This is where I stay when I am at the castle. I could not sleep in the bed that I used to share with you and so I moved all my belongings over here." His voice was wrought with emotion. "Do you know how much I have missed you Vienna; no, you couldn't possibly understand what it was like to be without you day and night."

I swallowed hard. "You could have found somebody else… apparently, I did."

He started towards me and I backed up until I hit the door. My bottom lip was quivering.

"Do you hear the words coming out of your mouth Vienna? I thought we were straight about who you were…has nothing I said sunk into that thick noggin of yours?"

I stammered. "Don't scold me Rainey; I don't like it when you're cross with me."

"Well then, don't say such stupid things and I do mean STUPID! You know there will never be anyone else for me. If you are insinuating that I should have had one night stands, then you have forgotten what our love is all about. You wound ne Vienna."

I was trembling. All I could manage was a lame "I'm sorry Rainey; please don't go."

"Go? Why do you think I would and where would I go? My whole reason for being is standing right here. Oh no, My Lady, I am not anywhere near through with you…that is, if you want **me**? Why are you shaking Vienna? Are you afraid of me?"

"No, no I'm not; only that you might leave me." I managed to murmur.

"There is no way I am leaving, but I think you're afraid that I am going to do this."

He put one hand on the closed door so that I couldn't move and reached around behind me with his free hand and unzipped my dress. He pulled it off my shoulder until my bare skin was exposed and kissed it tenderly. I took a deep breath as he tucked my hair behind my ear and kissed my neck and then my face and my eyelids and finally my lips. I threw my arms around him and told him that I had been so afraid that he'd never want to touch me or kiss me.

"There is no chance of that My Lady. Now, will you come and lay with me? I need to hold you and kiss you and feel your warmth upon my cold body."

"Oh yes Rainey, I need that too!"

He picked me up and placed me on the bed. "I'm not sure the lady of the house would approve of my dirty feet all over her satin coverlet." I laughed.

"I know that lady intimately, and believe me; she doesn't care about such things."

"What does she care about?"

"Me, I hope she cares about me." Rainey's eyes were very moist.

I touched his lips with my fingers. "She loves you Rainey."

"Then say it Vienna…say it."

"I love you Rainey Quinn! Oh, how I love you Rainey Quinn."

"And, that's no more than I love you Vienna LaFontaine."

He lay down beside me and pulled me into his chest. I wrapped myself around him and we lay together not saying anything for a very long time. I could feel his heart beating rapidly and as he relaxed the rhythm gradually became slower and calming. He was the first to break the silence.

"I wasn't totally honest with you when I said that I never lost faith that you were still alive. There was a time last year when I didn't think I could live another day without you. If it wasn't for Ava and the boys…well, I just don't know."

I had never heard such sadness in his voice ever before. "You just broke a piece of my heart Rainey. I am so sorry for what I put you all through."

He made an attempt at joviality. "Because of course it was your fault that there was an earthquake the second I turned my back on you."

"It probably was as I was always tempting fate." I said solemnly.

"You said those exact words the night before the quake and the worst day of my life."

"I promise I won't temp fate again Rainey. I should listen to you and Meggie more."

He laughed. "We know that is not going to happen so let's just agree to be more cautious. I was the one who was tempting fate by taking you to Nazeth on the Labour Day weekend for we know nothing good ever happens to me then. This year we are going to stay in bed all day."

I smiled. "Sounds good to me. I hope my so called photographic memory starts kicking in soon because I don't recall that it was Labour Day."

"It will Honey, give it time." Then he leaned over me and asked me a silly question. "Do you want to be my girl again?"

I answered him honestly. "I've always been you girl Rainey… even when you didn't want me, and even when I didn't know who I was. I will be your girl forever."

"Oh, I have always wanted you Vienna, but never as much as I do now. I know I don't want to live without you ever again…so, will you marry me and be my wife again?"

"I'm confused Rainey, aren't we still married? Oh, please tell me that I don't need to get a divorce from Anton? That marriage wasn't even legal was it?"

"I don't think so, but I still want to marry you all over again." He reached over me and picked up one of my little jewellery boxes from the night stand and opened it before me. "Do you want to wear my rings again Vienna?"

I covered my face crying and laughing all at the same time. "Oh Rainey, I was so afraid to ask you about them. I feared I had lost them or that Anton had disposed of them. Put them on me, put them on me!"

"Not quite so fast My Lady…I have a few conditions that I hope you will agree to."

"What? There are conditions for me being your wife again…I can't imagine."

"It's not as bad as you may think. Can you promise me that you won't take off on me again to meet with strange men in back alleys? There is to be no more conniving with witches and you must never run away from me to have another child without me ever again. Can you live with all that?" Rainey looked at me pleadingly.

I was trying to keep a straight face because I found his 'so-called' conditions amusing. "I can definitely promise that there will be no more meetings with men, not only in alleys, but anywhere, but for the 'witch thing'…how will I know because they don't always show their true colors you know? I doubt that we will ever be blessed with another child, but if we are, you have my guarantee that I will not leave your side. Now, can I have my rings please?"

"Don't make light of this Vienna for I am serious."

"Suppose if I don't agree to your demands?"

"There are many rooms in this castle that no one knows about but me, and I am not above holding you captive. Apparently, it can be done."

He was trying very hard not to smile but didn't succeed.

"Are you telling me in a- round-about way that you have discovered more secret rooms in this castle?"

"We'll get into that later, but for now, you need to know that I am serious. So what's your answer?"

"Oh yes, I can see that you are serious. Now, put **my** rings on my finger, please."

"Yes Ma'am!"

He slid them on my ring finger on my left hand and they immediately fell off.

"I was afraid of that; they are now too big for you now." He said.

"I want and need to wear them Rainey. What can we do? I don't want to wait until we can get them to a jeweller or until I put weight on." I whined.

"You are still impatient aren't you? There may be some adhesive tape in the bathroom." He got up and headed for the bathroom and turned at the door. "You'll be here when I get back, right?"

I threw a pillow at him.

He returned and stopped at the chest of drawers and withdrew what appeared to be a very large book and placed it on the floor by the bed. I asked him what was in it.

"One thing at a time young lady." He wrapped the tape around the rings several times until he was satisfied that I wouldn't lose them. I told him that I would never take them off again.

"What about when you go to bed and wash dishes and make bread?" He asked jokingly.

"Like I do the dishes or make bread?" I laughed.

"Could happen; someday we may be penniless. You know a lot has happened since you've been gone. There have been changes to the household staff. Did you like the new girls you met this afternoon?"

"I liked them very much…Jeanette and Caren, they are sisters, right? I was informed that Caren is pronounced Car-en; it's Irish isn't it? I didn't see hide or hair of the MacLeods though."

"You were right about them Darlin; they were up to no good."

I said in my 'I told you so' voice. "Oh, really! The Mrs. came on to you, didn't she?"

"That'll be enough of the cheekiness lass. I think they had their eyes on a much bigger picture than being the hired help and their true colors soon made an appearance." "I wish I had of been here to see you send them packing."

"Wasn't me Luv; Johnny, Amma and Rosy all had a say in their dismissal and without severance pay or references, I might add."

"I can hardly wait to hear about their transgressions."

"They don't warrant any more discussion. There is an envelope waiting for you in your parlour from your father. It was here waiting for you when I got back from Andorra."

"What was in it? Are we any clearer on the skeletons in the LaFontaine closet?"

"Don't know, never opened it. We'll do it together when you are ready, and by the way, I phoned our parents to tell them of your safe return. That's where I went when I left the dinner table. I told them you would call them tomorrow."

"Of course you did; thank you for doing what I should have. I'm sorry for lashing out at you earlier Rainey. I should have known that you could forgive me, but I know how jealous you are, and my insecurities about myself made it easier to accuse you instead of waiting for an explanation as to your intentions towards me."

"My intentions towards you may not always have been honourable, but that was a long time ago, and now the only intentions I have are to keep you with me forever. Now, do you want to hear about my visit from the Grey Lady?"

"Quit kidding Rainey!"

"I almost wish that I was, but I swear that I am not and I have proof."

"Are you going to tell me that you photographed her because that is virtually impossible?"

"Oh, so now it is you who doesn't believe in the unfathomable? I have had a lot of time to contemplate on the peculiar and unexplained happenings around here since you have been on your long holiday…" He paused to smile at me and I jabbed him in the ribs. "Contrary to popular belief, the exhuming of Taty's soul, so to speak, from room 6, **IS** what is impossible. You know that don't you? What I am going to tell you now is also beyond the realms of sanity, yet it happened. If someone else was to relate this story to me, I would say they were delusional or under the influence of hallucinating drugs, but that is not the case as it happened to me. Come, sit up, and I will tell you my bizarre tale."

He pulled me up to quickly that the pain in my hip caused me to whinge.

"Oh Lordy, I've hurt you! It's the hip that Zoe told me about isn't it; will it help if I massage it?"

"It's all right Rainey, don't worry. I never know when or why it acts up. Massaging does help, thank-you, but unfortunately, you are working on the wrong hip."

We both laughed. "Of course it is! It's the left hip, the one with the teardrop. Please tell me that the surgery won't destroy that beautiful natural tattoo?"

"No, the incision will be a lot higher; that's what Dr. Z told me anyhow. I'm surprised you remember that birthmark?"

"Why? I love it just as I do all of you. Do you think Dr. Z knew your real identity?"

"He didn't know Rainey, I am sure of it. He was my friend and I had so very few…"

"Why is that Vienna? Did Anton want you all to himself?"

"No, I didn't care to go anywhere or meet anyone until after I went to volunteer at the galleria Before that I was recuperating from the accident and subsequent coma, and dealing with being pregnant by a man I didn't know."

"Were you ill with Liliana as you were with Ava? God, I wish I had of been with you."

"I do too my darling, but not to fear as I had an easy pregnancy. You would have loved me Rainey for I gained 55 pounds. I was nice and plump…just the way you like me."

"You know I love you no matter what you weigh, but I have to be honest, I do worry about you when you are so slim. Did the extra weight affect your hip?"

"Be careful what you wish for Rainey because I may just be your pudgy little girl again if Mrs. D has her way. You know what? Now that I think about it, my hip didn't bother me at all. Perhaps all I need is some cushioning."

He retrieved the book he had set on the floor and placed it between us. "Are you ready?"

"I am…**Avanloch, the Grey Lady!**" I exclaimed. "What is this, and wherever did it come from?"

"And that is what I am about to tell you my dear. She came to visit me the night before we found out that you had been found. Do you think that you can sit still long enough for me to chronicle the events of that night?"

"Can I ask questions along the way?"

"Only if you cannot restrain yourself which I know is going to be very difficult for you." Rainey's eyes sparkled mischievously and I told him that I would do my best and that he had the floor and not to leave anything out. His narration took half an hour or so. He had my full attention throughout although I wanted to interrupt him a dozen times. However, when he said that the line of the McAllister's may have died with Stewart I could be silent no more.

"That can't be so Rainey! I exclaimed. "A travesty like that could not have gone undetected for over a century. No, it is just not possible."

"I don't know Honey, and it may be that we never know the real truth." He patted my hand. "These few pages that Ava has translated may just be the tip of the iceberg. Let's wait and see what else Avaleena has to say." He flipped to the back of the book and showed me some rough sketches. "I haven't had time to go over these in details yet because when we got the phone call from Stu…well, nothing else was important as getting you home. But I believe the drawings are of the original layout of Avanloch, perhaps drawn by Avaleena." With that he closed the book and placed it on the bed behind us.

"Is that it then?" I asked disappointedly.

"It is for now. I shouldn't have even told you about the damn encounter with the Grey Lady and subsequent happenings today. Ava is going to be upset with me as I promised her I wouldn't tell you. I'm sorry Vienna; you must be overwhelmed. You just got home and I am bombarding you with trivial matters. I shouldn't be kissing you and making you say you love me. Not that it is any excuse for my behaviour, but I have been on edge ever since Stu informed us that you had amnesia and that you had married. I have been scared to death that you wouldn't remember me and wouldn't love me anymore. I have demanded things of you and never once have I asked you what you want, and so, I am asking you now, what do you want and need from me Vienna?"

I took his fidgety hands in mine. "You never made me say 'I love you', for I do, and if you hadn't kissed me, I would have thought that you didn't want to and couldn't because of what I had done. I have also been scared to death that you wouldn't be able to love me again, but I know you do. Do you know what love looks like? Look into my eyes and you will see it shining and it shines only for you. Thank-you Darling for taking me back into your life for it is only you that I want and need."

He smiled. "You are my life Vienna. Will you dance with me My Lady?"

"What took you so long to ask me My Lord?"

He took me in his arms and rested his head upon mine. "I see you didn't get any taller while you were away. I'm glad because I like you just the way you are."

I asked him if 'away' was the way we were going to address my absence.

He said, "Yes."

"Are we going to be all right Rainey?" I asked solemnly.

He lifted my chin up and I looked into his dreamy azure eyes. "We *are* all right Vienna. Why would you think we wouldn't be?"

"I never want to see Anton again, but I do need to contact Somner. I need to know what he knows, and why he kept it from me? Are you okay with that?"

"Yes, because I need answers too. As soon as we get you acclimatized to life here we'll give him a call. Were you worried that I wouldn't want you to talk to him?"

"No, but suppose Anton comes looking for me and Liliana… what then?"

He kissed my forehead. "The minute the man sets foot in the British Isles he'll be arrested for kidnapping and falsification of legal documents, such as your hospital records and marriage license. No, I am not at all concerned that he will come after you. I'm quite confident that he won't risk his freedom to pursue you despite what he said."

"You don't know him like I do Rainey."

"Believe me Sweetie, precautions are already in place. I would never gamble with your and our daughter's welfare. But, we can install a more sophisticated security system if you like."

"I have always felt safe here Rainey, but I don't plan on being a prisoner in my home. I know you would protect us with your life, but you can't be with us all the time."

"Who says I can't be? Anyhow, if you want bodyguards, we'll get them."

"No thank-you. I had them in Spain and…do you hear giggling?"

Rainey laughed. "Guess who?"

"Come in girls; we have been expecting you." I called.

The door opened and there stood our five girls. Rosy asked what we were doing.

"Why, dancing of course." Rainey answered.

"But, there isn't any music." Zoe said.

"You'll soon learn that music follows these two wherever they go as they make their own." Ava responded and let Lili down who was squirming to get out of her arms. She made a bee-line for me, but Rainey scooped her up and I beckoned the rest of the girls to join us. We encircled them and had a big family hug.

"Mrs. D wants you to come down for tea and cake." Rosy said.

"Didn't we just eat an hour ago? I told you Rainey that she'll fatten me up."

"I think she only wants to make sure that you are really here Honey. I think we spent a little too much time with that damn book that we lost track of time."

"Dad, you didn't…"

"It's all right Ava; I'm glad he did. I can see by the look on Rosy's face that she has no idea what we are talking about. Perhaps you can enlighten her as the rest of us go to tea? Make sure that she understands that we have a lot more investigating to do and that tomorrow we start by visiting the rooms beyond the stairway."

Now poor Rosy really looked confused. Rainey ruffled her curly locks. "The book is on the bed. Ava will tell you everything and no exploring on your own, you hear? Don't be shocked at what Ava is going to tell you Rosy. We have just scratched the surface and to be perfectly honest, I think that Avaleena may have been a very deranged woman."

"Avaleena…what does she have to do with anything?" Rosy asked in bewilderment.

"All will be revealed just as Rainey promised, but it might take some time, so just be patient Rose. Ava, I think that Zoe can aid you in the deciphering as her Spanish is excellent, and she will be unbiased." I suggested.

"What a wonderful idea Mama. Zoe, would you care to help us?"

Zoe said she hoped that she could and would be delighted to assist.

As soon as the door was closed I told Rainey that we would probably have to enlist the aid of our French Spaniard friend again if we decided to take the revelations of the book seriously.

"Why on earth would we involve Roberge?" He asked somewhat dumbfounded.

"Do you not remember discussing Roberge's father with him? He said that an alternate pronunciation and spelling of the name Farradan was Ferrani? And, wasn't that the name of Avaleena's lover… Jacques Ferrani? This all happened a very long time ago so there is probably no rhyme or reason as to what I am suggesting."

"I don't know how you picked up on that Vienna, but you may be right. How strange would it be if Roberge's family is the rightful heirs of Avanloch?"

"Don't even go there Rain; it has to be just a coincidence, the name thing." I so hoped.

"If I have learned anything from you Honey, it's that there are no coincidences."

"Let's put the whole thing aside for now and go to tea."

"You don't have to have tea, Tia…hey, that rhymes. Mrs. D is making you the special coffee that Rainey brought home for you." Tanny assured me.

"Very good Tanny." I laughed. "Did you make it back with the coffee we bought in Saragossa Rainey?"

"That **you** bought my dear. It came home with me from Andorra. We have been saving it for you, but I did send a pound or two over to Meggie."

"That was very thoughtful of you Rainey, thank-you."

I said that I wanted to go down the main stairs and we started for them. Rainey took Lili from me and said that we would have to board them up as he didn't want her playing on them. I nodded in agreement remembering how they had to be barricaded for Ava and Rosy so long ago.

"What kind of adventures are we going to have Tia; you won't have to go away again will you? Tanny asked.

"No, my sweet girl, not for a long, long time." I stopped at the top of the stairs. "Just a minute…where are my bracelets Rainey? Are they still here or have you found the rightful heir?"

"Yes sure Vienna, because I made that a priority while you were gone."

I couldn't tell by his tone whether he was joking or being sarcastic so I apologized.

"It's okay Babe; I knew you were going to ask about them sooner than later, so get them if you want. They are in your silver jewelry box where you always kept them. I have to warn you though that they are cursed."

I grimaced at him and told them to go on without me. I ignored the pain in my hip and ran to my bedroom and freed the magnificent bangles from captivity for I was sure they had been in the rose box ever since I had been gone. I slid them on my wrist and felt energized. Cursed, they weren't!

Rainey was not pleased that I had not taken him seriously. "So, you are going to wear them after all? I tell you that they are the devil's trinkets and it means nothing to you. Are they not the cause of Katarina's death and maybe even her daughters'? Who knows how many others have suffered because of them? What about me when I bought them for you and came home and found you gone, and then because of them, I lost you in Andorra, and it seems they have also played a role in Anton's strange fixation that you were the fabled Katarina?"

"I won't wear them if you don't want me to Rainey, but I love them because you bought them for me. I promise they will not be the cause of anymore misfortunes."

"You can't promise that Vienna, but wear them as it appears you must."

"Who's Katarina and why are you mad at Tia, Rainey?" Tanny asked almost crying.

Rainey took her hand. "I'm not mad at her Honey; I could never be. Katarina is just someone Tia used to know. I'm sorry Vienna; I told you I was touchy." He flashed me a crooked little smile.

"Let's get going then. It's already way past time that these two babes were in bed, and we haven't even had tea yet."

"Tia, will you tell me and Lili a bedtime story?" Tanny wanted to know.

"Yes, my darling. Tonight I will tell you the tale of a damsel who was lost but was rescued by her hero." I winked at Rainey. "Then tomorrow and in the many days to come, there will be tales to tell of mysterious rooms, and silver bracelets, and strange lands, and friendly ghosts, and kings and queens, and all the princesses that live in a magnificent castle."

"Will you tell me a bedtime story too My Lady? Do I get to sleep in the big bed tonight and will you tell me how Emerald and Laddy came to be?" Rainey asked sheepishly.

"Sleep? Who says there is going to be any sleeping?"

"Really Vienna…in front of the children?"

I called back to him over my shoulder as I reached the bottom step and made a dash for the kitchen. "Yes, really Rainey!"

His laughter echoed through the long hallway and I knew at that moment that together we could overcome any obstacles that may have the nerve to confront us.